Planning done, I slipped back to the office door and used my powers of Cat Magic to lock it. Then, I sauntered around the desk, sat behind the crouched witch, and gave him my most innocent and winsome meow.

The man jumped several inches in the air and fell to the side, executing a rather flailing roll. Once he had scrambled to his feet, breathing hard and hands raised as if to defend himself, he finally spotted me and relaxed.

"What in tarnation..." he muttered, crouching down again so his silhouette would not be visible through the frosted glass of the office door. "How the heck did you get in here?"

The witch scowled at me, so I cocked my head in a way that I knew threw humans into paroxysms of adoration over my cuteness, and meowed again.

"I ain't gonna pet you. Now get lost," he whispered fiercely, making flapping motions with his hand.

Well. Fine.

Any restraint I might have been inclined to show this trespassing miscreant vanished like a plate of scones left unattended in Sebastian's presence. I dropped my "adorable cat" act and replaced it with The Death Glare—that look all cat owners know, and fear. The unfortunate witch had just enough time to realize the enormity of his mistake. An expression of horror transformed his face as I launched myself at his head, all eighteen claws extended.

LOVE, LIES, & HOCUS POCUS

CAT MAGIC

A LILY SINGER ADVENTURES NOVELLA

LYDIA SHERRER

Chenoweth Press

LOVE, LIES, AND HOCUS POCUS: CAT MAGIC

A Lily Singer Adventures Novella

Copyright © **2018 by Lydia Sherrer**

All rights reserved.

ISBN 13: 978-0-9973391-9-2

Published by **Chenoweth Press 2018**

Louisville, KY, USA

Cover design by Molly Phipps www.wegotyoucoveredbookdesign.com

To my overlords, er, cats—Gizmo and Gadget—who taught me everything I know about their magnificent species

ACKNOWLEDGMENTS

This book exists for two reasons: the wonderful support of my Kickstarter backers, and the enthusiastic love of my readers for Sir Edgar Allan Kipling. Without you, I never would have created this delightful tale.

I am also indebted to my cats, Gizmo and Gadget—the former who taught me about a cat's love for her human, the latter who showed me the annoyingly regal, yet magnificent nature of the feline race. Together, they are Sir Kipling, a cat's cat, yet devoted to his human's ultimate happiness.

Much thanks to my editor, Josiah Davis, whose fingers are as swift as the coursing river, and my wonderful cover designer, Molly Phipps, for her artistic vision. I'm indebted to my beta readers for their feedback, and my street team for helping to spread the word about Sir Kipling's adventures.

Most importantly, I want to thank my family, specifically my husband, who cared for me while I was completing this project, suffering through the first trimester of my first pregnancy. David, I look forward to the day when we read this together with our son, and tell him this was the book I wrote while he was busy making me sick as a dog.

A NOTE FROM THE AUTHOR

Ever wish you could get an inside look at the thoughts of a cat? Me too! That's why I wrote *Cat Magic*, the first Lily Singer adventure devoted solely to our intrepid feline hero, Sir Edgar Allan Kipling, magical talking cat extraordinaire.

For fans of the *Love, Lies, and Hocus Pocus* series, this is a fun side adventure that can be read at any point during the series, though it happens chronologically after the fourth book (*Legends*).

For new readers, welcome! I hope you enjoy this cute little standalone that revels in the joy of snarky cat humor and magical adventure. Once you are done with this novella, there is a whole series waiting for you to indulge in, so be sure to check it out starting with Book 1 - *Love, Lies, and Hocus Pocus: Beginnings*.

Happy Reading!

CHAPTER ONE

THE FIRST RULE OF CAT

*T*he First Rule of Cat is simple: never beg.
Ever.

Begging is the fine, immovable line that separates cats from dogs, and it is never to be crossed. Cats do not ask, we tell. Whether or not we are obeyed, of course, is another matter entirely.

"I already told you, Kip, you are *not* coming with us." Lily Singer, a wizard who also happens to be my human, stared down at me with a dour expression, hands on hips. The fact that I was the irresistible picture of feline perfection—large and sleek, with long, silky hair as gray as the shadows but for the white splashes on my front paws, tail-tip, and throat—did not soften her expression. Not even the white markings around my nose and eye which gave me the dignified look of a mustached and monocled gentleman could make her smile today. Faced with such stern resolve, I tried a different tack.

"You know, the last time you went off without me, you got yourself kidnapped. We wouldn't want to repeat that episode, now, would we?" I lifted one front paw and licked it slowly, giving her plenty of time to remember the unpleasant particulars. Normally, there would be no question of my accompanying her. For one thing, Lily was my human, and therefore my responsibility. For another, being a wizard meant trouble followed her wherever she went. I hardly dared take my eyes off her.

Lily shook her head, stray bits of her chestnut hair waving at the motion. The sensible bun at the back of her neck never seemed capable of restraining it all, and inevitably a curl or two escaped. "That was completely different, and you know it. Besides, Sebastian is coming. You might as well deputize him, because the friend he and I are visiting is highly allergic to cats and you will *not* be accompanying us, cat magic or no."

I stared up at her, yellow eyes narrowed to slits as I considered the Second Rule of Cat. It was slightly more complicated than the first: always give humans what they need, not what they want.

That might seem a tall order. After all, what do cats know? Quite a bit, I can assure you, and I more than most, since I had been cursed with human intelligence.

Horrible, I know.

My human calls it magic, but calling a cat "magical" is redundant. The very state of being a cat has a magic all on its own. Take physics, for example. We always land on our feet, we go wherever we want regardless of doors and locks, and we can fit into impossibly small spaces. Like vases. And goldfish bowls. And any box we come across. But in doing so we don't defy the laws of physics, we simply have a better understanding of them than humans. Ergo, Cat Magic.

To be fair, I have more than my fair share of magic due to a bothersome incident involving a witch, a demon, and an ancient tablet of unimaginable power. I might be persuaded to speak of it later, if you bribe me with salmon. Fresh salmon, mind you, and a side of cream.

But I digress.

The point is, regarding the Second Rule of Cat, that no matter how much we might appear to care only for ourselves, in actuality, our greatest concern is the welfare of our humans. Well, perhaps second greatest concern, but who is keeping track? The question I needed to answer was, what did Lily need more? My presence? Or absence?

Lily, obviously assuming she had won the argument, adjusted her glasses, gave me one last narrow-eyed look, and went back to packing. I allowed her to mistake my thoughtful silence as acquiescence and lifted one back leg to wash as I considered my next move.

Dogs think they have a monopoly on being man's best friend. They are wrong. Unlike dogs, cats understand that the most important part of friendship is tough love. Dogs are all mushy licks and worshipful groveling. They serve humans because they have an instinctual need for approval, and humans fulfill that desire. But because dogs are hard-wired to please, they haven't the faintest idea what humans actually *need*.

A cat's love is much more sensible. We don't give a squirrel's tail what humans think of us, which gives us the freedom to do what must be done.

Let me give you an example. Dogs foolishly think they can protect humans from the perils of the world with barks and growls. They assume that if they can make their human happy, everything else will be fine. Cats, on the other hand, understand that life is much more complicated. We don't waste our precious time protecting humans—naps won't take themselves, after all. We focus on making them stronger so they can protect themselves. We teach them the secret art of unassailable confidence, how to ignore people that annoy them, and the effectiveness of sneak attacks. We make them more self-sufficient.

Like us.

Now, I know what you're thinking: What about all the cats out there who are just plain mean?

I told you the Second Rule of Cat was complicated.

Cats differ on their interpretation of "what humans need." One might argue that whatever is good enough for a cat, is good enough for a human. Therefore, whatever cats want is what humans need. This philosophy is largely to blame for the phenomena of "dog people"—those humans who mistakenly assume they do not like cats simply because they have not yet met the *right* cat.

The right cat knows what their human needs: fuzzy cuddling and purrs, or indifferent stares and claw-avoidance training. Or, maybe their human is just a miserable scumball, in which case all bets are off. In any case, I take *my* duties as a cat very seriously, and derive utmost pride in ensuring my human's ultimate health and happiness. What happens along the way, of course, is all about building her character. She will thank me eventually.

What made the current situation complicated was that my human takes a great deal more looking after than most. So much looking after, in fact, that I am not able to teach her all the skills she needs to survive, but must employ a more "paws-on" approach. This is primarily because—in true cat fashion—her curiosity is stronger than her common sense. Oh, and because of the whole wizard thing.

No, she is not a witch. She is a wizard.

The witch in the equation is Sebastian, her closest companion and future mate—not that she realizes it yet, but then humans can be rather dense when it comes to the opposite sex. Cats, on the other hand, have a nose for such things. In any case, Sebastian was a skilled witch with plenty of alley cat smarts to counterbalance Lily's underdeveloped survival instincts. He would be coming by later to pick my human up, and together they would venture forth to visit this supposedly cat-allergic friend for a few days. But would his presence make up for all the important things only I could provide?

"Kip, did you hide my underwear again? You know that won't keep me from leaving, right? I can just buy more." My human's thoroughly annoyed voice drifted out of her open closet door where her various grooming implements resided, along with those ridiculous things called clothes that humans insisted on wearing. I once suggested she simply grow fur. Then she could dispense with the bothersome necessity of shopping and spend all that extra money on fresh salmon for me. She did not take kindly to my suggestion. I haven't the faintest idea why.

"The only thing I have done to your underwear is ensure they are coated with the proper amount of fur. It's cold outside. What kind of cat would I be if I allowed my human to freeze to death?"

She made no reply, but I could hear her eyes roll from my perch on her bed—we cats have very acute hearing. Left hind leg clean, I switched to my right and tried to regain my train of thought.

Ah yes. Wizards and witches. What is the difference, you ask? Well, in Lily's words, "Wizards are born, witches are made." But I prefer to think of it as the difference between cats and dogs. Wizards, like cats, have all the power and know it. Witches, like dogs, want power but do not have it, and so must break the First Rule of Cat to get it.

5

They call what they do "trading," not begging, but to a cat it's all the same.

I have not yet shared this helpful comparison with my human's witch. While I know it would make Lily smile, I suspect Sebastian might be inclined to take offense. So, let's keep it between us, shall we?

Don't misunderstand me. I have the utmost—well, at least a moderate amount of—respect for witches in general, and Sebastian in particular. I have less respect for dogs, but that's because they are filthy and uncivilized. They dare to chase *me*, for catnip's sake, the great Sir Edgar Allan Kipling, Magical Talking Cat Extraordinaire. What savages. Witches don't chase me, at least not usually, so they're much more tolerable.

Dogs—and witches—have their uses, of course. But they work best when employed sparingly, and from a distance. Lily always seemed to agree, and for many years we lived a simple life, content in each other's company. I ran the household and made sure all surfaces were properly covered in fur, while my human kept my food bowl full and a warm lap in reserve at all times.

But magic changed everything. Completely aside from the dangerous and disruptive adventure which our magical lifestyle seemed to engender, something far, far worse had insinuated itself into our household. For with magic came expectations, and we all know how disgustingly inconvenient expectations can be. Upon my "Enlightenment," as I call it, Lily realized that she and I could understand each other perfectly, and from that point onward she expected me to do all sorts of ridiculous things like "behave" and "obey."

As if.

I acted as swiftly and decisively as possible to impress

upon her that obeying was for lesser beings, like dogs. To an extent, I was successful. But every now and then—all right, nearly every day—she forgets and tells me to do things as if she actually expects them to happen. Like right now. I was still undecided on whether or not I would let her get away with it.

"How do you know your friend is allergic to cats? What if that's simply a ploy to avoid admitting her inability to handle my magnificence? It has happened before."

"You mean that time with Mrs. Pettibone? Kip, she ran out of the house because you waved your tail under her nose after I specifically told you to stay away. She broke out in red blotches and could barely stop sneezing." Lily emerged from her closet, arms full of clothes and a resigned expression on her face. Using a sticky roller—the bane of my existence—she meticulously removed all my hard work before carefully folding and tucking each item into her suitcase.

"Humph," I grumbled. "I was conducting an experiment. Sacrifices must be made in the name of science."

"Or you were just annoyed that she called you a mangy street cat and said you probably had fleas."

I paused my ministrations long enough to give her my signature stare. "If I recall correctly, by the time she fled the house screaming, you were muttering hexes under your breath yourself."

"That's not the point. The point is that she really was allergic to cats, and so is my friend. Therefore, you are staying *here*. Furthermore," she continued, straightening to eye me with pursed lips, "I don't want you wandering about and getting into trouble while I'm gone. It won't kill you to remain in the house for a few days. You can catch up on all that sleep you complain about missing. I've asked Penny to look in on you every day to make sure your food and water are topped off and that you remain where you're supposed to be."

I did not deign such nonsense with a response. She acted as if I were some naughty puppy in need of a sitter. Lily knew she couldn't keep me confined, whether by mundane or magical means. But she seemed to think her exhortations, combined with third party monitoring, would do the trick.

Were I a normal cat, I would have rebelled by hiding under the couch. But, since I was a civilized feline, I decided that sulking was beneath me. Instead, I resolved to go about my business exactly as I pleased. After all, stupid rules had only themselves to blame for not being followed.

At least the unlucky soul saddled with "looking after" me was none other than Penny, my human's assistant at her place of work. While a cat's duties are fairly simple—eat, sleep, tend to your human, repeat—humans seemed to delight in taking on odd and rather superfluous tasks. My human, for instance, is a Book Guardian at a small women's college. She spends her days fussing over dusty tomes as if they were her kittens and roaring like a she-tiger at anyone who so much as looks cross-eyed at them. The boring human term I believe is "archivist" or "librarian." But having been on the receiving end of her wrath—it isn't my fault I don't have thumbs, how was I supposed to put the books back on the shelf?—I think you would agree that Book Guardian is a more accurate title. And it is not just mundane books she guards, but wizard ones as well. For beneath this college's library is hidden...you'll never guess... another library.

Shocking, isn't it? I thought so, too.

Supposedly, it is a top-secret archive known only to wizards, but whoever said that has obviously never met me.

In any case, it was not long after my Enlightenment that I made my first excursion into this magical abode, all the while allowing my human to think she had "let" me in. After a thorough inspection, I gave it a solid "B" for soft things to lie on and an "A-" for the quality of its "up" spaces. There were many interesting things among its shelves that made my nose tingle, which I rather like. But in the end I stuck with an overall "B" rating because of the giant, deformed stone squirrel atop one of the wooden cabinets. I don't know what species of squirrel a "gargoyle" is, but the hideous thing has no tail, barely any fur, and a lumpy, misshapen face. Its eyes always seem to follow me, and my nose itches so violently when I approach it that I nearly always sneeze.

There are many strange and amusing things that happen in the library above and library below that keep me entertained. Once, a particularly dense student brought her lunch into the sacred "stacks" and was caught *eating it while reading a book.* Silly human. I suspect everyone within the surrounding three blocks heard Lily's cry of outrage once the unfortunate student was discovered. The girl certainly won't be breaking library rules again any time soon, not after her lengthy visit to my human's secret torture chamber. What, don't believe me? Just because I have not seen it doesn't mean it's not there.

When not distracted by dim-witted students or piles of paperwork, my human retreats to the library below to practice magic. She is quite good, though I usually prefer to observe, just in case, so I often accompany her—sometimes with her knowledge, sometimes without.

That is why, though Lily had already assured me her trip was purely "social" and would involve no magic whatsoever, I was still tempted to ignore her command and stow away in her car anyway. One can never be too careful when it came to wizards.

The only thing that held me back was, in fact, the Second Rule of Cat. Contrary to popular belief, I was not in the habit of raising my human's blood pressure simply because I enjoyed watching her squirm. That was Sebastian's job. Though, if one was inclined to be technical, I did allow him to go about it with complete freedom, perhaps even encouraging him a time or two. But that's beside the point. Regardless of my own desires, my presence would most likely detract from Lily's enjoyment of her friend's company, and she had few enough friends as it was. With Sebastian accompanying her, I could not argue that her safety would not be looked after—that witch was the only being besides my human's wizard teacher, Madam Barrington, whom I trusted to keep her more-or-less in one piece. Sebastian did tend to attract trouble like catnip attracted cats, so his presence was somewhat of a double-edged sword. But I knew he was trustworthy and had plenty of tricks up his sleeve.

This did not mean I intended to stay in the house, of course. With Lily gone, who would guard all her books? Penny would surely appreciate the help. In any case, my nose was tingling that morning, which was always a sure sign of adventure on the horizon. The sight of my human zipping up her suitcase and hauling it to the front door did not give me any ill feelings of foreboding, so I surmised that the coming adventure would be best found among the silent shelves of my human's library. After all, when the wizard is away, the evil denizens of the deep come out to play. At least, I hoped they would. I hadn't gotten to maul anything in far too long, and my claws were going positively dull.

Silent as, well, a cat, I hopped down from the bed and

followed my human into the living room, where I took up a position on the back of the couch to observe the proceedings. It was not long before I heard the dulcet tones of Sebastian's radioactive scrap pile approaching. That is my human's name for it, in any case. Since her first encounter with the artfully arranged layers of trash coating the car's interior, she has refused to set foot in the vehicle. Sebastian calls it theft insurance. Lily calls it disgusting. I choose to remain silent on the issue.

To be fair, the trash is not just a symptom of Sebastian's laziness. He actually uses it to ferment aged pizza, a delicacy preferred by a certain mold fae named Grimmold whom he employs from time to time. Unfortunately, I am strictly forbidden from interacting with any of Sebastian's fae minions. The humans seem to think I would be inclined to eat one. Silly humans. I could tell from the little creatures' smell that fae would taste positively awful—like plants, to be exact. Which does not mean I wouldn't enjoy their squeals of terror as they fled from my razor-sharp cla— I mean, no, of course I would never *dream* of chasing Sebastian's little friends. What kind of monster do you think I am? Alas, my plight would be far less painful if the dratted creatures did not flit about in such a tantalizing manner. I swear they do it simply to torture me.

The life of a cat is positively agonizing. Some days, I don't even know how I survive.

In any case, Sebastian's sense of interior decorating meant that Lily insisted on taking her car for the trip while Sebastian left his at the apartment. The clank and puff of his aged steed was not yet within human hearing range, so Lily was oblivious to its approach and hurried back to the bedroom to complete her preparations.

While she was thus distracted, Sebastian finally arrived,

parked, and mounted the front steps. But instead of ringing the bell, he peered through the front window, brown eyes searching. Spotting me on my perch, he grinned and pointed down at the doorknob with one eyebrow raised.

I considered my options for a good long second, then took it upon myself to be helpful and let the witch in instead of bothering my obviously busy human. Hopping down to the floor, I...what? Did you expect me to give away all my trade secrets by describing how I managed to unlock and open a closed door?

Humans. So demanding. Suffice it to say: Cat Magic.

"Hey, Kip. You ready to have the house all to yourself?" Sebastian asked, closing the door carefully and crouching down to give me his trademark dazzling smile—which, by the way, doesn't work on cats. His long, nimble fingers scratching under my chin and down my spine on the other hand, were another matter entirely. I rewarded him with a purr and a head-butt on his knee to show my acceptance of his offering. He chuckled, his dark, unruly hair and rumpled clothes the picture of unabashed disarray. After a sufficient amount of time spent showering me with adoration, he straightened his lanky form and glanced around for signs of Lily. "Bedroom?"

I twitched my tail in affirmation and sauntered toward the hall. It was a pity the only person who understood my meows was my own human—something about the nature of my Enlightenment and the magic connecting us. Fortunately, Sebastian was as clever as they came and picked up on my cat signals with little trouble. He followed me dutifully down the hall as I acted the gracious host and showed my guest around the house—Lily's room first, of course.

Nosing open the bedroom door, I hopped up on the bed and settled down, tucking my feet under me to observe the action. My human calls this a "catloaf" position, but I resent such comparison of the noble cat to a common bakery item.

"Kip, is that you?" Lily asked from her clothes dresser, back to the doorway. "Will you do me a favor and keep an eye out for Sebastian? He should be arriving soon if he isn't late again."

Sebastian, who was doing a very poor job of hiding his mile-wide grin, leaned against the doorframe and stuck his hands in his pockets. "Hey, Lil."

My human gave out a most satisfying squeak and half spun, one hand clutching her dresser for support, the other over her heart. After shooting me a truly dirty look that I knew held little promise of salmon and cream, she turned said glare upon her guest.

"Don't *do* that, Sebastian. Just because I adjusted my wards to let you come and go freely does *not* give you permission to saunter into my bedroom unannounced."

"What do you mean?" The witch spread his hands wide, almost as innocent looking as me. "Kip let me in. I assumed that meant I was welcome to make myself at home."

Lily's lips made a tight, white line as she looked back and forth between the two of us. I blinked lazily in response, having accomplished my mission for the day.

"Whatever." She threw up her hands and turned back to the dresser, grabbing a few last things before shooing her friend out the doorway and down the hall.

I yawned, enjoying a brief respite after a job well done as I eavesdropped on the humans now headed for the living room. Lily was grilling Sebastian, ensuring her witch had brought enough spare clothes and toiletries. After she had gone through her own checklist twice, she sent Sebastian outside with the baggage and got to work raising several wards that would keep her abode secure from strangers while she was away. I decided it was time to make my appearance.

Taking advantage of shadows and my human's own inattention, I "appeared" on the back of the couch just as Lily finished her casting and turned around, eyebrows lowered. They lifted as she spotted me.

"There you are. I thought you might be sulking under the bed or something, since I said...well...you'll be fine, won't you? It's just a few days."

"I would be more fine if you added a cream dispenser beside my water bowl."

My human's worried look broke as her lips twitched upward—which, naturally, had been my objective all along. "Only if I also get you an exercise wheel."

"Agreed."

"In your dreams, buster."

I sniffed disdainfully.

Lily stepped forward and picked me up. It was not something I generally enjoyed—lap snuggling was my preferred method of human contact—but she obviously needed reassurance, so I allowed it. With gentle fingers she stroked my ears, then hugged me tight. I purred loudly, assuring her of my continued, if rather exasperated, affection. She was my one and only human, and I would do anything for her. Well, anything she *needed*, anyway. And I did appreciate the ear rubs.

Setting me down, she gave me one last, stern look. "Behave. Please? At least stay out of trouble and don't run Penny ragged. The poor woman has to manage everything while I'm gone, and she doesn't need you adding to her stress, all right?"

"I promise to do nothing Sebastian would not approve of."

"Sir Edgar Allan Kipling!"

"Oh, very well. I promise not to get into trouble..."

"That's better. Penny will be by every morning to check on you before she goes to the library. Now, have a good time napping and I'll see you in a few days."

With that, she opened the door and stepped outside. Sebastian was waiting at the bottom of the steps and gave me a wave. "Be sure to eat all the ham and cheese scones for me while we're gone!" he yelled, eyes sparkling with mischief.

"Shush! Don't encourage him." Lily pulled the door shut and the lock turned with a click. I felt the magic of her wards slide into place as the sound of their footsteps faded; then car doors slammed and an engine rumbled to life.

"...unless absolutely necessary." My meow echoed in the empty house, and I allowed myself a moment of smugness before I got back to cleaning myself, confident that trouble would come knocking all too soon.

CHAPTER TWO

THE DELICATE ART OF BUZZSAWING

*H*ave you ever tried to out-wait a cat? If you have, it probably didn't work. This is because we spend our entire lives waiting—for food, for pettings, for our next nap—and so are masters in the art of sitting and doing nothing.

While I have all the natural advantages that come with my ancestry, I was unusually restless the next morning. I considered striking out on my own for the library, but two things held me back. First, I needed Penny to see me in the apartment, so she would assume all was in order. Second, and most important, it was raining. No amount of adventure was worth getting soaked, short of my human's imminent demise. Therefore, I decided to commandeer a ride from Penny instead.

Penny is a decent sort. She likes cats and helps my human maintain her sanity, which is more than could be said of some. She is a "mundane," as wizards refer to normal humans clueless to the existence of all things magical. Wizards are strict about keeping themselves and their affairs off the mundane radar, so I was limited in what I could allow Penny to guess about me. Fortunately, mundanes are excellent at rationalizing away anything out of the ordinary, especially where cats are involved, and Penny already knew me for a—ahem—shall we say "precociously clever" feline. Other terms have been applied to me, but "dratted hellion" and "troublemaking ragamuffin" don't have quite the same ring.

Penny, in any case, was not one to call names, and I greeted her with a friendly purr and raised tail as she unlocked Lily's front door a little before seven thirty.

"Why hello there, Mr. Kipling!"

For some reason, she had never quite grasped that I was a Sir, not a Mr., but I suppose I couldn't hold it against her, especially not when I could smell tuna coming from somewhere inside her purse.

Penny bent down to stroke me and coo, but with treats on the line I was all business. Bracing my paws on her knee, I nosed in her bag, trying to determine which of the many foreign objects within it contained her offering.

"Goodness, what a smart kitty you are, Mr. Kipling." Penny laughed and stood, hand reaching inside her purse— if she were lucky, she would never realize exactly how clever I actually was. I remained calm and dignified, eyes peeled for the tuna I knew would soon be materializing. "I thought you might be a little lonely with Lily gone, so I whipped up these homemade cat treats. What they sell at the store is so unhealthy, you know."

At that particular moment, I wasn't concerned with where she had gotten the treats, just so long as the treats found their way into my food bowl, posthaste. A single, somewhat plaintive mewl escaped me—purely on instinct, I assure you. The smell of fresh tuna was impairing my cognitive abilities.

Finally, Penny's hand emerged holding a little plastic box filled with round balls of delectable squishiness. She went to the kitchen and popped open the container. The rich wave of aroma which assaulted my senses overcame the last vestiges of my self-control and I twined around her ankles, meowing my immediate demands for tribute.

"There you go, and I'll put the rest of it in the fridge for tomorrow."

Busy satisfying my baser urges, I did not bother watching where in Lily's food cave Penny had secreted the rest of my treats. It didn't matter. I would find them tonight. Normally I knew better than to set paw into my human's food cave, but this particular item was mine, made especially for *me*, and human ideas of rationing were pure ridiculousness.

While I ate, Penny brought in the mail and puttered around the kitchen. Lily had left a few instructions scribbled across a notepad on the counter for her. I had already checked them, of course, to ensure they met my approval and did not contain anymore silly rules.

"Well, I guess I'll see you tomorrow, then, Mr. Kipling," Penny finally said, bending down to scratch my ears as I used one paw to clean tuna juice from my whiskers. "You have a nice day, hear? I'm hoping it'll be quiet at the library. Nothing like staying indoors with books when the weather is this miserable."

"I could not agree more, Miss Penny. Though I suspect you will be seeing me sooner than you expect." The girl didn't understand a word of my meow, of course, but she beamed down at me like a proud mother all the same.

"You are such a darling little thing. Sometimes I almost fancy you can understand what I'm saying."

If only you knew, human. If only you knew.

With one last pat, she rose and gathered her purse and coat, heading for the front entrance. I employed my powers of Cat Magic to shadow her, staying close on her heels as she opened and closed the door. The moment I was out I made a dash for her car, eager for shelter from the rain while Penny busied herself locking the apartment. Her heels made a muted clacking sound in counterpoint to the rain as she descended the steps and headed for the driver's side door.

Vehicular stowaway was a skill I had perfected soon after my Enlightenment, and it was particularly useful on days such as this when the sky above became the color of cat litter and inflicted water on every unprotected surface, conditions which no self-respecting cat would endure. What about tigers, you ask? Don't they love water? Well, every family has a crazy uncle, and tigers are the crazy uncles of the cat family. India may be hot, but so is Atlanta in August, and I managed to survive without lowering myself to the level of *bathing in water*. Tigers just needed to find themselves humans with air conditioning.

In any case, I was *not* a tiger, and would happily use every bit of Cat Magic I possessed to remain dry. Which meant I had to infiltrate Penny's car. The first step—positioning for launch—was complete. In the next step things became tricky, and timing was everything. The best moment to slip in was when humans were busy arranging their belongings. That gave me the chance to ooze onto the floorboards and hide under the driver's seat. My long fur made everyone assume I was too large to secret myself into the many nooks and crannies I employed on a regular basis. That is often humans' greatest mistake; you should never assume anything about a cat. I admit, it was a tight squeeze, but cats are half liquid anyway—another feline trait humans always seem to underestimate.

Penny, much like Lily, kept her car neat and tidy, and I easily slipped beneath the driver's seat and settled into a somewhat flattened ball...cube...lump...all right, fine! Loaf. I settled into a catloaf. You would think the English language would be sophisticated enough to describe our mannerisms without equating us to baked goods. You would be wrong. I suppose I can withstand the indignity for the sake of clarity. But know that I do so under extreme duress.

Regardless, I enjoyed a warm, comfortable ride to the library. In all honesty, if Lily wished to curtail my stowaway proclivities, all she had to do was adopt Sebastian's tactic: stuff so much trash beneath her car seats that there was no room left for a cat. Not that I would be sharing that particular insight with my human any time soon. I liked my incognito rides, thank you very much.

We arrived at the library in no time, and I slipped out from under Penny's seat and into the bushes to wait for the coast to clear. I can't turn myself invisible, after all, no matter what you may think. Though, at this time of morning with no one else in the library, it would not have been difficult to stay on Penny's heels all the way through the front doors. But no, I had my own secret way of infiltrating the building which gave me much better access to the out-of-the-way bits in which I preferred to lurk.

Once Penny had disappeared through the front doors, and I had waited for a few early-rising students huddled under umbrellas to hurry past, I made my furtive way around the outside of the library. Like many of the buildings of this human college, the library was quite large and very old. Its towering red and gray walls smelled of aged stone and moss, a bit lost amid the overwhelming aroma of damp earth that surrounded me as I slunk from bush to bush, trying to keep out of the wet. Much to my displeasure, the leaves were sparse this time of year, and branches did little to halt the drip, drip, drip of rain onto my lovely—and freshly cleaned—coat.

Deciding that discretion was useless in the face of water, I abandoned the bushes and made a beeline for my secret entrance, not stopping until I was safely ensconced in the dry embrace of the library's ground floor.

The McCain Library, as it is officially named, had a bit of an odd layout that lent itself to my secret wanderings. The original building containing the vaulted, gothic-style reading room was attached to a newer section remodeled to hold the "stacks." Why humans come up with all these complicated terms, I'll never know. As far as I was concerned, it was all books, books, and more books. But for whatever reason, the three floors of stacks were offset with the three floors of the main library, so that stack number one was halfway between the first and second floors, and stack number two was halfway between the second and third, and so on. This made for marvelous nooks and crannies to hide in, not to mention the maze of ducts and crawl spaces that a clever cat might use to great advantage.

For the time being, however, I avoided the upper floors. Being rather damp and put out, I retreated to the utility room near the basement archives to clean myself in peace and get a bit of shuteye before beginning my patrol. That was where the furnace was located, you see, and I had discovered one special place just beneath it where I could bask in the flow of warm air. Understandably, it was my favorite refuge in the whole building. While not quite as divine as the sunbeams in my human's office, this spot was at least reliable and out of the way.

Several hours later, I calculated I was revitalized enough to mosey upstairs and ensure Penny was getting along. After that, it was time to begin exploring. My whiskers had been twitchy all morning, and I just knew there was something in the library in need of my feline attention.

After carefully checking the door to the basement archives—all was secure and in order—I made my way up to the first floor. I found Penny in the world history section, re-shelving a cart of books. Though her official title was Assistant Administrative Coordinator, there was only so much coordinating a person in a quiet library on a small college campus could do, so I often found Penny assisting with librarian duties. I left her to it; as a being with opposable thumbs, her time was well-served in such organizational tasks. I sometimes wished I had been endowed with human powers of grasping—everyone knows that if cats possessed opposable thumbs, we would rule the world—but I had come to accept the fact that my paws were meant for greater things, such as kneading couch cushions and swatting overly friendly dogs.

Leaving Penny to the joys of her opposable thumbs, I conducted a thorough patrol of the rest of the library's seven floors, searching for the source of my whisker twitches. But my investigation uncovered nothing more than two cases of book abuse and one student hidden in a reading nook eating a banana. I considered bringing a librarian's attention to the girl dog-earing pages of *Das Kapital*, but decided that any maltreatment named after a dog was ironically fitting for such a book and left her to it. By the time I circled back to the banana-eater, the offensive object had disappeared from view, and all was quiet. Since no books appeared to be lying about in stained tatters from their supposedly lethal proximity to food, I surmised my intervention was not required and continued my restless prowling.

I had to admit, despite my devotion to my human and the protection of her library, I did not quite understand her obsession with rules when it came to books or, well, everything. Sebastian's mind made more sense to me, and I was glad he was slowly rubbing off on her. She needed it. A lot. They would be good for each other, if I could ever get them to admit it. But that was a job for another day. Today, I needed to discover what nefarious plot was afoot that kept making my whiskers twitch like a nervous mouse—a comparison which, I can assure you, no cat appreciated.

Speaking of mice, I decided to retreat to the ground floor to do a bit of pest control. Since I had begun to frequent the library, the very scent of my presence was often enough to deter any rodent so unwise as to set its disgusting little paws within my domain. But there was always that one foolhardy individual. Perhaps it had been dropped on its head as a mousling, or perhaps the little vagabonds had some sort of bet going—whoever could bring back a bit of book spine from the seventh floor would win the cheese pot.

Well, not on *my* watch.

I had just settled into a comfortable stakeout of one of their usual hidey-holes in the utility room when I was stricken with the most terrible nose itch a cat could possibly endure. I sat up, rubbing a paw across my face in vain. That's when I noticed it—my collar had grown warm.

Now, my collar is no ordinary object. Not only is it a thing of great beauty—finely tooled leather inlaid with silvery metal—but my human had enchanted it with many wards. It came in handy when I had to do things like attack wizards who tried to blast me into a pile of cinders, or face down demons with claws the size of kitchen knives who fancied me for an after-dinner snack. I appreciated the help, since singed fur smells absolutely terrible and is impossible to clean. You have to wait ages to shed it, and in the meantime your life is pure misery. Don't bother asking how I know; it's embarrassing and I won't tell. Just remember that having a wizard for a human is no walk in the park. Not that I let my human take me on walks. Putting a cat on a leash is paramount to waterboarding—pure torture, I tell you, and a crime against the good name of cats everywhere.

But let's not get distracted.

The point is that my collar was a thing of great power. But beyond my own human's spells, it seemed to have something...extra. Perhaps it had to do with the magic that precipitated my Enlightenment. Whatever the reason, it was in the habit of growing warm when something connected to my human was being threatened.

Mice forgotten, I immediately went on full alert, mind darting to all sorts of horrible scenarios where Lily was being attacked and I wasn't there to protect her. Yet that familiar dread deep within the essence of my cat-hood which I normally experienced whenever my human was in danger did not materialize. Instead, I simply felt mildly annoyed.

Well, that wasn't very helpful.

And don't give me that look. It wasn't as if my Enlightenment had come with an instruction manual. Most of the time, I was just as clueless as the next cat when it came to magic. I simply did a better job of hiding it. You see, humans assume that when you refuse to respond to a question, it's because you know the answer, but don't want to share it. Since I respect my reputation as a cat too much to go around doing something as un-cat-like as *answering ques-*

tions, humans assume I know what's going on. It is a useful mistake that I have never felt inclined to correct.

Of course, sometimes I know exactly what's going on. But how, and why, are none of your business, so keep your nosey questions to yourself.

In this case, all I could surmise was that, while my human herself was safe, something connected to her was being tampered with. Giving up the futile effort to relieve the itch in my nose, I abandoned my stakeout and made a beeline for the door to the basement archives. The door was situated on the ground floor and was kept locked at all times. Beyond the door, steps descended into a cool and quiet room containing rows upon rows of shelves, cabinets, and various other storage devices. It was through the broom closet of this archive that one might gain entrance to the library below, or the Room of a Thousand Mischiefs, as I liked to call it. Due to an appalling lack of imagination—or perhaps the desire to remain inconspicuous—Lily referred to it simply as "the Basement."

Now, I would like to go on record and state that I cannot be held responsible for my human's poor decisions, even if she *can* understand me when I point them out. Humans are stubborn things. They have all these grand ideas about being a "superior species" and forget that we cats domesticated *them*, not the other way around. The audacity of the human race is indeed something to behold.

Despite my uneasiness, the door to the archives was securely locked, and there was no scent of strangers—nor magic—upon it. Next, I headed up to the first floor where my human's office was situated. To my knowledge, she did not keep anything magically sensitive within its walls, but it did not hurt to check.

After waiting behind a corner for one of the administrative staff to leave their office and disappear down the hall, I finally slipped out of my hiding place and crept toward my human's door. Right away, I could tell something was wrong. My nose twitched, but not with the familiar prickle of magic. This was a twitch of disgust as it was assaulted with the stink of rotten eggs. The scent would have been barely noticeable to a human, but to my sensitive nose it was overwhelming.

I edged forward with care, and was unsurprised to find Lily's office unlocked. She always kept it locked when she was away, though Penny had a key should she need to access something in Lily's files. Penny, however, did not use rotten-egg-scented perfume.

But I knew who did.

The last time I had encountered this scent, it was accompanied by a large demon who tried to eat me. Unsurprisingly, I objected, and the ensuing altercation left me rather hypersensitive to the smell. Sulfur, I believe it was called, and it was the unmistakable sign of a witch nearby using demonic magic. I could not think of a more appropriate odor to announce their presence, though wet dog might have done the trick just as well.

Now, I feel I must say a word about witches, lest you come away with the wrong impression. Throughout the long history of magic, wizards and witches have most often been at odds. According to what I have observed and overheard from various sources, that is because the easiest way a non-wizard can gain magical power has always been to make deals with demons, and demons are about the nastiest and most despicable beings to ever exist. They are even worse than squirrels, if you can believe that. Demons always have their own agenda, usually involving death, destruction, and entrapment of souls, and are much better at manipulating humans than humans are at manipulating them. Having seen such demonically influenced witches myself, I cannot blame wizards for their opinion that the only good witch is a dead witch.

But, of course, there are always exceptions to the rule, since demonic magic is not the *only* option available to witches—just the easiest, strongest, and most alluring. Sebastian is a shining paragon of witchly virtue, if I may say so myself. Except for a few foolish encounters in his youth, he has kept himself to dealings with the elusive fae, beings who are incredibly picky in their contact with humanity, since fae are the sworn enemies of demon kind and humans have long proven themselves to be unfailingly corruptible and untrustworthy.

Taking all that into account, it might be easier to understand why Lily and Sebastian's friendship was so unique, and why I could trust that troublemaker with my human's life, yet be greatly displeased to learn that witches were about in McCain Library, snooping into my human's private things.

At least my day was finally starting to get interesting.

The smell of sulfur was not strong enough for a demon to actually be present, and I could detect no more than one human in the office, but I was taking no chances. With the utmost care, I eased into the room, keeping to the shadows along the bottom of the many bookshelves which covered every available wall space. Once secreted beneath the visitor's chair—which stayed next to the bookshelves because my human used it as a footstool—I took stock of the situation. My nose had been right. A single man crouched behind Lily's desk, rifling through its drawers with occasional nervous glances at the office door. He was a runty type, with longish, unkempt hair and a thin nose which seemed to be permanently scrunched in disgust—well, if he spent much time around demons, I could not blame him.

I did not know what he hoped to find in my human's office—Lily was careful to keep all traces of her wizardry safely hidden at home or in the Room of a Thousand Mischiefs. She could not maintain wards on her office or the basement archives that restricted general access, since employees of the library had legitimate business in both locations on a regular basis. I suspected she had some sort of passive wizardry in place to warn her of trouble, but I hoped for this unfortunate witch's sake he had not triggered it. Not only did Lily not need to be bothered with such a trifling, but I did not think even this piece of scum deserved to be on the receiving end of my human's steely-eyed displeasure. I would deal with him and that would be that.

Comfortably hidden beneath the chair, I began to formulate a plan. I had to not only instill the appropriate amount of terror in my victim so he would think twice before invading my human's private space again, but I also needed to notify the library staff of his misdeeds. All without revealing my presence, of course. Well, I supposed it would do no harm for the witch to see me, since he would not be rushing to tell anyone how he had been royally thrashed by a cat.

Planning done, I slipped back to the office door and used my powers of Cat Magic to lock it. Then, I sauntered around the desk, sat behind the crouched witch, and gave him my most innocent and winsome meow.

The man jumped several inches in the air and fell to the side, executing a rather flailing roll. Once he had scrambled to his feet, breathing hard and hands raised as if to defend himself, he finally spotted me and relaxed.

"What in tarnation..." he muttered, crouching down

again so his silhouette would not be visible through the frosted glass of the office door. "How the heck did you get in here?"

The witch scowled at me, so I cocked my head in a way that I knew threw humans into paroxysms of adoration over my cuteness, and meowed again.

"I ain't gonna pet you. Now get lost," he whispered fiercely, making flapping motions with his hand.

Well. Fine.

Any restraint I might have been inclined to show this trespassing miscreant vanished like a plate of scones left unattended in Sebastian's presence. I dropped my "adorable cat" act and replaced it with The Death Glare—that look all cat owners know, and fear. The unfortunate witch had just enough time to realize the enormity of his mistake. An expression of horror transformed his face as I launched myself at his head, all eighteen claws extended.

What happened next is what I liked to call The Delicate Art of Buzzsawing. It is not a step I take lightly, and it is only applied to the most lowly of miscreants: kidnappers, murderers, cat-haters, and the like. Luckily for my target, it was winter, and he was wearing a jacket that more or less protected his upper torso, so I focused my mincemeat-making activities on his head and neck.

The doomed witch screamed and flailed about in a blind panic, knocking over Lily's chair as he stumbled backward. Soon enough, the initial shock passed, and his brain kicked in, ordering his body to switch from hysterical flailing to attack mode. Being no stranger to fights, I anticipated this and released my hold before he had a chance to land any blows. Dropping to the floor, I slipped between his blundering feet and clawed my way up his left leg. His screams reached a new pitch of terrified agony as he attempted to unlatch my claws and teeth from his crotch, vision impaired by the blood trickling into his eyes. If you have ever attempted to disengage a cat in full attack mode, you will understand the insurmountable difficulty the witch faced. He eventually seemed to realize the futility of his efforts, because he let go with one hand and staggered to the office door, wrenching at the handle with bloody fingers.

It did not turn.

He fumbled at the lock.

It did not budge.

Believe me, when I want something to stay locked, it does, and in this particular case I was not quite done punishing the witch for rejecting me. It wasn't long before reality dawned on the hapless man: he was trapped in a room with a crazed cat who was busy ensuring his inability to procreate. This realization seemed to be the tipping point, for the witch finally began screaming for help, his cries interspersed with colorful obscenities aimed at yours truly.

To his relief, I am sure, help was not long in coming. In a place as quiet as a library, such a ruckus does not go unnoticed, and I soon heard running feet. One of the librarians appeared on the other side of the door, jerking the handle and trying to figure out what in the world was going on while the witch cursed, cried, and begged for mercy. I only dug my claws in deeper. It took another good minute for Penny to arrive, key in hand. Based on the mutter of voices outside and the sound of her stern reprimands, I could tell nearly everyone in the library had crowded into the hallway, flocking to the commotion in predictable human fashion.

As soon as I heard Penny's key slide into the lock, I knew my work was done and released my hold on the trespasser's groin. Dropping to the floor, I galloped to the corner of the room and scaled one of the bookshelves, reaching the very top just as the door opened. My victim was far too busy blubbering and clutching at the door to have seen where I'd gone. At the prospect of escape from the room of horrors, he literally fell forward through the door, his legs apparently not functioning properly—why, I have no idea, I can't imagine what was wrong with them.

To my delight, Penny leapt back with a scream at the sight of the witch's bloody face, and the man, instead of falling into her arms, did a face-plant on the rug. I observed the proceedings from my perch atop the bookshelves, purring in satisfaction as campus security was called and someone ran to get a first aid kit while Penny interrogated the trespasser.

In the end, I think the best answer Penny ever got for what had happened was that the man thought Lily's office was the bathroom, somehow locked himself inside, and then fell down and hit his face on the desk. I could attest that all those things had, indeed, happened at some point or another, though I was disappointed by the man's lack of imagination. The spectacular nature of his injuries deserved a much more dramatic explanation—ninja squirrels armed with forks, for instance, or an alien abduction at the very least.

Once campus security finally arrived and hauled the miscreant away, Penny had a chance to examine the crime scene. I watched her carefully, aware that she knew exactly what cat scratches looked like and had not been at all convinced by the witch's story. She tutted at the blood stains he had left on the carpet and various objects around the room, no doubt making plans to notify the janitor. She also carefully rearranged Lily's desk, cleaning up the mess the witch had made of my human's papers and belongings.

Finally, she began a careful examination of the whole office. At first, I thought she was looking for the perpetrator of the attack—that is, me. But she did not investigate the normal places one might search for a cat. Instead, she focused on the floor, walls, door, desk, and other flat surfaces around the room. At one point she even turned her attention to the ceiling. I thought for a moment I had been discovered, for she looked straight at where I lurked atop the bookshelf. Thankfully, there was enough room for me to scoot back against the wall and remain invisible from below, and Penny did not go in search of a ladder, so I concluded her glance was mere coincidence. She eventually finished whatever she was doing and left the office with a puzzled expression, carefully locking the door behind her.

I spent the next few hours cleaning blood from my fur and taking a nice, long nap. I was pleased with my day's work, but a nagging tingle in my whiskers told me that I had not seen the last of this adventure. Whatever that witch had been after, my intervention had ensured he left empty handed, which meant he, or some other miscreant, would be back tomorrow to finish the job.

I did not slip out of my human's office until late in the evening when the library was being locked up for the night. To my great relief, the rain had stopped. I had a pleasant, if chilly trip home under the dark gray sky while I busily planned the next day's excursions.

CHAPTER THREE

AN UNEXPECTED VISITOR

*O*ur morning routine proceeded just as before, with Penny arriving bright and early to offer me a cheery smile and several much-appreciated scratches. I had decided the night before not to raid my human's food cave for the remaining tuna treats. No doubt Penny had enough suspicion swirling around in her head already, without me adding The Case of the Disappearing Cat Treats to her list of inexplicable occurrences. The last thing I needed was for her to call Lily and mention any oddness—my human would know exactly what I'd been up to.

No, instead I sat patiently on the kitchen floor, trying to contain the occasional tail-twitches of impatience as Penny extracted the tuna treats and warmed them up to a comfortable temperature—a thoughtful, but unnecessary gesture. I would rather have not waited the extra sixty seconds, but alas, she was not Lily and therefore was oblivious to my polite suggestion to *GIVE ME MY TREATS THIS VERY INSTANT OR SUFFER THE WRATH OF—*

Okay, so I forgot all about wrath and ruin as soon as warm, juicy tuna filled my mouth. I decided to let things slide, this time. After all, we cats can't hold humans' ignorance against them. It takes decades of careful observation and tireless research to understand even the most obvious of our communiqués, so it is not surprising that the subtleties of our everyday speech are lost on them.

These thoughts consoled me as I ate and Penny brought in the mail. By the time I was finished, she was heading out the door, and I had to scramble to slip past her unseen. My whiskers were still wet with tuna juice, which annoyed me, but I was forced to endure it a little longer as I executed my usual maneuverings to catch a ride to the library. The sky was no longer molten gray, nor assaulting the earth with its offensive water, but the temperature had dropped, and I much preferred Penny's warm floorboards to traipsing about in the cold myself. I needed to conserve my energy in case I was called upon to buzzsaw another miscreant.

Since it was no longer raining, I took my time circling the library building after disembarking from Penny's Taxi Service. I wanted to give the grounds a thorough inspection after yesterday's incident. As I slipped through the grass and around bare bushes, the early morning frost bit into my delicate pads. I conjured up dark thoughts of Cat Displeasure and Disapproval and aimed them at the accursed weather. If the cold had any sense, it would go north where it was actually wanted, or at least expected. Somewhere like the North Pole. Or Ohio.

Refocusing on the task at hand, I sniffed delicately around the back of the building, paying special attention to the maintenance entrance. To my great non-surprise, I found footprints and the faintest whiff of rotten eggs. Someone had been there last night, snooping around. And by someone, I meant a witch with a death wish, of course.

What? Don't look at me like that, I'm not threatening to

kill anybody. I've simply spent enough time around Sebastian to know that anyone so imbecilic as to meddle with demons has a swift and unpleasant end coming to them. "Like playing with fire, if fire could invade your mind and possess your soul without you even knowing it," as he once said. Personally, I tried to avoid fire as much as possible, so I wouldn't know. What I did know was that witches bled just the same as everyone else, and I intended to make whoever had been poking about my human's library regret their curiosity.

Information gathered, I raced to my special entrance and made all haste inside. To my relief, the door to the archives was secure, as was Lily's office, and after a thorough patrol of the entire premises I could not detect even the tiniest trace of witches or their smelly demon minions. This brought the threat level down from "Deigning to Actually Run" to "Forgoing a Nap to Keep Watch." Yesterday had already seen us at the highest threat level: "Buzzsaw Mode." Below "Forgoing a Nap" there was simply "Keeping a Cat's Eye Out." Technically, there did exist a threat level higher than "Buzzsaw Mode." I call it "You Have Touched My Human, Prepare To Die." However, I tried to reserve that level of energy depletion for only the most dire of situations. The nap regeneration required after such an outburst was considerable, and no threat save my own human's imminent harm was worth the trouble.

And so the morning wore on, with me keeping watch in the form of cat-naps staged in various locations around the library. What most humans don't realize about cats is that our eyes are the least effective of all our senses. While we give our eyes a rest, our ears and whiskers are just as alert as always, attuned to every scrap of sound or thrum of movement. Yet despite my alertness, I discovered nothing more alarming than an errant student using her cell phone on the third floor—a crime almost as great as bringing food into the library.

Finally growing bored with my lurking, I decided to find out what Penny was up to. My search ended in Lily's office, where the assistant was filing forms and leaving a few stacks of papers on my human's desk for her later perusal and approval.

I was about to wander off again when Penny picked up the phone and began to make a call. Curious, I stationed myself beneath a visitor's chair to listen.

"Oh, hello, Lily! Just checking in like you asked...Yes, yes, everything at the library is fine, though we did have a strange man, er, hanging about yesterday. But security took care of it...What? Oh no, nothing to worry your head over, he was just loitering about with no chaperone...No, no, Mr. Kipling is fine. I saw him just this morning. He is quite enjoying those home-made treats I told you about. You really should let me give you the recipe, you know store-bought treats are full of all sorts of chemicals that—oh...yes, of course, you have to run, I'm sure. Well, have a safe trip home. I'm sure Mr. Kipling will be pleased as a pickle to see you tomorrow. Bye, now!" And with that, she hung up.

I waited, curious to see what would happen next. I hadn't the faintest notion why Penny had left out the screaming, blood, and intrusion into Lily's office. Perhaps she just didn't want to worry Lily on her vacation. After all, the incident would be the talk of the month, and my human would not fail to hear the particulars when she returned, exaggerated out of proportion, of course. But, I supposed I could understand Penny's reticence. It was human nature to downplay and ignore things they could not understand, and in this case it worked to my advantage.

Penny remained at Lily's desk for some time, appearing lost in thought. When she finally left, I hopped up on my human's work space and inspected everything, just to be sure. But all was in order, so, bored once again, I decided to visit the front desk and practice my "invisibility" skills. There was a convenient spot just under the librarian's station where I could safely curl up and listen in on conversations. The trick was getting there without being spotted—not that I have ever been spotted, of course. I'm quite disappointed you even considered the possibility.

Several strategic slinks later, I was stationed beneath the front desk with no one the wiser, and I settled down to listen. McCain Library was not a terribly busy place, even when school was in session, so most of what I heard consisted of occasional phone calls and the librarians speaking quietly to each other. Every now and then a student would come to the desk with a question, but I only kept half an ear on such mundanities, my attention distracted by the tiny squeaking noises I was picking up from the walls behind the librarian's station. Those dratted mice. One of these days—

"Excuse me, young lady. I was wondering if you could help me."

The voice above me snapped my awareness back to the front desk as a strange shiver passed over my skin. A man's well-kept shoes, made of expensive leather, had appeared in front of me. Even as my ears pricked, I was aware of the tingle in my whiskers and the involuntary, restless twitch of my tail. Every hair stood on end as my instincts screamed *snake*. Charming, mesmerizing, and deadly, snakes were the archenemy of cats, and I could tell by his voice alone that this man spelled trouble.

"Of course. How can I help?" Heeled feet shifted and I

knew one of the librarians had given the visitor her full attention.

"Well, I am a good friend of Lily's, and she asked me to bring her this little package when I had the chance. Could you point me in the direction of her office?"

"Oh...well, Ms. Singer isn't in today, but you're welcome to leave the package here at the front desk. I'll make sure she gets it."

"Oh, no need for that. It's a very valuable item, and I promised I would not pass it off to anyone else. She mentioned I could simply leave it on her desk if she was not available when I came by, so I'm sure you would not mind showing me where it is?"

"I...I..."

Something odd was going on. The librarian's voice was distant, as if she were barely aware of what was happening, and my whiskers were itching like mad. There were no odd smells coming off this man, but that only meant he had not recently called upon any demons. There were other ways to manipulate.

Like I said: Snake.

Moving carefully, I oozed over to the librarian's side of the desk and gently laid a paw on her foot. When she didn't respond, I unsheathed my claws a fraction, letting them barely prick the skin.

"Oh—I'm so sorry, sir, I-I don't know what came over me. I'm very sorry, but—but non-staff aren't allowed in the offices without an appointment. Ms. Singer is very strict about the rules."

I half expected the Snake to press the issue, but he simply gave a winsome smile—I could tell because the librarian's heartbeat quickened—and made his excuses.

"No need, my dear. I'll simply look around a bit at your

magnificent building and then be on my way. I'm sure I can catch Lily next week."

"All right. H-have a nice day..."

The librarian still seemed confused, but as she was in no danger, I knew what my duty was: to keep my eyes on the Snake. He was clearly up to no good, and I couldn't let him out of my sight for even a moment.

You humans might consider it quaint, but animal instincts give us a superior edge for a reason. There are some things we animals just *know*. Behavior is one of them. Most humans are a pretty even mix of behaviors, and give off vibes as simple as "friendly" or "unfriendly." But some humans have a stronger air about them. Sebastian, for instance, is very foxlike, though he has a rather prominent streak of magpie as well: messy, playful, and inclined to hoard. Madam Barrington, my human's wizard mentor, is an eagle through and through. Proud and strict, she can pin you beneath that disapproving gaze of hers and turn you into a terrified rabbit, no matter how brave you think you are. Not that she has ever had reason to disapprove of me, of course. Lily, unsurprisingly, defies description. If I could put her neatly into a little box of predictable behavior, my job would be ten times easier. The problem with my human is that ninety percent of the time she sticks to her comfortable habits and lulls you into a false sense of security, so that when that other ten percent of the time kicks in, she takes you off guard. But I suppose I enjoy the challenge. After all, Sebastian is responsible for ninety-nine percent of her ten percent of unpredictability, so if I really wanted my life to be normal, I would just get rid of Sebastian, which, of course, is out of the question.

Unlike my human, I knew exactly what to expect with this Snake. Well, I knew he would be sneaky, untrustworthy, and dangerous, at least. Which is why I kept my distance as I shadowed him about the library. He did, indeed, seem to be interested only in the beautiful gothic architecture, the sight of which often made my human sigh in pleasure. Yet his gaze was too sharp, his demeanor too casual to fool me. He wore a suit of gray and had his winter coat draped over one arm. The package he had claimed to have was nowhere in sight, which made me even more suspicious. For a long while I could only see the back of him. His shock of blond hair was stylishly swept to one side and neatly combed—another mark against him. I never trusted men with perfect hair.

After a while, he headed for the stairs and descended to the ground floor, making his unhurried, meandering way toward the door to the basement archives. I crept closer, ready to leap into action if he showed even the slightest sign of misbehavior. But he only laid a hand against the door and stood there, stock still, as if listening. I hunkered down beneath a nearby chair, eyes fixed on his back, which was much more relaxed than my own quivering form. Once again, I could smell no signs of demonic magic, and yet I could *feel* something. Something lurking.

Something evil.

That's when the man turned around and looked right at me. His eyes locked with mine, and I was momentarily frozen in shock. One eye was hazel green. The other was ice blue.

The moment was broken when he sank into a comfortable crouch, eyes not leaving me as they approached my level. I involuntarily arched my back and hissed, the only appropriate response to such an aggressive stare.

"My, my, my. What is a little kitty cat like you doing around here, hm? Perhaps a stray who wandered in?"

I growled deep in my throat; I couldn't help it. Everything in me was blaring alarms and flashing threat level "You Touched My Human," even though Lily was not here, and not in danger. Perhaps it was just the overpowering aura of snake that this cretin exuded. It was wreaking havoc on my normal, sanguine behavior. Or, more likely, it had a magical origin. I hadn't felt this on edge since that incident with the greater demon, and even then, the evil in the air hadn't been this oppressive. There was something more in the hallway than just the Snake and myself. Something bigger, a shadow of some kind. The presence felt like the exact opposite of the entity who had Enlightened me and charged me with Lily's care. Then, I had been surrounded by light and peace. Now, a feeling of malevolence hung in the air.

The Snake remained silent in response to my growl, though a gleam came to his eyes and a little half-smile lifted his lips. "No, you aren't a stray, are you? You are much, much more. Why don't you come over here and we can get to know each other better?"

"Over my dead body," I hissed. If I hadn't been so unnerved by those eyes, I might have launched an attack then and there on mere principle. This creature did not belong anywhere within a hundred-mile radius of my human.

The Snake chuckled. "Tut tut, such disagreeable manners. Perhaps I ought to teach you a lesson in politeness?"

I didn't know what he meant, but I didn't like it and I let him know, no longer afraid my warning growls would disturb the library's peace. For the time being, at least, this Snake wanted to remain inconspicuous, so if I attracted someone's attention, I hoped he would vacate the premises.

"Shhhh, someone might hear you..." the Snake whispered, eyes locked on mine and expression still casually amused. I ignored him, upgrading my growl to a hissing yowl. At that his brow furrowed and his eyes seemed to burn blood red with displeasure. "Silence!" he hissed, his voice turning strangely sibilant as he gave a command he obviously expected me to obey.

Well, "obviously" he had never met a cat before. I increased the pitch of my yowls and took a few swipes in his direction, just to drive the message home: get lost, buster.

A flash of surprise crossed his face. Whatever he had been expecting had not happened, and now that it was clear I wasn't going to shut up, he seemed less inclined to continue our little game. Standing swiftly, he gave me one last narrow-eyed look through those mismatched orbs, then turned to go.

His retreat was timely—for me, at least, if not for him. I had only just ceased sounding the alarm when Penny came round the corner at a trot and ran smack into the taller man's chest. As he caught Penny and steadied her, I took advantage of the confusion and darted down the hall into the utility room where I could peek around the corner and ensure the Snake actually left.

The man exchanged low words with a flustered-looking Penny, pointing to the chair I had been stationed under. I caught the words "cat" and "stray" and knew exactly what story he was feeding the assistant. It was almost true, even, and combined with the look of concerned helpfulness on his face and his respectable appearance, meant he would most likely get away without another call to security.

Penny looked worriedly down the corridor in my direction, but, bless her heart, turned to escort the man up the stairs toward the front desk. Since it was a women's-only college, men were discouraged from loitering about unless they had an escort or a legitimate reason to be there. I wondered why the Snake hadn't sent a less conspicuous female witch the day before—there was no doubt in my mind that this man was in charge of whatever mischief was afoot. Perhaps female witches were all smart enough to give the Snake a wide berth.

Though I still felt a little shaken, and my tail refused to cease its impression of a bottle-brush, I crept carefully after the pair, using my ears rather than my eyes to keep tabs on them. Whether the Snake was just abnormally perceptive, or whether he had some magic that detected my presence, I didn't know. But I was taking no chances where he was concerned.

To my great relief, the man left the building without a fuss, though his absence did little to calm my nerves. It was obvious that, whatever he wanted, it involved the Room of a Thousand Mischiefs. There was nothing else a witch might find of value down in those archives. The man yesterday must have been looking for some sort of key in Lily's office, or perhaps information on the portal to enter the magical library. Whatever it was that they wanted, they would be back again to get it, probably sometime after-hours when I wasn't around to run them off like the mangy dogs they were. And against the Snake...I wasn't sure I could go head to head with him and be sure of a satisfactory ending. Not that the Room of a Thousand Mischiefs didn't have other protections. Only a wizard could enter it, since only a wizard could cast the spell necessary to give them passage through the portal. Witches couldn't use magic the way wizards could. They could only pander to other magical beings, like demons—or fae, in Sebastian's case—and use their "borrowed" power in a limited number of ways.

And yet...perhaps it was time to call Lily home. Just because witches couldn't enter the library below didn't mean there wasn't plenty of other mischief they might get up to, like laying a trap or spying on my human. Or, perhaps they operated under the false impression that they *could* gain access. Anything was possible.

I was still considering these worrisome thoughts, secreted behind the edge of a bookshelf near the main entrance, when a very old, very wizened man came slowly through the front doors. Evening was getting on, and most of the students had left, so the library was empty but for a few librarians and the odd professional scholar.

The man supported himself with a cane that appeared as antique as himself, and he wore a suit that could not have been much newer. Atop a head of snowy white hair sat a black bowler hat. The hat was faded in that way a beloved object gets when you simply can't part with it, even though it is far past its prime. I have several cat toys in just such a state, but don't tell Lily, because she's always trying to throw them away. She doesn't realize that the tattered toys are the most fun.

I wouldn't have given the old man a second glance, except that I couldn't seem to take my eyes off him in the first place. Whiskers twitching, I watched him carefully as he approached the front desk. He carried himself with great dignity, yet from the bow in his shoulders and shadows on his face as his gray eyes swept the lobby, he seemed weighed down by a terrible sadness.

My eyes didn't leave him as he coughed politely, getting the attention of the librarian on duty who was organizing books on a re-shelving cart in the back. When she came over, he took off his hat and gave her a smile.

"Good evening, young lady. Might I bother you to

inform Madam Barrington there is someone here to see her? She usually works late on winter evenings, I do hope she is in." The man spoke with an old fashion turn of phrase, and the curious way he replaced his "w" sounds with "v" and "th" sounds with "z" made me think he was not from around Atlanta. Or America, really.

The librarian gave the man an odd look, probably as thrown by the accent as his appearance. "I'm sorry, sir, but Ms. Barrington is retired. She hasn't worked here for several years. Her replacement, Ms. Singer, is not in at the moment, but you can certainly leave a message for her."

The old man's face fell, and his shoulders drooped further, piquing my curiosity. I wiggled carefully from my hiding place and crept closer as he replied. "Hmmm, Singer...Singer...no, I am not familiar with that family name. I do not suppose the Madam left an address?"

"No, I'm sorry, sir. But she and Ms. Singer worked together. I'm sure if you leave me a way to get in contact, Ms. Singer would be happy to pass on your message to Ms. Barrington."

"No, no, that will not be necessary." The old man shook his head, and from my new hiding place beneath a book cart by the lobby wall, I could see the many lines of age and weariness marching across his face. "She will hear soon enough...soon enough."

With that, he turned and began his slow, unsteady way out the arched front doors. I remained where I was for a moment, considering. Wizards could generally sense when other wizards were nearby. While I was not attuned to the energies of the Source, the place from which wizards drew their power, there was more to Cat Magic than simply landing on one's feet and curling up in fish bowls. If that man was a mundane, then I was a mere house cat.

I decided the library could do without me for a bit, then sprinted for the ground floor where I could slip out unnoticed. Considering the old man's speed, I calculated I could easily catch him before he disappeared into the night, but there was no sense lollygagging.

Dashing around the outside of the library's brick exterior, I made a beeline for the visitor parking lot and saw I was just in time. The man was carefully, laboriously lowering himself into the seat of a car as old and rickety as himself. Not having time for anything more subtle, I threw caution to the winds and leapt right up into his lap just as he reached to close the car door.

To my relief, he didn't have a heart attack, something I am sure Madam Barrington would never have forgiven. He did, however, give a startled yell and raise his cane, causing me to rethink my vulnerable position. I quickly hopped from his lap to the passenger seat where I'd have room to dodge in case he decided to start laying about with that stick of his. Once he got a good look at me, however, he seemed to calm down considerably.

"Now, what is this, eh? Are you lost, pussycat?"

I glared at the man, incensed and at my limit after my stressful encounter with that blond witch. "By all the salmon in the sea, why does everyone insist on using demeaning epithets when addressing the feline race? You humans wonder why cats look so angry all the time? Perhaps because we are nature's perfect killing machines, and yet you stupid humans keep picking us up and kissing us and calling us things like pussycat. I don't care how cute you think we are, we are predators. We kill for a living, or at least we would if you'd let us out into the back garden. Not that we mind pettings, warm laps, and tuna treats, but still. Give us a little respect, for catnip's sake."

Silence descended, and I realized that the old man, far from being properly cowed, was actually amused. His eyes, so shadowed and sad before, had gained a little twinkle, and the few hairs that remained of his eyebrows had risen high, almost disappearing beneath the brim of his bowler hat. "You seem to have quite a bit to say on the matter, *Miezekatze*. So does that mean you are lost? You seem too handsome a fellow to be a stray. It is obvious someone loves you very much."

My indignation eased a little at his words, and I lifted a paw to lick it slowly, making it clear that I was immune to both his praise, and his apparent amusement. I had to maintain some sort of dignity, after all.

"Not lost, then, pussycat?"

My tail twitched in annoyance, but I let it pass.

"Well, you had best go back to your master. I am an old, tired man with no one left, I would be poor company for a lively fellow like yourself." He reached as if to lift me up and no doubt deposit me outside his car, but I gave a little growl and smacked his hand, claws safely sheathed. I needed to find a way to make him understand. If only he would realize I wasn't a normal cat.

An idea came to me, and I arched my back and bent my head as if begging for scratches. He obliged with a little smile, and his fingers soon found the tooled leather of my collar, mostly hidden beneath my long fur.

"What is this, now, little one?" he muttered. As I had hoped, he sensed it was not a normal collar.

Picking me up gently and setting me in his lap, he parted my fur and took a closer look at the dimmu runes engraved in the metal studs of the collar, giving me protection from various types of magical harm.

"Very interesting...are you a wizard's companion, then, pussycat?"

Resigning myself to the name, I nodded my head. It was not a normal motion for a cat and came across as more of a head bob, but at this point I was reduced to miming.

"Ah, very good. Did Madam Barrington send you?"

I shook my head.

"Hmm..." He thought for a moment. "This *Fräulein*, Ms. Singer. I know of no wizard family of that name. Are you her companion?"

I nodded.

"Interesting indeed, *Miezekatze*. I suppose, then, you saw me in the library. Do you live there?"

I wasn't sure how to respond to that, so I attempted a shrug, something I saw Sebastian do on a regular basis whenever he didn't want to give a straight answer to Lily. Unfortunately for me, cats were not really made for shrugging. The best I could come up with was a sort of wriggling crouch, so I gave up the attempt.

"*Meine Güte*, you are an odd little fellow." He looked down at me, expression now thoughtful. "If you spend time in a library, perhaps..." Trailing off, he seemed to become lost in thought. I waited patiently. My human got like this on a regular basis. Wizards seemed prone to becoming lost in the intricacies of their own mind and only came out of it when they had reached some brilliant idea or clever solution.

The old man eventually grunted, as if agreeing with himself on some point. Then he looked back and forth, peering through his windshield into the winter night. It was cold enough that no one was out and about, and indeed, I was a bit worried that the old man would catch his death, sitting there in the cold with barely a sliver of meat on his spindly frame. But he seemed not to mind the chill, and once he was satisfied no one was about, he flicked his fingers through the air as if tracing the alphabet. Shapes formed in streams of gold, and I was soon surrounded by faintly glowing letters, all within easy reach. I stared at him, impressed. I had seen Madam Barrington—and even Lily on occasion—silent cast, using only their willpower and the sharpness of their mind to control spells that most wizards needed to speak aloud to activate. But I had rarely seen either of them do it as effortlessly as this old man.

"Go on, then, pussycat. If you live in a library, perhaps you can read and write. Tell me your name."

It was a bit of a crude solution, but far better than the charades I'd been forced to pantomime for Sebastian on more than one occasion. Lifting a paw, I daintily tapped each letter I wanted, spelling out a sentence for the wizard. It floated above me, glinting in the darkness.

I AM SIR EDGAR ALLAN KIPLING.

"Well, Mr. Kipling, it is a pleasure to meet you, I am sure."

My tail flicked in annoyance, and I wondered if correcting him was worth the effort.

"Tell me, now, why did you jump into my lap, eh?"

I considered my answer, not honestly sure what had driven me to it. To tell him where to find Madam Barrington, perhaps? Or was it the way his whole being was overshadowed by a loneliness that triggered something deep inside me? No matter how indifferent we may seem, cats really do care for humans. We don't want to see you unhappy, we just know it is necessary on occasion. In this case, the old man's sadness was absolutely *un*necessary, and if I could do something about it, I would. In any case, he might be of use.

The glowing letters were still there, having resumed their proper order once my previous sentence was complete. My paw flicked out once again.

I NEED YOUR HELP.

"Ah, so you *are* lost, *Miezekatze?*"

NO. PERHAPS WE SHOULD DISCUSS SOMEWHERE WARMER.

My sentence was messy in my haste to get my point across, but the old man seemed not to mind. In fact, he laughed.

"*Ach*, I forget, sometimes. As old as I am, if I did not spell my coat to keep me warm, I would never venture out of doors. Forgive me."

With a grunt and a groan, he leaned to the side, reaching for the car door that still sat open. I was concerned he would fall over with the effort, but he managed to haul the old thing closed with a slam, rusted metal creaking as it went. As soon as the noise faded, I noticed a change in the air. Even though the car had not been started, and no heat blew through the decrepit-looking vents, the interior grew increasingly warm. The old man must have cast another spell, once again silently manipulating magic as if it were nothing.

"Better, eh?"

I meowed in agreement, hopping off his lap to take up a more dignified seat in the passenger-side chair. The glowing, floating alphabet followed me.

"Now, tell me what you are about, my young friend. Where is your mistress and why have you accosted an old man in the dark?"

I was about to protest when I noticed the gleam in his eyes and the crinkles around his mouth—well, extra crinkles. There were already so many it was honestly hard to tell. Was this what my human felt like when Sebastian teased her? If so, he needed to do it more often—with my help, of course.

MISTRESS ON VACATION. I GUARD LIBRARY BELOW. WITCHES SNOOPING ABOUT. MIGHT COME BACK TONIGHT. HELP ME WATCH?

Relinquishing formality for the sake of brevity, I finished my explanation and waited while the old man read it and reached up to stroke the few white bristles that still held on to his chin. Finally, he muttered to himself and sighed.

"*Ach du grüne Neune*...I am too old for this, my friend. I came here only to...but never mind, that is not important. I am long past my prime, and wish only to sleep. To rest. You can find other help, yes? Perhaps I can call your mistress?"

I studied him for a moment, looking not just for what was obvious, but what was not. Though he did indeed look tired, he also had a strange longing on his face, as if his words were more for himself than for me. This seemed a clear instance of the Second Rule of Cat, and so I did my duty with no small amount of satisfaction.

NONSENSE. OLD PERHAPS BUT POWERFUL. MISTRESS TOO FAR AWAY. YOU ARE WARM HERE. WAIT WITH ME. YOU WILL ENJOY FIGHTING WITCHES. THEY SCREAM LIKE LITTLE GIRLS.

The old man chuckled. "What a bloodthirsty *Katze* you are. Though with witches, I cannot blame you." His expression darkened, and I decided not to mention Sebastian any time soon.

SO YOU WILL STAY.

"*Oy...Scheisse*, you are a clever cat. But my old bones cannot take a night sitting in a car."

YOU ARE A WIZARD. MAKE CAR MORE COMFORTABLE.

"*He*! Cheeky little *Miezekatze*. I ought to teach you a lesson. Familiars were more respectful in my day. Perhaps your mistress is too soft on you.

I AM A CAT, I responded, as if that explained everything. Which, of course, it did.

"Indeed. Ahhhh...well. I have nowhere to be and no one to wait for me. What is an old man to do, eh? At least I will have company this night."

I WILL PURR FOR YOU.

"A generous offer, young sir. Will you also be taking the first watch, then?"

OBVIOUSLY. CATS ARE NOCTURNAL.

"Well, then, that settles it. I am too old to stay up all night anyway. You wake me when the witches come, eh?"

DO NOT WORRY. I WILL SAVE ONE FOR YOU.

"Humph. Cheeky little thing." He chuckled to himself as he shifted about. First, he carefully took off his hat, setting it out of the way on the dashboard, then he leaned back his seat to get more comfortable. No doubt he had already cast a spell to make the seat cushion softer or some such wizardry. I waited until he had settled, then climbed onto his chest, curling up to purr him to sleep as I kept watch out the window, McCain Library looming dark and quiet before me.

It was not until his shiftings had subsided and a light, wheezing snore began to whistle from between his lips that I realized I had forgotten to ask his name. Even more curious, he had made no attempt to offer it.

CHAPTER FOUR

A MOST SATISFACTORY ENDING

The old man must have had a cloaking or avoidance spell of some sort on his car, because the security patrols that occasionally passed by in the night did not give it a first glance, much less a second, despite the fact that it was occupied by a loudly snoring wizard. I was not unduly bothered by the snoring, since I was on watch anyway. It did make it difficult to hear noises outside, but I decided that was the price I paid for picking an old man as my partner in crime. Crime prevention, that is. The side benefit of making trespassing miscreants beg for their mothers was just icing on the cake.

It was late into the night, indeed nearing the hour of dawn, when I finally had the premonition of trouble. Even though I possessed a good vantage from which to watch the library's front and side, its rear was hidden from me, and I knew the witches would not be so foolish as to use the front door. And so even though my hair suddenly stood on end and my whiskers twitched most irritatingly, I had neither seen, heard, nor smelt anything amiss. No matter, I knew when to trust my instincts.

The wizard's floating letters had faded soon after the old man had fallen asleep, so I simply uncurled from my comfortable perch upon his chest and laid a soft paw on his cheek. His response was a resounding snore.

Changing tactics, I decided a thorough ear licking would do the trick. Ears were a safer bet than faces. Despite humans' lack of physical prowess, when startled awake by unknown sensations upon their sensitive faces, they often reacted with violent spasms that even a master of agility such as myself might fall prey to. And with a wizard of such caliber, who knew what magical defense he might resort to in a semiconscious state. My collar would most likely protect me, but it was best not to tempt fate.

Slightly hampered by a multitude of ear bristles, I proceeded with my plan and was soon rewarded with a snort and a disgruntled mumble, at which point I hopped over to the passenger seat and out of the direct line of fire, just in case.

"Verdammte Feen...sind wieder im Jägermeister..." The wizard, far from stirring to wakefulness, rolled over with a creak of old bones, and his snores once again filled the rickety vehicle.

With a tail twitch of displeasure, I assumed the proper stance and resorted to that time-honored tactic of cats around the globe: I began to sing the song of my people. It was the only reliable way to draw humans from the warm depths of their slumbers, though a cat's inevitable success in this regard was usually followed by a hail of pillows and house shoes. Since neither item was available within the cramped space of the car, I felt safe from that particular repercussion.

"Heiliger Strohsack! Zum Donnerwetter, what is all that noise?"

"Well, if you didn't sleep like a deaf lump of petrified wood, I wouldn't have needed to resort to it. Though I feel it only fair to point out that you snore loud enough for a clutter of cats."

"*Ach...mist...*it is only you. Can an old man not get a peaceful sleep? What has your tail in a knot, eh?"

I stared at the wizard, aforementioned appendage twitching, waiting for him to make letters appear. It was at times like these when I lamented my lack of eyebrows. Humans used them to great effect, yet failed to realize that cats had very little in the way of facial expressions, instead using our tails and ears for nearly all communication. Cats do not, in fact, meow at each other. Besides the occasional hiss or yowl to express our deepest displeasure, we would make nary a noise if it weren't for humans and their hopeless ignorance. We invented meowing to communicate with them, since they seem completely oblivious to our tails.

The wizard, apparently, was less dense than most humans, and soon letters appeared before me, glinting ever-so-faintly in the dimness.

MY WHISKERS TWITCHED. SOMETHING IS WRONG. NEED TO CHECK LIBRARY.

"*Du willst mich wohl veralbern...*" the old man muttered, rubbing his eyes. "So your little pussycat whiskers told you to wake me up, eh? *Oy,* I am too old for this..."

STOP BEING A PANSY AND GET UP. WE HAVE WORK TO DO.

The old man froze for a moment, as if his mind needed a moment to unravel the words floating in the air. Then he gave a wheezing chuckle and shook his head. "Serves me right for running about with another wizard's familiar, and a *verdammte* cat, at that. *Ach,* at least there is a bathroom inside."

I ignored his insinuation and instead focused on the mission.

YOU ARE FAMILIAR WITH INSIDE OF LIBRARY?

Another chuckle. "More so than you might imagine, little *Miezekatze*."

GOOD. TRESPASSERS USED REAR. TARGET IS ROOM OF A THOUSAND MISCHIEFS.

"*Was is das*? A thousand mischiefs?"

THE LIBRARY BELOW.

"Ah! We simply called it the Basement in my time. Less chance those nosey mundanes might overhear and get suspicious."

HUMANS. YOU HAVE NO IMAGINATION.

"*Quatsch*! We invented the written language. Who is the uninventive one now, eh?"

CATS INVENTED DIGNITY. ALSO PURRING.

The old man smiled. "A valid point, *Miezekatze*. Now, are we going to sit here jabbering like a flock of hens? Or are we going to do something useful?"

AM WAITING FOR YOU OLD MAN. DO NOT FORGET CANE. GOOD FOR THRASHING.

"Do not tell me how to fight witches, you young whip-per-snapper. I have been dealing with those dirty *Hosen-scheisser* since long before you were a wee kitten."

MAYBE. YESTERDAY SAW WITCH WITH RED EYES. VERY BAD. BE CAREFUL. ALSO WATCH MY TAIL. UP IS GOOD. DOWN IS BAD. I doubted we would have time to stop for Scattergories, and hoped my tip on the tail would help.

The old man grew sober and gave me a firm nod, then gathered his hat and walking cane and began the laborious process of hauling himself upright and out of the car. I hopped down to the floorboards and slipped out as soon as he opened the door, sniffing the air and checking our surroundings for danger while he puffed, grunted, and muttered curses behind me. The air was bitingly cold after the warm interior of the car, and I wondered if I could convince my human to add a warming spell to my collar. I deserved it after all the work I was doing in her absence.

Fortunately, there were no security guards about, though I suspected the wizard had ways of making himself scarce in the event they did appear. I could smell little in the frigid air, at least not at this distance. A closer examination of the library would reveal if my whiskers had been right.

Once my companion had finally leveraged himself from his vehicle and shut the door, I led the way stealthily around the back of the building. For an old man, he was surprisingly quiet when he wanted to be. He carried his cane, rather than using it as a support, and seemed to stand a bit straighter, a bit prouder. Whatever had bowed him over with such a weight yesterday seemed to be forgotten, or at least put aside for the moment.

Upon reaching the back door, it was clear I had been right. Not even the frost could cover the smell of demonic magic, and though my floating letters had vanished as soon as we exited the car, the old wizard did not seem to need my warning to know there was trouble afoot. His brow was wrinkled—well, more so than usual, anyway—and his sharp eyes glinted in the light of nearby street lamps.

He examined the door with a calculating gaze, then reached for the doorknob and turned it gingerly. It did not budge, which boded ill for us. Whatever villains had invaded my human's domain were smart enough to lock the door behind them.

Before the wizard had a chance to cast his own unlocking magic, I raised myself to place both paws on his thigh and, when he looked down, carefully shook my head. I had no idea what wards or enchantments my human might have known to cast against demon magic, but she was much more likely to have wards in place to foil common wizard spells. I did not want my compatriot to damage, or be damaged by, her safeguards.

Instead, I trotted around the old man and stared up at the doorknob with narrowed eyes, doing what I do best.

There was a faint click, and I purred in satisfaction.

"*Ach*, a useful little pussycat you are, indeed. Does your mistress know you can do that?" asked the old man.

I twitched my tail in unconcern, waiting patiently as he eased open the door, then slipped ahead of him to scout, tail held high like a flag. The library was dim, but certain lights were always left on for security reasons, so I did not need to worry about my companion falling over a table in the dark. I led him carefully through the ground floor and toward the door to the archives, halting just before the last corner and dropping my tail in a signal to halt.

Surprisingly, he did. It was nice to be around humans who actually paid attention. Leaving him a little ways back, I peeked around the corner with care, whiskers twitching. Against the wall next to the archives door slouched a man I had not seen before, though he looked similar enough to the Snake that I would not be surprised if they were related. His white-blond hair shone faintly in the dim light, and he had several rings in his ears and tattoos showing around the collar of his shirt. He seemed to be chewing his lip and staring at the far wall, lost in thought.

Some lookout.

I returned to the wizard and thrashed my tail back and

forth in agitation, baring my teeth in a silent hiss in hopes that he understood the presence of a threat. With a wink, the old man put a finger to his lips and, very carefully, sidled up to the corner to peek quickly around it. His eyesight would not be able to pick up all the details I had seen, but there was enough ambient light that the figure of the man would be unmistakable.

The old wizard returned and patted me on the head, I suppose his way of congratulating me for doing my job. I attempted to roll my eyes—it is much harder for cats to do than humans, but Lily always uses the expression with such aplomb I must admit I have grown fond of the gesture. The wizard ignored me, of course, and crept back to the corner. I had only a moment to wonder what he was up to before I heard a soft thump from the corridor beyond.

I joined my compatriot and found the "lookout" collapsed on the floor, sound asleep. Well, that was quite handy. I wondered if that spell was just as effective on dogs, and if there was any way I could learn it.

As we carefully skirted the body and approached to examine the door, I began to notice an odd quality to the air. It felt heavy and sticky, and made my skin twitch all over. I fought the urge to sit down and wash myself clean of the odious atmosphere. Looking behind me, I could see sweat beading on the wizard's forehead as he eyed the door with worry. Whatever made my skin itch clearly affected him as well, but I didn't have time to worry about it.

There was no need for me to unlock the archive door— whoever had come before had left it cracked. I considered what to do, whether I should go ahead and spy out the situation downstairs, then come back to inform my friend, or if it was better to rely on the element of surprise and storm right in.

Before I had made a decision, however, I felt a tap on my back. The old man had touched me with his cane and was now gesturing down the hall. We retreated around the corner, then he bent over his cane to whisper at me.

"There is bad magic down there, pussycat. Black magic. I sense no trace of a summoning, but there is something very bad down there all the same. It might be too dangerous for you, small one. Perhaps it is best if you stay here, yes?"

Even if I had my floating letters, there was no way I could explain to this wizard that I was no mere familiar, no simple pet with an enchanted collar. I could not explain, even to Lily, that the one who had made me her guardian was far more powerful than the puny demons witches used as their minions. Even a greater demon—whose claws and teeth were far larger than mine—was no real threat as long as I was quick on my feet. I definitely couldn't explain the feeling that my end lay elsewhere, hidden in a distant and far darker future. I felt that, when my time came, I would know it without a doubt. And this was not my time. Not by a long shot.

But, since I could explain none of this, I twined around the old man's legs instead, rubbing and purring reassuringly with tail upraised.

"*Ach*, very well, then. *He!* Not so fast, now, *Miezekatze*," he whispered sharply as I began to head back toward the door. "Come here and sit still. I will make it so I may see through your eyes and hear through your ears. Useful, yes? Then you can go running off to get your tail singed."

I sat patiently while he muttered to himself, as if trying to remember something he had not thought of in a long while. Finally satisfied, he bent down as far as he safely could without falling over, using his cane for balance and support. With a wrinkled, bony finger, he tapped me lightly on the nose and I jumped back in surprise, sneezing several times as the magic spread. It tickled worse than dust, but finally seemed to sink in and settle.

"Off with you, now, puss puss." The old man grinned down at me, obviously amused by my reaction.

Instead of obeying, I gave him a look of deepest disdain and sat, taking a long moment to lick one paw and run it over my abused nose. The wizard leveraged himself upright with a grunt and leaned on his cane, watching with raised eyebrows as I showed him just how little I cared for his silly orders. Finally, when I was good and ready, I turned and sauntered around the corner and down the hall, keeping close to the wall as I approached the cracked door. Nose to the gap and ears pricked, I ensured the coast was clear beyond before squeezing through and heading down to discover what awaited me.

I was not pleased with what I found.

The air was even worse down in the archives. My skin felt like I had sat on an anthill—something even the most idiotic cat was smart enough to avoid—and the need to stop and wash myself with all possible vigor was quite distracting. Worse, however, was the oppressive weight of evil in the air. I'm not sure how to describe it in human terms. Animals sense things differently than our two-legged companions, though perhaps it might be compared to the human notion of a "sixth sense." Oddly, the room held no stench of rotten eggs, the smell I had come to associate with a demon's presence. Rather, there was a cloying, sickly sweet odor that irritated my already itchy nose.

My senses told me a single human occupied the room, and I could hear whispering at the far end of the archives where the broom cupboard was located. Remembering how easily the witch had spotted me yesterday, Cat Magic and all, I decided an indirect approach was best. I slunk between the tightly packed rows of archive shelving, each shelf supported at the top and bottom by a mechanical frame so they could be moved back and forth to provide access to whichever books the humans desired. Staying within the shelving enabled me to traverse the room unseen as I cautiously inched nearer to the broom cupboard.

The closer I crept, the more my skin crawled, and not just from the atmosphere. I could now clearly hear the whispers coming from the corner, though the words I caught were strange and unfamiliar, as if in some ancient tongue. As I listened more closely, I realized there was not one, but two voices. One voice I recognized instantly—the unctuous charm of that Snake was unmistakable. The other voice, however, was even more disconcerting. It sounded like a *real* snake, its hissing, sibilant words so soft and deadly I could feel my back arching and hair bristling in instinctive response.

I finally found a gap between the shelves where I could crouch, eyes peering out to lock on the back of my nemesis. He was wearing a leather jacket and jeans this time in place of his fancy suit, though the clothes had a new smell to them, as if they'd just been bought. I searched about to find the source of the second voice, but my nose hadn't lied. There was no one else there.

Well, no *one* else.

Some*thing* else was in the room. I could feel it even more strongly, and though both voices seemed to be coming from the Snake as he bent close to the cupboard door, the air about him was blacker than black. It shifted and oozed, forming oily-looking tendrils of shadow that reached out as if to spread throughout the room, but were held back by some unseen force.

I suppressed the rumbling growl forming in my throat, hoping the wizard could see this creature as clearly as I could—hoped he could see it, and knew what in the world to do about it. This was more Sebastian's expertise than mine. He had dabbled in the demonic in his earlier, foolish days, but had fortunately wised up before it was too late. From then on, he had kept strictly to his fae connections, and given how much the fae hated demons, he had learned even more about how to counter the forces of darkness. I could only hope my wizard companion knew as much. My teeth and claws were formidable weapons, but I doubted the Snake would be quite as foolish and incompetent as the lackey he had sent to break into my human's office.

Whatever the case, I felt the urge to move, to do something. I couldn't let this filthy reptile stand there, working who knew what sort of mischief on the library my mistress was sworn to protect. If only the old man would—

"Whatever you are doing, witch, cease and back away from that door."

I started in surprise at the voice, realizing I had focused so completely on the threat before me that I had forgotten my surroundings. I could almost be forgiven—that old wizard was as quiet as a cat when he wanted to be, and had somehow managed to approach without even the intruder noticing his presence. He stood, now, about fifteen human paces from the Snake, leaning on his cane, his face a cloud of thunder and his eyes nearly sparking with the lightning inside them. I decided then and there that this was one wizard, old though he was, whom I did not want to anger.

Though as momentarily startled as I, the Snake seemed unperturbed by the interruption. He straightened and spread his hands wide. "There is no need for hostility, my good sir. I simply left my coat in this cupboard earlier and forgot to retrieve it at the end of my shift. The latch seems to have jammed and I'm having trouble getting it free. The library is closed, by the way. Should I summon a security guard to help you find your way out?"

"*Blödsinn*! You are no worker here, you filthy *Hackfresse*. Do not try my patience with your lies. I have a mind to send you to your maker just for defiling this place. That demon inside you would be pleased, yes? He would enjoy feasting on your soul so much sooner than anticipated." A nasty glint had come into the old man's eyes, and he bared his few remaining teeth in a crooked, crocodile grin.

Though the Snake did not flinch or blanch at the old man's words, I could sense a rising tension in him, and I coiled my muscles in response, ready to spring forward at the first sign of an attack. But the man's smile remained fixed as he dropped his hands and stepped forward, his eyes wide and fixed on the wizard. I remembered those mismatched eyes and gave a little shudder, glad not to be on the receiving end of their intensity.

"No need for insults, old man. If you truly knew the power of he who dwells in me, you would not be so confident. His power is vast, but he is not greedy with it. Come, let us speak like civilized men. There is enough treasure here for the both of us. If you would lend your aid in gaining entry, I could certainly make it worth your while." The Snake gestured to the old closet door, the invitation clear.

I looked back and forth between the two, tail thrashing in anticipation of the old man's explosive indignation. Perhaps he would even begin the fight then and there, and I could leap onto the Snake from behind while he was distracted.

But, to my utter astonishment, I found the wizard's face unnaturally calm and relaxed. My ears flicked back and forth in confusion as I tried to understand his sudden change in demeanor.

"...talk..." the old man muttered, eyes wide and vacant, fixed on the Snake's face.

"Yes, yesss. We will simply talk. I can teach you a great many thingsss."

That other voice, the truly serpentine one, made me narrow my eyes and dare to slip out of hiding to get a better look. Something was going on, and I needed to find out what it was and stop it. Though I risked being spotted, I crept level with the Snake so I could see his face. That's when I realized his mismatched eyes were glowing a deep, blood red.

"...talk...yes...no need for fighting." The old man seemed completely relaxed at this point, and his eyelids had begun to droop, his body sagging over his cane.

With a jolt, I remembered the last time I'd seen those eyes glow red, and how confused and angry the witch had seemed when I hadn't obeyed his command to come, as if he couldn't even imagine the possibility I would *not* obey. I didn't need Sebastian's demon expertise to recognize a snake in the act of hypnotizing its prey. Whatever evil force resided within this good-for-nothing, it obviously preferred to fight with guile rather than strength. But then, what else could I have expected from a snake?

A feather-light sensation touched my paw, and I jumped back in surprise, barely avoiding collision with the shelves. I couldn't suppress a hiss of fear and disgust as I batted at the oily, red-black tendril of ooze that had reached across the floor to snare me. And not just me. Like a spider's web of filth, the fingers of ooze were reaching out in all directions. Some had even arrived at the old man's feet and were beginning to twine about his cane and ankles as he ·stood, oblivious, caught by the Snake's gaze.

Fortunately, the witch seemed too engrossed with his prey to notice the noise I had made, and I took full advantage of the vile creature's inattention. Now was the time to do what I did best.

Slipping back between the shelves, I ran to the end of one and scaled it, more concerned with speed than stealth. I had no idea what that web of filth on the floor might do to me. It looked sticky, and the last thing I needed was to become trapped in it—not to mention how disgusting it would be to clean out of my fur. So, once I had gained the top of the shelves, close to the ceiling and a good foot or two above the humans' heads, I took a running leap and flung myself off the metal frame, aiming for the Snake's face.

I landed in an explosion of righteous fury, claws digging deep into skin as I swiped at the Snake's accursed eyes, his obvious source of strength. Whatever spell had been woven over my companion broke, though whether because the witch closed his eyes, or because I was yowling to wake the dead, we'll never know. I had to focus on my balance as the Snake screamed and stumbled about, but I did notice the old wizard cursing colorfully as he struggled to free himself from the oozing tendrils. A flare of orange light and a sizzling sound assured me the old man had his situation under control, so I concentrated on digging two mismatched eyeballs out of their sockets.

Much to my disappointment, I had only barely gotten my claws hooked into one eyelid before the witch managed to get a firm hold on my neck. He wrenched me off, tearing his own flesh as my claws came free, then flung me away with a yell of fury. I soared through the air, still caterwauling my defiance.

A shelving unit abruptly halted my glorious flight, and I think I lost a few moments after that. When the blackness pulled back and I managed to stumble to my feet, the smell of burnt flesh filled the room. Several of the small tables used for examining documents, normally in a neat row against the wall, now lay strewn about, most of them in pieces. I turned to find the old wizard beating the Snake about the head with his cane, bowler hat askew and screaming obscenities that I am quite sure the witch deserved.

"You *Arschgeige*! You *Flachwichser*! How dare you come into my library and muck about with your filthy demon magic! You are a *Fickfehler* with a maggot for a mother and a slug for a father. Take that, you *Schlappschwanz*!"

The witch lay in a puddle of bubbling black ooze, looking as if he had fallen there—perhaps thrown by a spell or tripped by an overturned chair—and must have only had enough time to raise his arms in defense before the wizard was on him with his cane. I had assumed the cane was of simple carven wood, a fragile antique. Yet the loud THWACK THWACK and punctuated yelps from the witch indicated this particular wizard's cane was made of sterner stuff.

I was only able to enjoy the show for a few moments before the witch managed to scramble back and get his feet under him. Though my wizard companion was surprisingly robust for his age, he had not the speed and agility of an adult in his prime. Before the old man could stop him, the witch had darted off behind the shelves. I could hear him racing between them, and I sped off down the room to intercept. But I only managed to swipe at his heels with a hiss as he shot out from between the shelves and took the stairs two at a time.

I was about to follow him up when I heard a grunt and a moan behind me. Was my friend injured? He had not seemed so, but perhaps in his rage he had ignored some hurt. I myself was beginning to feel the aches and bruises of slamming into those shelves. As much as it irked me, I decided to let the obviously beaten witch flee for his miserable life. He would not be returning any time soon.

Loping back around the shelves, I saw that the old wizard had managed to right one of the chairs and sink into it, looking very weary. I reached him and began to rub on his ankles, meowing my concern.

"*Oy*, calm down, pussycat, I am unharmed. Just tired. So tired." He paused to cough, and I made a mental note to show him the water fountain on the way out. "No, I have simply not used this much magic for many long years. It takes a toll on you, it does. I will be all right. Well, as right as one can be at my age. Just let me rest."

The poor man's head drooped pitifully, and I feared he would fall asleep where he sat, though perhaps a little nap would do him good, as long as he didn't topple out of the chair. I hopped into his lap and curled up against his chest, lending him my warmth and purrs. Human scientists have all kinds of things to say about a cat's purr, but we have no need for their wisdom. We are perfectly aware of what we are capable of. Remember, cats are innately magical, in a sense, and it is well known among us that our purr has a power of its own. It does not heal so much as it makes things better. Whatever is happening, the precise and deliberate application of a purr will improve the situation.

And so we sat for some time, the wizard resting, and I worrying. It did not seem likely, but if the witch happened to regain his courage and return, I believe the old man would have been hard-pressed to defend himself. As I lay there administering EPT—Emergency Purr Therapy—I wondered why the Snake had not put up more of a fight. Judging simply by the malevolent presence of whatever demon he was channeling, there was a much greater power there than he had brought into play. And yet, the old wizard's taunt about the demon consuming his soul, and that unseen barrier holding back the tendrils of shadow, got me thinking. Perhaps the witch had—wisely—put such restrictions on the demon that, even though the power he could use was limited, the power *it* could use on *him* was just as weak. If that was the case, it showed a level of restraint and shrewdness that I had not yet observed in witches who dabbled with demon kind. It boded ill for us if we could not rely on the Snake to be the instrument of his own destruction. But, at least in this instance, it had worked in our favor, once I had broken his hypnotic hold over my companion.

Despite my fears, not a thing disturbed us as I waited for the old man to regain his strength. Not even the mice were stirring, having been startled into hiding, perhaps, by the commotion. I was just closing my eyes to relish the memory of the Snake getting the fear of wizards beaten into him by an old man's cane, when I felt my patient stirring.

"*Scheisse*, dratted *Katze*, I shall sleep the night away and be found by the morning watch at this rate. Off with you now, I have rested enough."

I hopped down from the wizard's lap, looking about the room with a critical eye. It was a mess, frankly, though at least my companion had possessed the wits to not use any spells that might have damaged the precious archives. A bit of black goo had splattered onto the metal shelving, but other than that the only real damage was the tables. I looked up expectantly at the old man as he rose with a grunt and began to mutter to himself.

All right, so I suppose I had spent enough time around Lily and Madam Barrington to have known not to worry. I was just used to Lily's approach to magic: do everything possible the normal, mundane, way and use magic only when necessary. It made sense for a wizard who lived and worked on a daily basis with mundanes. Perhaps this old man lived as a hermit and did not give thought to it, for in the blink of an eye he was mending wood and "disappearing" oily filth from every surface. How, you may ask? Unlike my human, I did not question magic. She needed to know *how* it worked, and *why*. She followed rules, for if she did not, the power she wielded might slip from her control.

Me? I had a much more practical relationship with magic. I was a cat, it was only magic, and so it did as it was told. See? Simple.

While the old man cleaned up, I did a thorough inspection of the entire archives, ensuring nothing was damaged or out of place that we had missed. I was also looking for any nasty surprises the Snake might have left behind. But I found nothing. Even the door to the broom cupboard seemed back to normal, once the faint traces of taint in the air had been whisked away. The oppressive presence of evil had fled with its master, and good riddance to it.

Once things were as good as new, I turned toward the steps, ready to bid the library goodnight. But the wizard did not follow, and when I looked back to examine him, I found him before the broom cupboard door, one wrinkled hand laid against it, staring down at its scratched surface with such sadness that I felt the urge to jump in his lap and comfort him. Except he wasn't sitting down, so I couldn't. Instead, I padded silently over and rose to brace my paws on his leg, giving a concerned mewl when he didn't respond.

The noise snapped him out of whatever dark place his mind had been dwelling, and he looked down at me with a deep sigh.

"Pay me no mind, little one. When you are old and everyone you care for has passed on, you may understand. It is a lonely life. I simply wish...but no, she was too bright a flame to ever be tamed." He sighed again and dropped his hand slowly, as if loath to be parted from the battered old door. "Everything of value I have left in the world is within this cupboard, preserved with the hope that I might do a little good, even after I have passed on. You will look after it for me, yes?"

I gave him my best approximation of a raised eyebrow. You know, that look of amused and somewhat annoyed incredulity that humans seemed to favor.

"*Ach*, of course, you are already looking after it. I can see you make a fine guard cat. Your mistress was wise to leave you in charge."

I dropped back down to my haunches and purred smugly.

"Well...I suppose we should be going, then, *Miezekatze*? I, for one, am in need of a hot bath and a long rest. Who knows if I will awake this time. Perhaps she will be waiting for me on the other side..." His muttering trailed off as he turned and followed me passively up the stairs and out of the library, making sure everything was carefully shut and locked behind us. As I had suspected, the Snake had roused or dragged off his lookout friend when he had fled, and there was no sign of anyone else in the silent building.

The old wizard was kind enough to drive me home, which I much appreciated. I gave him directions using the glowing letters as we slowly chugged down silent and empty streets. It was nearing dawn, and I was ready for a wash and a long nap myself.

When we arrived at my human's apartment and the wizard had turned off his car, he simply sat in silence, making no move to open the door. I waited patiently, hoping he was thinking about a certain letter in his possession.

"Your mistress, she knows Madam Barrington, yes?" he finally asked, giving me a beady-eyed look.

YES. LILY SINGER IS MADAM BARRINGTON'S STUDENT.

"Ah. That explains...Well, I suppose she could be trusted to deliver a letter and respect an old man's privacy, eh?"

UNDOUBTEDLY

"You and your vocabulary, *Miezekatze*," the old man said with a grin and reached out to scratch me under the chin. "It makes an old man smile."

YOU ARE WELCOME TO VISIT ANY TIME. I COULD FIND MORE WITCHES FOR YOU TO BEAT WITH YOUR CANE.

A second chuckle turned into a cough, and the man slowly shook his head. "No, I do not think I shall return again to Atlanta. Too many memories...*Ach*, listen to me. I am just a foolish old man. Here, now, take this." Reaching inside his coat, the wizard withdrew a crinkled envelope, sealed and labeled with, "Mme Barrington."

He hesitated, obviously unsure how to hand it to me, and I took advantage of this to have a last word.

BEING ALONE IS A CHOICE. IF YOU EVER CHANGE YOUR MIND COME FIND ME. I HAVE

PLENTY OF STORIES TO SHARE. ALSO PURRS ARE GOOD FOR YOU. YOU SHOULD GET A KITTEN.

I took my time to get my point across, choosing my words carefully in hopes that he would remember them. I knew I could not fix every human's problems. But I also knew I could fix *some* humans' problems—if they let me. My human was the exception: I fixed her problems whether she wanted me to or not.

The old man read my words slowly, his mouth quirking to the side when he reached the part about a kitten. Finally, he looked deep into my yellow eyes and gave me a grave nod. There was still sadness in his gaze, but perhaps a little peace as well as he held out the letter to me. I was moving to take it when I suddenly remembered a question I had been meaning to ask.

WHO ARE YOU?

The wizard chuckled and shook his head. "No one of consequence, *Miezekatze*. Those who need to know will find out, and those who do not will soon forget."

Well, I knew I wouldn't be forgetting any time soon. Madam Barrington would know. I'd have to ask when Lily delivered the letter.

Ducking beneath his hand, I gave his chin an affectionate rub and curled my tail under his nose, making him sneeze and laugh. Then, and only then, did I finally take the letter gently between my teeth and jump down from his lap, slipping between his legs as he opened his door to let me out. I trotted up the apartment's steps and turned to watch as his sputtering engine broke the crystalline silence of the cold night. The old car shuddered as it backed out of its parking space, then rumbled off into the night. I did not stay to watch it disappear, but slipped inside my warm and welcome abode to carefully lay the letter on my human's desk.

Purring contentedly at a most satisfactory ending to my adventure, I finally retired to my favorite spot on the bed for a much deserved and long overdue nap. I might have been tempted to waste time worrying about my human's reaction when she returned and heard about the whole affair, but I knew better. Sleeping was a far more productive activity than worrying, and we cats have always excelled at being productive. And so it was with an untroubled mind that I settled down for some serious sleep, content in the knowledge that I would soon be reunited with my human—and more importantly, my human's endless supply of ear scratches and milk.

EPILOGUE

*M*y human returned late that morning, all in one piece but ready to get back to the solitude of her own house, I was sure. Sebastian helped bring in the luggage, then gave me an acceptable tribute—scratches in all my favorite places—before snagging a handful of scones and heading off to business of his own.

Lily had already made herself a strong cup of black tea and begun to unpack before she noticed the letter on her desk, at which point I was summoned to the living room for the inevitable interrogation. I had spent a long time considering exactly how much to tell her, and finally decided on an acceptable level of fact that would convey the important points without inciting hysterics.

"What in the world is this, Kip? This wasn't here when I left."

"Indeed. I can assure you it is exactly as it appears."

My human sighed and put a hand on her hip. "And?"

"And you had best give it to Madam Barrington as soon as may be. Also, I'm coming with you when you do."

"And?"

I gave her a quizzical look. After all, just because I was going to tell her what had happened while she was gone didn't mean I had to make it easy.

She finally gave up our staring contest and threw her hands in the air. "And where did it come from? Who put it there? What's in it?"

"A wizard. I did. I have no idea."

My human's eyes bugged out slightly at the mention of a wizard, and her lips pressed together in such a perfect impersonation of Madam Barrington that I had to suppress a smug look of amusement.

"Stop being obtuse, Sir Kipling. I just got back from a tiring trip and have no patience for your nonsense. What happened while I was gone?"

I calculated I could get away with one, perhaps two more deflections, but decided to acquiesce without further obstinance. After all, the point was to tease, not distress. "I patrolled the library, as was only proper, and found several witches poking about. I ensured they were ejected by the appropriate authorities, but suspected they would be back. Last night, an old wizard came to the library asking for Madam Barrington. I explained to him where she was, and he helped me rid the premises of one last witch who snuck in after hours and was muttering foul things at the broom cupboard door. He left the letter with me, to pass on to you, to pass on to Madam Barrington."

As I spoke, my human's eyes got wider and wider, and I believe the only reason I made it all the way through without interruption was pure shock on her part. Finally, she seemed to find her voice.

"WHAT?"

I laid my ears back, offended by her shriek. It seemed hysterics were inevitable, despite my careful wording. I endured the onslaught, trying to protect my sensitive hearing as my human ranted and paced, alternating between berating me for not calling her home, and worriedly listing all the horrible ways I could have been hurt. She seemed torn between anger and relief. I watched her closely, ready to hide under something in case her relieved side won and she tried to squeeze me to death to reassure herself I was still alive. Considering her current reaction, I was grateful I would not be present when she returned to work on Monday and heard what had happened in her office.

Finally, she collapsed on the couch, her worry and distress spent. I began to purr loudly, knowing it would calm her, as I slowly picked my way over the cushions and settled onto her lap. She glared down at me, but as I ignored her completely, she finally sighed and scratched my ears.

"I swear, one of these days you will be the death of me."

I kept my opinion on that particular matter to myself, instead focusing on more constructive matters. "There's no need to worry. Aren't there ways to ward against witches? Or at least demonic magic?"

"Of course there are, and the Basement entrance is warded so heavily not even an army of witches could break through. Beyond that, they can't cast the spells that give them entry. But that isn't the point. The Basement was originally meant as a place of peace and learning; we didn't want to have to surround the place with so many wards that it was impossible to even get into the library. That would defeat the purpose."

"Well, perhaps in light of recent events, the purpose should change, at least temporarily. Besides, I'm sure Sebastian has some tricks up his sleeve you wizards don't know about. Ask him about it. The point is, it's nothing to get upset over. I took care of things while you were gone, and that's that."

My human groaned. "You have a very odd opinion of what I should and shouldn't worry about."

"That's because I'm a cat. We're smarter than humans, you know."

"Uh-huh."

"And much more practical."

"So you say."

"At least Penny is none the wiser," I pointed out, though even as I did, I wondered.

"Small blessings. Isn't that what my mother always said? Concentrate on the small blessings?"

"You should take her advice," I offered, then settled down for a good purr and a nap. Lily needed it after all that excitement.

My human fell silent as she stroked me, gazing at the letter still held in her hand. Fortunately, it was already so bent and wrinkled that her little bout of hysterics hadn't done it any harm. "Who was the wizard who helped you, anyway? Anyone I know? Not John Faust, surely?"

I felt her tense and gave my tail a flick of annoyance. "Of course not, silly. Don't you think I would have contacted you immediately if *he* had shown up? It was no one you knew, I don't think, but someone acquainted with Madam Barrington, long ago. He seemed quite at home in the library."

"Well, that's not surprising. Odd people show up from time to time to see the Basement. It is a repository of magical knowledge, after all. I know Madam Barrington has many contacts throughout the country. I've only ever met a fraction of them. I suppose we'll find out when we deliver the letter."

"I suppose we shall."

We both fell silent, settling into the comfortable relaxation of being safe at home with the companion of our choice—me with my human and my human with me. The clock on the wall ticked quietly as I let my eyes drift closed, mind busy considering a great many things.

This was the end of an adventure, perhaps, but I was quite sure there were more to come. As I had often lamented, my human was too much of a trouble-magnet for me to expect a respite, though I suppose I wouldn't have had it any other way. In any case, I was ready for the next adventure, Cat Magic and all. I just hoped I could catch up on my sleep before it arrived.

The End...or is it?

IF YOU ENJOYED THIS STORY, go to the next page and keep reading to find out where it all began with Lily, Sebastian, and Sir Kipling in Love, Lies, and Hocus Pocus: Beginnings.

LOVE, LIES, AND HOCUS POCUS: BEGINNINGS

CHAPTER 1: ENVIRONMENTALLY FRIENDLY BURGERS

*L*ily Singer wished she could simply say her date was going badly and leave it at that. But such a gross understatement was against her nature. To be accurate, she would have to admit it was in the top five worst, if not in the top three. This wasn't totally unexpected. Most—actually, all—of her dates were men she'd met online who, inevitably, weren't as cute as their profile pictures suggested. Awkward and bookish, she found it much easier to start virtual, as opposed to real, conversations. Speed dating and blind dates were out of the question due to her abysmal social skills. Well, that, and the fact that she was a wizard.

No, not a witch. A wizard.

"Soo...when you said you had diet restrictions, what you meant was you could only eat burgers?" Lily asked, trying to keep the sarcasm out of her voice. Though she suspected the only way her date would notice sarcasm was if it was dressed up like a cheeseburger.

"Huh?" Jerry Slate, a good hundred pounds larger and

ten years older than his picture online, looked up from his second burger to stare, confused, at her face.

"When we were setting up the date, you asked if you could pick the restaurant because you said you had diet restrictions," Lily reminded him.

"Oh, yeah. I have a sensitive stomach. I can only eat 100% pure beef burgers, and they have to be grass-fed. Free-range, you know? None of that GMO stuff. This place uses the best ingredients out there."

Lily resisted the urge to roll her eyes, consoling herself with the thought that it was better to be taken to a gourmet, environmentally friendly burger restaurant than, heaven forbid, a *normal* burger restaurant.

Looking to the side, she gazed longingly through the restaurant's front windows to the sunlit street, busy with lunchtime traffic. If only she knew how to teleport, she could escape this awkward situation with minimal embarrassment.

"So..." she tried again. "How is your gaming campaign going?"

"Oh, it's fantastic," Jerry enthused past a mouthful of half-chewed but—let's not forget—grass-fed burger. Not slowing his consumption of burger, fries, and a handmade root beer float, he launched into a detailed description of his gaming group's latest campaign against...someone. Lily couldn't remember who.

It was a topic she could safely rely on to keep him talking for a good while, though it bored her almost to tears. Boredom was preferable, however, to the awkward silence interspersed with chewing sounds she'd suffered through for the first half of their date.

Funny, she'd thought that, in person, Jerry would be more inquisitive. That was before she'd been aware of his burger obsession. As she absentmindedly separated the carrot coins from the rest of her salad and stacked them into a tiny, walled fortress between her and her droning date, she realized he hadn't asked her a single question beyond the perfunctory "How are you?" since they'd met outside some twenty minutes before. From the time they'd entered the restaurant, his entire attention had been devoted to ordering and eating, though he had, at least, disengaged a few brain cells long enough to inform her of the best items on the menu.

Come to think of it, he hadn't been very inquisitive online, either. But Lily was good at asking questions through virtual chat. It was like doing research with a search engine. Type in a question, then browse through the resultant dump of information to find your answer.

When asked a question, especially if said question had anything to do with himself, Jerry was obligingly verbose. He went into great detail, as long as that detail involved the hundred different titles in his grunge rock music collection, or his daring feats in the latest sneak attack against his group's unsuspecting, now-no-longer allies.

It wasn't as if she'd had soaring expectations. She'd just hoped for some intelligent conversation about, oh, say, books. Or history. Or philosophy. Or anything that mattered, really.

Some people improved upon face-to-face acquaintance. Jerry was not one of them. Neither was she, come to think of it. But she, at least, didn't bore anyone with loving descriptions of each book in her expansive personal library unless she knew, for a fact, that the person was a bibliophile.

Hands nervously smoothing down the dark fabric of her pencil skirt, she cast about desperately for an excuse to end the date. She intended to block Jerry Slate from her dating profile as soon as she got home.

Through the babble of obscure gaming jargon coming from the other side of the table, an idea came to her. She concentrated on the fork she held in her hand and whispered the words for a simple heat transference spell, her other hand wrapped around the power-anchor amulet she wore tied to her wrist like a bracelet. Her body heat began to seep into the piece of metal, making it grow warm as she grew cooler. When she judged it was sufficiently hot, she made a startled gesture, dropping it dramatically onto the table as she jerked back in her chair.

"Ouch!" she yelped.

"Huh?" Jerry said, stopping mid-sentence. It seemed to be his favorite word, along with *oh*.

"I wasn't paying attention and tried to pick up my fork. It's very hot. I think it burned my hand. They must have just washed it in an industrial washer."

Jerry reached forward to touch the fork experimentally, hand stopping short as he felt the heat emanating from the offending utensil.

"Gosh, that *is* hot. Are you okay? You don't look so good." Jerry's brow furrowed in confusion. Not even he was absentminded enough to miss the fact that their silverware had been sitting, quite cool and harmless, for a good fifteen minutes since they'd sat down.

Lily made a show of feeling her forehead, hoping to redirect his attention. "I feel all clammy. I should probably go home. I could be getting sick. Thanks so much for the food!"

With a touch of guilt, she fled the restaurant, not looking back. If she had, she would have felt better. Jerry's momentarily stunned face quickly smoothed over as he noticed the untouched burger at her place and, obviously not wanting to waste food, began to demolish it as well.

———

THE WARM SUMMER air felt good on her face as Lily drove her Honda Civic down Ponce De Leon Avenue, heading back to Agnes Scott College campus. Her soft, chestnut brown hair frizzed in the humidity, despite being pulled back into a severe bun. At least it wasn't whipping around her face and getting stuck in her glasses, as it would've been had she worn it down.

Verdant foliage and colorful flowers crowded around the sidewalks, businesses, and houses lining the street. The abundant plant life was one of the things Lily loved most about Atlanta. It made the place feel less like a big city and more like a well-tended neighborhood. Plus, it reminded her of home in the Alabama backwaters.

Pulling into the college's employee parking lot, Lily gathered her things and headed across campus toward McCain Library. Though originally founded as an elementary school in 1889, Agnes Scott had become a college by the early 1900s. McCain Library, built in 1936, consisted of four main floors, a grand, vault-ceilinged reading hall, and three attached floors dedicated to the stacks. It was a beautiful example of how Gothic architecture could meet utilitarian building needs and, along with the other Gothic and Victorian red brick-and-stone buildings around campus, made for a scenic and relaxing atmosphere.

Though it was Saturday, Lily preferred to take refuge in the library and bury herself in paperwork rather than go home and risk the urge to mope about. The tall ceilings, majestic architecture, and quiet atmosphere would calm her in a way no amount of tea or chocolate could. And, of course, there was the comforting smell of books.

She passed a few groups of girls relaxing or studying on the green—it was a women's college, and non-employee males were discouraged from hanging around campus. On this sunny day in early summer, the blue sky and warm grass had lured most students outside to study, so she saw only a few scattered girls working quietly in the library's grand reading hall as she made her way to the librarian offices.

Her office was a spacious room on the first floor, with a high ceiling and expansive windows. Tall bookshelves covered most of the other three walls, and a large, mahogany desk dominated the center of the room.

With a sigh, she dropped her purse onto one of the two visitor's chairs—both currently pushed up against her bookshelves as stepladders—and sat down at her desk. The desk's dark wood surface was polished to a shine, and each item on it was arranged neatly. Her computer, pencil holder, and file organizer were placed just so, cleaned spotless, and free of dust. Her shiny, brass nameplate was centered and aligned perfectly parallel to the edge of her desk. It read:

*Lillian Singer: Administrative Coordinator/Archives
Manager*

It was a prestigious position for Lily's relatively young twenty-five years of age. But the fact that the previous archives manager, Madam Barrington, had taken Lily under her wing and personally groomed her for the job had made Lily the obvious choice when Madam Barrington retired a year ago. Beyond the Madam's training and endorsement, however, Lily had been well prepared for the job. With four years of undergraduate work-study in the stacks, not to mention two years as head librarian after graduation, her BA in history and minor in classics were just icing on the cake.

Of course, Lily's love of books, organized nature, and library experience weren't the only reasons behind Madam Barrington's choice. The real reason was she'd needed someone to take over as curator of the "Basement"—a secret archive beneath McCain Library containing a private collection of occult books on magic, wizardry, and arcane science. Being a wizard herself, Madam Barrington had recognized Lily's innate ability soon after she'd begun her freshman year. The older woman had considered it her duty to keep the then-young and inexperienced girl's insatiable curiosity from getting her killed. Madam Barrington had always been frustratingly vague about exactly *who* owned the books. Her job, and now Lily's, was to care for them, study them, and act as gatekeeper to their knowledge. Only once had Lily seen Madam Barrington allow access, and that was to a very old gentleman who'd arrived late one night and whispered something in the Madam's ear. When Lily had asked how she would know to let someone in, Madam Barrington had simply smiled her mysterious smile and said, "You'll know."

Lily's worries had faded over time, as not a single person had ever appeared requesting access in the year since she'd taken over. Though the Madam was tight-lipped on the subject, Lily got the impression there weren't many wizards left in the world. Of those who did still exist, only a select few knew of the Basement's whereabouts. That was fine with Lily, as the Basement was her own personal heaven. Knowledge was the next best thing to life itself, and knowledge of the unknown and mysterious was something she'd craved ever since she could remember, long before she had found out she was a wizard and started learning the craft under Madam Barrington's tutelage.

That thirst got her into trouble on some occasions. But just as often, it resulted in exciting discoveries which added to her already encyclopedic mind. Having all of Agnes Scott's stacks, archives, and considerable online research capability at her fingertips was a dream come true, not even counting the Basement.

Now, having settled into her leather desk chair in the sunlit office, Lily relished a moment of glowing satisfaction as she surveyed her domain. Taking a deep breath, she let the disappointment and frustration of an abysmal date fade away, refocusing instead on all the good things in life. Books. Tea. Chocolate. Cats. More books. Who cared about men and dating when you had all that at your fingertips?

Speaking of men...

There was a flourishing knock on her office door and, without waiting for an answer, a tall, lanky man with mussed brown hair came swaggering through. His untucked shirt and worn pants gave him a disheveled look, though he walked as if he wore the finest Italian suit in all the world. On a leather cord around his neck hung a triangular stone with a hole in the middle. She'd always wondered what it was but wasn't one to ask personal questions.

His grand entrance was marred slightly by the absence of her visitor chairs in front of her desk, which interrupted his smooth transition from swaggering in to lounging handsomely across one of them. Instead, he had to reverse direction and pull a chair over from a bookshelf before settling his lanky form into it.

Lily hid a smile, trying to look stern instead.

"Sebastian, how many times do I have to tell you, you're not supposed to be wandering around campus. This is a *women's* college, and private property."

"Pish." Sebastian waved a hand unconcernedly. "If you're so worried about it, call security." His eyes were bright with mischief. As if to emphasize his complete lack of concern, he reached into his pocket and drew out that silly coin he was always playing with. He liked to roll it over his knuckles and perform other sleights of hand, knowing it annoyed her when he showed off.

Lily rolled her eyes. She knew that he knew that she wouldn't call security. At least, not until he'd annoyed her to the point of losing her temper, which wasn't often.

"And to what do I owe the pleasure of your visit?" Chin propped in the palm of her hand, Lily raised a skeptical eyebrow in his direction and did her best to ignore the coin. Unlike most men, Sebastian picked up on sarcasm like a child picked up candy—every time, and with great glee.

"Oh, you know. Just paying a social visit. It's been *far* too long, don't you think? How's the ol' biddy doing these days?"

Lily's eyes narrowed. Sebastian practically oozed casual nonchalance, which meant he was up to something.

"I'd like to hear you call her that to her face. And your aunt is just fine. The last time I visited her, she was enjoying a day in the garden."

"Still kicking, eh?" Sebastian snorted, twirling a bit of his bangs around one finger. "Far be it from the great Madam Barrington to grow old and die like the rest of us."

Lily frowned. "That's quite disrespectful. You know very well that wizards tend to live longer than everyone else. If you're going to insult my mentor, at least have the decency to do it behind my back."

Sebastian laughed, making a dismissive gesture. "Lighten up, Lily. It was just a joke. She *did* disown me, after all. I'd say that at least gives me the right to make jokes about her."

Unlike his elderly relative, Sebastian Blackwell was a witch. No, not a wizard. A witch. The difference came from the source of their power: a wizard's was innate, cultivated through discipline and study, channeled and shaped by will and word, often supplemented by a collection of arcane objects; a witch's was entirely acquired through the delicate art of give and take. Many beings—spirits, demons, and magical creatures—were happy to give aid or favors to the right person in exchange for the right thing. Others could be tricked, a few could be forced, and some were to be avoided altogether.

To drastically oversimplify, wizards were born; witches were made. Though Madam Barrington was always vague when it came to wizard culture, Lily at least knew that not all children of wizards were wizards themselves. It was genetic, like eye or hair color. The stronger the wizard and purer the blood, the better chance of passing on the gene, or whatever it was that enabled wizards to manipulate magic. So, being old, proper, and a traditionalist, Madam Barrington viewed witchcraft as disgraceful and lowly, not to mention dangerous. Only "shameless fools with no true ability" engaged in such activities. Sebastian's view was, since he couldn't be a wizard, he might as well be something. And anyway, he made a very good witch.

Lily happened to agree with Sebastian but never said so to her mentor. It took adept social skills, a clever nature, charisma, and force of will to live such a life and come out on top. She would make a dreadful witch, as evidenced by how terrible she was at interacting with anyone except the few friends—or annoying acquaintances in the case of Sebastian—with whom she was comfortable. The ease with which Sebastian glided around social situations made her quite jealous. He was everything she wasn't: handsome, confident, popular, and good at whatever he put his mind to, though he rarely put his mind to anything unless absolutely necessary. For, as it turned out, he was also lazy, untidy, and undisciplined. He would have made a terrible wizard.

Putting a note of briskness in her voice—she *did* have paperwork to go through, after all—Lily fixed Sebastian with a stare and asked more firmly, "What do you want, Sebastian? I know you're up to something."

"Well it sounds terrible when you put it like that," he said, grinning.

"Sebastian," she said in a warning tone.

"Okay, okay. I'll get to the point. You're no fun," he grumbled, hands raised in surrender.

"I have plenty of fun. It's called reading books."

"Uh-huh. Right." Now it was Sebastian's turn to roll his eyes. "Anyway, I need your...consulting services."

"You mean you need my help?" Lily asked sweetly, a smug smile pulling at her lips.

"No, I need you as a consultant, one professional to another." Putting his coin away, he straightened in the chair, smiling and spreading his hands wide in a disarming gesture. It was obviously meant to reassure her, but she was not impressed.

"Really? Professional? Since when are you a 'professional' witch?"

Sebastian adopted an indignant look. "Since a while. Can't you just see it? Sebastian Blackwell: Professional Witch!" he said dramatically, lifting his arm to paint an imaginary sign in the air. "I have business cards and everything." His hand dove into the back pocket of his jeans and produced a rather bent card, which he flipped onto her desk with a flick of his wrist.

"Fascinating," Lily commented, voice fairly dripping with amused sarcasm as she examined the card. The front showed a headshot of Sebastian—handsome without trying, as usual—beside his name and contact details printed in an overly curly font. The back had a stylized monogram in purple and gold.

"And what services do you offer as a 'professional' witch?" she asked, fighting the urge to laugh.

"Oh, casting out evil spirits, contacting loved ones who've passed on, consulting the fates, various potions. You know, the normal stuff superstitious rich people believe in."

"Charlatanry, you mean?" Lily asked, eyebrow raised again.

"Hey! I *can* actually do most of the stuff people ask for. When they want something impossible, like talking to their dead pet parrot or predicting the lottery, I make something up to keep them happy. Ignorance is bliss and all that. No harm done."

Lily gave him a hard stare over her glasses. She hated that saying. Ignorance was one of the least blissful things in the world, in her opinion. She believed that "the truth will make you free," a saying which was carved into the rafters of McCain Library's grand reading hall. But she reminded herself that Sebastian wasn't her problem and got back to the point. "So, what do you need my 'consulting services' for?"

"Well, I got hired for this job, see, and I've run across something more up your alley than mine."

"Is that so?" Her tone remained disinterested. She'd been pulled into too many of his wild schemes not to be hesitant. Though, to be fair, she'd egged him on in many of those schemes, whenever there was knowledge to be had or a new spell to try. Curiosity often got the better of her, and Sebastian knew it.

"Yes, it is so."

"Explain."

"I was hired to cast out this evil spirit, and it turns out the spirit isn't evil. He's actually a pretty nice guy. The real culprit is a spell put on the house almost a hundred years ago because of some jilted lover. The spirit has stayed behind to warn people away from the house ever since. So, even though he has, technically, been haunting the house, even if I get him to go away, that doesn't fix the problem, and I won't get my money."

"Let me guess: You need me to come figure out what the spell is and get rid of it, right?"

"A very astute conclusion! I'll give you an award later." Sebastian gave her a lazy smile and a wink.

Lily was not amused. "You know, you really shouldn't insult the person you're asking help from," she said, giving him a level stare. "And I still haven't heard any compelling reason why I should help you."

"Ah, yes, well." Sebastian backpedaled a bit. Lily knew his good looks and charming ways usually got him what he needed, so she took delight in giving him as much trouble as possible. A very small part of her liked to watch him squirm. Well, maybe not so small a part.

———

CONTINUE THE FUN IN LOVE, Lies, and Hocus Pocus: Beginnings. *Prepare for magic, shenanigans, and more adventure than you can shake a stick at!*

THANKS FOR READING

Thanks so much for joining Lily, Sebastian, and Sir Kipling on their adventures. Keep up to date with the *Love, Lies, and Hocus Pocus* universe by signing up to my mailing list at www.lydiasherrer.com/subscribe for new release alerts, behind-the-scene sneak peeks, and book giveaways.

Reviews are essential to a book's success by helping other readers discover stories they might enjoy! Plus they are a great way to show support to your favorite author. Please consider taking a moment to leave a review.

If you want to explore more of the Love, Lies, and Hocus Pocus universe, then come join my motley crew on Patreon www.patreon.com/lydiasherrer. You'll get awesome rewards like exclusive monthly short stories (found nowhere else), snarky swag, and series backstory.

I'd love to connect with you online! You can find me at:
www.lydiasherrer.com
www.facebook.com/lydiasherrerauthor
www.instagram.com/lydiasherrer
www.twitter.com/lydiasherrer
www.youtube.com/c/lydiasherrer

Award-winning and USA Today-bestselling author of snark-filled urban fantasy, Lydia Sherrer thrives on creating characters and worlds you love to love, and hate to leave. She subsists on liberal amounts of dark chocolate and tea, and hates sleep because it keeps her from writing. Though she graduated with a dual BA in Chinese and Arabic, after traveling the world she came home to Louisville, KY and decided to stay there. Due to the tireless efforts of her fire-spinning gamer husband and her two overlords, er cats, she remains sane and even occasionally remembers to leave the house.

Sir Edgar Allan Kipling is a domestic medium hair (he likes to think he's descended from Norwegian Forest Cats. Let's not shatter his dream). He adopted Lily when he was a kitten after she clearly demonstrated she was incapable of surviving without him. Since his "Enlightenment," he has developed a number of hobbies, including reading and watching soap operas (to better understand humans, he says). In 2017, he won runner-up in the Stephen Memorial Book Award for "maintaining feline dignity under trying magical circumstances." His favorite food is salmon, or if he can't get that, cream. If the world is in ruins and all else fails, milk will do.

KAIKAKU

The Power and Magic of Lean
A Study in Knowledge Transfer

By Norman Bodek

PCS Press
Vancouver, Washington

Copyright © **2004 by Norman Bodek**

PCS Inc.
PCS Press
809 S.E. 73rd Avenue
Vancouver, WA 98664

bodek@pcspress.com
http://www.pcspress.com

Printed in the United States of America

Printing number
1 2 3 4 5 6 7 8 9 10

The cover is a stereogram designed by Gene Levine

Library of Congress Cataloging-in-publication Data

Bodek, Norman.
     Kaikaku: The Power and Magic of Lean - A Study in Knowledge Transfer

     p. cm.
     Includes index.

ISBN 0-9712436-6-2
1. Production management.   2. Industrial Management.
3. Organizational change.   4. Organizational behavior
5. Manufacturing processes.

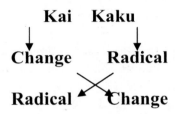

Kai   Kaku

Change   Radical

Radical   Change

Kai-kaku are Chinese characters meaning "innovation," a 'transformation of the mind,' 'working with others to achieve radical change,' and 'to bring new and vital energy to your organization.' Kaikaku (innovation) and Kaizen (continuous improvement) are the central themes of this book to help you change your mindset about manufacturing and to recognize the power of people creatively working together. (Kaikaku is Japanese while Gaige is the Chinese pronunciation of the characters)

The cover: The picture on the cover is a stereogram. Hidden for your discovery is a three dimensional picture (3 D) by the artist **Gene Levine**. Relax you eyes, focus six inches beyond the book or look at the blank space above the picture to see either your reflection or a subtle light. You can also look at the cover cross-eyed by holding your index finger three inches in front of your nose. Or hold the cover right up to your nose, focus as if looking off into the distance and slowly move the page away. With patience and a little practice you will see the magic happen. For help go to:
http://www.colorstereo.com/texts_.txt/practice.htm or to:
http://www.magiceye.com/faq_example.htm

LEAN

Lean is an all out war against waste of both manufacturing inefficiencies and underutilization of people.

The Power and Magic of Lean is to discover those hidden treasures within your company: to find and eliminate all of the non-value adding wastes and to bring out the infinite creative capacity from every single worker.

Testimonials

"Your manuscript came in on Saturday morning and I have had the pleasure of reviewing it over the weekend. I am enjoying the stories, the humor and the educational flavor that dominates the book. Also, I better appreciate your greatness as a thinker, a leader and as a human being."
– **Don Dewar, President QCI-International**

"I want to say that, over the past decade and half, I have watched the growth of the TPS/lean movement you started, and the tremendous benefits it has brought to U. S. industry and the returns to the nation in terms of growth and competitiveness. I recognize the vital and seminal role you played in transferring the basic concepts and techniques of TPS /lean to this country. You are the founding father of today's revolution in manufacturing in the United States, and the country owes you a debt of gratitude for it. Knowing that, one day, these transfers will be recognized as historic in nature, and I am honored to have been associated with you during the key period."
– **Carol Ann Meares**

"I just finished your book and the only thing I can think of to say is - WOW!!!! The story of your travels and learning's a great framework for what I think is the most easily to understand description of "lean" (concepts). I earmarked some parts to read over again."
- **Chuck Yorke, Manager, Organizational Development, Technicolor Corporation**
-
"Norman has always had fascinating stories about his travels around the world, the people he's met, and the things he's learned. Some of the most fascinating of these stories concern his friendship with Mr. Shigeo Shingo. As you read through this book, it is my sincere hope that you will appreciate the years of learning that went into its' creation, as well as the great many things that Norman has brought to this country, and the world."
- **Bill Kluck, President NWLEAN.net**

I thank Norman for opening the door to Japan and bringing such valuable knowledge to the world. Virtually every Lean tool or principle you are likely to encounter has Norman's fingerprints on it. Read this book, and follow Norman through his wonderful journey of learning. And may you be so fortunate to join Norman Bodek on his next study mission to Japan.
– Jon Miller, President Gemba Research

"The book is just great. The style is almost conversational and your sincerity and enthusiasm shine through every paragraph. The stories are fascinating."
- T.V. Suresh, President, Tao Consulting , Chenai, India

"As the Toyota system transitioned into a lean movement in North America, Norm Bodek was in the front row observing the translation. He met the leading figures of TPS and worked with them, as well as with Americans, and he captured a wide-angle picture of what actually took place. Since lean continues to be counterintuitive to conventional business thought, he also has an interesting take on where it might lead."
- Robert W. Hall, Editor-in-Chief, Target, Association for Manufacturing Excellence

Your latest work is very fascinating. You introduced Japanese Management techniques to the United States in the 1980's before anybody else. Also you brought Japanese professors to hold seminars while consulting the American corporations. It would not be an exaggeration to say that your ability and effort made it possible for an effective Japanese management to stay in the culture of American Corporations. I have a very warm respect towards your grace of integrity.
- Dr. Ryuji Fukuda, Fukuda & Associates

"Norman Bodek played the key role in the spread of lean techniques around the world. In this wonderful book, he tells how it all happened. Along the way, he weaves in lessons derived from his interaction with the original developers of lean production ideas. I couldn't put it down."
- Alan G. Robinson, Co-author of *Ideas Are Free* and *Corporate Creativity*

Author's Dedication

This book is dedicated to Dr. Shigeo Shingo who through his tireless efforts and academic brilliance conceptualized and developed Just-In-Time (JIT), the Toyota Production System (TPS), and what is today called Lean thus bringing untold additional wealth to the industrialized world. He has opened a new door of opportunity to change the very nature of work life in a factory.

Dr. Shigeo Shingo

My deepest hope is that as you learn the wonderful things about Lean Manufacturing that you will apply them to the work place to both make better products to serve your customers while at the same time create a better workplace for your employees.

I want to also thank Irv Otis, former VP with American Motors, Chief Industrial Engineer with Chrysler Corporation and adviser and consultant to the chairman and CEO of American Axel and Manufacturing, Richard E. Dauch, who continually urged me on to write this book, to Jon Miller, president of Gemba Research for his carefully review of the text, to T. V. Suresh of Tao Consulting in Chennai, India for his language ability, to Bill Kluck of NWLean for his great editing skills and wonderful advice, to Tsuey-Hwa Lai for her drawings and design advice and to Gene Levine for his artist cover. I hope you can see his 3 D stereogram.

Foreword by Jon Miller
President Gemba Research

The process improvement methodology we call "Lean" has taken hold and is changing how we work and how organizations create value for customers. We see Lean spreading rapidly beyond manufacturing to areas such as healthcare, government, financial services and education. Lean is not just a buzzword. If it is, it has been buzzing Toyota for the last 50 years.

Lean has been called variously Just In Time, Kaizen, and World Class Manufacturing but it is essentially the study and implementation of the Toyota Production System. The transformation in how we view customer-supplier interactions has come about as a result of our understanding of Lean principles. The story of how these ideas were brought to American industry is the story of Norman Bodek's career.

Norman is a unique and privileged individual. Norman has launched a *kaikaku* - a great transformation in awareness and in actual business. The term *kaikaku* means much more than *kaizen* (process improvement). It is a large and fundamental change of policy, practice, or awareness. As you read Norman's story you will appreciate where Lean came from and how it transforms us.

American industry has learned many things in the last 25 years. There are many challenges remaining, not least of which is to continue to be competitive in an increasingly competitive world market. I believe that the Lean movement will continue to transform American business for the next 25 years. Norman's story reminds us how much we have learned, and that the best is yet to come.

I have spent more than half of my life in Japan, and I speak Japanese fluently. I am well aware of the challenges of doing business in Japan and with the Japanese. Norman didn't speak a word of Japanese when he first ventured there 25 years ago. I can tell you, he had no idea what he was getting into! Perhaps it took that type of curiosity and courage to encounter so many of the greatest minds in industry of the last half century. I thank Norman for opening the door to Japan and bringing such valuable knowledge to the world.

Norman Bodek himself has been transformed over the years. On his first trip to Japan, he knew nothing about the secrets of Japanese quality and industrial productivity. Today he is the wise and seasoned teacher and a true leader in Lean thought. Virtually every Lean tool or principle you are likely to encounter has Norman's fingerprints on it. Norman has taught us these things, and today he teaches us that we must reduce waste and improve profit but also strive to improve the quality of work life for people.

All of us, whether we are business owners, trainers, academics, Lean Managers, consultants, or writers who make a living from Lean today owe thanks to Norman Bodek and his pioneering work. One way or another we all trace our lineage through Norman to a small group of very tough-minded but brilliant Japanese teachers who shocked us with what kaizen can do. Norman was the bridge that brought the sensei and their teachings to America.

Even after 25 years, Norman is still bringing us new knowledge from Japan. Read this book, and follow Norman through his wonderful journey of learning. And may you be so fortunate to join Norman Bodek on his next study mission to Japan.

Foreword by Bill Kluck
President NWLEAN

I first met Norman Bodek in the fall of 2001 when he first participated at an online discussion at NWLEAN (The Northwest Lean Networks[1]). He said, "Software is unnecessary, focus on the more important issues of focusing on waste, and getting your workers involved."

Norman had written the 'Forewords' for a number of my favorite books published by Productivity Press. Norman called me to discuss NWLEAN, and was very generous with praise about our website, our listserv discussion groups, and other initiatives we have to help companies get relevant information on how to proceed with their lean implementations. That phone call was the beginning of what I consider a very special friendship.

It became rather clear to me that, without Norman, there might be very little knowledge and practice of lean in the United States. You see it was Norman who sought out the Japanese experts, brought them to the U.S., published their books, and helped to popularize their efforts.

Norman has always had fascinating stories about his travels around the world, the people he's met, and the things he's learned. Some of the most fascinating of these stories concern his friendship with Mr. Shigeo Shingo. I may be biased, but as an Industrial Engineer, I've always had a special respect for Shingo's work. To me, Shingo was a can-do type of engineer, never afraid to get his hands dirty, not afraid to make a mistake in order to develop something new and innovative. Norman spent considerable time with

---

[1] NWLEAN can be found on the Internet at http://www.nwlean.net/.

Dr. Shingo, and I'm happy he's decided to share some of this in his new book.

In the spring of last year (2003), Norman spoke at the Institute of Industrial Engineering (IIE) Lean Conference in Portland, Oregon, and I introduced Norman at his session. He told one particular story with some regrets that he did not spend more time with Shingo while he was still alive, even if it was to just carry his briefcase during engagements and site visits. Norman seems to have a sense that there was still much more to learn, and that the world is that much less productive without him.

I have heard him speak and present on the topic of worker involvement (through Quick and Easy Kaizen) on many occasions. He has personally seen this powerful technique save literally millions of dollars, in both Japanese and American companies. Yet it continues to be a tough sell to most Western companies, which believe that thinking and intelligence is the job of management, instead of for all of our workers. Norman continues to spread the word at every opportunity, showing companies how to gather tremendous gains, which are sitting right under their noses.

Norman contributes articles to a wide variety of industry magazines, and is a regular contributor to NWLEAN's FEATURE ARTICLE section. Here you will learn of his accomplishments in the competitive world of publishing, and how he worked to bring lean concepts to the Western world. I am still learning from Norman. I expect he still has much to teach me. I hope to have the chance to carry his briefcase for many years to come. It is my sincere hope that you will appreciate the years of learning that went into this book, as well as the great many things that Norman has brought to this country, and the world.

Table of Contents

Introduction

"Failure to change is a vice."
Hiroshi Okua, Chairman Toyota

A parallel exists between 1979 when my journey of discovery started and the year 2004. Back then Japan was perceived as a nation of 'copiers' with nothing for us to learn or fear from them. We were richer, stronger and more innovative. It was comforting for us to just ignore their growth. And what happened? Toyota, Honda, Panasonic, Yamaha, Sony, Fujitsu, Hitachi, Toshiba, Fanuc, Kyocera, Nikon, Fuji Film and others swiftly rose to become manufacturing giants through their quality and productivity growth efforts and many of our industries were either threatened or they disappeared. We just didn't know what was happening until it was too late.

And today we look at Japan once again as a nation struggling with its debt, with its deflation, with its recession, with its economic decline as if there is nothing for us to learn or fear from them, and 'boy' are we wrong.

In the 1950's the Toyota Production System was born giving Toyota their eventual competitive advantages – bringing them to their current state as the world's most successful automotive company with 50 billion dollars in the bank and a net worth greater then General Motors, Ford and DaimlerChrysler combined.

You may not have heard of Norman Bodek before, but if you've have heard of Lean, Cellular Manufacturing, Kanban, the

Toyota Production System, JIT, SMED, TPM, QFD, Quality Circles, Hoshin Kanri, Poka-yoke, Visual Factory, Quick and Easy Kaizen, or Kaizen Blitz, you are familiar with my work. I played a major role in discovering these wonderful gems and bringing them out of Japan.

You may know most of the tools and techniques discussed in this book but my goal here is to deliver this information in a way to give you a fresh perspective on the importance of implementing a total system of continuous improvement. I also want to share with you some of the stories of what I found, whom I met and the importance of these discoveries to world-class manufacturing. I hope it will be both an informative and fun experience for you.

I will tell you the story of my adventures with Dr. Shingo, Mr. Ohno, Dr. Fukuda, Dr. Deming, Phil Crosby, and many others. I hope that you will recognize and apply the great competitive power that you can derive from their knowledge.

It was all truly magical because when I started in 1979 I hardly knew anything about manufacturing, did not speak Japanese, did not know a single soul in Japan, and didn't know about any of these great people at all. I would say that I am a slow learner but somehow I intuitively knew the importance of the Toyota Production System and I was persistent in tracking down these powerful geniuses whose work has completely changed the world of manufacturing.

Once at a Chinese restaurant I received a fortune cookie, which said, "You have the talent to recognize the talent in others." I am very grateful for this gift. I have met people with great talent who in the last 50 years have changed the very face of manufacturing and through their genius new and substantial wealth has been created for all of us to share.

In these last twenty-three years I have gone out of my way to meet and learn from many of the world's leading professors, management consultants, practitioners and leaders of industry in quality and productivity improvement. They have filled my life with wonderful stories that I want to share with you. This book will tell you about whom I met, how I met them, and what I learned from them. I hope as you read the book you will be able to understand and fully appreciate the wisdom created by these geniuses. Then hopefully you will be able to put together a complete continuous improvement system within your organization.

Since 1979, I have been to Japan 59 times, visited over 250 manufacturing plants, published over 100 Japanese management books in English, and have been privileged to meet and represent some of the truly great geniuses. It was these geniuses that discovered the new tools and techniques that helped to advance Japan from a nation noted in 1960 for making "junk," to one of the most advanced nations in the world.

Now I will share with you the adventure of how I discovered these great people, the importance of their ideas and how you can put them to use in your company and in your life.

Norman Bodek

1

The Journey Begins

__Two dreams – to make the best possible products__ __for our customers and to create the best quality of__ __work life for our employees__. They must go hand and hand!

It was in 1979 when I noticed in the business section of the New York Times, an article referring to the decline of productivity in America. For some strange reason I was fascinated and it started me on a journey to find out what this really did mean and what had caused the decline. I went the very next day to the Greenwich Connecticut Library to study.

I rarely ever go to libraries. I would much rather buy a book. When I was very young I was fearful of not returning a book on time, afraid that the police would come and get me or having to pay those late fines. However, I do love owning and reading books and love having my shelves filled with them.

From my initial research at the library, I found very little information on productivity but what I did find pointed me to Japan. At that time Japanese industry was leading the world in both productivity and quality improvement. Statistics showing Japan's success were easy to find, but the reasons for this success were pretty much a mystery to us in the West.

Fascinated with the subject, I started a company called Productivity Inc. with a monthly newsletter also called *Productivity* and made a commitment to discover those hidden secrets. Milton Glaser,[2] a very famous designer and a close friend of a teacher of mine, gave me a company logo and also gave me ideas on how to produce a newsletter.

The first newsletter was published in June 1980, and looked at Quality Control Circles (QCC) as one of the key ideas for Japan's manufacturing miracle. Wayne Reiker kindly gave us a copy of his QCC training material. We also wrote briefly about Dr. Deming, and Dr. Juran, two key players in productivity and quality improvement. Mentioned also was The Toyota Production System but at the time we didn't at all understand the real power and importance that Deming, Juran and Toyota played in the vast manufacturing changes taking place. We quickly found wonderful new ideas but had little understanding how they all fit together.

Most of our improvement programs, Six Sigma,[3] for example, are wonderful but it is only a small part of what is needed to be a world class manufacturing company. Too often in the West we jump on the bandwagon, sub-optimize a management technique, instead of developing a long-term strategy for competitive advantage. I hope as you read this book you will be able to see all of the parts needed for your success.

---

[2] Milton Glaser did the I Love NY symbol, Dylan covers, and was the only designer to have his own exhibit at the Modern Museum of Art in New York City.

[3] Six Sigma – There was a discussion on the NWLean website (http://www.nwlean.net) about, "which should we do first Six Sigma or Lean Manufacturing?" It is like comparing a window on the front door with the complete house, both necessary for you comfort but one much larger than the other. Six Sigma is a methodology and set of tools used to improve quality to 3.4 or less defects per million or better. See the Index for a definition.

When we look back at the 20th century's manufacturing geniuses I am sure that the names of Dr. Shigeo Shingo and Taiichi Ohno will rank with Henry Ford and Frederick Taylor.

> *Taiichi Ohno, former VP of Manufacturing at Toyota, visualized the new production process while Dr. Shingo invented the tools and techniques to make it happen.*

They helped to revolutionize the way manufacturing is done or should be done. Dr. Shingo and Ohno created what is known as the Toyota Production System, Just-In-Time or Lean manufacturing.

> *The words Toyota Production System and Just-In-Time are often used to mean the same thing but in Japan the Toyota Production System is the whole system while Just-In-Time is considered as only a part – delivering to the customer the products exactly on time, not before or after, in the right quality and in the right quantity. Lean manufacturing is just another name for the Toyota Production System. In this book Toyota Production System, JIT and Lean are often interchanged having the same meaning.*

After World War II, Shingo started to study and teach a basic understanding of how to improve the process of manufacturing. While most of the world's manufacturing companies attempted improvements by bringing in new technology or speeding up machines, Dr. Shingo brought a fresh approach to the subject. He recognized the dichotomy that operations (machines primarily) were on one level and process (the way we do things) was on another level.[4]

---

[4] Imagine a control chart with an X and Y-axis both on the same chart filling the same space but can be seen from different dimensions.

Most people only saw the conversion of raw materials through a series of machines, tried to improve the efficiency of each machine, while Dr. Shingo was able to stand back and help us maximize the efficiency of the entire factory. Manufacturers at the time arranged machines by type[5]: punch presses, lathes, etc., and allowed mountains of inventory to pile up and to be moved all over the plant,[6] while at Toyota machines were arranged into process flow cells. From Dr. Shingo's discovery inventories were reduced by over 90%, quality went from plus or minus 3% to Six Sigma (3.4 parts per million), manufacturing costs were drastically reduced, and the time line to deliver products were shortened from months to hours to Just-In-Time, just when the customer needed them.

> *Toyota in 1980 had reduced the set-up time on an 800-ton press to less than 10 minutes while similar operations in American and European auto factories were ranging from four to six hours.*[7]

I ordered recently a portable computer from Dell with all of my special features. Seven days later Federal Express delivered it to my office (the day before my trip to the mid-west). Prior to Just-In-Time it would have taken a few months.

If I could have given a Nobel Prize for exceptional contributions to the world economy, prosperity, and productivity, it would surely have been to both Dr. Shingo and Mr. Ohno. Their work has brought enormous new wealth to the world.

In fact, when Dr. Shingo was alive I did contact the Nobel Prize committee in New York only to be told that there was no category for him. It was ludicrous.

---

[5] We called these machine centers 'smokestacks.'
[6] Mercury Marine for example: in building an outboard motor shaft moved inventory 29 miles throughout the plant.
[7] Longer changeover the larger the inventory.

There is a Nobel economic prize but the Nobel people in New York could not comprehend the extraordinary value in Dr. Shingo's work to the well being of the world.   Fortunately, years later I met Dr. Vern Buehler, professor at Utah State University, and the two of us established the Shingo Prize for Manufacturing Excellence.[8]

Dr. Shingo had the intellectual knowledge and taught thousands of Toyota engineers the fundamental principles of manufacturing. As a consultant he was able to apply the Lean techniques at many companies in Japan and outside of Japan.   Ohno had the power as senior manufacturing officer at Toyota[9] to drive the process through Toyota and all of their subcontractors. I had the privilege of knowing both of them and being their American publisher.

The following are some of the books I found in Japan and had translated into English. A full bibliography is in the back of the book:

The Study of the Toyota Production System from an Engineering Viewpoint by Dr. Shigeo Shingo – to gain an understanding of the Toyota Production System, improvements of processing, inspection, preventing defects, improving transportation and storage, improving operations, poka-yoke, kanban, JIT, separating man and machine, non-stock, and SMED. It is the first book in English and the real bible of the Toyota Production System.

Managerial Engineering by Dr. Ryuji Fukuda – develop a reliable method, create a favorable environment and keep every

---

[8] I did not consciously leave out Mr. Ohno. In retrospect it probably should have been a joint prize. It was just that at the time I was much closer to Dr. Shingo.

[9] In the 1930's Mr. Toyoda tried to borrow money and was denied. He decided never to go to the bank again, now 70 years later Toyota through kaizen has $50 billion dollars in cash and probably owns the bank.

worker practiced in the method = the driving power for managerial success. CEDAC[10] and OET[11] explained.

A Revolution in Manufacturing- The SMED System by Dr. Shigeo Shingo – the key ideas on how to reduce all of your changeovers to less then 10 minutes.

Zero Quality Control – Source Inspection and the Poka-Yoke System – by Dr. Shigeo Shingo – a fresh and original approach to improving quality by detecting errors before they become defects. Dr. Shingo believed that 100% defect free work was possible.

Introduction to TPM – Total Productive Maintenance and TPM Development Program – Implementing Total Productive Maintenance by Seichi Nakajima – the first introduction of TPM to the western world through the eyes of the creator of the system. TPM's basic premise is that a new machine is in its worst condition.

Toyota Production System by Taiichi Ohno – here is the philosophy behind the system from the co-creator, simple words that built Toyota into the world's most successful automotive company.

Quality Function Deployment: Integrating Customer Requirements into Product Design by Yoji Akao – the original book from the creator of QFD.

JIT Implementation Manual: The Complete Guide to Just-In-Time Manufacturing by Hiroyuki Hirano – originally sold for $3,500.

5 Pillars of the Visual Workplace- The sourcebook for 5S Implementation by Hiroyuki Hirano – introducing 5S techniques.

---

[10] CEDAC = Cause and Effect Diagram with the Addition of Cards, a powerful process to gather ideas from all employees to solve problems.
[11] OET = On Error Training. We will explain this in detail later in the book.

Kanban and Just-In-Time at Toyota: Management Begins at the Workplace by Japan Management Association – details on how kanban works and can be applied.

The Canon Production System: Creative Involvement of the Total Workforce by Japan Management Associations – another view of how a magnificent company produced their products.

20 Keys to Workplace Improvement by Iwao Kobayashi – a simplified but powerful series of techniques to bring the improvement process to your company.

Management for Quality Improvement: The 7 New QC Tools by Shigeru Mizuno – *t*hese are the advanced quality tools used in Japan.

Japanese Management Accounting: A World Class Approach to Profit management by Yasuhiro Monden and Michiharu Sakurai – JIT brings a whole new look and approach to manufacturing accounting.

Toyota Management System by Yasuhiro Monden – looking at Toyota's approach to marketing, sales management, product development, financial management, international management, etc.

Workplace Management by Taiichi Ohno – additional wisdom from the master.

The New Standardization by Shigehiro Nakamura – *a* fresh approach to involving all employees in standardizing and improving workplace activities.

Hoshin Kanri – Policy Deployment for Successful TQM by Yoji Akao – Hoshin Kanri is used to communicate company policy to everyone in the organization.

Handbook of Quality Tools by Tetsuichi Asaka and Kazuo Ozeki – *a* teaching manual, which includes the 7 traditional and 5 newer QC tools

Kaizen Teian 1, Kaizen Teian 2 and The Idea Book by Bunji To-zawa (Japan Human Relations Association) – a review of the Japanese suggestion systems

CEDAC (Cause and Effect Diagram) - A Tool for Continuous Improvements - a detailed look at the tool that won the Deming prize in Japan.

The Shingo Production Management System – Improving Process Functions by Shigeo Shingo – looking at value engineering, CAD/CAM techniques and information management.

Non-Stock Production – The Shingo System for Continuous Improvement by Shigeo Shingo - teaching how to implement non-stock production in your plant.

One-Piece Flow – Cell Design for Transforming the Production Process by Kenichi Sekine – reconfiguring your traditional assembly lines into production cells

Some other great books published:

Handbook for Productivity Measurement and Improvement by William F. Christopher and Carl G. Thor – this is a great compendium of articles from the world's leaders in productivity measurement and improvement.

The Visual Factory by Michel Greif – visual management can make the factory a place where workers and supervisors freely communicate and take improvement action.

The Hunters and the Hunted by James B. Swartz – a great manufacturing novel

Plus many others. From these books and other material found in Japan we ran hundreds of seminars each year, produced training material, videos, CDROMS, study guides, newsletters, conferences, etc.

2

Introducing Dr. Shigeo Shingo

We learn from our mistakes![12]

Dr. Shingo defines process as "a flow by which an object is transformed from raw material into finished product," as opposed to operations which is "the flow of tasks performed by human workers on products," the focus needs to be on improving processes and not operations.

The old saying, 'you can't see the forest from the trees,' is quite appropriate. When I was younger this saying confused me and when I first met Dr. Shingo his definition also did not deeply register within me, but as I started to work and learn from him I began to realize his deep genius. When you can understand you can then begin to see the magic that comes from Lean, Kaizen[13] and the other powerful techniques developed from Dr. Shingo's unique perceptions about manufacturing.

---

[12] Making mistakes is our most powerful way to grow and learn and yet we often punish people to prevent them from doing so. Madame Curie and Thomas Edison for example both made tons of mistakes, learned from those mistakes, corrected themselves, and went on and discovered magnificent things to help humanity.

[13] Kaizen means continuous improvement.

Of course, you want both machines and people to work correctly but with the wrong emphasis you put your energies in the wrong direction. For example, we were thoroughly convinced by our accounting systems to maximize productivity from our machines "push the metal out the door," was our motto. "Keep those machines turning out the product." Dr. Shingo told us to first stop to see that the customers were happy buying those products, and then he asked us to shift out attention to insure that we were using and maximizing the proper system – reducing our costs and eliminating all defects. As you read further I am sure you will gain clarity from the clear perceptions given to us by Dr. Shingo.

The week before Dr. Shingo died his son drove him to the train station. Mrs. Shingo then pushed Dr. Shingo in his wheel chair first up an elevator to the platform and then they took a bullet train from Fujisawa to Osaka, Japan, around a four-hour ride. In Osaka, the client met them at the station and drove them to their plant. He consulted with his client then Shingo told his wife he didn't feel well and asked her to please take him to the hospital.

A week later at the age of 81, November 14, 1990, he died of cancer.[14]

All he knew really in his life was how to work. He lived with Umeko his wife in a very small house in Fujisawa, called it a "rat house,' around 100 miles south of Tokyo with virtually no land for gardening. There they raised three boys. One son Ritsuo Shingo is now the president of Sichuan Toyota Motor Co., Ltd in China.[15]

---

[14] Mrs. Shingo never told Dr. Shingo of his illness. He just accepted the pain and continued to work.
[15] Mr. Toyoda the former chairman of Toyota said a year ago in China, "If it wasn't for Ritsuo Shingo's father Toyota would not be where it is today."

Dr. Shingo would line up his clients a year in advance, filling up almost every day of the week with consulting assignments. He would visit the factory floor and help his clients solve problems and constantly challenged them to be better.

"The job of a manager is to get things done through other people. The manager is not usually able to do the job alone. Management defines the system. Workers work within the system. Only management can change the system and the system MUST be changed continually if quality is to be improved!" - Shingo - Zero Quality Control: Source Inspection and the Poka-yoke System

To attain the goal of continuous improvement Shingo was relentless in stimulating people to change for the better. "Can't be done "and " impossible," were not part of his vocabulary. He knew there were many ways to solve problems, like there were many paths to reach the top of Mt. Fuji.[16]

Dr. Shingo was never satisfied. He was happy with the progress of his clients but pushed them relentlessly to be better. Isn't that the heart of continuous improvement?

---

[16] Mt Fuji is the highest mountain in Japan 3776-meters high, and the symbol of Japan. More than 200,000 people climb to the top of Mt. Fuji in a year. I was told that when traveling on the bullet train in front of Mt. Fuji that I would only see the mountain if 'I behaved," and if not it would be covered by clouds.

Whenever Dr. Shingo left a client he gave them homework to work on. Just like at school we need to learn and work afterwards in our quest for competitive excellence. **Dr. Shingo expected his clients to have the work completed before he came back a month later.[17] He didn't want them to waste time and he didn't want them to waste his time.**

After a day's work he would have a simple dinner often prepared by his wife in his hotel room and then start to write. He wrote something almost every day.

The art of writing every day stimulated Shingo's mind to learn and to rethink ways for continuous improvement.

He wrote about his learning from the day's consulting assignments and produced 25 books on manufacturing management.[18]

He was completely dedicated to his work. He couldn't stop consulting. He had encyclopedic knowledge of manufacturing and was able to solve virtually every manufacturing problem presented to him. I knew Dr. Shingo for around nine years, published his books in English, arranged to have them translated into 17 other languages, brought him to America twice a year to speak and consult with companies, traveled with him throughout the states and in Japan, set up lectures at conferences and watched his magic on the factory floor.

"When I first heard about statistics in 1951, I firmly believed it to be the best technique around, and it took me 26 years to be completely free of its spell."[19]

---

[17] Try this with you employees. Give them improvement homework projects to do.

[18] Five of these books were published in English.

[19] Shigeo Shingo - ZQC: Source Inspection and the Poka-Yoke System

I once asked Dr. Shigeo Shingo, **"Who really discovered Lean, you or Taiichi Ohno? "** Shingo looked at me and quickly said, **"I did, for I was Ohno's teacher**." At a later time I asked an ex-Toyota group manager, Chihiro Nakao, who worked with both Shingo and Ohno a similar question, "Who really discovered Lean, Shingo or Ohno?" His answer was, **"Which came first the chicken or the egg?"**[20]

Of course, both Dr. Shingo and Mr. Ohno played significant roles and it was through their conceptual genius that Lean was born.

Years back, APICS[21] invited Dr. Shingo to keynote their annual conference in Las Vegas, Nevada. It was a very eventful moment in my life. I acted, as both Shingo's host insuring that everything would go on schedule, and also it was my job to introduce Dr. Shingo to the conference attendees. I arose early that morning gathering everything necessary to assist Dr. Shingo. Quickly I went to the dining room and bought four bananas, as Shingo liked to use bananas to open his talk about wastes in the manufacturing process.

After buying the bananas, I quickly ran over to Shingo's room to make sure he was dressed and ready to speak. Mrs. Shingo traveled with him, ironing his shirts, cooking rice in the room with her rice cooker and taking care of all of his needs. He normally had his breakfast in his room. At the time Shingo had difficulty walking so I had to provide a wheelchair and then slowly I wheeled him along to the conference hall. I carefully arranged for everything, except I forgot to have my own breakfast. Re-

---

[20] Even though both Shingo and Ohno jointly developed JIT, Dr. Shingo is not as well known in Japan as Ohno. I sold over 100,000 copies of Dr. Shingo's SMED book in English while only around 10,000 copies were sold in Japan.
[21] APICS is the American Production and Inventory Control Society - The Educational Society for Resource Management

membering that I bought four bananas, feeling that three were enough for his presentation. I took one of the bananas peeled it and ate it.

It was very impressive for there were over 3,000 people in the conference hall waiting to hear Dr. Shingo speak. I spent only a few moments introducing Dr. Shingo, invited him to the stage, handed him the microphone and then sat on the stage behind him.

Dr. Shingo looked at the vast crowd and then pointed to me and said, "Norman Bodek has thrown off my entire talk this morning. I originally saw four bananas and based my calculations on the four bananas and now I see that he has stolen one for his breakfast, leaving only three bananas."

Imagine how I felt? My face turned a thousand shades of red.

Dr. Shingo liked to use the bananas as an analogy. "When you buy bananas all you want is the fruit not the skin, but you have to pay for the skin also. It is a waste. And you the customer should not have to pay for the waste.

> *Waste elimination is the heart of the Toyota Production System. Lexus's new motto "The Passionate pursuit of perfection," symbolizes this unending quest to eliminate wastes in the manufacturing process and also to find more innovative products to please their customers.[22]*

When buying an automobile you want to pay only for the value adding[23] not for the manufacturing wastes. If defects are

---

[22] We will discuss waste in more detail later in the book.

[23] Value adding are the steps in manufacturing to convert raw material to finished goods: milling, grinding, stamping, attaching, etc.

made while manufacturing why should you the customer have to pay for the cost to produce those defects – it is a waste and the customer should not have to pay for those wastes."

This concept of waste is really the heart of Lean manufacturing.

When Shingo and Ohno shifted their attention from machine improvements to the elimination of all non-value adding wastes, light bulbs started popping off in their heads. They knew that this would give Toyota its competitive advantage.

I believe that if you understand exactly what waste is you can quickly move Lean throughout your company, but honestly there is so much "garbage," complexity, thrown around that just confuses the power of knowing and implementing Lean concepts.[24]

Dr. Shingo, in his work as a teacher and consultant was always precise with only a few exceptions. He would want to start his lectures exactly on time but never in all the years I worked with him would he end his lecture on time. At the APICS' conference in front of the 3,000 people he would not want to leave the stage – he had a burning desire to teach people the principles of the Toyota Production System with the hope that they would immediately put them into practice within their companies. They were not complicated concepts but they did require you to understand their importance, how they differed from the past and most importantly that you would put them into practice.

Once, Dan Bills, the CEO of Granville Phillips a manufacturer of vacuum testing equipment in Boulder, Colorado, told me the following, "If I was in Grand Central Station in New York City looking for a person but didn't know exactly what that person

---

[24] Yes, just keep it simple, get everyone involved in continuous improvement and eliminate those wastes.

looked like I would never find him/her. This is the same with waste. For years I did not know what waste was so I could never find it and remove it. We spent the bulk of our time trying to speed up our machines, bringing in new technology, trying to solve horrendous defect problems without really knowing the fundamental reasons why wastes were being created."

Granville Phillips' engineers knew they had defects but since they were always spending their time correcting problems they could never get to the real cause to eliminate them.

> *Getting to the root cause to eliminate problems and defects is close to the heart of lean manufacturing. Just solving a problem to allow it to occur again is such a waste of human ingenuity. Dr. Shingo would want us to spend a little more time up front, to investigate causes a little deeper to insure that the same problem would never happen again.*

It is like a modern doctor who looks at symptoms of a disease, like detecting a high fever in a patient and seeing a swollen knee giving the patient an antibiotic hoping that would solve the problem. Often the pill takes away the swollen knee and reduces the fever but the fever and swelling keep coming back until we can find the real source of the problem.

> *Last week I was in a supermarket and overheard the cashier talk about the pain in her wrist and that she didn't know what to do. I told her to be careful that many people on cash registers end up with carpal tunnel syndrome. She said, "I had it and the doctor operated on me." The doctor only looked at the symptom not the source of the problem. I told her that I once ran a company with hundreds of operators and never saw a case of carpal tunnel. I insisted that every operator hold their wrists straight while they keyed. I*

learnt this when I was 12 years old from a pianist who would hit my wrists with a ruler to force me to keep them straight. I told her to make sure that like a pianist you must keep those wrists straight. I also told the packer to remind her.

Does it ever happen to you? When you discover a problem and present it to others do they always have a very sound reason for the problems existence? I think most people are masters of procrastination and can find thousands of reasons why it is impossible to change.

A company in my area bought a very expensive automatic insertion machine to put chips into the integrated boards. The machine worked very fast but seemed to always make mistakes. This required that most of the boards go through 100% quality inspection; someone sitting in front of a microscope to see that every chip was placed and soldered properly.

When confronted, managers and engineers often say, "The machine just makes mistakes, can't do anything about it!" You cannot convince them otherwise.

Dr. Shingo would never accept that answer – you had to get to the root cause[25] and eliminate it. The Toyota Production System, which did visualize the entire factory as a one-piece flow[26] system cannot work unless those defects are eliminated. If one machine stops then the whole plant stops.[27] Producing defects is

---

[25] Root cause is the heart of the problem. Ask why, over and over again relentlessly until you discover the fundamental reason for the problems occurrence so that it never occurs again.

[26] One-piece flow is where a part is moved from one operation, one machine, to the next, one at a time with no interim storage, and no inventory building up between processes. I once saw 16 machines in a machine cell with one part moving between them.

[27] This was the theory and the goal of Ohno and Shingo and as you read on you will see how this was slightly changed.

one of the most significant wastes in the Toyota Production System.

Most of us have the same problem. We are surrounded by waste but without understanding what waste really is we can't identify it or remove it.

For example, take the whole idea of supply chain management.[28] We've always felt that it was necessary to have large amounts of inventory to supply products to our customers. We needed large warehouses to house the inventory; we needed to automate the warehouse to speed up the delivery process; we needed an elaborate accounting system to manage the inventory; we needed skids and forklifts to move the inventory around; we needed a vast array of shelving; we needed a large staff of people to do the moving and packing and shipping; we needed incoming and outgoing inspectors, etc – all adding to the cost of manufacturing, all is waste.

In all sports activities the score is always in sight. We might think that we are playing the game solely to win, but not really. We play for the exercise, we play to improve ourselves, we play for the companionship; we play for the excitement, the thrill. We feel good about the doing; we feel good about reaching for new heights, and, yes, if we lose our ego doesn't like it but the real benefits have been achieved just from the process. Winning is important but often it clouds the real issue. You can win next time; it comes as you improve. It is only a matter of time.

Dr. Shingo used the idea of the complete elimination of all non-value adding "wastes" as the target. And since in some sense there is always some waste we never stop improving. The meaning of the word subtly changes as we improve. We start at

---

[28] I was introduced to Supply Chain Management by BOSE who had offices in their plant for their major vendors – they did not need separate managers to do the purchasing for them, that responsibility was left up to the vendors.

the obvious, the gross and then we refine it.

3
Taiichi Ohno[29]

Ford, in the 1920's, was able to build a car in four days from the iron ore to finished cars onto the railroad cars. Of course, as Henry Ford said, "you can have any color car you want as long as it is 'black' and you can have any model you want as long as it is a model T."

Ohno, studying Ford, co-developed The Toyota Production System to deliver to the customer any color and any model car from a wide variety of choices within a week.

"All we are doing is looking at the time line, from the moment the customer gives us an order to the point when we collect cash. And we are reducing that time line by removing the non-value adding[30] activities."

---

[29] I published by Taiichi Ohno in English: *Toyota Production System: Beyond Large-Scale Production*, Workplace Management and *Just-In-Time for Today and Tomorrow* coauthored with Setsuo Mito.
[30] Non-value adding is an activity that does not add value to the finished product, like moving things or creating defects.

Taiichi Ohno and the author

Taiichi Ohno, the co-developer of the Toyota Production System, wouldn't allow anything to be written down about the system. He told me that he wouldn't allow anything to be written down for the process was always changing. But, I felt that the real reason was that he didn't want competition to understand what they were doing at Toyota.

In fact, when he finally put his theories in the book, *Toyota Production System: Beyond Large-Scale Production,* published in 1978 in Japanese, the management at Toyota was quite upset. The Toyota Production System had given Toyota a great competitive advantage and they did not want to share this information with other automotive companies.

> *Ohno continually wanted to reduce labor hours focusing on improving productivity, but Toyota with their lifetime employment system did not lay off workers. Thus, Toyota was forced to grow. Instead of laying off the weakest person, Toyota took the best people and gave them new challenging assignments.*

During one of our study missions to Japan we visited one of Toyota's subsidiaries, Toyota Gosei. I was walking outside one of their manufacturing plants with one of their managers when he said, "Soon after Ohno was moved from Toyota he became chairman of Toyoda Gosei."

> *In Japan, when you are a senior manager, it is common practice to move senior managers to subsidiaries when they are not chosen for a leadership position. This was very surprising in Ohno's case, for as vice president of production and co-creator the Toyota Production System, he was one of the major contributors of Toyota's success. It might have been his demeanor; he was very rough and also he wrote his book The Toyota Production System, giving others a clearer understanding of the power of the Toyota System. Publishing the book did not ingratiate Toyota's top executives. However, being chairman of Toyota Gosei is, of course, a high honor, but not the same as being president or chairman of Toyota.*

One day Ohno walked into one of the large warehouses at Toyota Gosei and said to the staff of managers around him, "Get rid of this warehouse and in one year I will come back and look! I want to see this warehouse made into a machine shop and I want to see everyone trained as machinists." And sure enough, one year later that building became a machine shop and everyone had been retrained.[31]

---

[31] "Ohno changed the structure of the workforce from the traditional foreman/supervisor/worker to a manager/team leader/team member relationship where, unlike the traditional system, the supervisor/team leader worked alongside the team members adding value to the end product. Problems with machinery, traditionally, were simply repaired and people hoped the problem would not recur. These new teams were taught to question the root cause of any problem and keep questioning until a solution was found. In time this had the effect of dramatically reducing production stoppages to a point where yields approaching 100% were not uncommon." - http://www.t-san.co.uk/

> *Ohno did not tell them how to do it. He just demanded that they do it.[32]*

Well, Ohno had a reputation of creating fear in others. He was often called "ruthless" in his desire to drive out waste from the Toyota system.

> *Suppliers supposedly lived in fear of not being able to deliver to Ohno's strict requirements; fear of being late on factory deliveries, fear of not being just-in-time, but somehow they all did conform and I was told that not a single Toyota supplier ever went bankrupt. And many of those suppliers now are world leaders in their product lines.*

Ohno knew the economic benefits to Lean, knew it wasn't easy to bring change, and was forceful in bringing it forward.

Another time I was standing inside a factory near Tokyo, in front of a newly purchased automated delivery system. The system allowed an operator to pick out the necessary parts to be delivered to the assembly line. It was impressive to see the operator and her proficiency using the automated system fulfilling orders. A former assistant to Mr. Ohno was standing with a group of the company's managers and he said to me, "Norman, what would Ohno have said about this automated warehouse?" I said, without thinking, Ohno would have said, "Get rid of it."[33] All the managers looked shocked. I am sure their minds were buzzing, "How can we get rid of it?"

Once confronted with a problem Ohno was sure that they would find the answer. He didn't have to tell people how to do it. He knew they would figure it out for themselves.

---

[32] This was not easy for others to follow, but it was a very powerful way to empower other people.
[33] Inventory to Ohno was considered as a waste.

I learned from these experiences that there is value in shocking people into understanding that waste should be eliminated. Automation can institutionalize waste instead of getting rid of it. It is management's job to set a clear direction, but to let their people figure out how to go get there.

Ohno would have wanted all of the parts delivered directly to the assembly line without any interim storage.

I remember years back when Xerox was filled with so much pride when they built one of the world's largest and most automated warehouse to ship their products. Dr. Shingo and Ohno both would have laughed that a company would spend so much money to move material around.

But, Ohno was also very practical. In fact, people living in the Toyota City/Nagoya area of Japan are noted for their 'Scottish Blood,' they don't want to waste money. One day on another visit to Toyota Gosei I noticed a batch of rubber hoses being machined in parallel. This confused me for we were taught about one-piece flow and here was at least fifty hoses being worked on at the same time.

I asked Ohno about that operation. He said, "Yes, we want one-piece flow but we also want to produce the parts the least expensively[34] and for that particular operation it pays us to machine a group of parts at the same time." This was a great moment for often when we learn something new, like the Toyota Production System; we think we must follow absolute rules to get there. Ohno was saying that he wanted one-piece flow but he wasn't going to waste money to do it.

---

[34] The Toyota Production System is a very practical system.

Ohno ultimately wanted one-piece flow and you can see this in many manufacturing cells, but parts are still held and moved in batches between cells.

Inventory is Like a River

When Ohno would speak to our study mission group, his lecture was always very simple and basic. He would start by giving us his famous 'river example.' "Inventory[35] is like a river of water and as it flows through the plant it hides problems and other wastes. It hides the machine problems, quality/defect problems, and many others. All of these problems add to the cost of manufacturing."

To address this issue Ohno recommended that we start by slowly reducing inventory, 'reducing the level of water in the river.' "As you lower the level of inventory, problems rise to the surface of your awareness,[36] then one by one you solve those problems and eliminate them, then you can lower the river again," Ohno said. You continue to do this eliminating those non-value added wastes.

Lowering the river of inventory is the heart of lean manufacturing. Keep this centered in your mind and practice it. People have a tendency to complicate things. It is only because they really don't fully understand and appreciate the simplicity and power of reducing inventory.

---

[35] Since Ohno's death Toyota has slightly reversed the trend to completely remove inventory and has additional inventory to protect them against disasters. But, Toyota is still the best JIT Company in the world.

[36] These problems could be machine failures. If one machine goes down, excess inventory allows the process to continue without having to immediately fix the machine. If there was a quality defeat inventory allows you to work without having to get to the root cause of the problem.

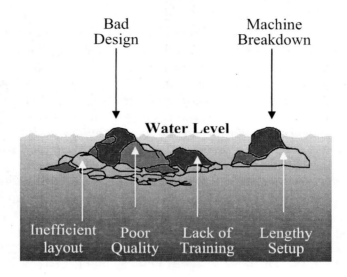

If you had a batch size of 100 parts, Ohno would tell you to lower the batch size to 99 and see what happens. If a problem occurs then solve it and then take away another piece.

The process of lowering the inventory levels led to the concept of one-piece flow, but when you cannot get to one-piece flow you use the Kanban[37] system and work with small batch sizes.

One-piece flow is producing only one part at a time then moving that part immediately to the next machine. The machine in a cell often has a device to hold the part while being machined then it is either moved automatically to the next machine or carried there by the worker. There is virtually no inventory built up between these machines.

---

[37] In December 1980 we interviewed Yasuhiro Monden, professor of accounting at the State University of New York at Buffalo and author of the *Toyota Production System.* We titled the article *Kanban – The Coming Revolution* for we liked the name kanban better than the Toyota Production System but kanban is only a subset and JIT became the term of choice.

Kanban means sign board or card and is used as a signaling or communication device to pull manufactured products through the factory. Using kanban a work center knows exactly what to produce, when to produce it, and in the quantity required. It drives the Lean system, and minimizes inventory. You can only produce a product when you have a kanban card; without a kanban you cannot overproduce products. The kanban creates a pull system as opposed to the old 'push' system. A process cannot produce a product unless the subsequent process goes back to the previous process and 'pulls,' causing the previous process to produce exactly what is needed.

On one of those visits to Ohno's plant, I saw a woman inserting a metal nozzle onto a small batch of hoses. In front of her was a board, around three feet by two feet in area. Nailed to the board were her procedures for assembly, examples of both good and bad hoses, a list of potential problems, the allowable tolerances for her to inspect her own work, and places for her to post her quality results and also to record any problems. It was not a computer printout. It was crude. It was simple but to me it was a very effective and powerful method to empower the worker to be responsible for the quality of her work.[38]

The last time I met Ohno it was at Toyota Gosei and I asked him what Toyota was now doing to improve. He said, "All we are doing is looking at the time line, from the moment the customer gives us an order to the point when we collect cash. And we are reducing that time line by removing the non-value adding[39] ac-

---

[38] Yes, you pass on as much responsibility to the worker as possible. People are capable of controlling and improving their part of the process, if you trust them and allow them to do it.

[39] Non-value adding is an activity that does not add value to the finished product, like moving things or creating defects.

tivities." Ohno kept it very simple – looking for and eliminating the wastes.

According to Ohno establishing the Toyota Production System took over twenty years. Once Toyota had made significant strides then JIT was slowly introduced to their subsidiaries. To spread JIT to the major subcontractors Ohno picked ten key people, one from each of the top tier suppliers to lead the effort.

These ten key people, known as a Toyota Autonomous Study Group, acted as consultants to all of the subsidiaries and worked closely together.

> *General Electric, when they acquired the automotive plants from Rockwell in the mid 1980's tried a similar approach to move JIT forward. The plant managers would meet for a full day each month at one of the eighteen plants. In the morning they were taught one of the JIT concepts. In the afternoon they walked through the plant acting as consultants. Imagine that you were a plant manager and that your peers would visit your plant next month – what would you do in advance in the plant to prepare for the visit? From what I understood the people in the plant went 'crazy,' making changes and moving JIT forward. It is such a simple approach but very powerful when peer pressure exists.*

One of those in the study group was Chihiro Nakao, who worked with Taiho Kogyo. Nakao, years later, left Taiho Kogyo, started his own consulting company, and has driven 'Kaizen Blitz'[40] throughout America.

One day in Japan, Nakao invited me to spend a day with him while he was consulting. This plant was a surface mount

---

[40] Kaizen Blitz - see page 177 for further information about the process.

technology company producing integrated circuit boards. Nakao gathered all of the managers into a conference room. He had consulted with this company around six months earlier and left them some homework, a tactic he learned from Dr. Shingo.

Two of this company's engineers showed us a large chart of how they set up a U-shaped manufacturing cell with around six different machines. They explained a number of the problems that occurred in setting up the cell and what they had done to solve those problems. They then explained the entire process within the cell telling us what each machine did and also where they did adjustments and inspection.

Nakao[41] then got up, took a red marker and crossed off the adjustments and inspection sections and said, "At Toyota we did not do adjustments and inspections within a cell.[42]" That's all he did.

What a powerful moment for me. I learned that you don't have to tell people exactly what to do. Nakao indicated that only value adding activities were to be done within a cell.

It was amazing how he could get to the heart of things in a few minutes. **He didn't tell them what or how to do anything. Telling them what they did and did not do at Toyota was enough to challenge and stimulate them to make the necessary improvements after he left.**

Nakao also pointed out simple things on the line like a ladies small inexpensive blow dryer next to an operator or an inexpensive mirror bought at the local hardware store placed behind the

---

[41] Nakao also told me that a machine should not be more than four times the size of the part, a simple but another very powerful idea to think about.

[42] Inspections and adjustments, if necessary, were done at the end of the cell or at the end of the production process in final assembly.

product to see things easier.[43] He laughed and said, "We try to get things done inexpensively but effectively."

I also was told that Toyota and the major suppliers instead of buying machines that would do 'everything possible needed in the future,' would build over 90%[44] of their own machines themselves to do the specific job needed at the time.

One day after taking my study group through an old Toyota assembly plant I met with Ohno and said, "Mr. Ohno, I do appreciate you allowing my study group to visit a Toyota factory but it is always an old factory not one of the new ones." He said a little annoyed at me, "Norman you do not understand the Toyota Production System. We don't need new machines.[45] We only use what is needed to get the job done, on time to the customer, and at the lowest possible cost to us."[46]

Lean starts with customer service and ends with customer service. You answer the following question, "How can I please my customers by delivering to them exactly what they want, exactly when they want it, in the right quantity and in the right quality at the lowest possible cost?"

---

[43] Most of these small ideas came from the workers. We will write about the Japanese suggestion system, Quick and Easy Kaizen later in the book.

[44] Imagine how much money your company would save if you built your own machines to do specifically what you wanted. Often we spend a lot of money to buy machines with fancy features that we might never use in the future.

[45] Prior to visiting Toyota I had been to many factories that to me looked much better, more modern, with newer equipment. I was, of course, embarrassed and felt uncomfortable being criticized by Ohno but it was a great learning experience for me.

[46] Funny though, I have a Lexus, a great automobile but I had to buy the auto drive feature, the automatic adjustable seats, and the seat warmer and other not used gadgets. I could not buy, here in America, exactly what I wanted.

4

Defining Waste

By learning you will teach; by teaching you will learn. **Latin Proverb**

What is waste? Ohno and Shingo originally listed seven types of waste:

1.   **Inventory** – wastes of stock – reduce the production period, reduce the setup times (which then allows a reduction in batch size, which reduces the work-in-process inventory), level the quantity produced by one-piece-flow – arranging machines into manufacturing cells, and adopting small lot production.

Inventory is reduced by synchronization of production – going backwards from finished goods to the previous process and only pulling forward exactly what is required, when it is required (JIT)

There are great dangers in holding inventory as it often is not saleable, deterioration comes with time, and there is a late detection of errors, etc. In Lean, stock is a liability whereas it is considered an asset in traditional accounting.

Nippondenso turns over inventory 350 times a year. Reduction of set-up was the key. Dana Corpora-

tion delivers frames to Toyota Georgetown 16 times a day. Create a new vision to match them and with time you will do it.

2.   **Motion** - Go back to the fundamentals of Industrial Engineering, video the process, watch the video and get engineers and the operators involved in finding ways to improve their movements and keep repeating the process continuously.

Improve motion by improving equipment, locate tools to facilitate ease of handling - required parts are positioned near at hand – only required parts arrive near or at hand one by one.

3.   **Transportation** or moving of things – rearrange the manufacturing process into cells to reduce movement.

Improve plant layouts; consider how you can eliminate transportation.

4.   **Defects** - apply six sigma techniques, use Total Quality Management[47] (TQM) and reduce defects to zero.

Inspect to prevent defective products not to find defects. Do 100% inspection not sampling – doing self-inspection (operator checks themselves), successive inspection (next person checks previous work), develop poka-yoke devices.

5.   **Waiting time** or delays – install kanban to move small batches of finished parts within the factory and set up U-Cells.

---

[47]Total Quality Management (TQM) is a comprehensive and structured approach to organizational management that seeks to improve the quality of products and services through ongoing refinements in response to continuous feedback.

Switch your thinking – waiting time of workers is more important than operation ratio of machines – machines can wait, people should not wait and watch machines.

6.   **Overproduction** that's ahead or behind schedule – do Just-In-Time and deliver the products exactly on time.

Eliminate storage between processes (drop the idea of economic lot sizes); adopt the SMED (Single Minute Exchange of Dies for quick changeover) system, level quantity and synchronize processes, adopt one-piece flow, and improve the plant layout.

7.   **Processing** – doing operations inefficiently, incorrectly, using the wrong equipment, people not properly trained.

Consider improvements from the point of view of value engineering and value analysis, is this operation required, why should this processing method be adopted?

To these I add three more:

8.   **Inspection inefficiencies** – reduce final inspection through poka-yoke[48] and other defect prevention techniques and eliminate in process inspection.

Poka-yoke are miss-proofing devices to absolutely prevent any defects from being produced. Poka-yoke is a system invented by Dr. Shingo, who encouraged all workers to look for opportunities and build very simple devices to prevent defects.

---

[48] For more information on Poka-yoke go to
http://www.campbell.berry.edu/faculty/jgrout/pokayoke.html

9.   **Excess costs**, including too much overhead – get the accountants to rethink the cost accounting system and find ways to continuously reduce your overhead costs.

10.   **Lack of creativity - underutilization of talents** – find ways to get all employees involved in coming up with improvement ideas to make their jobs easier and more interesting.

People traditionally come to work and are asked to leave their brains at home. Use Quick and Easy Kaizen[49] to develop people properly to fully participate in the continuous improvement process through the implementation of their own ideas.

From Just-In-Case to Just-In-time

The old manufacturing system you might call it the 'Just-In-Case' system.

> *Just-In-Case (as opposed to Just-In-Time) allows manufacturers to build up buffers of inventory to prevent failures from stopping the production flow. If one machine is stopped it does not prohibit other machines from working, for excess inventory is always available. But, when Toyota went to Just-In-Time it forced them to be more efficient. It was brilliant. Initially, it cost Toyota more to repeatedly stop production to solve problems. But ultimately, as problems were solved, the system made Toyota the most successful manufacturer in the world.*

In most factories there were mountains of inventory to protect against every kind of eventuality and the focus was on keeping those machines going at all cost. Ohno felt it was better to have the entire plant stop than to build in all of the redundancies to pro-

---

[49] Quick and Easy Kaizen is a process to get all employees involved in improvement activities and will be explained in detail starting on page 257.

tect against possible disaster.[50] If there was a bad snow storm and the factory had to close for the day; it was still better then to build up inventory 'Just-In-Case' these events would happen. Inventory was the first and most important waste in manufacturing.

At first, when starting, Toyota suppliers would build interim storage facilities to protect themselves against potential delays in shipping, but Ohno put a stop to this.

At a Toyota assembly plant I saw engines delivered in batches of 18 at a time, which meant that deliveries were done three times an hour. "What if there was a traffic accident or traffic jam?" a traveler asked.   "It is still better to have that entire plant stop and wait for the next arrival of engines than to build in a system to prevent those problems from occurring," said Ohno.

When I asked Mr. Ohno once where he got his ideas on JIT he said laughingly, "I learned it from reading Henry Ford's book *Today and Tomorrow, published in 1926.*"

On my return back to the states I went to the library and found a copy of the book, read it and noted that Doubleday was the publisher. I got permission from Doubleday and reprinted the book and sold tens of thousands of copies.

---

[50] Just-In-Case is the current system found at airport security stations. I used to be able to fly through airports allowing myself 10 minutes to board the plane. Now, after 9/11, we have to get to the airport one to two hours in advance. Time lost and security costs in the billions of dollars are terrible wastes. Losing 3,000 people was a terrible disaster, and we should go after the terrorists, but cigarettes, and car accidents take many more lives than the 9/11disaster and hardly anything is done to prevent them.

5

Dr. Shingo Asking Five Whys at Granville Phillips

"Don't tell them how to do it! Just teach them the principles of Lean, challenge them, and let them do it." **John Miller – Gemba Research**

In the mid-nineteen eighties I took Dr. Shingo to Granville-Phillips a manufacturer of vacuum testing equipment in Boulder, Colorado.

Granville-Phillips had brilliant engineers, but they took four months to bring a new product to market (and then the result was 97% defects in final inspection). Dr. Bills, the CEO of Granville-Phillips, asked Dr. Shingo to please look at their manufacturing process to see if he could help them become more efficient.

Shingo at first went to where the process originated. We went to watch the design engineers and then we followed a logical progression through the entire manufacturing process. At each stage engineers and managers would present problems to Dr. Shingo and he would carefully think and look and then instead of just giving the answer, he would ask the engineers some very basic questions. He loved to use the Five Whys, asking why five times. Five Whys is a simple but great technique to use to solve problems. It really gets people involved using their brains and challenging the 'status quo.' An example:

"Why do we get soldering misconnects?" an engineer asked Dr. Shingo. His answer was a question.

"Why doesn't the solder not 100% connect the pins to the board 100% of the time?"

"Sometimes the solder does not melt properly," an engineer would answer.

"Why does that happen?" asked Shingo.

"Maybe the solder's temperature varies," another said.

"Why would the temperature vary? Shingo again would ask.

At first the engineers stared into blank space until one said, "Something is causing the temperature to vary!"

"Why does that happen, what could cause the temperature to vary?" Shingo asked.

A bright light went on in the head of one engineer who said, "Maybe since the un-melted solder drops into the solder bath in chunks, not smoothly, the temperature drops at that moment, causing mismatches when the next board is entered into the bath."

This was a classic example of the "Five Why" process that Shingo was demonstrating. Continue asking "why" until the answers are exhausted and you have found the root cause.

"Brilliant," Shingo shouted. " Now what can you do to prevent the solder dropping in so drastically?"

Another engineer said, "We can reduce the incline for the

solid solder so that it would only slowly enter the melted bath."

For Shingo, there was always a fundamental reason for a problem and it only took some deep probing and a sense of never accepting a defect or that a problem could not be solved.

Another Example:

In one room a number of women were inserting microchips onto a circuit board. Immediately Dr. Shingo asked,

"Why are the lights so bright in this room?"

The answer given was that since so many errors were being made here they felt the women just needed more light.

Then Shingo asked, "Could the bright lights be one cause of the problems you are having?"

Suddenly an engineer realized that the bright lights could be causing glare to strike into the eyes of the operators.

"Yes," Dr. Shingo said, well pleased. "And how would you reduce the glare and give the operators enough light?"

"We should turn down the lights overhead and place lights underneath the boards," said another engineer.

"Absolutely," Shingo shouted with glee.

Yes, many consultants and managers feel that they are being paid to come up with the ideas, but when they do they take away the joy and the excitement from others. **We all love to discover for ourselves the causes of problems. When we do discover for ourselves our energy really moves inside us. When we are told the answers we might learn a little, but it is nothing like the**

magic of discovering things through our own questions. At that moment (when the light bulb goes off in our head) you can feel the excitement in the air and real learning takes place.

From four months to four hours, from 97% defects to three percent.

Dr. Shingo spent only two days at Granville Phillips but within three months after his visit the engineers there had reduced the time line on new products from four months to four hours, and the defect rate from final inspection dropped from 97% to only 3%, meaning only 3% of the boards required some rework not 97%. Imagine the satisfaction of their customers when they could get products earlier; imagine the satisfaction of the managers and the accountants when they saw the rework drop 94%; and imagine the joy the workers felt when the defects began to disappear.

6

My First Trip to Japan: A Thriller

"You can learn too much from experience.
A cat that sits on a hot stove will not sit on a hot
stove again but unfortunately the cat will not sit on
a cold one either." - **Mark Twain**

In 1980, I started a newsletter titled *Productivity,* and quickly discovered that the Japanese were the world's leader in productivity. When I did my initial research, I thought (like many others) that Quality Control Circles were the real difference between Japanese and American productivity growth. It was an important factor but there were other more significant reasons.

> *Quality Control Circles (QCC) are small group activities where workers get together in small groups periodically to solve quality and other problems found within their own work area. In the first issue of our newsletter in June 1980, we wrote about QCC stating that Japan went from 'junk' merchants to high quality producers thinking that Quality Control Circles could have been the answer.*

> *In that first issue we also wrote about Dr. Deming and Dr. Juran, and mentioned that they provided the Japanese with the basis for the QC Circle program – close but not really that accurate. We subsequently learned that it was Dr. Kaoru Ishikawa who developed QC Circles and that Deming and Juran played vital*

roles in the over all quality movement but had very lit-
tle to do with the success of QC Circles. Also men-
tioned in the newsletter was that American Airlines,
IBM, TRW, AMF, Eaton, Ford, General Foods, Polar-
oid, Buick, 3M, Hughes Aircraft, Westinghouse, and
Chicago Title Insurance already had successful Qual-
ity Control Circles programs.

To determine exactly what the Japanese were doing to enhance their outstanding productivity and quality I thought it was
necessary to go to Japan. Problem was, I did not speak Japanese.

I did not know a single soul in Japan nor did I have any contacts there. But I was determined. Maybe because I was totally
ignorant on the subject of manufacturing and the real causes of
productivity growth; I was like the child in the story of the Emperor's New Clothes; my naiveté might have allowed me to see
things others could not.

In November 1980, I attended a conference given by Industry Week in New York City attended by slightly over 100 people.
One of the speakers was Joji Arai, managing director of the Japan
Productivity Center's (JPC) office in Washington DC. Arai spoke
about some of the things being done in Japan to improve productivity and quality:

1.   No person had a private office, for they wanted to
        get a feeling of togetherness

2.   Each morning, people held an informal meeting

        Informal meeting – I saw, at the Takashimaya
        department store in Tokyo prior to opening their doors
        to the public, employees grouped around their man-
        ager. He asked them, "What can we do today to im-

prove our customer service?" Then he listened and, like a football coach, cheered them on to have a great day. He did this every day – a very powerful method to involve all employees in continuous improvement.

3.   Humanization of the work environment

I feel we, in the main, are 'light years' away from creating a humane working environment. Our emphasis is producing great products efficiently for our customers, but we put in very little effort on the human side of lean – creating ideal working conditions; bringing real quality of work life to our factories. We have a lot to do in this area.

4.   Inventory control systems

5.   In-house training

6.   Lifetime employment system

7.   Group decision making

8.   Management and employee participation programs

9.   Cooperation between design and manufacturing engineers

10.   Special emphasis on quality control

But, no real clues about the power of JIT and the Toyota Production system were mentioned at all. But he did tell us that JPC set up study missions for Japanese managers to visit American manufacturing companies. As he spoke he was looking for American companies that would be willing to be hosts for Japanese visitors.

For the past thirty years we in America had looked at the Japanese as a nation of copiers, surely as not an economic threat to our economy.

> *At the Japan Management Association (JMA) I was told the story of how at the end of World War II they visited the American Management Associations (AMA) offices in New York, took pictures and replicated everything including the size of the room, the blackboards, and even the size of the chairs. Yes, they did copy us for a time until they got back on their feet and then they improved. Unfortunately for us we were stuck with that old perception of Japan being copiers and did not recognize their incredible innovation and creativity. Today the JMA group of companies is probably ten times larger then AMA.*

The Japanese were making small cars more inexpensively than in America and their quality was improving each year and we thought that there was nothing for us to worry about. Many American companies allowed the Japanese to visit to study our manufacturing. We had that American spirit. We wanted to 'Show off our success.'

> *Japan was completely devastated after World War II and used America as a model to rebuild both their society and their industries. They needed and were grateful for our help in rebuilding their nation.*[51]

The Japanese came to visit our plants, told us how great we were and then took pictures of everything. They needed our help to reconstruct their society and we graciously allowed them to copy our technology without fully appreciating the ability of the Japanese.

---

[51] America, after World War II, was very unusual, instead of following, 'To the victor belongs the spoils;' we didn't take from our former enemies; we helped them rebuild their societies.

After Joji spoke I went over and introduced myself. I asked if he would arrange a reverse study mission allowing me to take American managers and engineers to visit Japanese companies. He said he would do it.

Of course, I had no real idea about the ramifications of what I was asking. It just sounded like a good idea at the time. This you will see as you read on is very typical of me: my mouth acts faster than my mind. I say things without knowing the full ramifications of what I am asking. I didn't know how to get travelers. I had no idea what to look for. But, maybe my ignorance was to my great advantage for it did happen.

Joji said he would get me twelve companies. So we set up a plan for the study mission to run in the first week of March 1981. We prepared the brochure copy, got a very nice design, showing in Kanji letters "Made in Japan," and I ordered around 25,000 mailing labels to promote the mission.

A few weeks later I called Joji and asked if he could please tell me the names of the Japanese companies that we would visit. I wanted to put their names on the brochure. I was told not to worry but that they would get us the 12 companies.

"Do you have any?" I asked.

"Not at this time," was the answer.

I was confused for I expected him to give me a list of companies. I didn't know what to do. I knew we needed three months advance notice to send out a brochure. It was a big financial gamble for me at that time. I didn't have a lot of options. Finally, a week later, I was given a list of company names and I put them on the brochure, only to find out later that not one of those companies had agreed to a visit.

I was literally shaking. I was at a loss for words. I didn't want to cancel the event and lose money. And within a few weeks 24 senior American managers had signed up for the study mission but I didn't have a single company to visit.

I did receive a call a few days later from Arai's office with the good news, "One Company had agreed to our visit."

I was livid. I was at my wit's end. What could I tell our travelers?

> *What a mistake I made. I told Arai I would 'sue' him. It was absolutely the last thing to tell a Japanese. They rarely sue each other. They spend an enormous amount of time and patience trying to work things out and looking for harmony, while it seems we in America are always in a rush to get things done now. It took me ten years to overcome that mistake with Arai. Thankfully, today we are good friends.*

Well, the way things normally work out in my life; I often get excited for nothing. Within the next three weeks Joji had found not 12 twelve companies but 16 visits for us. We now had the opposite challenge – we would exhaust the travelers traveling all over Japan.

I asked Joji to please cancel some of the visits, "We can't. We don't want to lose face."

> *Saving face – often the Japanese will not say 'no' to you. They will either avoid the subject or change it to something else. And since they spend so much time in building relationships to do business, called 'Nemawashi,' they are very careful not to cut off the communications.*

I learned painfully a few new valuable lessons working with the Japanese:

One, be patient. It just takes a lot of time to get things organized in Japan. They have to go and visit the companies, have a few drinks, sing a few Karaoke songs, and then wait.

Two, they can't say no easily.

Three, once done, the results do go off without a hitch for everything is so well planned.

On Friday of the first week in March, I met all of the travelers in Seattle the day before we boarded the plane. We spoke about the upcoming visits and how the days would be organized. We had a chance to get to know each other prior to this two-week study mission. We assigned everyone a "buddy," so as not to lose anyone.

Over the next ten years we ran close to 50 study missions and only once did we lose someone for a short period of time. As we traveled there was someone who seemed always to be last, last getting to the bus, last getting off the bus, last to lunch, etc. On the last day of this particular study mission we all arrived in Tokyo on the bullet train from Nagoya. When we passed the platform exit area you are required to show your tickets to an attendant. We all walked to the waiting bus and just forgot for the first time to do a 'buddy check.' This one traveler was walking far behind came to the attendant but he didn't have his ticket, which was held by our guide. He couldn't speak Japanese and they didn't speak English and they held him for an hour until we reached our hotel and got the message that he was still at the station. The guide had to go back to Tokyo station to get him released. Funny, when I took them to the airplane back to America, he was the last person to get on board.

In Seattle, we reviewed a little bit of information about each company: where they were located, what they manufactured, the number of employees, etc. But we could not tell them a single thing of what we expected to learn because we knew very little at the time about Japanese management and we didn't know what the companies were going to teach us. I trusted the upcoming experience to work, but I was pretty close to being a nervous wreck. Like Mel Brooks said, I had a lot of 'high anxiety.'

This first visit to Japan was a great success. It was exhausting but all of us felt it was very worthwhile. It was an experience filled with many unexpected events, bringing us very close to the power of Japanese management. For two weeks our heads were spinning from jet lag, long train and bus rides, and also from the new information being poured into us.

So much confusion to overcome! I thought that women, especially foreign women, were not allowed into Japanese manufacturing plants. But, once again, I was wrong. The truth I learned was that Japanese factory managers looked at us as Gaijins, foreigners, and to them it didn't matter what sex we were.

On this first trip with senior American managers we were looking to discover the secrets of Japanese management. How were they able to improve both their productivity and quality in such a short period of time? What were they doing that we were not doing?

I initially thought the success of Japanese industry was due to their quality control circles but quickly discovered that they were only a small part of the total quality and productivity effort.

Most of what I learned I truly did not absorb until many years later. I learned many of the fundamentals of the Toyota Production System but I did not fully understand nor appreciate the real power of it. However, I was most impressed on this first visit meeting Dr. Ryuji Fukuda, winner of the Nikkei QC Literature Prize awarded by The Deming Prize Committee, and being introduced to his on-error-training.[52] It was a very simple technique and I could see the enormous power in it.

In fact, he told me that he had just finished writing a new book including on-error-training in it. I jumped at the opportunity and asked if I could publish the book in English. He said, "yes." This was beginning of the magic in my life, just asking the question led to me becoming a book publisher. I, of course, did not know at all what I was asking for; I knew nothing about book publishing. Once again I made a commitment without fully understanding the ramifications. It took us two years to publish the book – it is part of the upcoming story.

I met Dr. Fukuda again on my second study mission and then asked him if we would come to America to speak at my upcoming conference to be held at the Waldorf Astoria Hotel in New York City. He said that he would be pleased to come and speak.

Dr. Fukuda accompanied us on the bullet train returning from Osaka to Tokyo. On the train I sat with him and his interpreter. I did not think that his interpreter was good enough to bring to America. **So my problem was how to tell Dr. Fukuda through this interpreter to bring another interpreter to America.** It was a challenge. But, miraculously, I was able to communicate subtly and intuitively enough to Dr. Fukuda to understand my need without offending the interpreter.

---

[52] On-error-training see page 130.

Since I had learned so much from the first study mission, I wanted to do it again in the fall of 1981. So a few months after this first visit, I tried to see how we could do another mission on our own.

We designed a brochure and then wrote to 300 Japanese companies asking permission to visit them hoping that 10 to 12 companies would accept us.

We were very lucky that some of the companies from the first visit allowed us to come back, like Canon, Fujitsu Fanuc, Sumitomo Electric, and Toyota, and new companies like Toshiba, Komatsu, Hitachi and others did accept us.

Around 18 managers joined us on this second two-week study mission including Jack Warne, at the time, Vice President, Omark Industries headquartered in Milwaukee, Oregon. Jack was great fun to travel with. However, on Tuesday of the second week after visiting six different companies, and hearing lectures from some top Japanese consultants, Jack said to me, "Norman, I am enjoying the trip but I really have not seen anything in Japan that compares with my company Omark. Our technology is better, my people work as hard and as smart, my plants are cleaner and as productive, and I think our quality is as good or even better."

I was a little embarrassed and didn't know what to say for Jack and the others had paid thousands of dollars for this trip and the power of Japanese management practices was not reaching them.

However, that afternoon the magic took over. We visited Nippondenso, a subsidiary to Toyota whose major products were manufacturing air-conditioners for the Toyota automobiles. In this particular plant managed by Mr. Ohta they produced starter motors for the Toyota vehicles.

> *Mr. Ohta was one of the key 10 people selected by Mr. Taiichi Ohno to drive the Toyota Production System through the top Toyota suppliers.*

They showed us how kanban[53] worked. In one machine center a worker would pick up a small colored disk, the kanban, which told him exactly what kind of motor to produce, the size, horsepower, the number of starter motors to produce and the time when they had to leave the plant. They were delivering motors to Toyota in small batches several times throughout the day.

Also we saw quick changeovers.

> *Quick changeovers were the real beginning, the very power of the Toyota Production System, which will be explained in detail later in the book. Question? How long will it take you to change four tires, fill your automobile with gasoline and clean the windshield? With luck maybe you can do it all in 45 minutes. How long does it take to do all of the above on Memorial Day at the Indianapolis speedway? In 2003 it took around 12 seconds. In 1979, Rick Mears beat A.J. Foyt Jr. by 15.36 seconds, in 1997, Arie Luyendyk beat Scott Goodyear by 0.57 seconds, in 1982, Gordon Johncock beat Rick Mears by 0.16 second and in 1992, Al Unser Jr, beat Scott Goodyear by 0.043 seconds. Remember and focus on this! In today's highly competitive world, one second could mean success or failure.[54]*

---

[53] Kanban means signboard or card used to pull the production process through the factory. It comes in many sizes, shapes and colors.

[54] We normally ignore the opportunities to make small but incremental improvements.

At Nippondenso we saw a daisy wheel surrounding a punch press with around four different dies. Mr. Ohta demonstrated the changeover, which only took a few seconds. This didn't mean that much to me for I knew at this time very little about manufacturing and the importance of quick changeovers. But this got Jack's attention. He started to get very excited as he saw something important to him and his company, and he understood immediately the ramifications of doing quick changeovers; he knew from this new knowledge how he could reduce his plant inventory back in Oregon by 90%. Within six months, he did just that.

Before leaving the plant Mr. Ohta took us all into a meeting room to teach us the concept of mixed model production.

> *Mixed Model Production is where you manufacture various products on the same assembly line. At the time General Motors, Ford and Chrysler would make only one model on one line. Once on a Toyota line I saw sedans, station wagons, even small trucks all made on the same line.*

The key to understanding mixed model production is takt time. Toyota using takt time was able to build so many different kinds of cars on the same final assembly line.

> *Takt time – the rate of customer demands. It is the target time you must meet per piece, in order to deliver the finished product to the customer exactly on time. Most of us were familiar with cycle time – the time it currently takes to produce the products. Takt time is the precise time per piece that we need to hit in order to deliver the products to the customer Just-in-time (exactly what the customer wants, exactly when they want it, in the exact quality and quantity needed by the customer). If the net available time in an eight-hour working day is 480 minutes, and customer de-*

mand is 240 parts, the takt time for these parts is 2 minutes per piece. The net available time per day is figured without regard to the number of people available, or the uptime percentage of the machines. It is simply the time available to produce.

Takt time synchronizes the production of many different parts for use in vehicle assembly and coordinates their supply to each process on the assembly line at the proper time. This keeps the production on schedule and permits flexible response to changes in sales.

Takt is a German word meaning 'time beat' or tempo like the beat used by the bandleader to keep the entire orchestra in tune with each other. This is the "beat" at which business operations must produce their goods and services to meet the "demand beat" of customers. The customers always dictate the operating specifications.

Mixed model production was not being done in Detroit at all at the time. This revolutionary concept meant that you didn't build the different model cars on a single assembly line.

You could build what the customer wanted one at a time. At that moment, at Nippondenso, we began to really begin to understand the power of one-piece flow.

We might have been the first Americans to be introduced to the concept of one-piece flow.

As Mr. Ohta was explaining the mixed model concept to us, our Japanese guide told me we had to leave to catch our arranged Bullet train back to Tokyo. If we didn't, we would lose our seats and might have to stand up for two hours on the next train. Well, I had no choice. Mr. Ohta would not let us leave until he felt that we had some understanding of mixed model production.

7

Discovering Shingo: Magic Moments

"If you are open to your growth potential, you will attract that for which you are willing to be responsible." **Rudi**

As we were leaving Nippondenso to get on the bus Mr. Ohta gave us all a flyer in English. On the train going back to Tokyo, and we did find seats, Jack, the others, and I read the flyer. It advertised a book written by a Shigeo Shingo titled, *The Study of The Toyota Production System from Industrial Engineering Viewpoint*[55] published by Japan Management Association (JMA). We could not tell from the flyer if the book was in English or Japanese but after Mr. Ohta's lecture it surely intrigued us. Strangely only Jack and I were interested in receiving a copy of Shingo's book.

At the hotel in Tokyo, I called JMA and asked them to please send two copies of the book over to us at our hotel. Two copies of this Green book arrived and Jack and I both read the book on the flight back to America. It was purely serendipitous as the book had only been published this month, November 1981, and Jack and I probably received the first copies of the books, 'fresh off the press.'

---

[55] This was the famous 'green' book giving the west the real essence of the Toyota Production System.

Jack and I unknown to each other both ordered 500 copies of the book. I wanted to sell the book to the subscribers to my news-letter[56] and Jack wanted every manager and engineer at Omark to have their own copy.

Omark had something very unusual but very powerful. Virtually every manager and engineer at Omark had been trained in the Value Analysis[57] technique.

They knew how to meet and work together to further new ideas. They knew how to take knowledge from a book, ask each other questions and get improvements implemented in their factory.

Value Analysis (VA), Value Engineering (VE), Value Management (VM) or Value Planning (VP) were originally developed by Larry Mills (General Electric) in 1943 as a process to add greater value to a company's products and services. They are methods using highly efficient procedures consistent with sound management techniques to achieve maximum performance, in the minimum amount of time required. Engineers and others are taught how to question each element of the product or process to find ways to add value.

I do see many people reading books, liking what they read, and saying, 'isn't that interesting.' Then put the book on the shelf never applying the knowledge or at least not using it immediately even though it could have given their company a real competitive

---

[56] When I ordered the books from JMA in Japan I asked for a trade discount. They offered me only 10%. It was much too little to cover my distribution costs. But, I raised the retail price from $21.00 to $29.00 to allow me to sell the books in America.

[57] In 1981, there were 400 certified value engineers in America while Toshiba alone had 1,600. This might account for the explosion of new electronic products developed in Japan.

advantage.[58] I know managers at companies that read the green book back in early 1982 but did not apply Just-In-Time until 15 to 20 years later.

Acquiring Real Power

The managers and engineers at Omark would read a chapter at a time, meet in small groups[59] to discuss the ideas and answer this very simple but powerful question, **"How can we apply this knowledge at Omark?"**

Within the next six months Omark became the best Just-In-Time Company in America. They vastly reduced their inventories, freeing up more than 50% of the factory floor space, moved out tons of unused shelving, sold off fork lifts,[60] improved quality, and cut leads times drastically. In fact, they had so much extra factory space that they consolidated two facilities into the freed-up space.

Often when I speak publicly, I like to mention one of the first things Jack did when he returned from his study mission to Japan was to install a metal bar on one of Omark's factory walls in Milwaukie, Oregon. A sign was placed over the bar saying, 'No inventory allowed above the bar.' Prior to this, workers would continue to produce each day to the capacity of the machine and place the finished pieces in boxes piled high against the wall. Now they could only put two boxes under the bar forcing them to stop the process and do something different, a simple but effective device to force a reduction in inventory.

---

[58] Question yourself, "What holds you back from applying your new knowledge?'

[59] The power of small group activities, (one person re-enforces another), can be seen in taking knowledge from a book and getting it applied. I highly recommend this exercise.

[60] In Madras, Chenai, India, a CEO starting JIT and reducing inventory sold off at a discount his skids to his closest competitor – we both had a nice laugh.

Too Much of a Good Thing

Funny the way life treats you! Jack Warne and I discovered the real power of the Toyota Production System. Through his ability, his keen understanding and his leadership skills his company became one of the real great Lean success stories. Omark became quickly the best JIT Company in America.

Probably too good!

For a few years later, a Mr. Blount, chairman of a two billion dollar construction company in Montgomery, Alabama, had heard about Shingo and went out of his way to meet him in Japan. He asked Shingo which American company was his best student. Without hesitation, Shingo said Omark.

Blount came back to America called his stock investment advisor and asked him to investigate this Omark Industries. He was subsequently told that Omark was a great company, a leader in their industry with something like 70% of the saw chain business.

Blount immediately contacted the chairman of Omark, John Grey, and said he wanted to buy the company. Grey laughed and said his stock was not for sale. Blount insisted and said "Come on there must be a price." Grey thought for a short time then doubled the current market price to around $44 a share.[61] Blount said, Okay, you got a deal." John Grey was astonished, but he sold Omark to Blount.

The deal was shortly consummated, resulting in Jack Warne now president of Omark losing his job. What was amazing

---

[61] In retrospect, if I were only smart enough to buy stocks in the companies visited in Japan and those I worked with in America I would have made a fortune.

is that Blount didn't realize that the key player in the deal was Jack Warne, and they let him go. It's like buying a shiny new car without the engine inside.

During this time I had begun the process of publishing Dr. Fukuda's book titled *Managerial Engineering*. It was my first venture into book publishing. The book was translated by Noriko Hosoyamada, subsequently twenty years later became my wife.

I liked very much the information contained in the book but did not fully understand all of the details so I decided to go to Japan and spend some time with Noriko and Dr. Fukuda. I was at first a little reluctant to spend the $5,000 for airfare and hotels but surely glad that I did break through my resistance.

On this trip Dr. Shingo and Mr. Ohno were speaking at a conference sponsored by Japan Management Association at the New Otani Hotel in Tokyo. I stayed at the hotel, met with Noriko and Dr. Fukuda, and also had a chance to hear Dr. Shingo and Mr. Ohno speak at the conference. (The conference was conducted in both Japanese and in English through simultaneous translations).

After Shingo's speech I walked over to meet him. "Mr. Shingo, I would like to introduce myself to you, my name is Norman Bodek." At first it didn't faze him at all as I was a 'gaijin,[62]' and you might know the old saying 'all Americans look alike.'

After a few minutes he looked up at me from his wheelchair with a smile on his face and said, "Oh, Bodek-san[63], how are you?" He remembered me as the man who had bought 500 copies of his book. I was thrilled to meet the 'great man' and I immediately asked if he would come to America to speak at one of my upcoming conferences and to visit a number of American companies.

---

[62] Gaijin is a Japanese word-meaning foreigner or non-Japanese person.
[63] San is just a note of friendliness.

At first, he was reluctant. At this time he was a little ill and needed this wheelchair to get around. But, after just a few moments he said that if his health allowed it he would come to America to teach. I also knew from his 'green book' that Dr. Shingo had written over 20 books in Japanese and I told him I wanted to get his books translated to share his information with the West.

He said that he would update some of these books and then get in touch with me.

It is amusing the way life has been for me, so serendipitous. I get such wonderful things without ever expecting them. Here meeting Shingo and seeing Ohno for the first time at the JMA conference was such luck on my part, not expected at all. And to put the "icing on the cake," I asked a JMA manager if I could buy all of the extra English conference proceedings notebooks to sell in America. He said, "yes," but then asked $100.00 per copy for 200 books. Reluctantly, once again, not knowing what I was doing I bought the books and miraculously sold them to my newsletter subscribers at $200 a copy which paid for my entire trip to Japan.

Now the 'green book' started to become very popular. I had promoted the book in my newsletter and sent it to a number of industrial magazines to review. In a short period of time we had sold over 15,000 copies.

Shingo did come the following year to America for three weeks and at one of our meetings he told me that he received a review of the 'green book' from a Canadian management magazine, which said, "The information in the green book is vitally important to industry in the West, but the writing style is 'Jangalese,' very difficult to read."

Another Magic Moment

Shingo was a perfectionist and this embarrassed him. He said, "Norman, I want you to publish and edit all of my future books in English." It was a wonderful moment for me and over the next few years I did publish a number of his other books in English, developed extensive training material and courses, workshops, seminars, videos, CD ROMS, etc. It was an amazing gift to my company and me. From those books came SMED[64], Poka-yoke,[65] and the real essence of the Toyota Production System. Shingo not only taught us the philosophy and theory behind JIT, but he also told us exactly how to do it.

A few years later we completely re-edited the Green book to make it friendlier to an American audience. After first selling the 'Jangalese' version of the Green book, we translated his masterpiece the White book – *A Revolution in Manufacturing, The SMED System.* SMED stands for Single Minute Exchange of Die – changeovers in less then 10 minutes. If we can reduce changeover times, the result is reduced inventories, faster throughput, and higher quality as we catch mistakes sooner.

Dr. Shingo gave us both very practical examples on how to implement Lean manufacturing and also gave us the theory behind it all. His books are classics worth reading.

---

[64] SMED = Single Minute Exchange of Die
[65] Poka-yoke means mistake or error proofing, ways to virtually eliminate all defects from the production process.

8

The Lobster Feast and
The First Changeover by Dr. Shingo

"Growth demands a temporary surrender of security."
Gail Sheehy

In addition to bringing Dr. Shingo to America for three to six weeks a year, I also asked him often to lecture to our study missions in Japan.

On many of my visits to Japan[66], I would include a special visit with Dr. & Mrs. Shingo in the town where they lived (Fujisawa). I knew many people in Japan; authors, consultants and others, but rarely was I invited to meet their family or visit their homes.[67]

But the Shingo's were different. They would always invite me to their house. I would call in advance and tell them my train schedule. Mrs. Shingo was always there waiting at the train station just outside my platform. Dr. Shingo would be sitting in a car nearby[68] and they would take me to lunch.

---

[66] Over the years I have been to Japan 59 times meeting Japanese publishers, authors, consultants and visiting over 250 manufacturing plants.

[67] A visit to a Japanese house was rare for me. Maybe it is just their custom not to mix business with their home life, or maybe they are embarrassed because their houses are very small in comparison to those in America.

[68] Imagine the 'great one' waiting for me, what an honor for me.

On this particular visit, Mrs. Shingo had specially picked out a Lobster restaurant near the train station. She knew I had the gout and that I was allergic to many kinds of foods, particularly most meats. I was very allergic to lobster, but had neglected to mention this to them.

Prior to sitting, I looked down and saw that the table was already set with a very large lobster in the center. At first I thought my eyes were playing tricks on me, for I saw the lobster move. I didn't say a word. I just stared at the dancing lobster and waited to see what the Shingo's would do.

I sat and waited. After a few moments, Dr. Shingo picked up his chopsticks, took a piece of lobster meat from the center of the dancing lobster, dipped it into some soy sauce and ate it. I was very confused. Believe it or not we were eating live lobster. It had been already carved carefully so that it would stay alive while we were eating it.

After a while I took a very deep breath and with my chopsticks picked up a piece of the live lobster and ate it. It was a very rare experience, but something I would never repeat again and luckily I didn't get a gout attack.

Another time Mrs. Shingo arranged for us to eat at a Chinese restaurant in Fujisawa. She preordered the meal and probably ordered 'everything' on the menu. But, my associate unfortunately didn't feel well and couldn't come to the restaurant. Mrs. Shingo told the waitress that there would be only three people to lunch not four. However, (never seen before in my life) the waitress served multitude of dishes, one dish at a time and placed each dish served in front of the three of us and also in front of the empty chair. I could only eat half of what was served on my dishes but ironically all of the dishes served to the missing person stayed on the table in front of the empty spot - probably twelve different dishes waited patiently for the person who would never come.

After lunch, we went, to Shingo's house. It was a very small house with almost no land around it. I wondered how they raised three children in such a small house. Dr. Shingo would almost always pull out some of his old books to show me and tell me which ones I should publish into English.

A Shingo Experience

On Dr. Shingo's first visit to America I took him to a Dresser, Inc. manufacturing plant, where they were producing gasoline fuel dispensing systems. After first meeting the management team we walked around the plant floor with a small group of engineers and managers.

Dr. Shingo stopped in front of a punch press. He asked us all to look at the operation and to tell us the percentage of **value adding time.** [69] He then took out his stopwatch[70] to time the operation.

We watched two workers in front of the punch press bend down and pick up a large sheet of thin stainless steel from the left side of the press. They placed the steel into the bed of the press. Then they removed their hands to press buttons outside the press, which indicated that their hands were out and clear of the press. The large press came down and formed the metal into a side of a gasoline pump. Then the two workers reached into the press, removed the formed sheet and placed the formed sheet at the right side of the press.

---

[69] Value adding time is the time when materials are being converted, altered by either machines or labor.

[70] Dr. Shingo was an educated industrial engineer and knew the power of working with a stopwatch.

"What was the value adding percentage?" Dr. Shingo asked us.

One engineer said, "100%, the workers never stopped working."

Another engineer said, "75%," and another said, "50%."

Dr. Shingo laughed and looked at his stopwatch and said, " Only 12% of the time was the process adding value. Adding value is only when the dies are pressing against the metal to create the formed sheet, the rest of the time is **waste**."[71]

Then Dr. Shingo asked them, "What can you do to improve the value adding time?"

An engineer immediately said, "You can place a table over here and put the raw inventory sheets on top of the table. This would help the workers. They wouldn't need to bend down. They could just slide the sheets directly into the press."

Another engineer said, "We could install a leveler to automatically raise the sheet metal to keep it at a constant height, similar to what you might see in a cafeteria when you reach for a dinner plate."

A third engineer said, "We could put a spring into the back of the punch press to force the formed metal to leap forward after the stamping."

Dr. Shingo laughed again as his message got through.

"Yes," Dr. Shingo said. "You all know what to do, so do it!"

---

[71] See page 39.

This was the magic of Dr. Shingo as a teacher and as the leader of the JIT movement in the world. In one sense he knew most of the answers but he knew the importance of stimulating others to think about how they could bring change to the production process. This was a very simple but powerful demonstration of how to challenge a group of people to come up with improvement ideas.

> *Looking back, when I managed a large group of people, I would be the one to come up with most of the ideas. I thought since I was the owner and the president of the company, it was my job to come up with new ideas. I was most fortunate to have had many new ideas come to me but I am sure I would have had a much more successful company if I had empowered, challenged and allowed my associates to be idea generators. People had to follow my ideas and implement them, for I was the 'boss.' I am sure they would have been more highly motivated and creative if I had given them the chance to implement their own ideas. Dr. Shingo taught me a great lesson.* [72]

For all of us watching Dr. Shingo, it was a great learning moment. For instead of telling them the answer, he asked them to come up with the ideas. He got their motors started. He got them to be creative. He knew the power in teaching was not to tell people what to do, but to get them to learn from their own questioning and experience it.

However, the managers, probably to show off, insisted on bringing Dr. Shingo to a new machine center that they just installed stating that the center had cost them $1,000,000. They wanted to show him a quick changeover. Dr. Shingo was not, at all interested in seeing the new center. He felt that if they followed

---

[72] The chapter on Quick and Easy Kaizen explains a great process to get lots of ideas from all employees. See page 257.

his simple principles, they could take their old machines and do changeovers just as fast without spending $1,000,000.

The First Changeover demonstrated by Dr. Shingo

Then we went over to another punch press operation. Now, Shingo said, "How long does it take you to make this changeover when you go from one product to another?

"Around two hours," was the answer.

"I want you to do it in less then 10 minutes," said Shingo. I heard lots of grumbles. One worker told me it was crazy. He had been working on this press for the past four years and it always took him around two hours to do it.

"I want to give you some suggestions on how to reduce the time it takes to do changeovers. So please ask me questions. Then I would like you to tell me how long it will take you to prepare for the changeover," Shingo said.

Shingo then taught them:

"First, I want you to make a "shim;" cut out a piece of metal and attach it to the top of the next die that you are going to use. This 'shim,' will make each die the exact same height so that when you do the changeover, you will not have to adjust the cam.

You can then just pull out the old die and slide the new one in without any height adjustment. Second, when the previous process is complete and you are ready to do the next changeover, blow a loud whistle to attract the changeover team[73], time it with a

---

[73] Like at the Indianapolis Speedway each person should have a set assignment.

stopwatch, chart the results, and post those results near the punch press machine.

Third, put a metal block under the inventory so the sheet metal slides in quickly. If the thickness of the metal changes you can easily put in another metal block to meet that thickness."

He told them about external activities (OED[74]) and internal activities (IED[75]), and how they could be examining each part of the change process to reduce the time of the changeover. He asked them for their ideas and many ideas were suggested.

He also told us to look at the dies as if they were tapes going in and out of your Sony Walkman. All you do is move them in and out without any nuts or bolts, and the tape stays locked. This kind of analogy helps to reduce setup time.

The discussion around the punch press only took around one hour. Then Shingo asked, "How much time do you need to get prepared to demonstrate a changeover?"

"Around three hours," was the answer.

"Okay, we will return after my workshop is over in around three hours to watch your demonstration."
We came back three hours later and watched the team do the changeover. They did it in 12 minutes. Everyone was so pleased with what they had done. Then they all turned and looked

---

[74] OED – Outside Exchange of Die - the things you can do while the machine is running, making sure all of the tools and inventory needed are ready and close by; checking to see that the next die is ready with all of the necessary parts, pre-heat the die if necessary, etc.
[75] IED – Inside Exchange of Die – the things that can only be done when the press stops. Maybe you can use cranes to lift the die, or pneumatics to move the die around, or change the clamping method to reduce the number of bolts and hoses, etc.

at Shingo who had a sly grin on his face. He said laughingly, "I told you to do it in 10 minutes not 12. Now, with a little bit more work I am sure you can do it."

We all laughed.

Changeover as the Heart of Lean Manufacturing

One day in the late 1960's Taiichi Ohno came over to Shigeo Shingo and said, "I want you to see if you can reduce the changeover time on this punch press from four hours to two hours. It is the only way that we can reduce our lot sizes." Again, this was a magical moment. Imagine if your client or your boss came over to you and asked that question of you and you knew that it had always taken close to four hours to do that changeover. What would you think? Probably that the client or boss was a little bit crazy.

But, Shingo said, "Okay!"[76] And then he sat, watched and studied various changeovers in the plant.

A few days later Ohno came over again and said to Shingo, "Two hours is not good enough we need to lower it to 10 minutes."

And Shingo said, **"Okay."**[77]   Dr. Shingo above all taught us to overcome our natural resistance to change.

Dr. Shingo then sat for days and watched changeovers taking place within the plant. And slowly the 'mist' lifted and he over

---

[76] A magic moment! How many people would have thought, "It can't be done. Impossible! The boss must be crazy." But, Dr. Shingo said, "Okay." And then he sat and watched the process of changeover again an again until slowly ideas for improving the process came to him.

[77] Shingo once said, "despite a tendency to assume that something can't be done, we find an unexpectedly large number of possibilities when we give thought to how it might be possible to do it."

time was able to accomplish Mr. Ohno's wishes and reduce the changeovers to less than ten minutes. [78]

Some Keys to Quick Changeover:

1.   Rethink the idea that machines can be idle, but workers cannot be idle.

2.   The ideal setup change is no setup at all or within seconds.

3.   Insure that all tools are always ready and in perfect condition.

4.   Blow a whistle and have a team of workers respond to each changeover.

5.   Establish goals to reduce changeover times, record all changeover times and display them near the machine.

6.   Distinguish between internal and external setup activities and try to convert internal to external setup.

Dr. Shingo started reducing changeovers on punch presses but felt that all process should be examined for changeover reduction.[79] When I initially would talk about changeover, I was often

---

[78] Vapor Rail, North America's premier vehicle door system manufacturer, held an improvement workshop at its plant in Montreal. The event converted its sheet metal area, in which door control panel boxes are manufactured, from batch to cellular, one-piece flow. The results, among other benefits, included an impressive 90% productivity improvement through reductions in cycle time.

[79] Jeremy Green with Eagle Group USA told me recently that he helped a manufacturer of small plastic bottles reduce change over time on a line from eight hours to 45 minutes.

confronted with the comment, 'What do you do with a screw machine?'[80]

"A shop we know outside Cleveland is a typical example. They were running lots of 100 to 500 pieces. It took 45 minutes to an hour to run some of those lots, and as long as eight hours to set the machine up for the next one. Using quick change tooling for the end slide, special quick change facing, and grooving tools on the cross slide along with quick-change chuck jaws, the shop managed to cut setup time from more than 18 hours to only 4 hours."[81]

Following Dr. Shingo's discovery of reducing set up times from hours to minutes, in some cases days to minutes; the cost of manufacturing worldwide has declined substantially.

Dr. Shingo is the father of the **Toyota Production System**, (Just-In-Time or **Lean Manufacturing**), *the true creator of **process re-engineering**[82]* and in my opinion, along with **Henry Ford,** one of the twentieth century's greatest manufacturing genius. Dr. Shingo called his technique **SMED** (Single Minute Exchange of Die – to make all changeovers in less then 10 minutes) and he felt it applied to every single process in the factory. It is the heart of Lean manufacturing. It is the heart of modern manufacturing.

Lean manufacturing is simply an American term that replaced The Toyota Production System, or Just-In-Time (JIT). Lean manufacturing means that you operate your facilities with the least amount of **waste**, that you are operating at the highest state of

---

[80] "You do your best to reduce the changeover time or you dedicate the machine to only one process and when you get the money get a new screw machine that is designed for quick changeovers." Dr Shingo

[81] http://www.production-machining.com/articles/030101.html

[82] Looking at the way products are manufactured from the viewpoint of the customer to minimize costs, deliver the highest quality, at the exact time needed by the customer.

efficiency, with the least amount of investment, the lowest number of employees, the highest state of quality, the shortest time line from order to delivery of the finished products, that you neither over nor under produce, and that you deliver the products to your customer neither early nor late – just exactly on time.

Hadn't that always been the goal of manufacturing? Yes, it is the goal but rarely lived up to until Lean manufacturing arrived.

Dr. Shingo taught the theory of the Toyota Production System to thousands of Toyota managers and engineers for many years, and Toyota made enormous progress in continuous improvement and improving the process flow, but the above dialog between Ohno and Shingo was the real magic moment in giving birth to JIT/Lean.

When you stand back and look at what Dr. Shingo did to reduce changeover time, you'll see how simple and logical it all is. I have found so often in my life that the simple things are the most powerful. Neither Ohno nor Shingo spoke of complicated things. "Just take out the waste," was their theme song.

Sure, sometimes the process appeared to be complicated, and the solution wasn't always readily available. One day I was standing with Dr. Shingo in front of an NC machining center. It was new and took a long time to make the changeovers. Shingo did not give them the answer, but told them to read his book and get groups together to question each other on how it could be done. **"Don't accept impossible as an answer. Some machines are harder than others, but you can reduce the set-up times substantially."**[83]

---

[83] Take videos of the process and show the videos in the meeting room with a group of engineers to study how to reduce the changeovers.

Inventory, to both Ohno and Shingo, was the key waste to be removed. The mountain of inventory hides most of the manufacturing problems. If you have a defect instead of getting to the root cause of the problem, excess inventory allows you just take another piece from the top of the inventory pile and threw the bad piece into scrap.

So with the emphasis on reducing changeover time, Shingo sat watching the changeovers for hours until finally 'light bulbs' started going off in his head.

The big break came when Shingo noticed a clear distinction between what can be done when the machine is stamping out parts and what only be done when the machine stopped. While the machine is processing you can be getting fully prepared for the next changeover.   Then he focused on finding ways to reduce what had to be done when the machine stopped.

I was told that in the early 1980's it was taking GM up to forty hours to make a changeover on a seven-ton press. I saw the same changeover at Toyota done in seven minutes.

It used to take Heinz Catsup, in England, four hours to make a changeover from one product to another.   Thanks to Dr. Shingo, it can now be done in eight minutes.[84]

Heinz, noted for their brand products like many other food manufacturers, dominated certain product lines and was the world's largest seller of catsup. They were confronted by the large food chains in England. Sainsbury and Tesco wanted their own private labels and Heinz had a choice either to confront the large chains and say no, causing them to find another source, or 'biting

---

[84] This was several years ago. They have improved the changeover time.

the bullet,' as the saying goes, and produce a slightly different product under the chains' private label.

Heinz, under the pressure of losing a lot of business from these powerful chains, decided to do the latter and produced a private label brand for Sainsbury and Tesco, and for other large chain stores. However, this put an enormous strain on manufacturing.

Since it took four hours to clean, alter and adjust the line for each different product—contents, size of bottle, labeling and packaging, it now required Heinz to have **mountains of inventory** to meet the new daily customer demands. New challenges were placed on manufacturing.

They could not predict what the product mix would be each day and the burden of that four-hour change over was affecting their bottom line.

To solve this problem Heinz studied the work of <u>Dr. Shigeo Shingo</u> and his *methodology that taught how to reduce set up time from hours to minutes*.

Heinz engineers and managers learned well, and they were able to reduce changeover times within a few days from four hours to eight minutes, resulting in a 90% reduction in finished goods inventory. They could now produce what was needed, when it was needed, and in the quantities needed by the customer. (**JIT**)

9

The Study Mission Process

*"Become a student of change. It is the only thing
that will remain constant."* - **Anthony J. D'Angelo**

The study mission groups would normally meet in San
Francisco or Seattle. I arrived early to make sure the arrangements were taken care of with the airlines.

>   *Once I was at the offices of Omark Industries
> in Milwaukie, Oregon one day prior to a study mission
> to Japan and reviewing my check list with the president
> of Omark. "Okay, does everyone have a valid pass-
> port?   The CEO said, "Yes." I said, "No, I forgot
> mine."*

>   *Imagine I, the leader of the mission left my
> passport back in Stamford, Connecticut. Boy, was I
> embarrassed. If I didn't get my passport within the
> next 24 hours the travelers would be off to Japan with-
> out me. Luckily I was able to call my office in Nor-
> walk, Connecticut and had my passport flown on the
> next flight to Seattle. The passport arrived two hours
> before takeoff.*

We normally booked all reservations business class, but if
United or Delta had extra seats in first class we would get them.

Once they 'upgraded' 10 of my travelers. To be fair, I went by age and upgraded the oldest travelers.

On arrival in Tokyo we would have to go through customs. In all the years of traveling to Japan this was the only negative experience we endured.[85] While all the Japanese nationals would wiz by the customs desk, we could take up to an hour waiting for someone to just look at the stamp on my passport. To me it was a mindless job.

After enduring the wait, the luggage was always waiting on the carousel. In 59 trips to Japan, never has a customs agent opened even one of my bags – maybe because none of them can speak English.

Once we picked up the luggage and cleared customs, we never had to lift our bags outside of our hotel room again during the entire two-week study experience. Just outside the luggage area was our guide who took our luggage away from us and had it delivered to our hotel door. When we traveled to our next destination, the luggage was picked up from outside our hotel door and delivered directly to the door of our next hotel room.

The hotel rooms at the time were small in comparison to American hotels. Once we did have a major problem at a small ryokan,[86] one traveler was over 250 pounds and over six feet tall, and found it very difficult to move around.

We are creatures of habit and some of the travelers were at first very reluctant to try to eat the raw fish and other Japanese food; but they loved the beer and sake. When McDonalds

---

[85] I would also include the traffic jams around Tokyo.

[86] Ryokan is a traditional Japanese inn, small but often very picturesque, with large bathing tubs and only Japanese food. Here we had a chance to take a traditional Japanese bath, wear kimonos, and sit around drinking Japanese beer.

opened outlets in Japan, a lot of the travelers would make a 'bee-line,' to get an American hamburger.[87]

On one of the trips I was having lunch with our interpreter, Noriko, at the Hyatt Hotel in the Shinjuku district in Tokyo. On our plates were various delicacies. At the end of the plate was a small whole cooked crab. I ate everything except the crab watching what Noriko would do. She also saved the crab for last, but she took her chopsticks and ate the crab whole. In 'Rome, you do as the Romans do,' so I picked up my chopsticks, took a really deep breath, grabbed and swallowed the 'sucker' whole. It was all part of the experience.

Normally our first day in Japan was Sunday. We would meet in the morning, review the schedule, and listen to a short lecture on Japanese customs. Here we learned that their most favorite drink (besides beer) was 'Pocari Sweat,' similar to Gatorade. The Japanese often use English words for their products but the meaning doesn't always make sense to us.

On Sunday afternoon we would do some sight seeing, maybe a Shinto Shrine or Buddhist Temple, looking at the rock gardens, the well groomed grounds, the hanging slips of paper (You can buy fortune slips at the shrines but you hang up the ones you don't like), see new cars being blessed by the priest, drink some holy water with the wooden ladles in front of the shrines, bow and ring the bells to the spirits, and just getting a feeling for ancient Japan and the Japanese spirit.

Each day of the week was filled with either factory visits or lectures from some Japanese experts. A lot of time was spent on buses, trains, or the bullet train. The bus rides were also oppor-

---

[87] On one trip Lester Shoen traveled with us. He started and owned U-Haul. Here was one of the richest men in the world, and couldn't wait to get to McDonalds.

tunities to discuss what we saw and what we learned from each visit. I would pass the microphone up and down the aisle. Often, when tired, out would come the beer and we would watch sumo wrestling on the bus TV.

> *Sumo is the ancient art of Japanese wrestling. Sumo has its roots in the Shinto religion. The matches are dedicated to the gods in prayers for a good harvest. The oldest written records date back to the 8th century. But it is probably more than 1500 years old. Each bout takes only a few seconds but there is a ritual they go through lasting around five minutes. The wrestlers go through rigorous training, up early each morning to work out for around five hours, then eat huge meals, drink beer, and sleep to gain weight. Konishiki, a former American Hawaiian sumo wrestler, was over 550 pounds.*[88]

Another blunder

On one trip I was with a group of senior managers from Dana Corporation. Included was Joe Magliochetti, the former chairman of Dana. The discussion on the bus was about comparing Japanese and American measures of performance. I, from my little knowledge said, "You have to drop the whole idea of using Return on Investment (ROI)[89] as a measure of performance. ROI forces short-term thinking. Here in Japan management is constantly focusing on the long term." Boy, did I get clobbered. They 'jumped' all over me as if I didn't understand what I had just said. I was really embarrassed, but what I didn't understand

---

[88] *http://www.artelino.com/articles/japanese_sumo_wrestling.asp*

[89] The problem with ROI was that it primarily looked at equipment investments and not at the investment in people. If you bought a new machine for $1,000,000 then you wanted the return to come back in four years. But how do you measure your investment in people?

until years later was that Dana (under the guidance of their CEO at that time, Woody Morcott), used ROI as their main measure of performance. I was attacking their 'sacred cow.'

Using ROI as the main accounting measure the big three automakers' just keep raising prices. But, as Japanese automobiles become more acceptable to Americans, US carmakers are con-strained to raise prices without the corresponding quality.[90]

> *Short life cycles of manufactured goods in to-day's market require manufacturers to recover invest-ment in a shorter time. The target cost is established as an attainable target, which will motivate all personnel to achieve. Now, the struggle begins.*[91]

In companies where target costing[92] is used, there seems to be a different culture and attitude. They place more emphasis on their relative position in the market and product leadership. Since more than 80% of product cost is already determined by the time product design and processing is complete, cost management must start (and is done substantially) at the design stage.

The Power of Seeing with Your Own Eyes

You can read a book, but end up doing absolutely nothing with the information. But when you visit a Japanese plant and see things with your own eyes, it is hard not to change your en-

---

[90] Each year Toyota, GM, and Ford expect new innovative improvements from their suppliers at lower costs.

[91] http://www.nysscpa.org/cpajournal/old/14979931.htm

[92] Before a company launches a product (or family of products), senior managers determine its ideal selling price, establish the feasibility of meeting that price, and then control costs to ensure that the price is met. The same logic as quality must be designed into products before they are manufactured. the same logic to determining the price of new products.

vironment when you go back. You say to yourself, 'If they can do it so can we.'

> *Years earlier I was president of a data processing company with offices in Greenwich, CT and Grenada, West Indies. In Grenada we were working a conversion for the New York Telephone Company. It was the hardest job I had ever seen. We had around 200 young ladies working with us. I could not imagine them understanding how to do this particular job. But, we needed the work. I knew that a similar job was been worked on in Jamaica. I looked at the women and said, "If Jamaicans can do this, then so can we." I didn't know how. I only knew that I did not want to be a limitation for them. Miraculously we did the job. We did it very well and ended up over the next ten years converting a good percentage of the telephone companies across America.*

One of our first impressions of many Japanese plants was their cleanliness and complete sense of order. I was not used to seeing this. My experience was that most American plants were just filled with dirt, dust, and clutter.

There are many ways to do business

On one mission I visited a bridge building company. It was cold outside and the workers had no heat at all. One of their managers told me, "We normally bid with two other companies on all of the bridges in the area. The local government then reviews the bids, and instead of giving the job to the lowest bidder, makes sure that each of us gets our share." I was amazed that he would say this to me, a stranger. But, if you are a bridge builder, it is a nice way to do business.

On one of the early missions we visited Nippon Steel. It was a very large plant, casting and making rolls of sheet metal. After walking through this huge plant and seeing how they made steel, we went into a meeting room to view a presentation on quality circle activities.

One worker showed us his idea on how to reduce energy costs. He noticed that to allow the steel to leave the oven, a door had to open. When the door was opened cold air came rushing in. This then required reheating the oven. He went home and spoke about the problem with his wife. She mentioned that recently shopping at a large department store there was no outer door being used, even though it was in the middle of the winter. When she went into the store she felt a curtain of hot air coming down to prevent the cold air from entering into the store.

"Why can't we do the same thing in the steel mill?" He asked his wife. The very next day he went to his supervisor to discuss the idea of installing a hot air curtain on top of the oven door. The supervisor agreed that it was a good idea, and asked the worker to implement his idea. "I would love to do it," he said, "but I do not know anything on how to handle electricity. The supervisor said, "Well let's see if I can get one of the electricians to teach you."

This was brilliant. Why not use this powerful moment to let a worker grow his talents from his own idea. Sure, there is an investment of time, but in the long run the individual and the company will be way ahead. The worker was taught how to use electricity to install a hot air motor, which saved the plant thousands of dollars.

10

SMED – Quick Changeovers – the Heart of Shingo and JIT

"I feel that the only consistent thing in my life is change." **Rudi**

Single Minute Exchange of Die (SMED) is a system developed by Dr. Shingo to reduce all changeovers to less then 10 minutes (1 to 9 are single minutes). Once changeovers are reduced drastically then in-process inventory can be radically reduced resulting in lower manufacturing costs and improved quality. SMED in essence is the heart of Lean manufacturing.

Some tales about SMED:

1.   At a visit to a GM plant, I watched a quality engineer checking with a gage the tolerances on some stamped vehicle side doors. I saw a small mountain of doors on the floor and I asked him, "How many doors have been stamped out since this door was originally produced?"

He said, "Oh, maybe a thousand or so."

"Well, what do you do if you find a defect - the door is then out of tolerance; you then have a thousand other doors to correct?"

His reply, "I would notify the die press people to make the necessary adjustments on future doors to correct the defect problem; then the new doors stamped would meet the exact specifications."

"But, what about the doors already stamped out?" I said.

"They are normally not too bad, not that much out of sync. When they get to the assembly line the worst thing they might do is use a rubber hammer to make them fit properly into the car.[93]"

2.   After visiting a Panasonic injection molding plant making vacuum cleaners, I told Dr. Shingo, "I visited a Panasonic plant and saw them taking over two hours to do a changeover. I thought they all could be done in less then 10 minutes?"

His reply, "Yes, they all should be done in less then 10 minutes; the people in that plant just didn't listen to me. They are ____."

He had very strong opinions, and did not hold back his comments. He knew the power of his teachings and he would never accept failure as an excuse. In fact, many years before Nike started to use the phrase, Shingo always said, **"Do it."** "Don't give me any excuses, just go ahead and do it."

3.   Chihiro Nakao, at one time probably the best changeover person in the world, once told me that he was always frightened of Dr. Shingo. If you knew Nakao you would wonder if

---

[93] I then knew why I had so many problems on the Buick station wagon I recently bought. In fact, whenever I would buy a new car I would put a blank pad of paper on the seat nearby to write down all of the problems. I was hoping that all of the problems would come within the warranty period. Today, when I buy a new car, I do not expect to have any defects – what a world of difference!

anything could frighten him.[94] But, Shingo would visit his plant at Taiho Kogyo once a month, review their progress and then always leave them with homework for the next month. He would challenge them to do something new, to eliminate some waste, and then just said, "Do it." Shingo expected and demanded the best from his clients and he would not want nor accept their excuses. And miraculously they did it.

Nakao then had to figure out how to do it before Shingo came back the next month. Dr. Shingo just would not listen to excuses. In one sense he was very critical and very rough but in another sense he had a real heart of gold.

The Power of SMED[95]

There are a number of potential advantages to reducing the time taken to changeover a production line. These include:

1.   Increased efficiency

2.   Reduced stock requirement

3.   Increased capacity

4.   Reduced work in progress

5.   Increased flexibility

Some keys to make SMED work:

1. Make sure that everything is prepared in advance and is

---

[94] Maybe an errant ball on the gold course would shake him up, but probably nothing else.

[95] Since SMED is one of the major keys to a successful Lean conversion, I repeat again these key points.

close by.

2. As inspiration put up pictures showing the pits at the Indianapolis Speedway where changeovers are done in seconds.

3. Blow a whistle to alert the changeover team when changeover is required.

4. Use a stop watch and measure every changeover to monitor improvement.

5. Post the changeover times right next to the machine.

6. Separate "External" and "Internal" activities - "External" activities are the work that can be done while the machines are running. While "Internal" activities are the work that can only be done when the machines stop. The intention is to do as much as possible when the machines are running.

7. Convert "Internal" to "External" activities. As an example, you can preheat the next die while the previous process is running.

8. You then want to reduce the time of the internal activities, like reducing the number of bolts or hoses, using compressed air or overhead cranes to move the dies around.[96] Shingo looked at the simple Sony Walkman as a perfect example. My first wire recorder took a long time to change but it only took a few seconds to change a

---

[96] Shingo showed a very clever bolt that had part of the screws filed away. Since the only important part of the bolting process is the last half turn by filing both the bolt and the hole in the die, he was able to just ram the bolt into the die and then only make a half turn to lock it all together.

tape cassette. He wanted you to envision the die changing like changing a tape cassette.

`"There are other important suggestions relating to SMED which include:

- Video a changeover then, get the team of operators and technicians that carryout the changeover to watch and analyze it see where operations can be improved.
- Maintain pressure on shorter changeover times and monitor / publish the times.
- Move whatever resource is available to a bottleneck machine to speed up the changeover.
- Do maintenance offline when possible – but target moving internal to external like doing repairs while the machine is operating.
- Put scale settings on all parts of the production line that have to be adjusted or moved to a different position for different products / sizes and keep a record of the required settings for the different products." [97]

Dr. Shingo came to America the next year to speak at one of my conferences, to run a public seminar, and to visit some manufacturing companies. He did this for the next eight years where he would accept my invitation to come over: sometimes once a year and sometimes twice a year, normally for three weeks at a time.

I would meet his airplane when it arrived in America and spend as much time with him as I could. On each trip he would make a checklist of every little thing that went wrong during his stay. He insisted that I meet with him for a review session on the final day prior to boarding his airplane back to Tokyo. I would dread this moment. Dr. Shingo would tell me everything that went wrong on the trip; he kept a shopping list of mistakes made:

---

[97] http://www.swmas.co.uk/Lean_Tools/SMED.php

1.   The car was not there exactly on time.

2.   At one seminar they did not have an extension cord ready for him.

3.   His interpreter came in a few minutes late.

4.   The lighting in the room was not exactly right.

5.   The 35MM slides were put into the carousel upside down.

Every little detail was recorded. He was very precise. He wanted everything to be 100% perfect. I valued and honored him for his willingness to come to America and teach. He did not come to America for the money. In Japan almost every working day was filled with consulting assignments.

I did not look forward to this final day. It felt like I was being 'roasted over coals.' However, this all changed when we started the Shingo prize and got him an honorary doctorate degree from Utah State University. Once he received his degree he became much more tolerant of our faults.

The Shingo Prize

Even if Dr. Shingo had made no other contribution to the world and to the knowledge base of Lean, he deserves a Nobel Prize for his innovation in the area of SMED and Quick Changeover alone. Quick Changeover has had that much impact in making Lean possible.

I spoke once at a conference at Utah State University and met Professor Vern Buehler who at the time was in charge of running conferences for the school. He wanted Shingo to come and speak at the school at one of their future events. I looked at this as a real opportunity, for I always wanted to get an honorary doctorate degree for Shingo.

I told Vern, "I believe that I could get you Shingo to keynote a conference and I would like you to try to get him an honorary doctorate degree. Also let us start a manufacturing prize at Utah State similar to the Deming Prize in Japan." Let us call it the Shingo Prize for Manufacturing Excellence and to sweeten the arrangement I offered to fund the prize with a $50,000 grant.[98]

Vern couldn't promise it but he said he would do his best to get the doctorate. A few months later he told me the school would be pleased to award Shingo his honorary doctorate degree.

Later on I brought Shingo to keynote a conference in Logan, Utah while we were having one of our first Shingo Prize committee meetings. I was the initial chairman of the prize. Vern and other professors had already assessed a number of American companies to be awarded the prize. It was a heated meeting. One of the board members had established strict productivity criteria for a company to win the prize. It was statistically bent and unfortunately not one company had passed the strict criteria.

Well, you can't have a prize without a winner!

---

[98] I told Dr. Shingo that I would give him 5% of what I grossed from our trainings using his SMED or Poka-yoke. We did not have a contract but I liked the idea. If he had patented his concepts his family would now be billionaires. I then told him I would like to use the money to start a prize and he agreed.

I told the group to please select the best companies to give the prizes to. But this board member insisted that no prize be given.

I went to Dr. Shingo and told him of our stalemate and asked him for his advice. He said, "Look, just treat this like a beauty contest where the most qualified person wins."[99]

He was a very practical man. I reported back to the board members and of course, everyone then agreed with Dr. Shingo and the prize was born, and has been very successful ever since.

Later that year I flew with Shingo to Logan, Utah for him to receive his doctorial degree. He put on his cap and gown and we wheeled him along with the others in the procession. It was a beautiful day and he gave a great acceptance speech. He was very happy and proud.

Afterwards he immediately printed new business cards and even printed up new pens to give away with his new honorary doctorate title on them.

When he died a few years later, Mrs. Shingo wrapped his body in his cap and gown. She knew how much it pleased him.

---

[99] Broaden your viewpoint. We wanted to establish a prize for manufacturing excellence to stimulate American industry to adapt and apply Dr. Shingo's ideas. It is so easy to get stuck when you don't 'see the forest for the trees.'

Dr, Shigeo Shingo and Takahiro Sakai, Interpreter

11

My Mental Transformation: There are 'Gems' Scattered All Over Japan

"I am always polishing my sword. I am always perfecting my style." – **Musashi Myamoto**[100]

To me it was very simple. I saw that the Japanese were swiftly catching up to America. They must be doing something that we are not. What was it exactly? I brought with me so many misperceptions about Japanese:

- I thought they were a nation of copiers.
- I thought the differences were due to their different culture not to technology or methodology.
- I thought their factories were small because they were small.
- They were only followers, traveling in packs, alien, unfriendly.
- They don't play fair and we let them get away with it.
- They don't follow the anti-trust rules that we followed.
- They have cartels that still exist with real power.

---

[100] Musashi was Japan's greatest samurai warrior winning 60 battles in his life. Author of *The Book of Five Rings*. Called the greatest book of its kind ever written – the backbone of successful business.

- It is Japan Inc. versus the world.
- They are always pure business.

But this attitude quickly changed as I got to know, like and respect the Japanese for their work ethic and ability to meet and overcome the enormous challenges they faced to succeed in the world.

Let us go back in time to our first study mission to Japan in February 1981 where we discovered some 'gems:'

1.   **Continuous improvement** - Japan had developed a system for continuous improvement, not just optimizing the separate parts. Since continuous improvement at Toyota and other Japanese manufacturers happens everyday, we in West could not see the strides being made.

> *This is where you should start. Develop a total system for continuous improvement not just going after the flavor of the month: six sigma, kaizen blitz, etc. They are all good tools but you should plan what the entire 'ship' you will build looks like before you start using the tools to build it.*

Like the Aesop's Fable about the tortoise and the hare, America was light years ahead of the Japanese at the end of World War II. We were the wealthiest most successful nation in the world with no real competition. So like the hare in the story, we fell asleep at the side of the road while the Japanese, focusing on continuous quality improvement and total employee involvement moved, slowly ahead. Slowly, but over time, they made enormous strides.

And now in 2004 many people ignore Japan[101] and think because of their economic difficulties that there is nothing to learn from them. Beware; let us not repeat the events of the past. We should study the best no matter where in the world they are.

2.   **Long term vision** - They looked at things with the long run in mind (not just profits this quarter). In fact, many of the companies had **100-year plans** broken into 5-10-25-50- and 100 year plans.

Wacoal, the lingerie company, told us the story of how at the end of World War II, they started to write their 50-year plan to be the finest manufacturer of woman's lingerie in the world.

"Developing products that women want, but that do not yet exist -- that is our forte. The process of transforming ideas into products is not an easy one.

Our first objective is to standardize product quality. By analyzing customer opinions and the results of monitor surveys, we acquire a clear grasp of the qualities our customers expect in terms of safety, appearance, comfort and durability. Prototypes are then developed, and subjected to rigorous testing and evaluation. We are constantly striving for quality improvements. We carefully manage the quality of our cutting and sewing processes, based on our own original quality standards. Only those products which fully satisfy these standards are delivered to customers.

We were the first company in the Japanese apparel industry to achieve ISO9001 certification, for our production process allows no compromise in quality

---

[101] Japan is the second largest industrial power in the world.

and is based on a sense of professionalism extending well beyond our customers' expectations.

For over half a century, Wacoal has nurtured a corporate culture in which creative people can tailor Western apparel for Japanese women. Now our focus is expanding from women's beauty to women's lifestyles. We have adopted the new business concept of addressing both "physique" and "emotions" with our products. We want to ensure that we address mental as well as physical beauty. We want to make sure that we are inspired by each woman's individuality, her lifestyle and her values. Our search for a new level of beauty has already begun."[102]

Every company we visited had a long-term vision and included in the vision was how the company would serve its customers. In the vision were value statements to inspire loyalty and appreciation from both employees and customers. We value them and we must treat them with honesty, integrity, and respect, always perceiving their best interests.

The Opposite Effect

In my earlier life I worked with a person who was fun to be with but had no morals at all. He once advertised a product for only $5.99 plus postage that was '100% guaranteed to kill all flies.' You would receive two pieces of wood and the following instructions, 'place the fly on piece of wood and use the other to smash the fly – it works every time.'

---

[102] From Wacoal's web site:
http://www.wacoal.co.jp/company/aboutcom_e/jigyo/index_e.html
I recommend that you review Japanese Corporation's annual reports to study their value statements; how their company's products will serve and better the quality of life in the world.

Well the age of a 'sucker is born every second,' once said by P.T. Barnum, is gone.

3.   **Kanban** (meaning signboard or card) is used to control work-in-progress (W.I.P.), and inventory flow production. Kanban facilitated a reverse production process – instead of following work orders to push manufacturing forward throughout a plant, the cards were used as part of a pull system – where the subsequent process would go back to the previous process to get only the necessary quantity of parts needed. Kanban was used to stabilize and rationalize the production process.

Final assembly determined the quantity and timing for the preceding stations. Daily lot sizes were very small. Shocking to most of our group was that economic order quantity (EOQ), something taught at all of the management and engineering schools in America, was being rejected here in Japan.

4.   **Quality Control Circles**[103] (QCC) where millions[104] of workers all throughout Japan would meet weekly in small groups maybe five to 10 people to discuss problems on the factory floor. They were taught how to identify, solve quality problems and use the quality tools:

- **Check sheet** - used to record and compile collected observations or historical raw data. It shows patterns or trends, which can be detected. You define the problem; describe the types of errors found; and place a check mark every time an error is detected.

---

[103] Quality Control Circles developed by Dr. Kaoru Ishikawa.
[104] The power of people's brains is neglected in the west! Every worker should be taught these tools. It is not too late. QCC takes knowledge traditionally only in the minds and hand of the quality assurance managers and trains every worker in these techniques.

- **Pareto Diagram** – takes the check sheets and visually shows the frequencies of problems indicating those with the potential greatest contribution for improvement.

- **Histogram** – is a graph that shows dispersion of the data and from this chart by analyzing the characteristics shown you can determine possible causes of the dispersion.

- **Control chart** – is a graph with limit lines that show acceptable ranges of quality, very helpful in showing abnormalities in the process.

- **Scatter diagrams** – showing various data points makes it easy to see variations in quality such as items that are expensive but offer poor performance or items that are inexpensive but provide good performance. Visualize the relationship between two variables and see how a change in one may affect the other.

- **Stratification** – or segregating possible causes of defects. A technique used to analyze or divide data into homogeneous groups (strata) collected about a problem or event from multiple sources that need to be treated separately. It involves looking at process data, splitting it into distinct layers (almost like rock is stratified), and doing analysis to notice differences that can lead to an understanding of the key causal factors.

- **Cause and Effect Diagram** – is used to record

ideas that come from brainstorming sessions to identify possible causes of problems and their possible solutions.

- **Brainstorming** - is a wonderful technique used by quality circle members to generate a lot of ideas. Rules of brainstorming:

  - define the problem
  - stay focused on the problem
  - no idea is a bad idea (every idea is a good idea for a good idea might come next and you don't want to shut down communications)
  - be careful of criticism
  - let people have fun
  - encourage people to develop other's ideas
  - one person should be designated to record all of the ideas mentioned
  - everyone gets a chance to talk.

All of the workers were encouraged to participate to solve quality problems. It was a way to both improve morale of the workers, to let them be a part of management, and to feel that they are more empowered on the job. You might call this "bottom up management."[105]

On a later study mission we visited Tokyo Juki, manufacturer of sewing machines. We saw groups of workers up on a stage[106] displaying the problems discussed in their quality circles;

---

[105] Bottom up management allows creative ideas to flow in both directions. It is a system that values input from everyone in the company.

[106] At Tokyo Juki this was a biannual event having workers put together quality circle presentations for senior management. What a wonderful way to empower people to participate in the quality circle process!

describing their process of discovery and the solutions they implemented to solve the problems.

I remember clearly when after a group presentation one of the members of the group came to the front of the stage and asked their senior management for comments. In the audience were the president and other key executives of the company. The president at first told the group members how pleased he was with their presentation. But, the person on the stage said, **"No, we don't want praise, we want you to criticize us so that we can make a better presentation next time." This was a Wow!**

5.   **Total Quality Control (TQC)**[107] was one of the key issues at every company visited. Everyone in the company was responsible for quality, not just the quality managers and inspectors. And most importantly, the quality effort was lead by the CEO who would speak about the subject almost daily. TQC was then built into every process including accounting, sales, etc.

> *The first shipment of cars from Toyota to America was so inferior, so poorly made, that they were put on a boat and returned to Japan. Then through attention to quality improvement and TQC slowly over the years Toyota went from producing 'junk, to producing the highest quality cars in the world.*

---

[107] Total Quality Control concept was originally articulated by Dr Armand V. Feigenbaum. The first edition of his book Total Quality Control was completed while he was still a doctoral student at MIT. The Japanese discovered his work in the 1950s at about the same time as Juran visited Japan. This discovery came about via his role as Head of Quality at the General Electric Company. Secondly, it was associated with the translation of his 1951 book: Quality Control: Principles, Practices and Administration and his articles on Total Quality Control. Feigenbaum argued for a systematic or total approach to quality, requiring the involvement of all functions in the quality process, not just manufacturing. The idea was to build in quality at an early stage, rather than inspecting and controlling quality after the fact. The term Total Quality Control (TQC) was changed year's later in America to Total Quality Management TQM).

In his book *Quality Control: Principles, Practices and Administration*, Dr. Armand V. Feigenbaum[108] strove to move away from the then primary concern with technical methods of quality control, to quality control as a business method. Thus he emphasized the administrative viewpoint and considered human relations as a basic issue in quality control activities. Individual methods, such as statistics or preventive maintenance, are seen as only segments of a comprehensive quality control program. He defined quality control as "an effective system for coordinating the quality maintenance and quality improvement efforts of the various groups in an organization so as to enable production at the most economical levels which allow for full customer satisfaction."

6.   **Kohei Goshi**, the 81 year old founder of the Japan Productivity Center, our host in Japan, said, **"Americans are very good at inventing, but we may be better at raising a baby."**

7.   **Robotics** - Everywhere we visited, the companies were experimenting in robotics, a technology invented in America but hardly being used at the time. At Fujitsu Fanuc they had a factory with no lights at night on the factory floor. There were robots making robots with only one person in the computer control room.

On this particular study mission I invited a reporter from Newsweek magazine to travel with us. He took pictures and gave us a full page in Newsweek. I thought our telephone would be ringing 'off the hook,' with people inquiring about our study missions but no one called. Afterwards about three weeks later I discovered that the telephone company inadvertently took

---

[108] I once went to hear Armand Feigenbaum speak and I understood his brilliance and importance to the quality effort but for me he was much too technical in his language and frankly put most of his audience to sleep. All he needed was to take a good speech course and then history possibly would have ranked him with Deming, Juran and Ishikawa.

our name and telephone number out of the yellow
pages and our telephone was not available from their
information operators. What a bummer! At another
time Steve Lohr, a New York Times reporter, also spent
a day traveling with us and featured us on the business
page, even using one of my pictures, but they only men-
tioned the name of the travelers without talking about
us. It must be my newspaper 'karma[109].'

8.   'The next process is the customer**, not just the
end user.' The average factory worker would never see or be in
contact with the external customer, the one who bought and used
the product – the customer service link did not exist for them.
But now, with the customer being the next person who gets your
product within the factory, you can now know whom to serve,
and you could get an immediate feedback to your quality and
productivity from them.

9.   **Lifetime employment** - Employees are normally
hired only after graduating high school or college. They are perceived as a long-term investment to be trained, and constantly
encouraged to develop new skills.[110] They are treated as part of a
corporate family.

Since workers were lifetime employees the
question arose, "What do you do with people that are
just not good workers?" Well, at first they are put into
groups with a lot of pressure coming from their peers
to keep up. But, some people after a while just lose
their energy. Well, if they couldn't convince the person
to do their job properly they would put them into a cor-
ner and just let them sit there with nothing to do. After

---

[109] Karma simply means, 'As sow shall ye reap,' you get in life back exactly ·
what you put out. Like Isaac Newton said, "For every action there is an equal
and opposite reaction." I'd better be careful from now on.
[110] You could see many diplomas up on the walls for employees who completed
and became certified in many different skills.

a while the person would either leave or get the message and start to put in the right energy.

On one of my later visits to Japan I went to a tuna canning company. With around 300 employees I asked if they had a lifetime employment system. "Yes, we do. Around 15 employees are lifetime members while all of the ladies you see on the production line are only part time workers." I laughed and saw how only in Japan would this be possible.

But the lifetime system was a key element for Japan's success. Young people out of school became dedicated to their company. They started off paid very little, often stayed at company housing[111], wore their company uniforms, worked and even socialized with their team of fellow workers, and worked late hours. But, there were rewards for them: each year they received raises, bonuses, continuous education and training, security (hardly ever were you fired), and were given a large retirement check when they reached age 55.[112]

Today as I am writing this book people often say since the Japanese are having so much trouble with their economy, What can we learn from them?' They did unfortunately hyper inflate their economy and the bubble did burst in the early 1990's forcing most Japanese companies to rethink and curtail their lifetime employment system. But Japan is still the world's second largest industrial power and there is still much to be learned from them.

---

[111] Housing is a real burden to the average Japanese especially near the big cities; people often travel up to two hours each way to get to work.

[112] A few managers would continue on to age 60 and if they made senior management levels they could go even further. At retirement employees were given a lump sum payment.

10.   **Jidoka**[113], looking at the factory like it had a human nervous system. If a defect was detected a worker had the power to stop the entire factory.

Using Jidoka lets us look at the factory like it was a human body. When we cut a finger the brain feels pain and sends blood and energy to quickly heal the injury. If we eat well, drink well, bathe often, live with some moderation, and exercise occasionally our bodies normally function without complaining. But when a problem occurs we feel the pain and immediately try to take care of the condition. Now consider a plant. Keep the machines and people well oiled, treated as if they were new and precious and they will continue to 'hum' along. But, when problems arise, we should immediately do whatever is necessary to get the machines and people back into harmony. To Ohno Jidoka was the another real power behind the Toyota Production System.

11.   **Andon**[114], a visual control system (part of Jidoka), which indicates what portion of the system is experiencing trouble:

> Green light – everything is all right
> Yellow light – I might need some help
> Red light – the machines stop and
>   supervisors and workers rush over
>   to help the worker in trouble.
>   When this happened it only took, at
>   most, a minute or two to solve the
>   problem, but what a great way to
>   get to the root cause.

---

[113] Jidoka or Autonomation is defined as manufacturing with a human touch. Every machine was fitted with an automatic stopping device. When some abnormality occurs in the process the machine stops and raises an alert.
[114] Andon means signboard a visual display system within the factory.

12.   **Kaizen – The improvement engine** - The Japanese managers told us we must be committed to continuous improvement, to have great patience, and to be persistent. Every employee must be perceived as a real asset with creative ability to solve problems they face daily. (Later on in the book we will introduce you to Quick and Easy Kaizen a very powerful methodology to capture and implement improvement ideas from all workers).

13.   **Wastes** - The "heart" of the Toyota Production System is the recognition and the total elimination of all wastes, worthwhile to re-look at some of these:

a.	Motion – use two hands if you can
b.	Transportation – cutting down on the distance that things move throughout the plant
c.	Producing defects, creating scrap
d.	Machines not functioning properly
e.	Inventory – having too much work-in-process
f.	Improper design of the process and the equipment
g.	Extra time to set up a new product
h.	Not utilizing the inherent talent of your workers
i.	Not managing correctly
j.	Waiting time, delays, people just watching machines[115]
k.	Inspection

---

[115] While machines in America are producing large quantities of parts, building up inventory, often workers just stand their watching the machines waiting for the machine to stop. I empathize with those workers. I never saw workers in Japan just standing, watching and waiting for machines to stop and I have visited over 250 plants there. To me it's a waste of the human being, the human creative capacity, to have them just stand there and watch machines.

14.   **Manufacturing cells** - At many factories we saw the machines organized into manufacturing cells with workers standing, not sitting, moving one part between machines; a worker would insert a part into a machine, held by a grasping device, then the machine would automatically process the part while the worker took the previously completed part and moved it to the next machine.   There was no inventory between machines.

15.   **Multi-skilled workers** - Many of the workers were multi-skilled, running many different types of machines. This allowed them to have opportunities to display their talents, intelligence and gave them the authority to make decisions and implement them.

16.   **The US Embassy** - I took a side trip to the US Embassy and met with the information manager who told me that the government spent tens of millions of dollars translating Japanese material into English.   My 'blood started to boil,' when I told him that he has been spending all of that money and couldn't find anything on JIT or the quality efforts in Japan.   "The Japanese 'are eating our lunch.   Maybe if you went to less parties you might have found the information that could have saved our industries."

17.   **Toyota** - Funny, but prior to the first trip to Japan we went to the General Motors plant in Tarrytown, New York where they were assembling Oldsmobile's.   We did this so that we would be able to have some ability to compare an American plant with a Japanese plant.

When we entered the Tarrytown[116] plant at first all you could see was mountains of inventory.   Here they were assem-

---

[116] At the Tarrytown plant we were introduced to the work of Sidney Rubinstein an independent consultant to GM setting up small group activities similar to

bling around 600 automobiles a shift on two shifts a day. On the factory floor they had 600 engines, 600 roofs, 600 tail pipes, 600 mufflers, 600 frames, 2400 to 4800 doors, 3000 tires, etc. Parts, boxes were piled almost to the top of the ceiling.

In the plant were also railroad tracks with a train sitting there waiting to be unloaded with another 600 car parts for the next shift. Also outside of the plant was another series of trains filled with car parts waiting to move into the plant the next day. We were told that waiting outside the plant were about a week's worth of parts. I believe at the time that GM was turning over inventory four times a year while at Toyota it was over 200 times.

Our guide took us along the assembly line. I noticed particularly one worker working on the line putting fluid into the brake lining of every other car. This was hard to believe. He moved so slowly. To me it was deadly. I asked the guide if this man rotated jobs. He said, "No. In fact we had one man, all he did for 43 years was put tires onto a hook; then the tires moved over to the line. Ironically, when he retired he only collected two retirement checks." Sure all the fun and excitement in life was over for him.[117]

Well, when we visited Toyota on that first trip and were also able to see the assembly line I particularly wanted to see the person putting in brake fluid into the cars. I did. But, he put brake fluid into every car not just every other one and he also put the windshield wipers on each car and also tightened a few

---

quality control circles. We were very impressed with his work but felt that Sidney was too secretive which prevented his work from spreading.

[117] Here is the work of the future. How to create a working environment for both advanced manufacturing and for the quality of work life for the workers.

screws on the dashboard.[118] This worker, if he/she wanted, could rotate weekly by posting their job on a bulletin board.

Today the workers rotate jobs every two hours.

At this Toyota final assembly plant the outside doors would open near the line. In fact, the wall of the plant were almost all doors allowing unloading to be very close to where the parts were to be assembled. This differed from the GM plant where there was a loading dock or the railroad cards forcing the use of movement of products throughout the plant from one side to another via fork lifts.

While we watched the workers on the finished assembly line the doors opened up near us and a small cart with 18 engines came in right next to the line. In fact, every twenty minutes 18 engines were delivered.

18.   **Innovation** – Whenever I could, I would go in Tokyo to Yodobashi Camera Store in the Shinjuku section or to Akihabara the huge discount electronic center. I would be on the lookout for the latest gadget to buy for my grandchildren or friends. On our first trip we thought that Japan was just a nation of copies but in these areas of Tokyo I would find on each trip something new and wonderful to buy: a new camera that was

---

[118] I do have a personal gripe with the unions in America who shouted their favorite slogan, "work smarter not harder." First of all, the average union worker was looked at as an extension of the machine and hardly ever was allowed to use their brains on the job and somehow the unions didn't fight management against that abuse. They thought that moving slowly was better for the worker than really moving at work. Unions were against what they called 'speed up.' However, to me I feel so much better when my energy moves. I love sport activities and I love to move around a lot at work.   And I just read recently that 40% of Americans are overweight, and probably a lot of that has to do with the way work is designed.

smaller, faster and cheaper, robot toys, pens, watches, walkman, great exciting computer games, very small calculators, etc.

I would buy these toy dinosaurs requiring hours for me to put together but my grandson Anthony would destroy them in just one moment.

19.   **Transportation** – The subway system was marvelous, always packed (imagine two million people passing through the Shinjuku station every weekday) – pushers shoving people in, those poor young girls being crushed, but the trains always ran exactly on time with a new train rushing in to the platform every few minutes. Ironically, the land of just in time had some of the world's worst traffic jams. It once took close to four hours to go from our Hotel in Tokyo to the airport, a trip that should have taken only 70 minutes.

20.   **PROFIT = SALES PRICE – COST**

We learned early on from Toyota that the old price formula had changed. It used to be SALES PRICE = COST + PROFIT. This allowed companies to automatically raise the sales price whenever costs went up, and profit was normally fixed as a percentage of the costs. Thus, if costs went up 10%, profit would also go up 10%, meaning that the higher the costs the more money the company made. Of course, competition was a constraint but when everybody played by the same rules the only loser was the customer. Somehow this process was allowed to exist for many years until Toyota changed the game.

The new game became PROFIT = SALES PRICE – COST. This meant that the sales price is fixed, and the only way that a company can make more money is to reduce their costs. This put

tremendous pressure on management to improve quality and productivity. [119]

    And it works. Every year innovative ideas are added to
new products but the cost of automobiles, computers, etc. goes
down not up. It shows you that competition can work to benefit
the customer.

A Radical Change is Happening at Toyota

> *On my most recent visit to Japan in November
> 23, 2003 I was told that Toyota is now reducing the size
> of their lines to mini lines with 20 to 40 people on the
> line and with three to four cars worth of parts as buffer
> stock. This is a radical departure from Ohno's and
> Shingo's ideal to have no buffer stocks at all. It was
> done to still allow people to stop the line to correct de-
> fects without stopping the entire plant. People were
> afraid to stop 300 or more workers from working.*

These trips were always filled with new discoveries.

---

[119] "Actually, it means that price is a variable (driven by demand) as is cost
(driven by improvement efforts), and profit is the by-product of good management." Bill Kluck, NWLEAN

12

Developing an Understanding of Japan

"If we don't change, we don't grow.
If we don't grow, we aren't really living."
Gail Sheehy

First Seminar on Japanese Management

It was February 1981 in Indianapolis when we ran our first seminar on Japanese management practices. Our speakers were Robert Hall, professor at the Indiana University, Dennis Butts, plant manager for Kawasaki Motor in Lincoln, Nebraska, Robert Patchin, director of Productivity Improvement at Northrop, Yasu-hiro Monden, professor at State University of New York at Buf-falo, and William Stewart, a specialist on productivity measure-ment. It was very exciting for us as it was a prelude to our first study mission to Japan from March 6 to the 21st.

Dennis was probably the first plant manager in America to do JIT; Robert Hall has written a number of successful books on Toyota; Robert Patchin was one of the early proponents of quality circles in America, and Professor Monden is now a famous profes-sor at the University of Tsukuba in Japan, the author of:

- *Toyota Production Systems*
- *The Toyota Management System: Linking the Seven Key Functional Areas*

- *Cost Reduction Systems: Target Costing and Kaizen Costing*
- *Japanese Management Accounting: A World Class Approach to Profit Management*
- *Cost Management in the New Manufacturing Age: Innovations in the Japanese Automobile Industry*
- *Japanese Cost Management*

We had dinner recently and I do intend to publish his new books in English.

Misogi: Experiencing a Japanese Ritual

All of our study missions for the first five years were two-week events. During the middle weekend we would go to the Tsubaki Grand Shrine in Suzuka, in the Mie peninsula between Nagoya and Kyoto. We wanted to give the travelers a chance to experience Japanese rituals. At Tsubaki we would be greeted by the priest and quickly led up the mountain past their shrines, and gates to a spot near a waterfall. We would remove our clothes and put on something that looked like a large baby's diaper.

Then the group, those of us who were brave enough, would go out into the snow and stand outside in front of the waterfall. To prevent us from freezing, we immediately participated in warm-up exercises. Then one by one we were led into the water to stand under the waterfall. This was a purification ritual practiced at Tsubaki grand shrine for 1300 years.

"The word MISOGI refers to the ritual cleansing of the body with water to remove both physical and spiritual defilements. Since Shinto lays great stress on purity and cleanliness, the act of cleansing the body assumes enormous importance."[120]

During the process you might shiver and shake a little bit but afterwards you feel proud of your accomplishment. All of us then would return to the Shrine's Hotel to shower, bathe in the hot tubs and then eat the splendid Japanese food while indulging in the beer, whisky and sake. It was a memorable event that none of us would ever forget.

What do Japanese do on Weekends?

On the airplane returning to the US I sat next to young man employed with NEC. He was in their marketing department and had worked for them for four years. I asked how many vacation days he had taken since he started, "I've never taken a vacation day in four years," he said.

How many hours do you work each week? "I normally get to work a little after nine in morning and get back home around nine to ten o'clock at night and do this normally for six days a week. I use Sundays to sleep, and to do my laundry."

Who Works a 40-hour Week?

Another time I visited an office in Tokyo and asked the president of the company. "How many hours a week does the average employee work? He said, "We normally work a 40 hour week." It was 6:00PM and I looked around his office and saw around 30 people working there. We both laughed. Yes, officially companies in Japan were reporting 40-hour workweeks, but actually the average Japanese works much, much more.

---

[120] For other details on Misogi go to detailhttp://www.tatsu.ne.jp/en/tours/misogi.html

What It Takes to Be Invited into the Club?

I met a manager with C. Itoh, one of Japan's largest trading companies, over 100 billion dollars in sales. We went to dinner and had some drinks. I think he had one too many, for he leaned over to me, put his arm around me and said, "Norman-san, we can do business together, but you will never be accepted in our 'club.' I have worked for over twenty years along side my group members, working very late hours almost every working day. You have not earned the right to be that close to us." On one hand I understood, but on the other it didn't make me feel that good about working with them.

What Would You Pay for a Round of Golf?

I sat on an airplane to Japan next to the CEO of a Japanese engineering company with over 5,000 employees working primarily in the oil fields in the mid-east. This was in the late 1980's, the heyday of the hyper economic explosions in Japan. During that time real estate values in Tokyo were doubling each year. My companion on the airplane told me that he recently bought three golf memberships near and around Tokyo for $1,000,000, $750,000 and $250,000. It was a crazy moment in Japanese history.[121]

Walls are filled with pictures

At Citizen Watch, the walls are filled with pictures. Most of the pictures show the improvements in set-up time. As an example, one picture shows a die with 56 seconds written under-

---

[121] Ten years later those memberships totally collapsed in value, many golf clubs went bankrupt. The Nikkei Golf Club Stock Index, where memberships were traded like stock had declined in the 1990's over 91%. A membership that once sold for $3,000,000 was selling at a little over $30,000.

neath, and to the right of that picture was another picture of the exact same die with 32 seconds written underneath. They went from 56 seconds to 32 seconds. This is significant for many reasons:

1.   You want to encourage everyone to be involved in continuous improvement.

2.   You want to reduce all of your set-up times to one touch if possible. Often when we make improvements, we sit back and 'gloat,' instead of just moving forward.

3.   Changeover time is one of the major wastes. As you reduce the time, you reduce the wastes. You can then reduce the work-in-process inventory and keep the correct takt time, allowing the entire plant to stay in flow to deliver the products exactly on time to your clients.

13

Factory Tours: A Feast for the Eyes

"In the long run; 'Lean' preserves jobs in this country because it is the only way to slow the movement of jobs to low cost labor markets."
James B. Swartz

On the study missions to Japan, after the initial introduction to a plant we normally were given jackets, safety glasses, and small earphones connected to receivers. Our interpreter would walk with one of the managers and would translate for us through a microphone transmitting back to us the questions and answers and descriptions of the things seen in the plant.

The plant visits normally lasted around an hour and then we went back to the meeting room where presentation would be given to us. At each plant a different topic was selected: JIT, kanban, distribution, logistics, quality, quality circles, etc. After the presentations were question and answer sessions. Often lunch was provided for us.[122]

---

[122] At Nippon Steel after our long walk along the continuous flow steel line we were taken to the plant dinning room and served a fabulous Chinese meal equal to the best Chinese restaurant in Tokyo.

Gift giving is a Japanese custom almost to the point of embarrassment. On my first trip to Japan I was not prepared. At many of the companies we would be given some gift to remind us of the visit. On all future trips I asked the travelers to bring with them corporate gifts to give out like: gold balls, knives, cups with the corporate logo, etc. And at the end of the visit we would exchange gifts.[123] Many of the Japanese gifts had their corporate logo.

It was a fun filled great learning experience for us all.

Value Adding Versus Non-Value Adding

Before the first study mission in early 1980, I was introduced to the concept of value adding versus non-value adding. Value adding is the essence of manufacturing, those steps that **convert raw materials to finished goods** such as milling, drilling, stamping, painting, polishing, gluing, buffering, lubricating, attaching, bolting, hammering, forging, melting, extruding, curing, laminating, etching, through hole plating, inserting, soldering and others. Non-value adding activities are the wastes we mentioned earlier – some necessary to do but surely to be continuously reduced.

A very valuable exercise to do is to take a stopwatch and calculate the ratio of value adding to non-value adding time. Take one product and follow it through the manufacturing process and record the exact time the product started into production,

---

[123] Giving gifts was not a common practice for me in the USA but here in Japan it seems to be everywhere. I appreciated the Japanese companies being hosts to my study mission with no charge to my company, and once they accepted us they were exceptionally gracious with their time. So on every trip to Japan I had to find appropriate gifts. It was a challenge for I wanted things that felt of value but didn't weigh too much since I had to carry them with my luggage. Often I would buy exotic Italian silk ties from Ferragamo and once even brought over a couple dozen Ping putters.

the time it was completed and record exactly the amount of time value was being added – the milling, drilling, etc. part. We found back in the early 1980's that in almost every American plant the ratio was 5% or less on value adding time and 95% was on non-value adding time.[124]

This was one of the great keys to the Toyota Production System, which was to find ways to focus on continuous improvement by reducing the non-value adding time. While most manufacturing in the past focused on innovation, better and faster machines,[125] Dr. Shingo recognized that there was more profit to be made by first reducing wastes.

The Most Valuable Part of This First Trip was Meeting Dr. Ryuji Fukuda

At Sumitomo Electric in Osaka, a manufacturer of electric products similar to General Electric, the study tour group entered the company meeting room, with the Americans sitting on one side of the room and around 10 Japanese managers on the other side. We were given green tea or coffee in lovely china cups and then one of the Japanese managers introduced us to the products being made in the plant.

Why did the Japanese allow us into their plants? I felt there were several reasons: to pay us back for helping them to reconstruct their industries; they also wanted contacts to visit American plants; they were always looking for international customers; they also realized the enormous value in this exchange ex-

---

[124] We discovered in 1980 this 5% to 95% non-value added to value added in a book titled *How to Win Productivity in Manufacturing* by Wm. E. Sandman and John P. Hayes.

[125] Speeding up machines, getting out more products, creating more inventory, often increases the non-value adding time, making the total process less efficient.

ercise – making a presentation to visitors and answering their questions was a very powerful learning experience. Someone years later gave a name to this process; they called it benchmarking.

After the introduction, their vice president of manufacturing, Dr. Ryuji Fukuda stood up and started to teach us On-Error-Training (OET), a very simple concept that he developed.

As I previously said, I knew very little about engineering and the intricacies of manufacturing, but I was impressed by OET; this was something I could fully understand and appreciate. Dr. Fukuda said, "The best time to train workers is when an error is first detected. It is also the best time to solve a problem." From a videotape in English we were taught the five rules to make OET work. It is an amazingly powerful and simple process:

On-Error-Training

1. Himself/herself Rule – the worker, who first detects the problem, becomes primarily responsible for finding the root cause of the problem, so that the defect will not occur again.

2. Quickly Rule – The problem must be dealt with within 30 minutes of detection. The problem must be solved immediately not later at a Quality Circle Meeting.

3. Actually Rule – The person plays back the process that transpired before the defect occurred and the defect is re-created, if possible, in front of the group.

4. Support Rule – The person who detected the problem becomes the person primarily responsible for solving it, but they do call over their supervisor and fellow workers – everyone stops

working and extends his support to the process of problem solving.

5. Don't Speak Rule – The discoverer of the problem is the person expected to solve it. He or she must be allowed the time to discuss the problem and attempt to solve it. Other workers can help but the supervisor or manager must keep quiet to give the workers a chance to solve the problem on their own. If the workers cannot solve the problem then the supervisors can, of course, offer their suggestions.

I was floored with the simplicity and brilliance of this process. Dr. Fukuda told us that OET in the first year reduced the rejection rate by over 90%. If we really want to empower people and let them grow then we should all do OET. We must invest, to allow people to stop the process for a short period of time to detect and eliminate the causes of defects. In the long run we will be far ahead. I keep asking others and myself over the years, 'why aren't we doing this very simple technique?'

As I mentioned earlier, I was so impressed with this presentation by Dr. Fukuda that after he spoke, I went over to him to meet him personally. In a brief discussion with him I asked if he would come to America to speak at one of my future conferences. He said, "Yes." He then told me that he had just finished writing his first book. Without thinking, without knowing really what I was saying I said, 'Can I publish your book in English?[126]' He was well pleased and again said, "Yes."

The problem was that I knew nothing about book publishing. It took me two years to learn.

A few months later I received a copy of Dr. Fukuda's book. On my next study mission, six months later, I went to Dr.

---

[126] *Managerial Engineering*

Fukuda's publisher (Japan Statistical Association) to negotiate a contract on the book.

Dr. Fukuda asked Noriko Hosoyamada to translate the book. After translation I read the book and was well pleased that my intuition was correct, the information was new, vitally important but it did need extensive editing. I gave the book to an editor and asked her to edit the first chapter. I didn't like it. I took the book to another editor and gave him the same test. I didn't like it. I then went to 10 other editors, probably made a lot of enemies in the process, until I finally found someone who really understood the power of Dr. Fukuda's work and was able to put it into easily understood English.

Publishing this book was a painful and expensive process. After editing we had to copyright the book, obtain library of congress and other catalogue numbers, select type style, create an index, get testimonials, and find a printer to print and bind the book. Like almost anything that is new it was not easy for us. But through learning how to publish this first Japanese book I subsequently was able to publish many Japanese books into English and created a book publishing company. We sold over 35,000 copies of Dr. Fukuda's book.

Magically I was able to get W. Edwards Deming, Richard Schonberger, Robert Hall, Wayne Rieker and Jack Warne to write testimonials for the back cover of the book. Deming said, ""With better quality at lower prices, a company captures the market, provides jobs and more jobs. A further important gain is happier employees – happy to have the privilege to take part in the company-wide improvement."

Wayne Reiker was a senior manager at Lockheed, noticed in 1971 the high quality products coming from Japan and convened a team of himself and five others including Don Dewar to find out what the Japanese were doing to get such high quality. They visited JUSE and were introduced to Quality Control Circles and came back with training material in Japanese with permission to translate the material into English. Don then trained quality control teams at Lockheed and the first US circles were born. Wayne and Don a few years later left Lockheed, opened up their own consulting companies, and taught and spread Quality Circles throughout America. In early 1980 Wayne gave me a set of his training materials to include in the first issue of our newsletter in June 1980.

The Schedule Board

During those early discovery days I was told that Americans would always be looking for big innovative breakthroughs, while the Japanese were looking for small incremental improvements, which would eventually lead to big breakthroughs. Since I was not an engineer, and initially knew very little about manufacturing, the little things seemed to fascinate me. On one trip with Dr. Fukuda at Meidensha Electric I was taken over to a large scheduling board hanging from the ceiling of the plant. This board scheduled all the main orders. (In this factory they were making large electrical generators).

At 8:00am and 4:00pm everyday the supervisors and managers would meet in front of the scheduling board. They would know which job was ahead or behind schedule; which workers were available, what equipment was available, etc. From this board they would allocate resources daily. It was easy to see, easy to keep up, and was wonderful for communication purposes.

Often we build very elaborate MRP computer systems only to find out that they are difficult to understand, people don't carefully look at them, and sometimes they have entry errors. This board seemed to solve all those problems.

The Training Room

The next day, Dr. Fukuda took me to a training room to watch a group of employees being trained in the latest management concepts. I watched, but not knowing Japanese I had no idea what they were learning and I had no idea why I was taken to this room. After observing the class, I noticed a large training manual in front of each worker. This excited me. I scanned the pages quickly, seeing lots of graphs and charts. I asked Dr. Fukuda to get me a set of the training materials. He sent me a set, and I asked for the rights to translate and publish the training material in English.

I subsequently worked out an arrangement to get the rights to translate and publish the training material in English. I agreed to pay Sumitomo Electric[127] $30,000 for the world rights to that material outside of Japan. Dr. Fukuda, however, told me to wait on the translation, as he would rewrite and bring them up to date for me.

Over the next year I received from Dr. Fukuda materials, which produced CEDAC[128], 5S[129], visual factory,[130] and a much greater understanding of Japanese management.

---

[127] Meidensha Electric is a sister company to Sumitomo Electric.
[128] CEDAC – Cause and effect diagram with the addition of cards. This was a variation of the cause and effect diagrams used in quality circles. Instead of working on a flat sheet, Dr. Fukuda added cards that could be better organized and moved around on the chart. For this technique he was awarded the Deming Literature Prize.

---

[129] 5S housekeeping is a very powerful employee involvement system that empowers workers to keep the plant in perfect working condition.

[130] In a visual factory every item has an exact place, is easy to find, easy to see, easy to store, easy to reach, well labeled, bright, cheerful and very effective. The goal is to be able to find every tool within 30 seconds, with everything totally organized and labeled. Floors are marked where items are to be placed, shelves all marked, and boards on the walls are outlined with the shapes of tools.

14

The Gemba Walk[131]

"A stumbling block to the pessimist is a stepping-stone to the optimist."- **Eleanor Roosevelt**

During a trip to Japan, Dr. Ryuji Fukuda took me to a Meidensha Electric plant[132] outside of Tokyo, and introduced me to the plant manager. I looked around the office, which had around 75 people all in one room with no dividers. All of the desks were pushed up close together with books and papers piled up high. No one had any privacy, not even partitions separating desks.

I noticed something very interesting, a group of engineers having a stand up meeting around one of the desks – not a bad idea as it cuts down the length of meetings.

At 11:00AM, the plant manager got up from behind his desk. He sat near the window in the center of the room to be able

---

[131] Gemba means factory floor, and walking around the plant could be the most important part of a manager's job. Instead of feeling that you must lead others, your real strength is bringing out the best from others, letting them develop their talents and letting them run the business for you. As you learn from the workers your job is to then disseminate your learning with everyone else – others in the plant and also sharing the power of this learning with your bosses.

[132] Meidensha Electric is a manufacturer of electric power equipment for the electric generation industry.

to observe everyone else. He asked me to join him on his daily walk; in fact he told me that he walked the plant twice a day every day and that **it was the most valuable part of his job.**

... it was the most valuable part of his job.

The plant manager said, "Norman, **I select a different theme** for every walk and this morning I am going to look at the quality charts to see if they have a real purpose for the company and for the employees; if people are keeping them up to date; to see how they're used; and to learn who looks at them and when they're looked at. I want to find out what is the real value of those quality charts.[133]"

It was a large manufacturing plant making electrical power equipment. As we walked over to the first department in the plant, the supervisor came over to meet us. The plant manager then inspected the quality charts[134] to see which ones were being displayed and if they were being kept up to date. All of the charts had current dates on them.

The plant manager then asked a series of questions to the supervisor about the usefulness of the quality charts including:

1.   Who's responsible for updating the quality charts?
2.   Do the other employees look at the charts?
3.   How often do they look at them?

---

[133] How many companies have quality charts up on the wall but no one really looks at them or knows how to really use them?

[134] At those American plants I had earlier visited I hardly saw anything displayed on the walls to inspire people to improve. Here in Japan almost every square inch of wall space was used to communicate some information to the worker: quality charts and statistics, ideas from the workers, safety figures, pictures of problems to be solved, certificates of courses taken by the individual workers, description of poka-yokes and change-over times, etc.

4.   What value do the charts have for the employees?
5.   Do our customers ever look at the charts?
6.   Do our suppliers look at the charts?
7.   Do you think the charts have an effect on the
        overall quality of the parts being produced?

The plant manager asked those questions and you could see the excitement on the face of the supervisor as he was answering the questions. I learned that there's enormous power in the leader asking questions and then **just listening** – yes; this is the key to ask the question and then to **just listen carefully**, not judgmentally.

When the plant manager looks at something with real interest, the people in the plant are interested in supporting the plant manager. They think, "If the charts are important to our plant manager then they must be important for us to keep them up to date." Well, the reverse is also true and when the plant manager shows no interest in an item, there is often a tendency for that to just fall apart. They think, "We have so many other things to do. If the plant manager doesn't look at those charts, they're probably not very important."

There was real learning going on as the supervisor was explaining the importance of the charts and how they played a vital role in the whole quality movement. To the supervisor, the charts were like a scorecard at an athletic event. Imagine going to a basketball game in which there is no score being kept. You would probably leave after a few moments. I saw a football game recently and the score was 28 to 4; people lost interest and started to leave the stands. It is the same in the plant and at work; we need both targets to shoot for, and we need to know the score to see if we're meeting or exceeding those targets.

I could see the real power in this walk; it was a learning experience for the manager to be educated by his supervisor and employees.   By selecting a different theme for every walk he would eventually cover all of the important aspects of running a plant. Imagine after one year the manager could do over 400 walks a year: safety, cost savings, people development, quality, reducing the time line, eliminating wastes, etc, and nothing would be 'lost within the cracks.' By asking questions and not telling, he encouraged his employees to understand the importance of their work. In reality, he was letting them run the plant – his job was to be the catalyst, to see that everyone was being motivated to keep to the highest possible standard.

My head was already spinning with a great many thoughts as I recognized how empowering this experience was for this plant. I also knew that I had to change the way I managed my company.[135]

As the leader, the plant manager sets the tempo and sets an example for the plant. It's up to the supervisor to follow the plant manager's example when he/she talks to the employees – to ask them questions and not always give the answers.

Then we walked to the next department to meet with another supervisor. Since this was done every day at a specific time, the supervisor was prepared and waiting for us to come by. The plant manager repeated the same series of questions to this supervisor and listened. Now, after he listened to this second supervisor he was able **to share** some of what he learned from the first supervisor. He was careful not to criticize the second supervisor and he was careful not to compare the first department with the second department. He shared with sensitivity some of the new things he observed and learned.

First we saw that all of the charts were kept up to date, and had real meaning for the workers in helping them sustain

---

[135] Not always easy to do.

their quality efforts. I fully realized the real power in the Gemba walk:

1.   When the manager shows an interest in something like quality charts, he is demonstrating that he feels they are important. Workers in the plant then ensure they are used and kept up to date.[136] If the plant manager does not show interest in them, workers have a tendency to stop keeping them up to date. "We have plenty to do to just do our job."

2.   By questioning the supervisor, there was an exchange of ideas on the subject. This was a learning experience for both the plant manager and the supervisor.

3.   The plant manager now shared what he learned from the first department with the supervisor of the second and subsequent departments. "Wow." This Gemba walk was a great communication device and I could see why the plant manager considered this the most important part of his job.

I was very impressed. What a way to run a plant!

After we completed the entire walk, which took around an hour, we came back to the office area. Because there was a lot of learning, and the first departments did not receive feedback from the later departments, the plant manager wrote a **summary memo** to post on the bulletin board to share everything he learned with all of the employees.

---

[136] Once in Scotland I was in a bottle manufacturing plant looking at the TPM charts. We had run an event three months earlier. Not one chart was kept up to date. The plant manager and the workers loved the training but without the plant manager following up people would just go back to their old ways of doing things – and TPM gets neglected.

Not everything was perfect, and there were a number of problems to solve, and new things to consider. He left it up to each supervisor and their employees to find a way to get these things done.[137]

The steps of the Gemba walk are:

1.   Selecting a theme for each walk

2.   Questioning the supervisors

3.   Listening attentively. This is a learning exercise for the manager

4.   Sharing what you learned as you walk through the plant

5.   Writing a short memo on what you learned and post it for others to see

6.   Follow-up to see that progress was made

---

[137] Another key is to empower the employees in the improvement process. If you make them responsible and then carefully follow up, a lot more power is given to the process.

15

5 S

"Become a possibilitarian. No matter how dark things seem to be or actually are, raise your sights and see possibilities - always see them, for they're always there."- **Norman Vincent Peale**

We noticed in a typical Japanese plant the use of the 5s' housekeeping technique. For many companies this process of keeping the factory in exact order with minimum waste drove their entire lean and quality improvement efforts. The 5s' vary, but normally are:

1. **Seiri** – 'sorting' - focuses on eliminating unnecessary items from the workplace. A visual method to identify unneeded items, red tag them, take them to a holding area for evaluation, and either discard or reuse them somewhere else in the plant. Sorting is an excellent way to free up valuable floor space.

2. **Seiton** – 'set in order' - focuses on efficient and effective storage methods. Ask yourself: what do I need to do my job; where should I store this item to be readably available when needed, and how many items will I need? Parts of the floor are painted, indicating where things should be

stored, where trash cans, brooms, mops, and buckets should be placed. Shelves are clearly marked, and tools hung on boards with an outline of the tool. There is an exact place demarcated for everything; you then know exactly where to go when something is needed.

3. **Seiso** – 'shine' - Once the clutter and junk is eliminated, the next step is to thoroughly clean the work area and you keep it clean – like the old days in the army when you had to shine everything prior to inspection. This gives people a better sense of ownership in their work environment and problems with equipment, contamination, oil leaks, vibrations, fatigue, breakage, and misalignment are revealed. The changes, if left unattended, can lead to equipment failure and loss of production.

4. **Seiketsu** – 'standardize' – is to set up procedures to insure that the best practices are followed. Workers should be allowed to develop those standards. McDonalds, Pizza Hut, and others are known for setting up and sustaining precise standards to deliver the exact same product to their customers.

5. **Shitsuke** – 'sustain' – probably the hardest to do as people resist change and seem to go back to their old way of doing things and within a few months are back to the old cluttered shop.

"Once fully implemented, the 5S process can increase morale, create positive impressions on customers, and increase efficiency and organization. Not only will employees feel better about where they work, the effect on continuous improvement can lead to less waste, better quality and faster lead times. Any of which will make your organization more profitable and competitive in the market place.[138]"

At many Japanese companies the walls are filled with charts, pictures, graphs, certificates, and kaizen ideas. The walls are used as communication devices, to stimulate and encourage continuous improvement, and are kept up to date.[139]

---

[138] Quoted from an article by Todd Skaggs, the President/CEO of Metaltek Mfg. Inc. located in Hodgenville, KY.
http://www.tpmonline.com/articles_on_total_productive_maintenance/leanmfg/5sphilosophy.htm
[139] Keeping the visual controls up to date is vitally important. Imagine going to a ball game and seeing only old scores. It does not make for an exciting game. People can lose interest in improvement activities if the scores are not kept up to date.

16

Discovering Books in Japan

"Everyone thinks of changing the world,
but no one thinks of changing himself."
– Leo Tolstoy

The first book I sold from Japan was Dr. Shingo's Green book.[140] It was published by JMA, but I became their major distributor. I didn't really feel I was a book publisher until I met and published Dr. Ryuji Fukuda's *Managerial Engineering*. As I mentioned earlier it took me two years to have the book translated, understood, edited, copyedited, typeset, and printed.

Since The Japanese Standard Association (JSA) originally published Dr. Fukuda's book in Japan, I negotiated with them for permission to publish his book in English.

While at JSA, I asked them to please recommend other books they published to consider for translation. They introduced me to Dr. Yoji Akao, and I published the original books on both Quality Function Deployment (QFD) and Hoshin Kanri – Policy Deployment for Successful TQM.

---

[140] Study of 'TOYOTA' Production System from Industrial Engineering Viewpoint.

Quality Function Deployment (QFD) is a set of powerful product development tools that were developed in Japan to transfer the concepts of quality control from manufacturing process into new product development process. Benefits of QFD are: reduced time to market, reduction in design changes, decreased design and manufacturing costs, improved quality and increased customer satisfaction.

Hoshin Kanri is a systems approach to the management of change in critical business processes using a step-by-step planning, implementation, and review process to improve the performance of business systems. For every business system there are measures of performance and desired levels of performance. Hoshin Kanri provides a planning structure that will bring selected critical business processes up to the desired level of performance.

In retrospect I made a major mistake, one of many. I thought that my object in publishing should be to replicate in English exactly the Japanese books maintaining the integrity of the original author. What I should have done was have each book rewritten into more understandable English. I wanted to be true to the author, but I also wanted to make the books of more value to an American audience. Adding additional chapters written by American practitioners also would have made the book of more value to American audiences.

Dr. Akao's books had great information, but were not easy to read or understand.

Quality Function Deployment starts with design of the product and provides specific methods to monitor quality throughout each stage of the product development process – to satisfy customers, and to translate customers' desires into design targets. QFD helps reduce costs in design and manufacturing while shortening the cycle time.

Here with QFD I had another 'goldmine' but I didn't fully appreciate what I found and published. But gratefully there were many others who appreciated the brilliance of Dr. Akoa, and the concept of QFD has spread like wildflowers. On February 4, 2003, typing in 'QFD,' in Google brought up 108,000 hits and Amazon had 325 books.

"In its simplest form, Hoshin Kanri is nothing more than a **system of forms and rules** that encourage employees to analyze situations, create plans for improvement, conduct performance checks, and take appropriate action. In practical application however, it is much more than forms and rules - **Hoshin is a philosophy of management!**"[141]

"Hoshin Kanri is like a ship's compass distributed to many ships, properly calibrated such that all ships (through independent action) arrive at the same destination, individually or as a group, as the requirements of the 'voyage' may require.

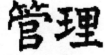

Hoshin = *a course, a policy, a plan, an aim*

管理

Kanri = *administration, management, control, charge of, care for*"[142]

---

[141] http://www.tqe.com/hoshin.html
[142] http://www.mcts.com/Hoshin-Kanri.htm

I led at least two study missions to Japan each year. Often after the travelers returned to the US I would stay an extra week to visit business book publishers.

> *I wish I had the money to publish thousands of Japanese books in English. In Japan, practically every American management book that does even fairly well is, within months, published in Japanese.[143] They relish new ideas coming from America. Unfortunately, we are reluctant to learn from other countries. It is the 'not invented here' syndrome.*
>
> *Also, since Japan has been in an economic slump in the 1990's, many people feel that there is very little to learn from the Japanese. It is foolish. Toyota's stock on December 12, 2003 was worth more than General Motors, Ford, and Chrysler combined. They must be doing something right. Like scientists, we must be willing to learn from anyone, anywhere.*
>
> *My teacher Rudi[144] once said, "When you want milk you go to the supermarket. All you want is fresh, good milk; you are not at all concerned with the color of the cow, or the age of the cow, or what the cow ate for breakfast." It should be the same with management information. We should want only the best available in the world and not care if it comes from Japan, China or America or anywhere else – we just want the best.*

At the Japanese publisher, an editor would review all of their latest books with me. I asked them to summarize the books and tell me the success of each book with Japanese managers. I

---

[143] I saw the revised edition of *The Goal* in Japan where it currently is on top of the best seller's list.

[144] Rudi was probably the world's largest oriental art dealer with a store in New York City. I studied with him from 1971 until he died in a plane crash in 1973. He taught yoga.

would also meet with Japanese consultants, professors, and various authors, giving me an opportunity to question them about their work. I would select a few books from each publisher, those that sounded the most interesting, or something new that sounded important.

When I returned home I would then give the books to a few other people proficient in Japanese to read for me. It was funny, but these readers never really liked any of the books. So I stopped working with them and used either my intuition, or accepted the evaluation of the Japanese book editors or from my meetings with authors. I then gave the books to Japanese translators. On average I published four of every five books translated. After translation and after reading each book, I felt some were just not right for an American audience, but four out of every five is not a bad average, especially when many of them were business best sellers.

Customer Service

Noticing the superior customer service in Japan, I thought that this could be another important area to investigate and bring information to America. When I first visited Japan in 1978 I was totally lost. I could not read anything, didn't even know how to take a bullet train.

I decided to go to visit Kyoto from Tokyo, but I didn't know how or where to buy a ticket. Standing in Tokyo station, probably the largest station in the world, looking lost, an older man came over and in broken English asked if he could help me. I told him I wanted to buy a ticket to Kyoto and find the right platform. He took hold of my arm, walked me over to the ticket office of the Bullet Train, bought my ticket, and took me to the correct track. I thanked him and gave him 200 yen (around 50 cents). He said surprisingly, "No, give me

500 yen." I was slightly shocked, but I gave him the 500-yen.

As I visited hotels and stores, I was deeply impressed with the quality of their food, the décor, and especially their customer service. I was particularly fascinated with the basement at the top department stores, where you could buy or taste every conceivable exotic food from almost anywhere in the world, including chocolate covered ants. You didn't have to go to France for pâtés, or Jamaica for mountain blue coffee, or India for mangos; it was brought here handed to you gift-wrapped.

Imagine going to a supermarket and buying some eels to take home, and then seeing them gift-wrapped for you. And they wrap the package impeccably, something I never really got a handle on.

In the basement of the department store are many, probably a hundred different shops. Each is separately owned, renting space from the department store. Of course, they are all forced to maintain very high standards of quality and customer service. When I stopped at one counter and asked, "where can I buy some rice," instead of just directing me they would take me to the exact spot, even if it were a considerable distance from their shop. It is nice to see this now being done at many American stores.

Seeing such great customer service in Japan, I added customer service books to my shopping list. One book recommended to me, written by a Japanese consultant, was about going to a store and standing there for four hours daily to just watch and observe customers shopping. He would look at their eyes, what they saw, what shelves would they go to, what sequence of products would appeal to them, in what order, what color appealed to them, and how they were being treated by the sales staff.

I invited him to speak at a Customer Service conference, but we in America were not ready for this. Most people in his session just walked out. He might have been just too subtle for us. We are a lot more action oriented. I could not imagine an American manager just going into store and standing there, watching customers shop for four hours at a time.

Fortunately I had very few competitors looking for Japanese management books. American book publishers were not willing to hunt down Japanese books and have them translated to discover if they wanted to publish them. The few books that other American publishers took were those that were presented to them already translated into English (very rarely done because of the cost of translation).

A major challenge for me was to find really great translators. Luckily I found Drew Dillon, a professor at Yale, and a few others.

Another Devastating Event

One day I got a call from a vice president working with Eliyahu M. Goldratt, who wanted us to publish their book, titled *The Goal.* I knew about Goldratt and his theory of constraints. He had a certain magic in his ability to sell to top American corporations. His software, called 'the black box' was used to eliminate the bottlenecks in manufacturing. It was rumored that he was getting a million dollars or more for his software. I jumped at the chance to publish this book and asked that he send up a copy immediately. It came. I put everything else aside and read it in one night. I knew it would be a big best seller. I gave it to two of my editors and we all agreed to publish the book. I called back the vice-president, and even told him three things to change to make it an even better book, and told him that we would gladly publish it.

My mistake!

This vice-president told me that they had decided to publish the book on their own. I was flabbergasted. I couldn't believe that he would send me the book, and then deny us the publishing rights. I felt like a child given some ice cream and then having the cone pulled away. I became emotional and told him this was a terrible thing to do. Then I made a fatal mistake. He said I could resell the book. But my ego was hurt; I said no and probably lost over one million dollars. The book is still selling strongly today. It was one of the biggest business best sellers this year in Japan. It is a very good book.

17

Fire the Quality Manager!

A problem cannot be solved with the same consciousness that created it."
- **Albert Einstein**

Whose fault is it when you can't solve quality problems? Who do you blame when you see all of that scrap? In the early 1980's when a company had severe quality problems they would often try to solve the problems by firing the quality manager and hiring another one.

Back in the early 1980's I was recommended by C. Jackson Grayson, president of the American Productivity and Quality Center in Houston, Texas to be a consultant for Jack Katzen, senior Vice president with AVCO Corporation. I would meet with Jack for one day a month. He wanted me to teach him all about quality and productivity. He would ask me a few questions and then we would dialog for the next six hours. It was lots of fun for me, for while I was teaching him I was really learning about the subject.[145]

A few years later Jack Katzen became the assistant secretary of defense and invited me to the penta-

---

[145] Strange, that if I am teaching properly it is my most important learning moment, as so many new ideas come to me.

gon. He introduced me to the other assistant secretaries and a number of generals and said, "I want you to meet the man who saved my former company AVCO $400,000,000." I smiled at the introduction and only wished I could have gotten my share. What do you think, would 10% have been fair?

At the time AVCO had a severe quality problem in their Connecticut plant, where they were manufacturing engines for the M1 tank. The tanks in Germany were breaking down during the war games. AVCO was getting a bad reputation in the US Congress. In fact, there was a group of senators that wanted to take away this sole source contract from AVCO and give the job to another manufacturer, or at a minimum to have half the engines made somewhere else. This could have meant the loss of over 1000 jobs.

Well, to solve the problem, AVCO (to show the US Army that they really meant business) found the culprit, and fired the quality manager. It is obvious, isn't it, that when something goes wrong it must be someone else's fault.

As you read about my attempt to help them with their problem – remember the old saying, "Solving one problem always leads to another problem." How true.

I remember on one of my later Study Missions to Japan I was sitting next to Don Ferrar, President of AVCO Corporation. On the flight over he turned to me almost tearfully and said, "Norman, why can't my people solve the quality problems?"

We spent the next two weeks visiting a number of Japanese manufacturing plants, and on the way back on the airplane I again sat next to Don Ferrar. After reviewing the highlights of the trip he turned to me and said, "After these two weeks I now realize that I am responsible for quality in my company. I must lead the effort to get it done." It was an amazing revelation and was the beginning of a great transformation for AVCO.

From being introduced to quality circles and Japanese management, we were now beginning to learn that to solve quality problems, everyone had to be involved and everyone had to be responsible. In fact, if we want to 'point a finger,' it should be at the CEO[146], not the Quality Manager.

Jack invited me to help the Stratford plant to move along their productivity and quality efforts. A group of senior managers met weekly and were somehow unable to get their program moving in the right direction. Jack got all of the directors together into a meeting room and at 8:00AM one morning told them that I would help them establish a productivity and quality process.

I first asked all eleven of them to give me a commitment that we would not leave the plant today until we could set up this agenda even if we had to work throughout the night. Nine of the eleven gave me their commitment and we got started. I then asked them to tell me the barriers that stood in the way to their productivity and quality improvement. Slowly, they came up with 34 barriers and we listed them on the blackboard. With some discussion this took around three hours. Then I asked them to vote on which

---

[146] A year later I asked Bob Bowman, the chairman of AVCO, to keynote my "Productivity the American Way" conference in Washington, DC. To really transform AVCO to become a high quality company, the leader (as the company's chief spokesperson) had to tell the world about their quality efforts. You must as they say, "Walk the talk." Also at that conference both Phil Crosby and John J. Hudiburg CEO of Florida Power and Light spoke about quality.

barriers we should remove first. I gave them all three votes indicating that they could use all three on one item or spread them around, but they preferred to spread them around.

Curiously, the highest votes related to removing the barriers that separated people in the plant. They wanted to involve all of the workers in improvement activities, but felt there were things getting in the way. They wanted to remove the private parking spaces for executives; they wanted the office employees and the factory employees to both use and remove the time clocks that separated them; and they did not want the president to build an executive dinning room. I then told them to act cautiously. First go back this week and meet with your staff and talk about the barriers that stood in the way of open communication but do not do anything until you get approval from your senior managers.

Well, someone squealed on me and phoned the president of this division, who was in Germany at the time. I received a call from him and he was screaming at me, "Norman, I told you to get me a productivity and quality program. I did not want you to take away my parking space and kill my new dining room."

Unfortunately, that was the end of my consulting assignment at the AVCO plant. We all want to improve productivity and quality, but we have those subtle hidden things that we are not always willing to surrender. The president could not correlate how his parking space and dinning room had anything to do with removing barriers to improvement.

But, what we learned from the Japanese was that there are many subtle barriers to improvement. They all wear the same uniforms and very rarely do they have a separate office, but I have seen some great executive dining rooms.

18

The Best Factory in the World

*"A great teacher is a great student and
great students are great teachers."*
Rudi

One day I called Dr. Shigeo Shingo and asked him, which one of his clients, in his opinion, had the very best factory in all of Japan. Without hesitation he said it was the Matsushita (Panasonic) Washing Plant in Shizuoka, a little over an hour by bullet train from Tokyo.

> *The Bullet train, in fact, all trains are amazingly on time in Japan. The bullet train called Shinkansen goes at speeds of 300km/h (180 miles per hour). The train cars are sparkling clean, seats comfortable and even the food in the dining car is very good.*

I asked Dr. Shingo if he could arrange a visit for me. He kindly called the plant manager Mr. Fukuda and set up an appointment for me to visit the plant.

My interests at the time were not just to see the manufacturing processes but to also see how well the workers functioned and treated their customers. With Dr. Shingo's blessing I was warmly greeted by Mr. Fukuda and the other senior managers. My first impressions were the cleanliness of the plant grounds, the fresh painting on the plant exterior, the outdoor athletic equipment promoting employee health, the flowers and shrubs, and I remember when I entered the building going through the reception area that every employee in the office, around a dozen people, bowed and greeted me with smiles into their presence.

I was taken to a meeting room, served tea and met with Mr. Fukuda and his team who gave me many details about their facility.[147] They were very proud of the plant and the fact that it was at the time the most productive washing machine plant in the world. I mentioned my particular interest in learning about their people and their development.

Mr. Fukuda told me that they originally hired only people who were very enthusiastic about sports. Of course, they wanted intelligent people but their main concern was their athletic ability. This they felt added to the enthusiastic climate that existed in their facility. In fact, many of the workers did participate in athletics and other competitive activities and were at the time the top company volleyball team in the nation. They were also the Quality Circle champions within Matsushita and also champions within their manufacturing area.

I noticed that when lunch break came many employees first went to the volleyball court or to some of the other athletic areas prior to having their lunch.

On visiting the manufacturing plant, I noticed the punch presses, which applied Dr. Shingo's quick die changing tech-

---

[147] Once I was accepted as a guest, and it wasn't always easy to be accepted as a guest, the Japanese manager always found time, even if just for a few moments, to greet me.

niques, and I was shown many poka-yoke[148] devices invented by the employees to absolutely prevent defects from occurring. Besides each poka-yoke was a card explaining its purpose, and who had invented it.

In front of every employee on the washing machine assembly line was a video screen. Since the line had mixed models, each washing machine being different, the operator could see while they were working the specific instructions and quality standards for each separate machine. Also the video screens were great for sharing news and solving problems together.

I noticed a person's name and picture on every machine. "That is the person in the plant today who can fix that machine. We do not have a maintenance department. Our engineers and workers are taught how to fix the machines. And maybe twice a year we might need some help from the outside."

Imagine a manufacturing plant without a maintenance department operating with super efficiency. They invest in their employees, through training, to raise skill levels to achieve a plant without a maintenance department.

Anything that added costs was attacked. So safety was a very key issue. You could notice the work of safety prevention teams throughout the plant.

Often we wait for a problem and then establish a team to go after the problem. Dr. Fukuda taught me early on that establishing safety teams and letting them roam, letting them look for things that might happen in the plant could be very fruitful. In one case a safety team found some flammable material that could easily explode. It is better to be proactive than reactive.

---

[148] Poka-yoke are mistake-proofing devices created by the employees to prevent defects from occurring.

They looked for new things that might possibly cause injury. As an example, not a single case of carpel tunnel syndrome occurred. In America, I believe there were over 200,000 cases last year of repetitive strain injuries, including carpel tunnel syndrome. Almost all of them could have been prevented if employees in teams observed other employees working. At Matsushita, teams developed checklists[149] to consciously discover potential safety problems before they could possibly occur.

Parts purchased from the outside were delivered to an automated system adjacent to the assembly line, and parts would automatically come down directly to the operators in small carts just prior to the washing machine being assembled.

However, even here nothing is perfect. When an operator discovered a defect the entire line stopped. Supervisors and other workers quickly ran over to the problem and had it fixed within minutes.

At most American plants the whistle would blow at the end of each work day signaling the end of a shift. In Japan often the workers know that they have to finish the production scheduled for their shift and either they would finish early or stay a few minutes later. At many of the Japanese plants we would see electronic counters displaying the goal of the day and the daily production. The worker then knew if they were leaving early or late. It was an excellent motivator to keep people focused on the job.

Imagine the level of respect given to every operator when they have the power to stop the entire plant to insure that not a single defect leaves the plant.

---

[149] Checklists kept by all of the employees are truly wonderful devices to pass the responsibility for improvement to the person doing the job.

Almost every available inch of wall space had been plastered with charts and pictures.   These were the results of their quality teams, their accident prevention teams, and other teams activities that were displayed to keep every one in the plant informed of improvement activities.   As the charts were normally created and maintained by the employees themselves, and scrutinized by senior management, they were very effective.

They had a very intensive Quick and Easy Kaizen system and you could see the hundreds of new improvements ideas implemented by the workers individually and within their teams.

> *Quick and Easy Kaizen is an adaptation of the American suggestion system, but instead of getting one idea every seven years, which is the American average; the average in Japan is two improvement ideas per employee per month.*

> *Quick and Easy Kaizen is not a suggestion system for someone else to implement ideas and it does not place additional burdens on supervisors and senior managers, for the worker that comes up with the idea implements it.*

The Four-Picture Technique

At Panasonic and other Japanese companies we noticed a series of pictures hung up all throughout the plant.   These were pictures of part of the factory or office.   People were then encouraged to make improvements.   A month later another picture would be taken of the exact same area.   The old idea of a 'picture is worth a thousand words' is very true.   A picture gives another perspective of the work place, and also acts as a reminder for the workers to come up with improvement ideas.   And more importantly, this technique works.   When you look at a series of pictures you can see the improvements that were made.

Take a Picture of a Part of the Plant or Office Once a Month

This was the first plant where I saw displayed four pictures side by side.[150]

Once a month a picture was taken of a certain spot in the plant and then people were encouraged to examine the pictures closely and then try to come up with improvements. This was a very simple but powerful graphic reminder that there are almost always opportunities for improvement. To make this system work the workers were encouraged to see these pictures and then to talk about them together.

I noticed multitude of certificates being displayed on the walls and hallways. Obviously, these certificates were there to recognize those people who had taken advanced training courses to improve their skills in some area. This plant was like an on-going university with everyone encouraged to get an advanced degree.

Throughout the plant were specific areas reserved for group meetings. You could see the chairs, tables, a blackboard, and sometimes a rug on the factory floor, and often the meeting areas

---

[150] It is great to display things for people to both be stimulated to improve and to show outsiders, visitors to the plant, the progress that they are making.

would have flowers, green plants, and pictures to make them much more pleasant.

It was a super efficient facility on every level with one sole purpose to serve their customers effectively. The customer was obviously - their prime focus. Continuous surveys were conducted to determine what the customer needed in washing machines to operate efficiently. In Japan, electricity costs are very high so the washing machines were designed with fuzzy logic to determine the needs of washing based on the size and type of the clothes being washed.

I learned from this visit that to be the most productive plant in the world was to build an environment where:

1. **Continuous growth** - people were encouraged to continuously improve their skills and utilize their energy.

2. **Reach the whole human being** - people's personal lives and well-being were always considered through athletic programs and job enrichment activities.

3. **Improvement ideas to eliminate waste** - wastes were continuously attacked through everyone's improvement ideas.

4. **Stay focused on the Customer** - the customer was always the key focus to insure not a single defect ever left the plant.

5. **Innovation** - product technology was continuously improved with the latest features to please and ease

the life of the customer. I saw here the use of fuzzy logic[151] incorporated into a machine.

6.   **Be the Best** - there was a desire that the washing machine would be most competitively priced offering the greatest lasting value.

7.   **Build it in-house** - Most of the parts for the washing machine were made in the plant.[152]

8.   **Synchronization** - trucks would come up to the side of the plant and unload parts in small containers that were feed into an automated parts delivery system that would bring the necessary parts automatically to the exact place on the assembly line where it was needed, at the exact time it was needed. The whole plant was completely synchronized.

9.   **Communication** - every worker on the assembly line had a video monitor in front of them with special instructions, with quality and production statistics to keep them informed of all happenings in the plant. Since the assembly line was mixed-modeled, each washing machine could be a different model.

---

[151] Fuzzy logic provides a simple way to arrive at a definite conclusion based upon vague, ambiguous, imprecise, noisy, or missing input information. Fuzzy logic's approach to control problems mimics how a person would make decisions, only much faster.

[152] Something happened in the mid-eighties where top managers started to re-engineer their companies to only manufacture key parts of the product and outsource the rest. In my opinion this has been shortsighted and companies have been losing a lot of their basic technologies. Even today there is a surge to send work to China – this also might be very shortsighted.

The screen would give the operator specific instructions on what to install or test on that machine.

10. **Ownership** - every manufacturing machine had an individual's picture. It was the face of the person in the plant that knew how to fix that machine. You knew who to call if there were any machine prob lems. The workers were trained to fix machines. There was no separate maintenance department. Maybe once or twice a year they had to call in an outside expert to help fix a machine.

11. **Poka-Yoke** - throughout the plant were hundreds of poka-yoke devices, created by the workers, to absolutely prevent defects from occurring. In front of each device was a small tag with the creator's name.

12. **Wall charts** - every wall was filled with charts, drawings, statistics showing their improvement activities. I particularly liked seeing four pictures. On the first of a month a picture was taken of some part of the plant. One month later another picture was taken showing the exact same scene. You could easily see all of the improvements made by the team in the last month. Even though this was one of the best plants they still had intensive improvement activities always going on.

13. **A spotless plant** - the plant was spotless; nothing appeared to be out of place. It even smelled good very unusual for a manufacturing facility.

14.   **Changeovers** - in the machine shop I saw changeovers conducted in seconds.

15.   **Empowerment** - while standing and watching the line, I saw the assembly line stop as they pulled off a washing machine that they felt could have had a potential problem.

It was a very interesting visit for me and their labor hours were the lowest of any washing machine plant in the world. I can understand now how it is possible to have both a super efficient manufacturing plant and also a place where people's concerns were also met. When you focus on manufacturing excellence, on the needs of your customers, and also on creating a facility that stimulates your employees, you can become what Dr. Shingo called, "The best manufacturing plant in the world."

19

Getting to Know Dr. Shingo

"Those who are not dissatisfied will never make any progress." - **Dr. Shigeo Shingo**

Mrs. Shingo told me a wonderful story about Dr. Shingo. During World War II, Dr. Shingo was a consultant and industrial engineer working in Taiwan in the ship building industry. After the war he became a consultant working with Japan Management Associations. After a few years he quit. He was married and had children but he resigned for he felt that JMA was charging their customers too much money for his time. It is not that the customers ever complained. It was just that Dr. Shingo had a very unique moral system.

His life was devoted to teaching others to improve, to be more efficient and effective with their processes to serve their customers better. He felt that his time also had a fair market value and he insisted on receiving what he considered as being fair.

Imagine the world's greatest manufacturing genius, saving industry billions and billions of dollars, establishing a fair criteria for his own worth. I never met another person like him on this globe.

On one of Dr. Shingo's visits to America we set up a two-day seminar in Cambridge, Mass. He taught more to the style of a Japanese audience than for Americans. In Japan, the teachers are highly respected and they are known for lecturing with very few questions coming from the students.

Listening to a lecturer who has very little humor and doesn't allow any interaction with the audience he can easily put me to sleep. Shingo was brilliant, the real great manufacturing master, but he was teaching new concepts, not so easily accepted by a US audience, and he was teaching through a translator, which added to the difficulty.

I had invited some of the top authors and professors from Harvard University to be our guests to hear Dr. Shingo. Well, on the first day during the question and answer session a participant asked a very simple question of Dr. Shingo. The question really disturbed Shingo for to him it meant that the person asking the question did not listen to what he was saying. Shingo, known for his brilliance and not his patience said, "That is a stupid question!"

It gathered a few chuckles and great embarrassment for the questioner. It was, of course, wrong for Dr. Shingo to say this in front of a large American audience not used to this kind of behavior. But what surprised me even more was that the professors from Harvard did not come back for the second day of the seminar.

Dr. Shingo in 1946 was wresting with the problem of process versus operation. This was the beginning of the JIT system. Most manufacturing at the time (and for decades thereafter) focused on maximizing each machine center, each department, with very little concern for the overall effectiveness of the entire manufacturing process.

If your job was to stamp out 5000 fenders little thought was given to the next process, which needed those fenders. Our engineering teachers taught us the concept of economic lot size (EOQ). Since every process had some form of set-up costs, original equipment costs, and maintenance costs we were taught by our professors that the best way to amortize those costs, were to keep that machine producing as many parts they could. The idea was that the inventory produced was a real asset/value to the company and that it would eventually be sold to customers. As real assets, which included the value added – the cost of material, equipment, and labor was placed proudly on the balance sheet even if eventually the assets had to be sold at a discount or even discarded as scrap.

I originally was a public accountant and had even passed the CPA exam. It took me a long time to realize that the accountants were part of the problem. Accountants insisted that we look at inventory as a great asset. In fact, as you go from a company with high inventory to a lean environment, you reduce inventory, freeing up a lot of cash. (You also pay the penalty of coming up with additional profits for Uncle Sam).

JIT attacked the entire theory of economic order quantity (EOQ). Dr. Shingo taught us and demonstrated that set-up was not a 'given.' It could be reduced drastically and we then could produce one-piece at a time with no real need for EOQ calculations.

I once took Dr. Shingo to lecture at Yale University where we met the professor who taught production engineering. Dr. Shingo confronted him and said, "Do you still teach economic order quantity (EOQ)[153]?" The professor shyly said, "Yes." The saying that you can't teach old dogs new tricks exists at every level of our society. As we drove away from Yale we both had a good laugh.

Over the years I have brought many Japanese consultants to America to teach, consult and deliver presentations to our conferences. I paid them whatever they asked for, some wanted $1,000 per day, some $2,000 per day, some $3,000 per day and the next group I will write about will insist on $5,000 per day plus first class airfare, and weekends on the golf course.

Dr. Shingo asked for $3,000 per day and once said, "Norman, I want you to treat me fairly. Money is not why I travel the world to teach, not at all. What is also important to me is that you make money with me." No one ever has ever cared if I made or lost money. They were brilliant people who had much to share with the world but Shingo was the real humanist. I remember working with many people, one professor I recall just looked at me as a vehicle to make money and never

---

[153] EOQ is essentially an accounting formula that determines the point at which the combination of order costs and inventory carrying costs are the least. The result is the most cost effective quantity to order. In purchasing this is known as the order quantity, in manufacturing it is known as the production lot size.

considered for a single moment if I was doing well in the arrangement. Shingo might have been at times on the factory floor real tough but I felt that he treated me as his fourth son. I felt that I lost a father when he died.

20

The Birth of the Kaizen Blitz

"A genuine leader is not a searcher for consensus but a molder of consensus." – **Martin Luther King, Jr.**

I met both Iwata and Nakao in Japan. Iwata was Ohno's assistant at Toyota Gosei and Nakao[154] worked at Taiho Kogyo. They were two people from the ten that Ohno used to convert all of the top tier Toyota suppliers to JIT. They wanted to start their own consulting company and I volunteered to help them get started in America. They came to one of our conferences to speak, and I also got them two consulting assignments, one an AMP plant and the other at Snap On Tools.

The plant manager at AMP said, " It was the best day of my life," but I couldn't convince either company to continue to work with us – imagine the millions of dollars lost by the company's unwillingness to learn new things.[155]

---

[154] Iwata and Nakao started Shingijutsu and brought Kaizen Blitz to America.

[155] Learning new things, this is the challenge to 'stick your neck out on a limb.' Most people are afraid of change and feel powerless to follow their 'gut' feelings. They are petrified of making a mistake. As long as other people are doing it they feel safe to 'jump on the bandwagon.' Just look at the Six Sigma today. Six Sigma is good to do but there is a middle management disease based on fear of being different and doing what is right, which I hope will stop being so contagious.

I did meet with the plant manager, George Koenigsaecker, at Jake Brake, a Danaher company in Bloomfield, Connecticut and arranged to run at his plant the first Kaizen Blitz. We initially called it 'Five Days and One Night,' meaning that you would learn and work for five days and get very little sleep during the week.

We promoted the workshop to our mailing list for fifty participants, sold it for $5000 per participant for the week, and completely sold it out. We gave Jake Brake five free attendees for letting us use their plant.

Iwata gave the initial lecture on a Monday morning, teaching the principles of the Toyota Production System.

The next day we all went into the factory in teams of around 10 people. Each team looked at one manufacturing process with the goal of rearranging the machines into manufacturing cells. We looked at the process carefully, each person taking one part of the process to study in detail. We calculated the cycle time, the time it was taking to do each job and then we determined the takt time, the time it should take to produce the product Just-In-Time. We especially looked at improving the value adding ratio and the elimination of wastes.[156]   We were also taught how to complete standard work sheets.

> ***Standard work sheets precisely show all of the tasks of a job including walking, and the time necessary for each task. They also show the sequence of tasks, jigs and tools needed, and the location of stock. They are used to show both the current process and the***

---

[156] This process is now called Value Stream Mapping whereby you follow the production flow and map out all of the value adding and non-value adding steps. The goal is to reduce, even eliminate, all of the wastes – the non-value adding steps.

future process with cycle times and takt times. The Standard Work sheets are used to map out the new processes to make sure that every operation will be done within takt time. Standard Work sheets detail the motion of the operator, the sequence of operations and how long it takes to do each task. It is used to determine opportunities for improvement. As we improve we revise the Standard Worksheets.

On Wednesday morning we went into the plant and completely mapped out five different processes showing the cycle times[157] and the takt times. This third day we started to plan how we would move the machines, how we would position the workers, and listed the many problems that had to be solved for the process to be run smoothly and takt time. Problems immediately rose to the surface.

Mr. Ohno taught us that inventory is like a river and that as a river it covers up of the problems in manufacturing. If there is a machine problem causing some downtime, the inventory stacked between processes can be used by subsequent processes until the machine problem is corrected.

When you focus on lowering the river, the mountains of inventory, problems pop up and have to be solved. This workshop forced problems to surface, and then be corrected.

On Wednesday night we moved 50 machines into their five machine cells. While doing this we also listed all of the problems and potential problems that had to be addressed to have the new lines running properly. The problems would be work projects for company engineers, managers and workers to solve over the next few months. The list was long.

---

[157] Cycle time – the actual time that it was taking the plant to produce the parts.

If we had quality problems, or people problems, or electrical problems, etc., we could always use the stacks of inventory to keep the plant going. But in Lean, in theory, when operating properly there is no inventory as a buffer between operations. A quality problem would stop maybe ten machines from working.

We were intentionally creating chaos – a good thing by the way, for when you do shake up things you can bring marvelous change to a company. But people should be treated more respectfully, and told what will happen, and be assured that they will all be trained and that everyone will be able to do the job well. It would be good to tell people that the change coming is not going to lose any jobs. Unfortunately, Lean does make manufacturing more efficient and many jobs have been lost in the US. In Japan people were protected by lifetime employment and are therefore willing to accept change.

On Thursday morning, after staying up after midnight moving the machines, all the participants began to work with the Jake Brake employees to explain how they now were going to work in their new cells. Many of the workers looked to be in a state of 'shock,' not knowing what was to be expected of them. The workers were not part of the teams. They really had no idea that overnight their work was going to change so radically.

In reality we treated the workers like pawns. Ohno had a reputation for being ruthless, callous with little concern for people at all. The net result would have been a much better experience for people if they were informed in advance about the changes and were also involved in the training along with their managers. Where they were used to running just one machine in the machine cell they would be expected to run many machines one after the other. Probably the biggest change for the workers were to stand not sit while they work.

For most of the engineers and managers in the workshop the most exciting aspect was the standard worksheets and rearranging the factory into work cells, but to me it was Jidoka which gave us an opportunity to look differently at the human being in the work environment.

For the past 100 years, people have been looked at as extensions of machines. People do work in factories today that machines as yet cannot do. In fact, today, I hear managers say that if we can't automate it then send it to China.

On Friday morning the five groups presented their case studies.

It was a glorious event probably, the most important moment of transition in American manufacturing history. The amazing thing is that it worked. The ex-Toyota managers leading the training had spent years working under Mr. Taiichi Ohno, former VP/manufacturing at Toyota, and Dr. Shigeo Shingo, independent consultant and the real brains behind Lean. This workshop was used effectively with Toyota and their suppliers to drive Just-In-Time (Lean) throughout their organization.

Of course, Jake Brake was in chaos for the next three months, late on their shipments, and all kinds of problems arose. But after those three months, the company was able to reduce inventory substantially, reduce defects, and deliver products to the customer exactly when they needed them.

We continued to run these Kaizen events in Japan and also at various other Danaher plants for the next two years. These events launched the careers of the famous Shingijutsu group in the United States. They have been very successful and

Kaizen Blitz's have been sweeping the country.   I read where
Freudenberg-NOK had run over 1000 events.

At the Jake Brake event we were taught a number of very
powerful concepts to make lean work: Jidoka (also referred to as
autonomation), adding human judgment to automated equipment,
the analogy of inventory acting like a river (hiding most manufacturing problems), and the use of the standard work sheets to improve the processes by rearranging the factory primarily into work
cells.

In the old "smokestack" factory, where machines built
enormous piles of inventory, the worker was there as an attendant
to watch the machines, to load and unload materials, to make adjustments, and insure that the machines were operating efficiently.
But rarely was the worker asked to think or make independent decisions to improve productivity and quality.

*Shortly after the first trip to Japan I remember
my visit to a cable manufacturer in Connecticut. I was
invited by the plant manager to see if I could suggest
ways for them to improve the quality of their products.
As I walked around the plant, I noticed a young lady
working at a machine that allowed her to spin two cables at the same time. She was fast and highly skilled.*

*I was introduced to the operator and began
talking to her, questioning her about the quality of the
cables being produced. While she was working, I
asked her if she had ever found any defects? She replied that when she first came to the plant (around nine
years earlier), she noticed some defects on a cable and
immediately stopped the machine. She then wrote up a
red tag and placed it on the cable and went back to
work spinning more cable. She related that, a short
while later, her supervisor came by, noticed the red tag,*

> *yanked it off the cable and said, "What are you trying to do, take away the job of the quality manager? Your job is to spin the cable and his job is to find the defects."[158]*

In the new lean machine cells the worker also loads the machine with material, but the machine is capable of holding the part while it is working on it. Visualize this: the worker loads a piece of material into a machine, and the machine holds and automatically drills the part. The worker then picks up the drilled part, which was completed in an earlier cycle, and takes it to the next machine where a fixture can hold the part to be further worked on. The worker then walks around the cell loading, unloading, looking at the part, and insuring the accuracy of the process.

In the old system the worker loaded the machine then just stood there and watched. Logically we are taught that it is all right for the worker to stand, watch, and not work as long as the machine is running. **In the lean system it is the reverse logic, the machine can stand idle but the worker continually moves.**

> *This would drive me bananas. I visited the Ford Engine plant in Cleveland where they spent over two billion dollars installing world-class machines, mostly made in Germany. The line was almost fully automated (except for pockets that required workers attendance) but often the worker sat by the machine reading a magazine or newspaper waiting for an abnormality to occur. What a waste of human talent!*

When operators are alerted to variability in quality and machine performance, and when they detect an actual problem that is occurring, they have the ability to alter the manufacturing process (even to the extent of stopping their machine).

---

[158] Thankfully, the times have changed for the better.

As I walked through a Toyota factory I saw large light boards with numbers hanging from the ceiling. Whenever a worker detected a problem, they were encouraged to pull a string or press a button that would at first cause a yellow light to go on which could be seen by almost every other worker in the plant. This yellow light alerted the supervisors and other managers of a potential problem. If the problem was unsolvable for the worker, he/she would again pull the cord or hit a button, which would cause red lights to go on, an alarm to go off, and all the machines in the factory would stop. The supervisors and other workers would then run over to help. From these lights they knew exactly what process was in trouble.

Thus one worker in trouble could stop everyone else in the plant from working. This Jidoka system forced supervision, management and the worker to get to the root cause of the problem so that it would never happen again. Ohno did not like work to stop, but recognized that by applying this type of pressure on people, the system would drive down defects and problems.

Imagine the power, the respect that this gives to every worker in the factory, with a policy that says we are willing to stop the entire plant from working rather than to allow a single defect to be passed on to the customer.

Jidoka is a strong part of lean manufacturing and I wonder how many American companies have adapted this part of Lean to their setting. The assurance of top quality for Toyota's automobiles is maintained through 'Jidoka.' This defect detection system automatically or manually stops the production operation and/or equipment whenever an abnormal or defective condition arises. Directing attention to the stopped equipment and the worker who stopped the operation, forces improvements to be made immediately. The Jidoka system shows faith in the worker as a thinker and allows all workers the right to stop the line on which they are working.

A good example of Jidoka is the Toyota power loom developed in the early 20th century. A problem existed with shuttlecocks that would stick and create defects in the cloth being produced. Before power looms, a weaver would be able to remedy any such problems before proceeding, but power looms continued mindlessly on, producing unacceptable quality that required the cloth to be unraveled and backed up, boosting costs and making quality suspect. The Toyota loom incorporated a simple stopper that was activated by a sticking shuttlecock, and thus the machine became more 'human,' and 'knew' when to stop. The end result was a *reliable* system that was cheaper to operate and produced *the expected quality*. Jidoka prevents products with unacceptable quality from continuing in the process.

We were taught how to use our stop watches to time out a process both on cycle time, what was being done, and also on takt time, the time that each operation should take for the product to be produced on time. Then the entire production areas were re-arranged to one-piece flow.

The Kaizen Blitz works very effectively. Talented people form teams and analyze a process and take out the waste. Many engineers and managers know what waste is, but they are reluctant to go out and do this on their own. It was a great event.

What teams of people achieved through the Kaizen Blitz process was truly a miracle.

21
Finding Books and Meeting Kazuhiro Uchiyama

Everybody wants to do something to help, but nobody wants to be the first. - **Pearl Bailey**

On my third study mission to Japan in early 1982 I went to the Japan Management Association (JMA) to meet with their chief editor,[159] Mr. Kazuhiro Uchiyama. The JMA, as mentioned earlier, published and distributed Dr. Shingo's green book. Dr. Shingo paid for the translation of his book and used JMA to distribute it.

I visited JMA looking for new books to publish whenever I took a study mission to Japan. I got to know Mr. Uchiyama, but initially he gave me a 'rough' time. Often I would write to him but never would he answer me back. It was very frustrating for me. Years later when we did become very good friends, I asked him why he never answered my letters. "Quite simply," he said, "I don't read English."

Actually, Uchiyama did not fully cooperate with me at the beginning until Dr. Shingo said, "Uchiyama-san, I want you to work with Norman Bodek, for he will publish all of my future

---

[159] Uchiyama's title was assistant editor but he really was in charge of their book selection and production process.

books in English." Then Uchiyama slowly became a real friend and helped me discover some really wonderful books from both JMA and from other publishing companies in Japan.[160]

Dr. Shingo arranged with Uchiyama for us to publish the SMED book in English at the same time the Japanese version was to be published in Japan. As soon as the Japanese manuscript was completed Dr. Shingo offered me a copy, but Uchiyama insisted that JMA do the translation. I was very reluctant to allow this to happen knowing the 'Jangalese' done on the original 'green' book. Uchiyama also asked for $12,000 for the translation. At the time it sounded much too high but I didn't know what my options were.

Well around three months later I get a copy of the English translation and it was a 'horror.' I knew that the information in the book was 'gangbusters' but I also knew that it would be cheaper for me to have the entire book retranslated then to have this Japanese version edited. I told this to Uchiyama. Now, I felt as if I was stuck to have to pay for the Japanese translation, which I would not use. I asked Uchiyama to be frank with me and to tell me what he paid for the translation. He did. He said, '$6,000.' I was amazed that he was going to make a profit on the translation, for he was also going to share the royalty with Dr. Shingo.

I was told of the Japanese idea of 'saving face,' so I told Uchiyama that I would pay the $6,000, but we never used a single page of that translation. Funny at the time, as I already told you I was a novice at book publishing. Also I knew that the average book in America cost around $25,000 to publish including editing, royalty advances, printing, etc. But, because I was such a neo-

---

[160] For the first few years in Japan, I had a rough time working with publishers who mostly treated me as a 'gaijin,' foreigner. But, when Shingo told Uchiyama to work with me, he did, and Uchiyama helped me open all of the other doors to the Japanese publishing industry.

phyte it eventually cost us close to $100,000 to publish this new book.

Because of the high cost of publishing and also the perception that we had a limited audience interested in reading *A Revolution in Manufacturing, the SMED System,* we put a retail price of $65.00 per book, more than twice the average cost of a business book at the time.

We started to sell the book to our newsletter subscribers. I received a couple of calls a few months later from consultants: one was from a partner in one of the big eight accounting firms who told me I had a 'lot of gall,' to sell the book for so much money. I thought this was strange, because he was using the book to charge his clients over $2,000 a day for his consulting, while the book only cost him $65.00. I received a second call from a consultant in Chicago, who told me how great the book was and that he was going to make a million dollars off it. He probably did.

The book eventually sold over 100,000 copies. It shows you that when you have a really good product, price will not stand in the way.

Dr. Shingo, on his own, put together a slide set with pictures and words in English on the SMED system. It was a little crude (with Japanese cartoon characters), but conveyed the real keys and the power of the SMED system. I distributed these slide sets for him and JMA and sold them for around $750 per set. We sold 'tons' of them.

I visited Uchiyama on every one of my trips to Japan. He would spread out a dozen or so books on the table in front of me and talk about the attributes of each book. To me they were all 'Greek', as I couldn't read a word of Japanese. It was hard enough for me to figure out how to eat at a restaurant.[161] I would listen carefully to Uchiyama and also to my intuition and finally selected, actually gambled on, some books to translate.   Luckily over the years I was 80% right – 20% of the books (once translated) I couldn't publish.

Another Funny Story

Uchiyama and Mr. Sai, manager of international affairs at JMA, took me to a Karaoke[162] bar. It was a private club in the Ginza[163] area of Tokyo. We sat in a small room on the fifth floor of the building, in a room with a small bar filled with smoke and a TV hung from the ceiling.

Since I was an American, they played very old American songs[164], and everyone started to sing. To keep them happy I also began to sing until Sai, a little drunk at the time, put his arm around me and said, "Norman I am so happy that you did not embarrass us for you sing just terribly." Well, 'you can't win them all.'

One of the books that Uchiyama recommended was *The Canon Production System,* which turned out to be a really great book. But he also told me to translate a book by the current chairman of JMA, which sold over 100,000 copies in Japan, titled *Man-*

---

[161] Most Japanese restaurants have a plastic display of their food on plates either in front of the restaurant or in their front window. It never looked that inviting but at least you would get some idea of what to order – the menus in Japanese were useless to me.

[162] Karaoke is a Japanese word meaning 'empty orchestra' or singing without live instruments.

[163] Ginza area is filled with stores, restaurants and bars with probably the most expensive real estate property in the world.

[164] The songs were really the old ones. I guess they used these to avoid any copyright infringement.

ager Revolution. I think we sold only a little over 1000 copies – not a profitable venture.

22

Shingo the Teacher

"Concerns for man and his fate must always form the chief interest of all technical endeavors. Never forget this in the midst of your diagrams and equations." – **Albert Einstein**

Whenever Shingo would teach, he, like Ohno, would only talk about the basics.   Ohno would talk about the river of inventory and Shingo would like to talk about SMED and Poka-yoke.

Dr. Shingo created a slide set to teach the principles of SMED.   After lecturing for an hour we would show the slides. They were crudely done but showed us what was possible, giving many different ideas on how to reduce changeovers.

A few years later we discovered a quick changeover game developed in Australia that we used in our seminars.   We let groups get together to play the game and try in the classroom to understand Shingo's principles of fast changeovers. It worked. In the class students easily reduced the changeover time showing them what was possible with the equipment in their factory.

The SMED training course we developed was another 'goldmine' for us.   Dave, our consultant spent almost two years of his life just teaching one customer, Kimberly Clark, the process. We ran over 110 workshops for them all over the world.   It allowed Kimberly Clark to reduce their lot sizes while continuing to deliver to Wal-Mart their Kleenex tissues Just-in-time.

> *Dave, our training consultant for Kimberly Clark, did something very unique. First he convinced a senior manager at corporate the value of the SMED workshop, then Dave called a plant manager with the senior manager's blessing to set up a workshop at the plant site. Dave did not stop there. He asked the plant manager to give him the names of supervisors and other key people in the plant and Dave called them all to set up the workshop. Curiously, even though Dave ran 110 workshops he was never allowed into a Kimberly Clark plant. All the workshops were run in classrooms outside of the shop floor.*

Poka-yoke was Shingo's second favorite topic. He wanted to ensure defects would not be made. He developed a very careful process to eliminate virtually all defects from occurring. For example:

1.   A worker adds value by assembling a product.

2.   The worker double-checks himself or herself before passing the part to the next process. He called this self-checking.

3.   The subsequent worker first checks to see that the previous process was done correctly. This, he called successive checking.

4.   And after final assembly the part was tested and inspected. Dr. Shingo wanted to ensure 100% inspection with 100% accuracy.

The above would eliminate many defects but some would still get through. Shingo then looked for a way to be 100% sure that defects could not be produced. Now, all companies have this as a goal but rarely is it achieved. One reason is that companies have limited resources, not enough engineers. But, Shingo said, "Let us ask every worker, not just the engineers, to come up with ideas on how to totally eliminate defects."

At first Dr, Shingo called his method of enlisting all of the workers to find methods or fixtures that would prevent defects as Baka-yoke, (Bata-yoke in Japanese means fool proofing). He used this term until a young lady in one plant started to cry saying, "I am not a fool." He immediately changed Bakta-yoke to Poka-yoke (Poka-yoke means mistake proofing).

For example, if an operator could put a part upside down and drill a hole on the wrong side of the part, putting a small notch on one side of the metal plate and creating a simple fixture to recognize the notch this prevented the operator from placing the part incorrectly.

At United Electric in Waltham, MA, they set up a poka-yoke initiative whereby one engineer, Paul Plant, worked with the operators to help them build the necessary fixtures. Within a year they had built hundreds of these simple devices to eliminate defects, with almost all of the ideas coming from the workers themselves.

As you walked through the plant you could see examples of the Poka-yoke devices with the name of the worker who came up with the idea. Paul was a resource for workers to help them get their ideas implemented. He did not come up with the ideas for them – they were the worker's ideas.

While visiting a Komatsu factory, I watched a worker insert bolts into an Excavator with an electric hand-held device. When the bolt was secure, a bell went off. If there was not enough torque on the bolt, the bell would not ring, telling the worker that the bolt required further tightening.

In another plant I saw a worker removing chips to put into a part. He was required to pull out the chips in an exact sequence. If the sequence was incorrect, or he missed a chip, the part could not be released to the next station. The poka-yoke devices used were very simple, inexpensive sensors to detect if the parts were taken out properly.

At a packaging station, simple sensors were used to detect booklets and instructional manuals, to ensure they were placed into each box.

23

Never Take No for an Answer

Real knowledge is to know the extent of one's ignorance."
Confucius

One year we invited Dr. Shingo for a three-week trip to America. His first stop was to work with Omark Industries in Oregon, then off to their plant in Wisconsin, next to Toronto to run a two-day seminar for me, then on to General Motors in Detroit, and the University of Nebraska.

Omark had established a Shingo prize[165] to stimulate continuous improvement between their plants. Milwaukie, Oregon was the headquarters for Omark. Dr. Shingo would go there to work with the officers, managers and engineers. This particular year the internal Shingo prize went to an Omark plant in Wisconsin.

Dr. Shingo spent only a day in Oregon, and then flew to Wisconsin to give the Shingo prize to that plant. From Wisconsin he then flew to Toronto. I was in Toronto and he was traveling with his interpreter, Noriko Hosoyamada, and Mrs. Shingo. He arrived in Toronto about 8:00PM and was very hungry. He said that he could not eat anything in Wisconsin.

---

[165] The Omark Shingo prize is a wonderful idea, whereby each plant at Omark would compete yearly for the most improved plant.

He was teaching a flexible manufacturing system, but when it came to his own food there was very little flexibility. He would not eat at a fast food restaurant. His preference was, of course, Japanese food. When desperate, he would accept some Chinese food, and if close to starving he might have some spaghetti at an Italian restaurant. Well, driving through Wisconsin he could not find a single Japanese restaurant, or Chinese, or even an Italian restaurant. I think he had only an egg and a bowl of rice cooked by his wife the whole day. Luckily that night in Toronto we went to a Japanese restaurant to give him sufficient nourishment before his two-day seminar.

Shingo gave, as usual, a very good seminar. And two days later I took Mr. and Mrs. Shingo and Noriko to the Toronto airport to catch a plane to Detroit. When we got to the airport, customs would not let him back into America. He had a tourist visa not a business visa. Portland officials had recorded his purpose as 'consulting with GM', which was in conflict with his visa requirements.

I didn't know what to do. So I put him on a plane to Windsor, Canada (across the river from Detroit) and I told Noriko to rent a car and drive into Detroit the next morning.

A good idea – but it didn't work. Customs had it all in the computer, and when he got to customs in Windsor, they wouldn't let him through. Luckily Noriko reached me at the hotel in Toronto and presented me with the problem.

Well, whenever confronted with a problem I always like to call the headman,[166] so I called the White House. I knew Roger

---

[166] Calling the headman – I once wanted to speak to the president of Macy's department store. I asked for information, called a Macy's store, and spoke to someone in customer service and was told that I could never get to the president; in fact she did not even know whom the president was or where his office was. I

Potter, Director of the White House Office of Policy Development in the Reagan Administration who once keynoted a past conference for me, and I thought he could help, but he was not at the White House that day. I then asked for the head of immigration and got the secretary. I told her that the world's greatest consultant was stopped at the border. She didn't know what to do.

Being totally frustrated, I called the customs agent in Windsor and said, "Look you are holding up the most important manufacturing consultant in the world. General Motors is waiting for him. I just called the White House and the chief of immigration to handle this." He said, "Is my ass going to be in a sling." I said, "If you don't get Dr. Shingo across the border in the next ten minutes you are a goner."

Miraculously, he let them through and Shingo was able to deliver the lecture on time. Miracles do work if you just get out of the way and give them a chance to happen.

Not the end of the story, when Shingo got home, his son (who works at Toyota) was pretty annoyed that his father was working with the 'enemy.' Shingo had to promise never to work with a Toyota competitor again.

To me the great lesson was to never take a 'no' for an answer.

---

asked for her supervisor. The supervisor also did not know the president's name or location. 'Believe it or not' but I made 20 telephone calls to reach the president's secretary and an hour later the president called me back saying, "I must speak to the person who had to make 20 calls to reach me." It was a nice conversation but I couldn't convince him to use me as a consultant – subsequently Macy's went into bankruptcy. Maybe, just maybe, I could have helped.

24

Introduction to TPM[167] – Another Billion Dollar idea

*"To believe your own thought, to believe
that what is true for you in your private
heart is true for all men—that is genius."*
Ralph Waldo Emerson

One day I was at the offices of Japan Management Associations (JMA) meeting with Mr. Uchiyama, assistant editor, and the publisher of Dr. Shingo's books. He said, "Norman, come with me. I want to introduce you to the people at the Japan Institute Plant Maintenance (JIPM) office. I had no knowledge about them. I never heard about JIPM. I didn't know what they did. And frankly I was not really interested in meeting people who just worked with 'grease.'[168] Up to that moment I had no appreciation at all to the real value of what maintenance did in a factory. I just didn't see at the time how maintenance fit into the overall scope of advanced Japanese management, especially the Toyota Production System.

But I trusted Uchiyama, and followed him to the offices of JIPM. That day, like so many others in Japan, was completely serendipitous; I discovered new and powerful things just by staying

---

[167] TPM = Total Productive Maintenance
[168] At this time I did not understand the ability required and the real value of trained maintenance people. They are important keys to make Lean work.

open and not saying 'No.' It was my naiveté. Maybe my ignorance of a subject has allowed me to be successful. My travels to Japan have been hard, but what wonderful gifts I have been given. Remember, I can't read or speak a word of Japanese. It is like I have this wonderful patron saint that just keeps guiding me.

Uchiyama brings me to this little tiny office at the JMA building and I meet with one of the managers there. This was a really strange meeting. It was very brief. The secretary general of JIPM hands me two books by Seiichi Nakajima: *Introduction to TPM: Total Productive Maintenance* and *TPM Development Program: Implementing Total Productive Maintenance*. There was no real discussion between us, for I did not know anything about TPM. I thanked Uchiyama and put the books into my briefcase.

It took me quite awhile to appreciate TPM, to understand that when you have cell manufacturing (whereby groups of machines are aligned together into one-piece flow) that when one machine stops or breaks down that all the machines in the cell must stop and wait until the one machine is fixed. This puts enormous pressure on maintenance and the operator to insure that those machines do not go down. If you have frequent breakdowns, JIT or lean just doesn't work.

I negotiated a contract for the books, and when I returned to America I gave the two TPM books to a Japanese teacher at Harvard University to translate for me. Believe me, once again I did not know what I was doing. You know the old saying, 'Ignorance is bliss,' was surely the case this time. For here I was spending tens of thousands of dollars without knowing what I was getting. I figured that since the translation was coming from a Harvard teacher it must be good – boy was I wrong.

A few months later I received one of the translations the

larger of the two books, and an invoice for around $25,000. I started to read the TPM book and tears started to roll down my face. I could not clearly understand TPM. The book was not at all clear. I felt sick.

However, grace was still on my side. I sent the translation to Noriko, my first translator in Japan. A few days later Noriko wired back to tell me the translator was leaving things out and was not accurate at all.

I was livid, but I bit the bullet. I didn't say a word to the Harvard teacher, paid her invoice in full, and was not too critical of her. Then I gave the book to Dr. Drew Dillon, professor at Yale University Language School, to totally retranslate. Drew was great, a master of many languages. The books, though rather expensive to translate, turned out to be a gold mine for my company and also for America. TPM is a vital and needed part for any successful Lean system.

TPM is a new way of looking at maintenance. A new machine is considered, in Japan, to be in its worst state, to be continuously improved and kept up to date as if new. The 'P' in TPM stands for **Productive:** not post-active (reactive), but pre-active (proactive). The goal of TPM is to keep the machine functioning in top performance, looking at every machine like we look at an airplane.

The Boeing 747 airplane first delivered in January 1970 is still flying internationally, 34 years later. Douglas DC 3's are still flying after 67 years in the air. How many of your machines on the factory floor are still operating at such peak performance?

Breakdowns should never occur, for they should be anticipated and prevented before they happen.[169] TPM promotes

---

[169] Just like the airplane, a machine, is not allowed to malfunction.

autonomous maintenance, through day-to-day activities – each machine operator, like a pilot or an airline mechanic, uses a checklist while working with their machines to insure that machines are operating at peak performance.   The worker checks daily, looking carefully at all of the gages, making sure the machine looks new, like a Navy ship before inspection. TPM promotes group activities, which dramatically increases productivity and quality, improves equipment life cycle and broadens the base of every employee's knowledge and skill.

Luckily, a few years later I found a training course in Japan called, 'Maintenance Miracle,' and like 'Five Days and One Night – Kaizen Blitz.' We ran the course at an American factory with Japanese masters, and taught it right on the factory floor, and it was once again 'gangbusters.'

This time we charged a little less money then the Kaizen Blitz event, $3,750 for the week per attendee but we filled it up with close to fifty attendees.   The attendees were taught in the classroom the principles of TPM, and then taken out to the factory floor to apply the principles.

During the week, the attendees were taught the principles of autonomous maintenance, fundamentally cleaning and inspecting techniques. After each morning classroom session, after learning some new ideas about how teams can work effectively to eliminate the causes of machine malfunctions, the attendees moved to the factory floor. On the floor, they would lock out a machine and then assign each member tasks. The target was to bring this machine up to a point of perfection.

After the day's session, working on the floor, the team continued to work in their classroom late into the night. No one made them work late. They just got caught up with the experience of learning.

During the summary session at the end of the week's activities, each member of the team presented what they and the team accomplished. They expressed what the week's event meant to them personally. I was amazed at how much was accomplished in such a short period of time.

One group found close to fifty abnormalities with one being so major that if not corrected would have caused the entire loss of a machine worth close to $350,000.

I remember sitting and listening to the final summary session on the morning of the last day. An Ezell Ramsey, an operator from a steel mill, LTV, in Gary, Indiana stood and told the entire audience about his week. "It was the best team learning experience of my life." Imagine!

It brought tears to my eyes. Here was a week's training that opened his energy in a whole new way. It allowed him to be part of a team where he participated equally with others, managers, supervisors, technicians, etc. His voice was equal. He learned from doing. Instead of just tending a machine, watching it all day, pressing buttons, having very little responsibility, rarely participating in the management process, this week he was fully recognized by a peer group of factory workers.

I then realized that only through team activities would we have a chance to change the work environment. The old structure of managers and supervisors telling people what to do, controlling their activities, and limiting worker's participation in the improvement process was archaic and had to change.

In summary we:

1.   Took off all of the covers from the machines.

2.   Cleaned the inside of the machines – imagine paying $3,750 to attend a course and then end up washing someone else's dirty old machines. Reminded me of Tom Sawyer getting people to white wash his fence and getting paid for it.

3.   We removed the oil pans from under the machines – the Japanese master told us machines should be made not to leak oil. We also want to put pressure on to keep the machines as if they were always brand new.

4.   We color-coded all of the pipes to show what they carried and which direction the fluid went.

5.   We color-coded the wires to indicate what they were for.

6.   The gages were made more visible and effective by marking in color the correct operating range.

7.   We tagged the machine indicating all of the abnormalities or minor problems to be fixed.

8.   Daily check lists were created for operators to use before turning on their machines – this was to ensure that the machine would always be kept in perfect condition, and that early signs of trouble would be detected.

It was a glorious event, a very important part of the Toyota Production System. If one machine malfunctions the whole cell goes down. We understood immediately how critical TPM was to the overall success of the Toyota Production System. I did not know this when I first picked up the TPM books in Japan.

Subsequently, I translated about a dozen books from JIPM, started a TPM newsletter, developed a number of training courses and ran TPM conferences – at one conference a few year's later 1000 attendees came.

The foundation of TPM is that machines are in their worst condition when they are brand new.

With TPM we expand beyond the typical maintenance functions to coordinate activities with JIT. To do this, JIPM came up with The TPM Loss Structure – 16 Major Losses to study[170] and to eliminate:

1. **Failures, breakdowns, major machine stoppages** – We view each machine like an airplane that can never malfunction, and we learn to do this through our team activities involving all employees.

2. **Setups** – goal is first less then 10 minutes, but eventually to have one touch exchanges. Maybe you have some old 'screw machines' that you just can't turn over quickly – so dedicate them to one process, and continue to find ways to reduce those set-up times on all of the other machines.

3. **Cutting tools/Jig changes** – all tools should be in perfect condition; every tool has an

---

[170] Everyone in the company should be part of one or more study groups to improve productivity and quality.

exact place, clearly marked, easy to find. Start to do 5S and vision the Indianapolis speedway so you can find tools quickly.

4.   **Start-up** – should be done quickly with everything ready to go. Use a stopwatch and whistle to gather teams, post the time it takes to do a start-up, and challenge teams to continuously improve them.

5.   **Minor stoppages** - each one investigated to eliminate – get to the root cause, get your teams working on finding ways to prevent these minor stoppages.

6.   **Reduced speed** – how often do we slow machines down from their rated performances with the idea that there will be less problems. Imagine having an automobile and being afraid to speed it up. Treat a machine similarly and bring it up to date to run at maximum speeds.

7.   **Defects and rework** – to be totally eliminated. Get all workers to brainstorm quality problems in team activities and teach and encourage everyone to implement poka-yoke devices to totally eliminate defects and rework.

8.   **Shutdown losses** – scheduled downtime – this must be kept to a minimum, on schedule to have a minimum effect on production.

9. **Waiting for management or materials** – if everything is within takt time, the machines and people are not waiting. Remember machines can wait (not people) and reduce work in process inventory by reducing batch sizes and set-up times.

10. **Operating motions** – unreliable methods, low skills/morale, downtime – get the IE's working to improve operations. Use videos and get engineers and workers into study groups to find ways of reducing motion – if possible, use both hands.

11. **Poor line balance loss**, lacking automation – study this to improve.

12. **Logistics** – correct all of the schedule problems.

13. **Inspection and adjustment loss** – build in poka-yoke devices and locking devices.

14. **Yield loss** – examine causes of problems and eliminate them.

15. **Energy loss** – proper care, oiling, tooling.

16. **Die/tool/fixture loss** – have a place for everything.

Smelly, Oily, Dark, Dirty

In our quest towards perfection a good place to start is to send out teams into the factory and ask each person to find 30 things to improve. At first they could be left to their own judgment or you could suggest the kinds of things to look for. Suggest that people look for those areas that are smelly, oily, dark, dirty, disorganized, unsafe, potential disasters waiting to happen, loose screws, etc.

Or you could teach them the fundamentals of waste elimination and have them go on a treasure hunt for waste.

This kind of activity, going through the plant looking for opportunities for improvement, is very powerful. Remember it is management's job to determine the what and the why but not the how. You really want to empower people to take more responsibility, to take more responsibility in the improvement of their own environment, in the quality of the products produced, in reducing costs, in responding to the needs and demands of the customer.

In this case we challenge people to help us improve the profitability of the plant (**the what**) and with this greater profit we will be more competitive in the marketplace, our customers will be happier and the workforce will both learn new techniques to enrich their job and also help to create a much cleaner and safer place to work. (**the why**)

But, we leave the details to the workers. (**the how**)   It is their job to discover the opportunities to foster improvement. When they make the discovery of what is needed to be improved, they also begin the process of ownership.

Of course, the next step is to have them find the solutions to the problems that they are detecting and to have them make the corrections themselves -- best in teams.

Why is it necessary for a factory or a machine to be dirty? Habit!

Dirt covers things preventing the discovery of deterioration. Dirt also creates an attitude. How can you be expected to feel really good about your workplace when it is filthy? How can you really feel good about producing high quality products when you are surrounded by dirt? Quality and smelly, oily, dark and dirty just don't go together. In the past maybe, and I say maybe, you didn't have much choice but today it is totally inconsistent with the new corporate competitive demands.

In the microchip field we have clean rooms, not a spot of dust to be found. A spot of dust could cover some minute part and cause a malfunction. And yet, fundamentally the machines in the clean room are the same as those in the older factories, maybe smaller but still they are made of metal or glass with lubricants, bolts, screws, etc.

When attention is given to cleaning the environment, making and keeping it spotless, a whole new attitude is created for workers about their company and about themselves. And cleaning is the first step to having a defect free environment.

We are told that the average factory's cost of manufacturing is 15% to 30% higher due to the maintenance of the machines and the environment. We are talking about total manufacturing costs -- waste in scrap, lubricants, defects, time searching, fixing things, maintaining things, etc.

I also challenge you to realize that you can reduce those excess costs significantly. There is a new measure being used called Overall Equipment Effectiveness (OEE) which is calculated by multiplying the availability of a piece of equipment times the efficiency or percentage of quality parts produced times the effectiveness of the equipment (running at full speed, etc.). You might find that your true utilization is somewhere around 30% instead of world class of over 85%. This indicates real loss of profits.

TPM is a totally new way at looking at the factory and is a vital part of your Lean efforts.

25

Shigehiro Nakamura

"If there is a way to do it better... find it."
Thomas Edison

Shortly after Dr. Shingo died, Mr. Uchiyama manager of JMA's book division and editor of Shingo's books in Japan came over to me and said, "I know how important Dr. Shingo was to you. I will find you other great consultants in Japan to work with." A few months later he introduced me to Mr. Shigehiro Nakamura who was a consultant and seminar leader with JMA. I looked at his resume and saw that he was able to teach some 23 different courses on manufacturing improvement. At first, I was a skeptic. I never met before anyone with that breath of knowledge. My skepticism lasted until we translated his book, *"The New Standardization,"* and I realized the great gift that Mr. Uchiyama gave me.

Mr. Nakamura showed me a video of robots working in a factory. As I watched he said that the robots were wasting motion. To keep this in perspective, to Nakamura every motion that did not add value to the product was a waste and should be eliminated, even for robots. He also felt that the improvement process never ends.

I found a few wonderful books by Shigehiro Nakamura that had been published by JMA, and we made arrangements to translate them into English. They were *The New Standardization and Go-Go Tools*. What was amazing about him is that he developed on his own courses and taught a dozen different courses on various Japanese management techniques. In addition he developed an excellent management tool, a chart to guide improvement activities, as well as innovative uses for video cameras.

Using the Video Camera

Whenever Nakamura would go into a plant, he would always be carrying his Sharp video camera, the one where you could see clearly what you were shooting. We spent a day at the Wiremold Company in West Hartford, CT. Nakamura took us to the plant floor and we stopped in front of an operator assembling some parts. Nakamura video taped the operator and then took us back into a meeting room to project the video up onto a screen. He then asked us to watch carefully and then to offer suggestions on how to improve the operation by reducing motion. Nakamura wanted us to suggest every small improvement possible – each second saved was part of the journey to perfection.

When you do look at a video, you somehow see things differently then when you are watching the person live. You can also freeze each frame. As we watched the video we were able to make many suggestions on how to save time: you could move that fixture, she should use her left hand instead of the right, you could move that cord over, the box on the table is getting in her way and should be moved, etc. We came up with many ideas on how to reduce the 'motion.'

However, it would have even been better if we had brought

the operator into the meeting room and asked her to come up with ideas on how to make her work easier and more interesting. She could then have participated with us, giving her reactions to our suggestions and have a greater sense of ownership in the improvements.

Of course, industrial engineers should be using these techniques. However, most companies do not have enough industrial engineers to cover every job. **Teaching workers about waste and giving them the opportunity to participate in making improvements adds a lot more power to the improvement process.**

The kaizen blitz used to improve a process, normally a week's activity on the shop floor or in the office, should also use the video camera. Since the kaizen blitz is normally a one-time improvement activity, the videos could be used to sustain continuous improvement.

Nakamura believes in the power of the video camera. He feels that its use can drive us to zero defects. Whenever defects occur, we should immediately go out with the video camera to capture the process, and then take it back into the meeting room once again to examine carefully the causes. This method can help us completely eliminate defects. Nakamura resists the idea that defects are an acceptable by-product of manufacturing.

Once I met Nakamura in Scotland where he was set to run a workshop at a bottling plant. Here they were making the little plastic whisky bottles you would find being served by airline flight attendants on airlines. Prior to the workshop, I had met the senior vice president of manufacturing for the entire company. I invited him to come to the workshop in Scotland.

To me the plant looked very nice, with the lines of small bottles moving along, but the VP said the place had too much waste. I was confused because the plant was almost totally automated. I asked Nakamura what was the VP talking about. He said, "Well, there is a lot of waste. The lines are much too long, with far too much inventory between processes.

Nakamura's Chart

Nakamura gave me a chart he designed. On one large page, a group of managers wrote out their long term manufacturing improvement plans – their road map to automation. I was very impressed. I realized how powerful it is to get a group of people together to determine their strategic goals, to encompass all of the major areas of manufacturing, to establish their common measures, and to plan a step-by-step approach to attain their goals of world-class competitiveness.

Basic steps to create a management chart:

1. Introduce flexible manufacturing systems (FMS) and factory automation (FA). ↑

2. Improve materials and production techniques – through materials innovation, technology innovation, and solving problems at the source. ↑

3. Improve production equipment – unattended operations, zero defects through source control. ↑

4. Develop better measuring instruments, jigs and tools – Using SMED and Poka-yoke. ↑

5. Standardize best practices – IE, QC and standardization. ↑

6. Improve operator skills

Establishment of Indicators:

1. Quality – defect rate, claims rate, rework,
2. Cost – costs of sales ratio, value indices
3. Productivity – output in $ per head, value adding time/operating time
4. WIP – Absolute quantity, days' WIP, inventory turnover rate
5. Headcount – headcount, ratio of direct to indirect
6. Startup speed – new product startup rate and market share, new equipment startup rate

Management by objectives:

1. Various management ratios – profitability, efficiency indicators
2. Standard labor hours – standard time, waste indicators (defects, rework, downtime, and skill differentials, etc., process time, office automation
3. Preliminary studies – for equipment investment, action against bottleneck processes

Then Nakamura divides the plant operations into specific areas to control. Each area indicates the relevant methods to use, refers to the top competitors in the world as benchmarks and then sets up five target levels to move the company to world class.

Example:

Quality Improvement – automatic inspection equipment, poka-yoke, abnormality monitoring, in-process inspection, quick turnaround time system, sequential inspection, rapid feedback on defects to previous process, QC analysis, and continuous improvement of standards.

Top benchmarked companies – Toyota, Matsushita – zero defect system established by means of in process inspection equipment. Fanuc – computerized checking by means of automatic inspection equipment.

Targets and levels:

0 – Defects tackled by labor

1 – Defects addressed by QC analysis and TQM activities

2 – Defects detected and promptly tackled by poka-yoke – quality built in by the process

3 – Defects tackled by controlling non-straight-through rate – abnormality control

4 – Defects tackled by countermeasures at the source - reduction in control points

5 – Expertise used to create equipment that does not produce defects – unattended operation

The following are the other areas to monitor with the highest target:

1.   Automatic control – FMA – unattended operation of the entire plant[171]

---

[171] We saw unattended operation of the entire plant at Fujitsu Fanuc whereby the plant had robots producing robots with only one person sitting in the computer control room.

2. Setup improvement – unattended setup with automatic error correction

3. Improvement of inter-process links – automated conveyance, unattended operation and stockless inter-process flow control

4. Anti-breakdown measures – abnormality monitoring, breakdown maintenance, preventive maintenance, corrective maintenance, equipment failure analysis using 5S, PM and training of operators – faults diagnosed and corrected automatically by the equipment itself (perfect zero-breakdown system)

5. Order receipt/issue system – Long term forecasting and planning system, order-entry system, orders from sales to factory, proactive control by means of forecasting system

6. System for selecting best production schedule – on line production employing CAD/CAM/CAT

7. On-line production control – All lines operating with CAD/CAM/CAT and FMS

8. Real-time data gathering

9. Standardization – Standards are minimized through planned time, etc.

10. Suggestion system – at least two suggestions per month per employee, concurrent engineering and specialized research taking place; design in activities

11. Work improvement – improvement of hard physical and dangerous work, improving team activities,

OJT improvement activities, new equipment developed and built and system for commercializing technology developed in-house

12.   Model line – world's lowest cost and highest quality, public dissemination and development of world-leading activities

13.   Long term specialized training system established

14.   Competition between plants – award scheme, visual controls

15.   Safety – autonomous control by each department

16.   Human Resources Development – technology transfer activities, OJT, job enlargement – multi-skills, small-group activities, development of expert engineers, and preparation of training – HRD allows people to cope with new fields by forming flexible project teams

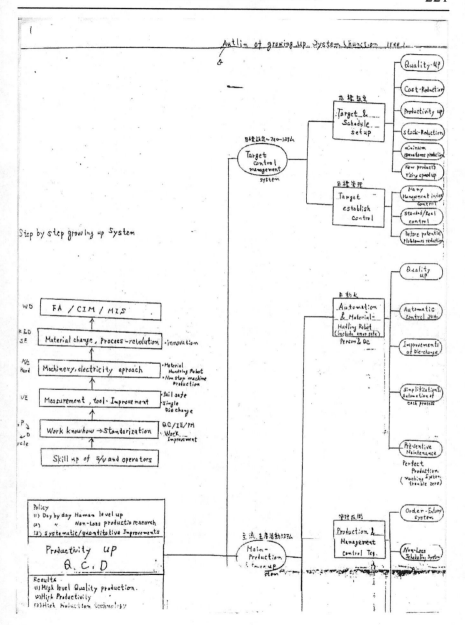

Outlin of growing up System (function tree)

Step by step growing up System

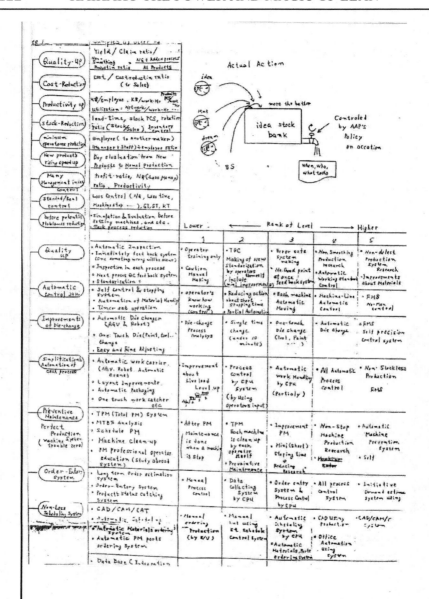

	ordering system			Materials, Parts ordering System	using system
On-Line Production System	• Data Base (Integration of Production's Information) • On-Line Information use work • Demand energy Control etc	• Manual Data Gathering System (by S/w)	• Manual (but One section) data gathering system by cpu	• CPU-Network using System	• Automatic Machine Production Control system FMS ←Same
Automatic Data Collecting system	• online data Gathering system • Lost time Control • Alarm system	• Paper using system	• Daily data Collecting System using/stool follow	• Only illregular finding & Control system	• Self Control system before orders and Product by CPU P-D-S Automatic control system
Tool & Die Service System	• Tool, Die, Paint Control System • Office Automation	"	• Control by CPU • Partial BA	• Integrated BA • Automatic tool, Die ordering System (FMS?)	• Quip joint to buyer ← SAME Network System
Standardization Using System	• ST, RT, KT Standardization • Know-how → Automation or Error safe System	• Operator training by using standardization	• Level up Action to ST, GT, KT	• TFP Improvement Team Action	① New. work & Machine system PLAN/construction ⑤ Safe system at AAP-Origines Technology & Machines
Proposal system	• Proposal team work (1 Idea/1 operator-Month) • Self Improvement system	• uncontroled Improvement occur and Apply Action	• Group Proposal System (BC group)	• Self Improvement system (3 Idea/day, M's by using IE, BC)	① Improvement target negotiation system (MAP Method) ② • High level machine Plan and construction by AAP Engineers
Work-Methods Improvement by operation guidelines	• Heavy/High Temp/Dangerous Work Reduction (Improvements by IE & tool→Mechanization) (low Cost) • Improvement Team action system	"	• Improvement team work by ARP's Polycy (update 2-3 H or monthly)	• TFP Team Improvement	Same ①, ② Same ③, ④
Model I-Line Making	• challenge / Champion machine or line making (High Level)	Each machine each production	Model machine challenges the perfect production	Model line challenges the perfect Production	Every Machine challenges the perfect production	Non-deffect Production is established Since 3 year ago
Open working (best working show)	• Display of open working • VTR/Automatic Loss time Data-Collector Analysis					
Manual Making	• Standardization Making team Action • Standardization→CPU	Each section each Training (T.T. is done by only meeting)	T.T. is done by using the general teaching materials and ARP2 Improvement Sample	Special Training by using high level Text	High Speed Training System Established	Long-run staff and operator Training System
Improvement Example publish	• T.T. Communication system (ex. wall newspaper) • Intimate education • VTR					
Presentation Ceremony	• Perfect Production challenge (Non-deffect production) • idea→improvements Ceremony	—				
Display system	• (Il-regular) Problem display (No-deff PCS, Maximum-stop) • Target/Practice Display	—				
Off the Job Training	• Education about safety • Training of finding some dangerous points in 6 work	Safty Education	Training of finding some dangerous points in a work. & Improvements		Application of Error Safe system	
Diagnosis about Safty	• Checklist diagnosis • Pre-check before machine opera (ion (about safety)					
Daily education ON the job Training	• 10 minutes/day Education • Self-Development • Man to man Training	New Employee Education only	Man to Man Training & Training	Team Training	Specialists training system (include other Training School)	Research & Development of New Technology
Job enlargement job-enrichment	• Many machines or Many Process operations • Aid to another section • Not operation					
Specialist Education	• Education manual preparation					

Nakamura's Three People Technique

Often we write standard procedures and place them in a notebook to be used by new employees. These procedures in most instances are there as 'security blankets,' just in case an employee leaves. But rarely can a new person pick up the written procedure and then go out and do the job – they normally need someone else to show them how to do it.

>   *Throughout my life I have rarely been able to read instructions properly. They are often written by people who have good editing and writing skills, but have very little real knowledge about how the product works. This three people technique is simple, and should be used by any one creating a procedure or a manual.*

Nakamura's technique is simple and brilliant:

You ask an expert on the job to write up a procedure.

You then ask three people to do the job following the written procedure. If the three people can do the job perfectly without any outside assistance then you have a very good written procedure. If any one of the three people makes a mistake, ask them to write (in their own words) corrections to the procedure.

You then give the new procedure to three new people, asking them to follow the instructions.

You keep repeating the above process until three people can do the job perfectly.

This process is so easy but so powerful. There are millions of manuals and procedures published that are so difficult to read and use. Try this!

26

Kaoru Ishikawa

*"Energy that does not move or change its level
creates congestion. This will end creative flow."*
Rudi

The real genius behind the Japanese quality movement was
Kaoru Ishikawa. Even though he didn't coin the term Total Quality Control (TQC), Ishikawa was the person who organized and led
the TQC efforts in Japan. He was instrumental in bringing Deming, Juran and Feigenbaum to Japan. He started the Deming Prize,
developed and created Quality Control Circles[172], the seven Tools
of Quality Control (with the famous Ishikawa Cause and Effect
Diagram), and was the head and helped to start the Union of Japanese Scientists and Engineers (JUSE).

---

[172] In April 1962, Dr. Ishikawa started a quarterly magazine 'Gemba-To-QC,'
(Quality Control for the Foreman) to educate and promote QC Circles. In May
of 1962, the first QC Circle was registered with JUSE from the Japan Telephone & Telegraph Corporation. In June 1978, 90,000 QC Circles were registered (average members of a circle was 8 to 12 people). Circle members started
off learning the seven basic tools, but many advanced to also learn and practice
industrial engineering methods such as motion study, time study, process analysis and statistical methods such as regression analysis, design of experiment,
value analysis, value engineering, and PERT.

In the initial period, foreman or first line supervisors played the role of leader
but this changed to only workers being members of a circle.

Ishikawa also argued against having separate Quality Assurance Departments. He wanted everyone, all workers, to be responsible for quality improvements.

I invited Dr. Ishikawa to speak on our study mission in Tokyo.

I think Dr. Ishikawa will most be remembered for his contribution to humanistic management. This is an area of management often neglected. It is funny that we strive to make innovative, quality products to serve the needs of our customers, but often we have very little concern about the quality of the lives of the people producing those products. We must change this thinking.[173] We need to find a way to enrich everyone's life at work and also produce products/deliver services that fill the needs and aspirations of our customers. In the past this improvement process was left to the manager, often overburdened to 'just get the goods out of the door.' To achieve a real quality of life the work environment must enlist and empower all workers to be responsible for the improvement process. Ishikawa got us started.

The basic philosophy of QC Circles is:

1.   Improve the leadership and management abilities of the foreman and first line supervisors in the workshop, and encourage improvement by self-development.

2.   Increase the level of worker morale and create an environment in which everyone is more conscious about quality, problems and the need for improvement.

---

[173] 'The shoemakers children have no shoes,' must become something from the past.

3.   Function as a nucleus for company-wide quality control.

The three basics of the QC Circle as an integral part of company-wide quality control:

1.   Allow all workers to participate in contributing to the improvement and development of the enterprise.

2.   Build in greater respect for humanity at work. Make work more worthwhile for all workers and create a happy and bright workplace.[174]

3.   Display human capabilities to their fullest and to draw out the infinite creative possibilities resting with each worker.

"Respect of humanity at the workshop level" means that QC Circle activities can create a pleasant and meaningful place to work, which is characterized by the following:

(1) People are not treated as a part of the machinery, but as human beings who are engaged in meaningful jobs, in which they can display their abilities and truly feel like devoting themselves to exploring their full potential.

(2) People can use their wisdom and creativity in the work they are engaged in.

(3) People can develop their abilities as they are given an opportunity to use their brains.

---

[174] Up to this point in time, factory work was based on Taylor's concepts of maximizing productivity with very little concern for the psychological, emotional, intellectual, and spiritual well-being of workers.

(4) People are not isolated from each other. People in the same workshop are organized and act as a group. This creates harmonious human relations based on bonds of brother-hood in the workshop.

(5) People can mutually educate themselves by sharing experiences.

(6) People are given an opportunity to be recognized by colleagues, superiors, subordinates, people in other workshops, and also by people outside the company. It is said the Japanese workforce is known for its high quality. Therefore it is all the more important to create a pleasant and meaningful place for them to work in."[175]

"It is a poor workshop where operators and foreman are considered to be part of the machinery and required to do a job specified by set standards. What constitutes a human being is the ability to think. A workshop should become a place where people can think and use their wisdom."

[175] QC Circle Koryo, General Principles of the QC Circle, edited by QC Circle Headquarters, JUSE 1980

27

Iwao Kobayashi

20 Keys

"A leader is most effective when people barely know he exists. When his work is done, his aim fulfilled, his troops will feel they did it themselves." **Lao-tzu**

Mr. Iwao Kobayashi wrote 20 *Keys to Workplace Improvement.* Probably the simplest book we published at Productivity and also probably the easiest way to adopt Japanese management concepts into a company. The book covers: 5S, quick changeover, scheduling, reducing inventory, maintenance, skill building activities, eliminating waste, value analysis, empowering workers, quality, developing suppliers, etc. Each key is further divided into five levels from novice to "world class" status.

It was always enjoyable meeting Mr. Kobayashi in Tokyo. Somehow we would inevitable end up eating at the fish restaurant at the Imperial Hotel in Tokyo. The waiter would come over, impeccably dressed, give us the menus, and then ask for our order. Mr. Kobayashi would always tell the waiter, "I want to order exactly what Mr. Bodek ordered." It was simple and sweet.

He invited me to keynote a conference he set up, gathering attendees mostly from his client companies in Japan. His book was so simple to understand and apply and amazingly he drew over 500 people at this conference. I gave a short presentation and then Mr. Kobayashi gave me a speaker's honorarium which I 'blew' that night eating at the La Tour D'Argent at the New Otani Hotel in Tokyo, probably the most I ever spent on a meal in my life.

Real Power

One of Mr. Kobayashi's clients was the Seiko Watch Company. They were so successful using twenty keys that they set up a separate consulting company with Mr. Kobayashi to teach 20 Keys to all of their suppliers and other companies in Japan.

The Twenty Keys

1. Cleaning and organizing
2. Top down and bottom up management
3. Team activities
4. Inventory reduction
5. Reduction in change over
6. Reducing motion and improving methods
7. Attaining zero defects
8. Improving process flow within the plant
9. Improving equipment
10. Improving the value added time
11. Improving quality
12. Improving supplier relations
13. Waste elimination
14. Empowerment
15. Improving and developing worker's skills
16. Scheduling techniques

17.   Getting to 100% efficiency
18.   Information systems
19.   Cost reduction
20.   Improvements in technology

Here again we see the building blocks of what is called Lean.

I understand that places at General Motors are using 20 Keys to drive their Lean efforts.

Once again it is simplicity, which is what is wanted. I meet so many people in life that take something very simple and then complicate it. Often they even develop their own language to mystify others in perceiving or misperceiving their 'genius.'

28

Union of Japanese Scientists and Engineers (JUSE)

"The function of leadership is to produce more leaders, not more followers." – **Ralph Nader**

In February 1981, at JUSE, we received a lecture on Quality Control Circles (QCC) from their Executive Director, Jungi Noguchi. From that lecture and our prior studies we thought that QCC was the real power behind the Japanese manufacturing success story. Of course it was important, for it enlisted the talents of all workers, but it was only part of the story. JUSE took a major role in improving quality of Japanese products through their educational and training programs and their emphasis on Total Quality Control: starting at the top whereby the senior officers lived, breathed, and always spoke about their quality improvement efforts.

Unfortunately, I and a lot of other people from America could never really get Mr. Noguchi to share with us the training material developed at JUSE. He allowed study missions to visit JUSE primarily to talk about QCC, but coveted their training materials. Surprisingly, he did share consultants and information with

Florida Power and Light (FPL)[176], as they applied to be the first American company to receive the Deming Prize, but I believe most of the training material at FPL came from Kansai Electric and from the JUSE books. Lucky for us that JUSE books were not under Noguchi's control, and I was able to publish many of their books in English.

I once approached C. Jackson Grayson, CEO of the American Quality and Productivity Center in Houston, and urged him to contact Noguchi with the thought that JUSE would agree to cooperate with this famous non-profit group, but Noguchi declined.[177]

I made one mistake with Noguchi, which could have been part of the reason for his lack of cooperation with me. I had Mr. Ichiro Miyauchi give the first lecture to my study group at JUSE. He spoke English and was very good. For our next visit to Japan I wrote directly to Mr. Miyauchi, without going through Noguchi, asking him to speak for our next study group to Japan. I subsequently learned that even though JUSE was a non-profit organization, they were still very protective of their domain.

---

[176] I did negotiate the publishing rights for *Management for Quality Improvement – the 7 New QC Tools,* edited by Shigeru Mizuno and found out that FPL had already translated that book into English. I met with Kent Sterrett, VP of Quality, in Florida and negotiated with him to use FPL's translation and in turn FPL bought 7,000 copies of the book. Wonderful luck for me as the 7,000 books paid for all of our publishing costs.

[177] Once Noguchi told me that he was not that pleased with Dr. Deming, for Deming once said, "I brought quality to Japan!" Noguchi, like many Japanese, value 'humility,' something Dr. Deming didn't adhere to.

29

Meeting Dr. W. Edwards Deming

"It is not enough to do your best; you must know
what to do, and THEN do your best."
W. Edwards Deming

On June 24, 1980, NBC aired their famous documentary titled "If Japan Can Do it, Why Can't We," which introduced many of us to Dr. E. Edwards Deming and Dr. Joseph Juran. Of course, both of them had been very well known in Japan since the early 1950's. In fact, Deming was invited to Japan by the Supreme Commander of the Allied Powers, under General Douglas McArthur in 1950, to help improve their quality. He gave his first lecture for the Japanese Union of Scientists and Engineers (JUSE) in Tokyo to a large audience of CEO's, (included in the audience was Dr. Ishikawa).

A Funny Sidebar (I hope it is funny to you)

One of the biggest problems in life has been listening to other people and getting caught up with their misconceptions. Once, when I was in basic training in the US Army, the captain stood in front of us and asked if anyone was a capable typist. I was an excellent typist, but I wouldn't raise my hand because I remember what Ira told me, "Norman, never volunteer in the Army; they will fool you, when they ask for a typist you will end up typing garbage." Finally, one of the sol-

diers spoke up and told the captain that he could type with one finger, so he got the job as company typist and spent the next two months indoors while I, listening to Ira, a friend, spent the next two months marching in the rain.

Well, I went to New York University Graduate School of Business for my master's degree and Dr. Deming was teaching statistics. I wanted to take his course but was told, "Norman, statistics is the hardest course at the school." So once again, listening to other's misconceptions, I didn't get to meet Dr. Deming until thirty years later. Funny, life has really given me every opportunity. But much too often I listen to other's prejudices instead of listening to my own heart – all of you take heed and listen to the Jiminy Cricket inside of you instead of those J. Worthington Foulfellow's, sly foxes, lurking around to misguide you.

Worth a revisit

"Deming biographers point in particular to a dinner at Tokyo's Industry Club on July 13, 1950, in which he told the presidents of 21 (in some interviews Deming says 45) leading manufacturers that if they would only use statistical analysis to build quality in their products, they could overcome their reputation for shoddy quality within five years. Deming is generally credited with the post-war introduction of quality concepts to Japan, although the reality is much more complicated, and there is considerable evidence that he learned as much from Japanese thinkers like Kaoru Ishikawa and Taichi Ohno as he taught them."[178]

---

[178] Quoted from http://courses.bus.ualberta.ca/orga432-reshef/demingobituary.html

The Key Moment

While Deming was not the first to introduce quality techniques to Japan he was probably the most important **'catalyst'** to help the Japanese move towards improving their product quality.

Recently I received a rare copy of the original transcript of Dr. Deming's eight-day lecture course titled Elementary Principles of The Statistical Control of Quality given 1950 in Tokyo. There were 230 first-class engineers of leading manufacturing companies. Deming, "GOOD QUALITY and UNIFORM QUALITY have no meaning except with reference to the consumer's needs."

He taught his audience to make a shift from The Old Way of thinking: "Design it, Make it, Try to Sell it," to The New Way of thinking: "Design the product, Make it, test it, Put it on the market, Test it in service, through market research, find out what the user thinks of it and why the non-user has not bought it and Re-design the product in the light of consumer reactions to quality and price."

"Quality is not built by making a great number of articles, hoping that some will be good, and then sorting out the bad ones. Your company or anyone else's whether it is in Tokyo or Chicago, will go bankrupt if it attempts to operate in the that way today."

"Inspection is not quality control, and quality control is not inspection." "You must build quality: you must make the product so that it has quality in it, if you want quality." "Control charts by itself will not improve quality or uniformity. You must take action on the process if you are to achieve any improvement."

> *Dr. Deming taught the power that can be derived from understanding and applying statistical control techniques to manufacturing. From these notes you can see the key role that Dr. Deming did play in the success of Japan.*

One of his most powerful contributions was, after his lecture to the JUSE attendees, he declined to accept the honorarium. He told JUSE to take the money and start a quality prize. Dr. Kaoru Ishikawa, the head of JUSE at the time and a very powerful figure in his own right, took Dr. Deming's advice and started the Deming Prize. The Japanese used the prize as a focal point to spearhead their quality movement.

Unfortunately, US companies rarely listened to Dr. Deming's advice, and allowed the Japanese to catch up to American quality and productivity and even surpass us. Dr. Deming was also most noted for his 'Deming Wheel,' plan - do – check - action.[179] Meaning you never stopped perfecting quality.

Plan – you decide what has to be done to improve quality.

Do – you put into action your quality plan.

Check – did you obtain what you intended?

Act – if you didn't obtain the results you expected then you make the necessary corrections and continue around the wheel endlessly until you attain your goals of perfect quality.

This was the foundation for continuous improvement.

---

[179] Walter A. Shewhart, considered to be the 'Father of Quality,' originally came up with the improvement wheel later adopted by Dr. Deming.

While the Japanese were on this unending search for continuous improvement, we in America were content with the old 'Military Standard,' of plus or minus three percent. If we produced 97 parts correctly it was acceptable. The problem is we neglected the other three percent.[180]

I remember at one of my conferences in the early 1980's when one of the lecturers told us about the problem with plus or minus three percent and the US Navy in World War II. A factory was making parachutes. **Imagine telling the Navy pilot that there was a three percent chance that the parachute wouldn't open.** To solve the problem they told the people folding the parachutes in the factory that they would use their parachutes to jump out of a plane; instantly they received 100% quality parachutes.

Dr. Deming began the process for the Japanese and also learned from them as you can see from his following 14 points.

Read the following carefully, once a week would be good:

#1 Constancy of Purpose

181

---

[180] I was told often in Japan that those 3% not happy each would tell twenty other people about your defects and their lack of satisfaction.
[181] Cartoons are by Pat Oliphant source and permission to reprint comes from The Deming Library video series, a production of CC-M, Inc. found at ManagementWisdom.com on the web. Thank you Bob Mason

1. ***Constancy of purpose*** – provide for long-range needs rather than only short-term profitability, with a plan to become competitive, to stay in business, and to provide jobs.

2. ***The new philosophy*** - We can no longer live with commonly accepted levels of delays, mistakes, defective materials, and defective workmanship. Transformation of Western management style is necessary to halt the continued decline of business and industry.

3. ***Cease dependence on mass inspection*** - Eliminate the need for mass inspection, and build quality into the product in the first place. Require statistical evidence of built-in quality in both manufacturing and purchasing functions.

4. ***End lowest tender contracts*** - End the practice of awarding
    business solely on the basis of price tag. Instead, require
    meaningful measures of quality along with price. Reduce the
    number of suppliers for the same item by eliminating those,
    which do not qualify with statistical and other evidence of
    quality. The aim is to minimize total cost, not merely initial
    cost, by minimizing variation. Purchasing managers have a
    new job, and must learn it.

5. *Improve every process* - Improve constantly and forever every
process for planning, production, and service. Search continually
for problems in order to improve every activity in the company, to
improve quality and productivity, and thus to constantly decrease
costs. Institute innovation and constant improvement of product,
service, and process. It is management's job to work continually
on the system (design, incoming materials, maintenance, improvement of machines, supervision, training, retraining).

6. Institute training on the job - Institute modern methods of training on the job for all, including management, to make better use of every employee. New skills are required to keep up with changes in materials, methods, product and service design, machinery, techniques, and service.

7. Institute leadership - Adopt and institute leadership aimed at helping people do a better job. The responsibility of managers and supervisors must be changed from sheer numbers to quality. Improvement of quality will automatically improve productivity. Management must ensure that immediate action is taken on reports of inherited defects, maintenance requirements, poor tools, fuzzy operational definitions, and all conditions detrimental to quality.

8. Drive out fear - Encourage effective two-way communication and other means to drive out fear throughout the organization so that everybody may work effectively and more productively for the company.

9. Break down barriers - Break down barriers between departments and staff areas. People in different areas, such as Production, Leasing, Maintenance, Administration, must work in teams to tackle problems that may be encountered with products or service.

10. Eliminate exhortations - Eliminate the use of slogans, posters and exhortations for the work force, demanding Zero Defects and new levels of productivity, without providing methods. Such exhortations only create adversarial relationships; the bulk of the causes of low quality and low productivity belong to the system, and thus lie beyond the power of the work force.

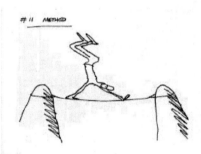

11. Eliminate arbitrary numerical targets - Eliminate work standards that prescribe quotas for the work force and numerical goals for people in management. Substitute aids and helpful leadership in order to achieve continual improvement of quality and productivity.

12. Permit pride of workmanship - Remove the barriers that rob hourly workers, and people in management, of their right to pride of workmanship. This implies, among other things, abolition of the annual merit rating (appraisal of performance) and of Management by Objective. Again, the responsibility of managers, supervisors, and foremen must be changed from sheer numbers to quality.

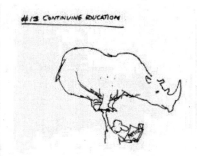

13.   **Encourage education -** Institute a vigorous program of education, and encourage self-improvement for everyone. What an organization needs is not just good people; it needs people that are improving with education. Advances in competitive position will have their roots in knowledge.

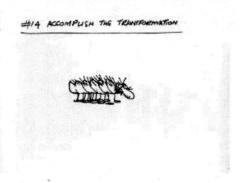

#14 ACCOMPLISH THE TRANSFORMATION

14. *Top management commitment and action* - Clearly define top management's permanent commitment to ever improving quality and productivity, and their obligation to implement all of these principles. Indeed, it is not enough that top management commit themselves for life to quality and productivity. They must know what it is that they are committed to—that is, what they must do. Create a structure in top management that will push every day on the preceding 13 Points, and take action in order to accomplish the transformation. Support is not enough: action is required!

*W. Edwards Deming, **Quality Productivity and Competitive Position** (Cambridge, Mass. MIT, Centre for Advanced Engineering Study, 1982).*

"Deming blamed management for most of America's ills, but perhaps his most revolutionary message to the managerial classes was his fundamental belief in the competence of the average worker and his or her willingness to work hard and work well, given an environment in which the worker is permitted to think and exercise control over quality. With 'empowerment' now the rage (if not necessarily the reality), that message has gained widespread acceptance.[182]"

After seeing the TV program 'If Japan can do it, Why can't we?' I called Dr. Deming's office to have him speak at one of my

---

[182] http://courses.bus.ualberta.ca/orga432-reshef/demingobituary.html

conferences. I also went to Atlanta to hear him speak for another group. During his talk he told the audience that we should all be prepared to stay for the next four hours. The schedule showed only an hour and a half but he insisted that he was going to speak for four hours. I understood if you wanted Dr. Deming to work for your company he insisted on having people sit in his course for a full four days. I liked his speech but I could imagine spending four days listening to him would be a challenge.[183]

Dr. Deming fooled us all for he only spoke for an hour and a half. I liked his presentation and went up to him at the end of his talk.

Fatal Mistake

I said, "Dr. Deming, I would like to publish all of your future books." His answer, "Norman, I don't write books." My fatal mistake was that I didn't say, "I will then write the books for you." It would have been easy. All I had to do was to attend his four-day workshop, tape it and then edit it into a book. I really lost out for it wasn't until maybe five years later in 1988 that Mary Walton wrote *The Deming Management Method* and it must have sold tens of thousands of copies.[184]

Root Out Fear

Is it true that most middle managers are afraid? Are they afraid of change? Are they afraid to make decisions? Are they afraid to make mistakes? Are they afraid that someone else will prove to be better than they are? Are they afraid that they will be

---

[183] The Japanese had an advantage over us. In their classrooms they very rarely would ask questions of the professors and teachers. They would just listen and take notes while in America I believe most of us are used to asking questions and being involved with the teacher.

[184] Well you 'can't win them all.'

re-engineered and gone? Are they afraid that they just can't keep up? Their favorite motto is 'Don't rock the boat!'

Dr. Deming recognized the evil in having any kind of fear in the workplace.

What has helped me very much in life is to just stop occasionally and turn around and say, "Look I got here through all adversity and I will surely continue to get to my next place – absolutely." I might be challenged by thousands of things, but I have confidence that I will survive and survive well. I am sure the same will happen to you.

30

The Impact of Dr. Joseph Juran

"Satisfaction lies in the effort not the attainment.
Full effort is full victory." – **Mahatma Gandhi**

In 1954, the Japanese Union of Scientists and Engineers and Keidanren[185] invited Dr. Juran to deliver a series of lectures to Japanese managers. Dr. Juran became world famous in quality when his *Quality Control Handbook* was first published in 1951. I went to hear him at a conference and was very impressed with his speaking ability. He was informative, interesting and entertaining. During his talk he mentioned that his claim to fame came from his carefully cutting out articles to read and filling them away in a file cabinet, until he became inspired to compile them into the handbook.[186]

---

[185] Keidanren was an organization of the top executives from the top corporations in Japan.

[186] Dr. Juran's talk inspired me to do the same thing at Productivity. I encouraged both William Christopher and Carl Thor to put together the *Handbook for Productivity Measurement and Improvement*. Juran's book, fifth edition, is 1872 pages while our handbook's first printing was over 1,500 pages.

Since I made it a habit to always go the source and never allow myself, to say it can't be done[187], I called Dr. Juran to interview him for my newsletter. He said "yes." It was a splendid moment, which came shortly after my first study mission to Japan.

I had prepared a few questions in advance and Dr. Juran was very articulate. At one moment I told Dr. Juran that I had recently been to Japan. He stopped, looked at me and said, "You are interested in me, and I am not interested in you. Let us go on with the interview." Luckily, I held my composure and got a very good interview. Dr. Juran with his son-in-law produced a video series, which sold at around $16,000 a set and met with great success.

In 1937, Dr. Juran conceptualized the Pareto principle, which millions of managers rely on to help separate the "vital few" from the "useful many" in their activities. This is commonly referred to as the 80-20 principle.

Both the visits to Japan of Dr. Deming and Dr. Juran had a profound effect on the Japanese quality efforts, helping them make their remarkable ascent from its pre-war position as a producer of poor quality to its current reputation as a world paragon of manufacturing quality.[188]

---

[187] Unfortunately so many people will not venture out of their sphere with the fear that they will be 'shot down.'

[188] Although Juran down plays the significance of his lectures there, the Japanese themselves do not. Nearly thirty years after his first visit, Emperor Hirohito awarded him Japan's highest award that can be given to a non-Japanese, the Order of the Sacred Treasure. It was bestowed in recognition of his contribution to "the development of quality control in Japan and the facilitation of U.S. and Japanese friendship", which significantly helped set them on the path to quality.

31

Life Time Employment System

"The best work is always performed under the most trying conditions." **- Rudi**

This brings up another discovery from our trips to Japan, the Life Time Employment System (LTES). To be competitive, we want to get the best ideas from everyone. But how can you expect people to come up with great ideas when those ideas will lead to their unemployment. Well, somehow the Japanese came up with their Life Time Employment system:[189]

1.   Young workers were hired after graduating directly from either high school or college.

2.   They were all given the exact same starting wage; college graduates made more than the high school graduates.

3.   Each year they were given a raise in salary and also a bonus.

---

[189] Born in Japan in the 1920's but did not take off until after World War II under the urging of General McArthur.

4.   They were encouraged to be part of a close-knit team. Often they all lived in the same company housing, wore the exact same uniforms, and socialized together. You often worked six days a week, went out and ate and drank with your team at night. You worked your tail off.

5.   The company invested in extensive training, knowing that the employees were not going to leave.

6.   It was noted that when the men reached around 30 years of age and the women were around 27 to 28, the company would help arrange marriages – often the women retired when they married.

7.   Age 60 was the retirement age when they would receive a 'lump sum,' package. If you were an exceptional manager you would work until you were 65, and some went on to age 70. If you were very good (but not part of the top echelon) you would be sent to a subsidiary company and act as a consultant with around 60% of your last salary.

8.   Since you were a permanent employee, the company demanded and they received extreme loyalty.

But like most good things they do come to an end and many Japanese companies in these last few years have been rethinking the lifetime employment system.

32
Quick and Easy Kaizen[190]

"Within each person is unlimited creative potential!"

On one of the earlier trips to Japan we were introduced to Japanese suggestion systems. At first, the travelers on the study mission could not understand them. Toyota and other Japanese companies we visited were receiving close to 50 written suggestions per year per employee while in America the average employee submitted one idea every seven years – I repeat: one idea every seven years. [191]

Not a single person on the early study missions could get a handle on what the Japanese were doing. Comparing the American suggestion system with its Japanese counterpart was like comparing 'apples and oranges.'

Actually even though they are both called suggestion systems; they are totally different. The Japanese system has all employees involved in continuous improvement activities, while in America it is a cost savings system; we don't want to be bothered with small ideas.

---

[190] Kaizen is a Japanese word meaning continuous improvement. I called a manager at one company and told her that I teach Quick and Easy Kaizen. She said, "Oh, we tried kaizen and it didn't work! How do you answer that?
[191] Statistics were kept by the National Association of Suggestion Systems (NASS) now called The Employee Involvement Association.

And quite frankly, in the early 1980's, workers in the American factory were not expected to think. It was as if there was a large box on the entrance door which said, **'Please, deposit your brains here, they will be returned to you when you go home.'**

"Quick and Easy Kaizen" is one of the more recent ideas to come out of Japan, an idea ripe for consideration by American industry. As with so many ideas that have come from Japan in the past decade or two, it is aimed at increasing quality, productivity and worker satisfaction, all from a very grassroots level.

"The basic idea is that each and every company employee is encouraged to come up with ideas, however small, that could improve his/her particular job activity, job environment, or any company process for that matter. More importantly, the employees are encouraged to implement their ideas and document them for review and consideration for incorporation wherever the idea might be applicable within the company." - Eugene Ruff-Wagner, C.P.M.

Canon Camera Plant

On many of our missions to Japan we visited a Canon Camera plant. As we walked through the Canon plant outside of Tokyo, I remember seeing cameras being assembled. At the time Canon employees were offering around 50 improvement ideas per year per employee. One clever idea was a wastepaper bucket with small wheels on the bottom. An operator, when finished with her assembly process, put the camera into the bucket and pushed the bucket over to the next operator. Simple, but it saved her time getting up and going over to the next station.

Not one of the travelers on the early study missions understood what was happening, so we basically ignored Quick and Easy Kaizen, thinking that it was like eating rice everyday or eating raw fish – something that was peculiar to the Japanese culture. In fact, many things that we saw, even though they impressed us, were sloughed off as being only peculiar to the Japanese; it gave us the excuse to just forget about it and not to change anything when we went back home.

When you read a book, or watch a television program, or go to a movie, or sit in a lecture room, you may appear to be interested, and then you go back to your normal life and not use a single thing you learned. When you see it with your own eyes, see it applied by other human beings, you still might not do anything immediately, but there is that 'seed' inside you growing. This may cause you to make some change in the future.

Toyota impressed the 'heck' out of us. We all recognized that something was happening here that was changing the world of manufacturing. And we also were told that Quick and Easy Kaizen was an essential part of the process that makes the Toyota Production System work.

And Toyota said:

"What sets us apart?

The Toyota Production System is at the heart of everything we do. Based on the concept of continuous improvement, or kaizen, every Toyota team member is empowered with the ability to improve their work environment. This includes everything from quality and safety to the environment and productivity. Improvements and suggestions by team members are the cornerstone of Toyota's success."[192]

---

[192] http://www.toyota.com/about/operations/manufacturing/

Toyota was telling us that the ideas coming from all of their employees were the CORNERSTONE of success. **If true, why have we continued to ignore that part of Lean?**

In the early 1970's, Toyota and other large Japanese companies started to introduce American suggestion systems, with the purpose of involving all employees more in continuous improvement activities. Quality Circle Activities were prevalent whereby small teams of employees, eight to twelve in a group, would meet periodically to solve quality and productivity problems. However, these quality circle activities normally only attacked two to five problems a year while there were thousands of small problems lying around the company often totally neglected.

Toyota expects everyone to participate in suggestion programs, but supervisors take the responsibility to help those workers who have difficulty participating. The supervisor encourages, challenges, suggests, and teaches the employee how to implement their ideas.

The Japanese, in studying American suggestion systems, felt it was a necessary vehicle to really get employees involved in solving all of those small problems. But they noticed that the American suggestion systems were not employee participation systems but cost savings systems.

> *In 1898, Kodak established the first American suggestion system, with the first submitted idea being, "Clean the windows," a small but probably important idea for the worker. But these small ideas became a pain for middle management, who felt it was their responsibility to implement suggestions, and nobody really likes to implement another person's idea. So the system quickly changed to a cost saving system. Once again we invented something great and then dropped it.*

Those companies that do have suggestion systems in America receive on the average one idea per employee every seven years, while the average in Japan today is two ideas per month, 24 ideas per year, per employee.

Typically the Japanese move slowly. At first they copied the American system and received only one or two ideas per employee per year, but when they understood the real power in implementing small ideas and how it inspired and empowered workers to be part of the continuous improvement efforts, it really took off. Toyota, Canon and other Japanese companies were up to 50 improvement ideas per worker per year.

Power to Help People Grow

I became fascinated with this system. I wanted to learn more about how it worked, so I went to the Japan Human Relations Association (JHRA) in Tokyo. This is the organization that was leading the Quick and Easy Kaizen efforts throughout Japan with their training programs, workshops, books, and magazines. JHRA only promotes Quick and Easy Kaizen. They dropped all of the other HR functions for they felt that Quick and Easy Kaizen was the best way to develop human resources within a company. The NHRA[193] (in the United States) has a similar mission to help develop people within a company, but to what extent do they promote anything, similar, to Quick and Easy Kaizen?

---

[193] NHRA (National Human Resources Association) states its mission, "In today's dynamic workplace, human resource professionals are expected to add value to their organizations. In addition to managing traditional human resource functions, HR is expected to contribute to such key organizational challenges as facilitating mergers and acquisitions, improving productivity and quality, improving the ability of an organization to bring new products to market, and to continuously improve the company's return on its greatest asset...its people."

I attempted to visit JHRA' offices in Tokyo but they were difficult to find. In fact, Tokyo, to me is the hardest city in the world to get around. Most signs are in Japanese, there are very few street names, you find buildings by knowing the block number, which are not necessarily in any kind of logical order, or you just hope that the taxi driver knows where to go. On one occasion the taxi driver was totally confused driving me around and around the area; frustrated, I just got out to walk, only to be drenched by a sudden downpour.

At the JHRA, I met the general manager Mr. Kenjiro Yamada and the leading trainer Mr. Bunji Tozawa[194] and asked them to suggest books on Quick and Easy Kaizen[195] for me to translate and publish in America.[196] Mr. Tozawa was the author of close to 20 books and personally runs over 100 workshops a year on Quick and Easy Kaizen in Japan and all throughout the Far East.

Virtually every Japanese company is doing Quick and Easy Kaizen. Why not, it makes a lot of sense to bring out every workers talent in making improvements.

It's like playing 'tug of war,' pulling that long rope and only a few of the leaders are really pulling – how in the world can you win the game unless everyone is pulling in the same direction?

---

[194] Bunji Tozawa is the current president of JHRA and my co-author of *The Idea Generator – Quick and Easy Kaizen*. Bunji ran a public workshop a year ago in Bangkok, Thailand and 500 people showed up. Question, have you ever had Quick and Easy Kaizen training? Why not?

[195] The system was earlier called Kaizen Teian, (Teian means suggestion), but was changed later on to Quick and Easy Kaizen, an employee empowerment system.

[196] I published ***Kaizen Teian 1 and 2**, The Improvement Engine, The Idea Book, The Service Industry Idea Book,* and *40 Years, 20 Million Ideas – The Toyota Suggestion System.*

HR associations' in America initial role were to develop human resources, but somehow lost that focus to payroll, hiring, OSHA, and other 'housekeeping' functions. JHRA only focuses on developing human resources and feels that when employees implement their own creative ideas, they have the best opportunity to learn and grow on the job from their own ideas.

JHRA keeps annual records on the Quick and Easy Kaizen systems for over 600 companies showing:

1. The total number of ideas submitted.
2. The number of employees participating.
3. The average number of ideas per employee per year.
4. The economic effect per employee per year.

Matsushita (Panasonic), Isuzu, Sanyo and others claimed to save over $3,000 per year per employee. Imagine Panasonic claims over $175,000,000 was saved in 2002 from their employees' improvement ideas. Why in the world aren't we doing this in America?

5. The average rewards given per employee.
6. The average yen (dollars) invested per employee.
7. The participation rate (% of employees submitting at least one idea per year).
8. The implementation rate (% of ideas implemented).

To learn more about the system, I asked Mr. Yamada and Mr. Tozawa to arrange a company for my study groups to visit. On one trip I asked them to get us permission to visit the company that offered the most suggestions in all of Japan. It was Tôhoku Oki Electric Co. of Fukushima, and they were getting 570 suggestions per employee per year (roughly two written ideas per employee per workday – 'mind-boggling.')

This really caused a lot of confusion with the travelers. When we arrived at the plant, I met the president of Oki and he told us all about how the system worked for them, and how he felt it was the center of their success. It led all of their improvement efforts.

I then asked the president of Oki if he could please introduce us to person who had submitted the most suggestions in all of Japan. He had submitted close to 5000 ideas in the previous year. He would go home each night and with his wife's help he would write down 20 ideas. When I met him I asked him to please show me his job. He took us to a room where a machine was producing parts without any human interference. He had, over the last year, figured out a way to totally replace him self.

In Oki's lunchroom we saw tables stacked with large overflowing notebooks filled with the thousands of employees ideas. It was crazy. We couldn't understand it, and so we all just laughed it off as something totally nutty. (In retrospect not one of us had enough sense to ask the right questions).

It is like looking at Tiger Woods and saying, 'Well, he is just a peculiar phenomenon and not considering that his success had come from his relentless dedication to continually improving his style every single day.'

Believe me it has taken me close to 20 years to understand what I saw earlier at Oki. I will try to share this learning with you.

What impressed me so much at Oki was that there was real dedication and excitement of the workforce in continuous improvement. Everyone was involved. The system helped the company out of their financial problems and the morale in the company was one of the highest I have ever seen.

There was a reward system, for each implemented suggestion. The worker received 150-yen reward, around 75 cents at the time.

Improvements can come from one big leap of innovation or they can come from very small steps.

Claudia Washington's Idea

Claudia Washington's job at Technicolor Corporation (Detroit) is to pack video's and DVD's. When reaching for the bubble wrap on the floor she has to bend and twist to reach the roll. These are unnecessary motions and extra steps to take. It is an unsafe condition possibly causing her to trip and possibly leading to a repetitive strain injury. Claudia through her Quick and Easy Kaizen training was taught to find ways to make her job easier and more interesting.

Claudia's creative idea was to hang the bubble wrap on a very simple square fixture to eliminate bending and twisting and making her work area safer. Just imagine how she felt when she was asked to be creative on the job; told that she did have very goods ideas on how to make her work easier and more interesting; empowered by her supervisors and managers to make the improvements necessary; came up with this creative idea on her own and participated in the improvement. She just didn't give her idea to someone else to do for her.

Yes, Quick and Easy Kaizen is a WOW!

Along comes Ken Van Gundy another worker at Technicolor who notices the new fixture. Another light bulb goes off in Ken's mind and he replaces the bubble wrap with inexpensive wrapping paper. And it works. It works very well.

Ken then sees that the paper on the square bar when pulled, rolls off unevenly. He replaces the square bar with a round bar.

Ken's next idea is place a pen at the end of the round bar to prevent the wrapping paper from falling off.

Prior to these four suggestions two semi-trailers of bubble wrap was delivered to Technicolor each week taking up a lot of shelf space. Also forklift drivers were constantly moving bubble wrap around the factory.

Claudia and Ken made their work easier, safer and much more interesting and also saves their company over $99,000 a year. It is amazing what can happen when you empower people to be creative at work.

Each step is a separate suggestion. Each step is an important part of the creative learning process. It might sound silly, but sometimes the small step approach could be more successful then the giant leap. And doing small steps is possible for each worker, while taking those giant steps is something rare and special for only a select few in the company.

At Technicolor Corporation (Detroit) in July 2002, I ran a workshop for twenty of their managers on Quick and Easy Kaizen. Prior to the workshop in 2001 they received 250 suggestions from 1800 employees with 113 of them implemented. In 2003 they received 12,500 suggestions with 5,800 of them implemented. In January 2004, they received 2,683 suggestions with 1,009 implemented.

A funny aside: during the initial workshop Gary Smuda (one of Technicolor's plant managers), stopped me and said, "Norman, I have been sitting here for the last two hours and I have not heard anything new." You can imagine how this shocked and embarrassed me in front of the workshop attendees. But I didn't react badly. I just said, "Gary you are right. I am not teaching things that are new but, Gary you are not doing this – you are not getting two ideas per worker per month."

Then shock waves went off in his head, and he realized the truth in what I just said. Subsequently Technicolor calculated that their Quick and Easy Kaizen system had saved them $4,600,000 in non-production costs and probably an equal amount in production costs in 2003. The key to Gary was when he realized that each employee had the ability to make their job easier and more interesting by their own improvement ideas – they had these ideas 'bottled up,' inside them, but management never asked them for their ideas.[197]

The employees would sit in the lunchroom having the answers to many problems and would say, "Those managers just never listen to us. Why don't they fix that shovel? It is easy to do. I am not going to tell them for they wouldn't listen to me anyway."

Now Gary listens. In fact, every day at 4:00PM Gary meets with his immediate staff and they review all the ideas submitted by the employees. Their goal is to give immediate feedback to the employees and also to see how they can help the employees implement the ideas.

Michael Miller's Idea

Michael Miller worked on the assembly line packaging new videos for Blockbuster, Hollywood Video stores and others at Technicolor, Detroit. His job was to close around 8,000 to 10,000 jewel case covers a day; the jewel case houses the CD movies. Imagine doing Michael's job everyday of the week?

Well, when Michael was introduced to Quick and Easy Kaizen, empowering him to make his work easier and more interesting the 'light bulb,' went off in his head. He got two pieces of wood, tied them together with pieces of cardboard and adhesive tape, and placed them against the assembly line. This simple contraption automatically closed the 'jewel' case covers without him

---

[197] See page 319 for a copy of an interview from Quality Digest magazine with Gary Smuda.

Quick & Easy TIP	
Before Improvement	After Improvement
ONE PERSON STANDING closing TOP OF MULTI PACK	I put corner on conveyer so it can close by it self

The Effect: Close Boxes by it self, save person and money

Date: 1-17-02   Name: Michael Miller

What Michael did with his idea was to totally replace himself. How many of you would do this if you had the chance?

In a recent lecture in Cleveland, Ohio I showed Michaels idea and asked the audience, "Raise you hand if you would do the same thing as Michael." Out of 50 attendees only one person raised their hand. Another attendee laughed and said, "Yea, he raised his hand because he owns the business."[198]

Consider that even a bad Kaizen idea can somehow lead to a better solution. So cultivate, not kill off the flow of ideas when you don't like one. Edison had hundreds of bad ideas; Madame Curie had many failures, but through perseverance and a willingness to learn from their failures they both eventually succeeded. You should give hints to lead your employees to find better solutions. Cultivate it; don't kill it. Your critical reviews might sound very logical, but they may shut off people and crush future innovative ideas. "I gave an idea but they didn't like it so I will never offer another one again." Stop, just stop playing the 'Devil's advocate,' and try to find a new way to inspire people to grow. Criticism is like stepping on a fragile flower, while constructive review will bring new life to the Kaizen activities.

To make the Quick and Easy Kaizen process work:

1. The employee notices a problem or an opportunity for improvement.

2. The employee gets an improvement idea, writes it down and submits it to their supervisor.

3. The employee implements the idea, writes up the idea on the Kaizen form and puts it into the Idea box.

---

[198] But shouldn't we develop the kind of organization where everyone would replace themselves to make the company more productive. Of course, they would have to trust management that the reward for these ideas would not result in "unemployment."

4. Within 24 hours, managers review and give positive feedback. A must!

6. If a larger improvement idea is approved, the employee should take leadership to implement the idea. They just don't submit an idea for someone else to implement.

7. All implemented ideas should be posted to share with others.

And praise, praise, praise!

Awards are also a nice way to show appreciation for people's special efforts to help the company succeed. At some Dana Corporation plants, the names of people who have submitted two ideas for the month are placed into a barrel for prizes. Last year they offered two tickets to a Raiders football game as the prize. That month they received the highest number of ideas ever. You might like to also have some of the workers talk about their implemented ideas at group meetings.

Sometimes when I run a Quick and Easy Kaizen workshop and mention that the average company in Japan gets two written ideas per month per employee, some of the managers in the room just freeze up – their minds just stop working. 'How in the world can I handle '240 ideas from my workers?' They just don't hear or believe my next phrase, which is that the employees implement their ideas, not the supervision. There is fundamentally a lack of trust between supervisors and their workers as if they are all out there ready to just take advantage of the company. Yes, of course, you do need a new mindset, and supervisors have to build up trust and learn to listen to the ideas from their workers. For me it is quite simple. I just say, "If Japan can do it, Why can't we?" And instead of being afraid of too many ideas we should look to it as proof of an energized workplace.

Kaizen educates at the job site, Kaizen means knowing when to eliminate, reduce, change an activity, Kaizen promotes personal growth of employees and the company, provides an opportunity to provide guidance for employees, serves as a barometer of leadership, Kaizen does not conflict with productivity or quality efforts, each Kaizen is small but the cumulative effect is tremendous (like ants, bees building their hills and hives). Three objectives: participation, development activities and effect. You want to make Kaizen part of your culture.

Kaizen means not accepting the status quo. Managers should explain the real objectives and targets to each department. Kaizen is simply changing the way we do our jobs that is all there is to it. Learning about Kaizen is nothing more than learning how to do the job. Kaizen begins with identifying existing problems. It presumes acknowledgement of one's own prior willingness to tolerate a problem. People thus have to admit there is always a better way to do things.

The power behind Quick and Easy Kaizen is contained in the definition of Kaizen:

1. Change the method; meaning that once the change is made you can't go back to the old way of doing things.

2. Kaizen is small ideas, in fact, the smaller the better. Engineers and managers are constantly coming up with new innovative ideas – they must innovate for the company to survive. Innovation takes time and is costly to implement but Kaizen is just day-to-day small improvements that when added together represents both enormous savings for the company and enormous self-esteem for the worker.

3.   Kaizen is also done within realist or practical constraints. Often when change is suggested to supervisors and managers, there are host of reasons why it can't be done:

- Not enough money
- Not enough time
- Not enough man/womanpower
- We have to many initiatives going on at this time – lean, six-sigma, 5S, supply chain, etc.
- The bosses are to busy and won't allow us to change
- We have too many rules and regulations to overcome
- We have to worry about ISO and standardization
- The old way is always the best
- It is difficult times
- We might make a mistake

Fundamentally, there is just a resistance to change.

But, Kaizen is only small changes and can be done by the worker himself or herself with very little investment of time.

Try it! I guarantee you will love it.

Why?

During the late 1980's I started to take Dana Corporation managers to Japan. From one trip Woody Morcott, the CEO and chairman, came back and realized:

"Why did we hire 55,000 brains and only use four of them?"

"Norman, I never ask those very powerful four words –

What do You Think?"

Woody then asked all of Dana's employees to submit two ideas in writing every month, and implemented 80% of them. It is now ten years later and Dana is still getting on average two ideas per month with 80% of them implemented.

For additional information on Quick and Easy Kaizen you might like to read the book I co-authored with Bunji Tozawa.

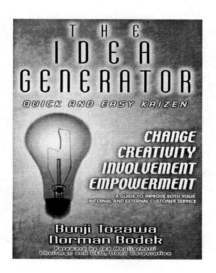

The Idea Generator – Quick and Easy Kaizen
By Bunji Tozawa and Norman Bodek

33

A Gallery of Great Geniuses

"What is central to business is the joy of creating."
Peter Robinson

Philip B. Crosby

In January 1980, *Quality is Free* by Philip Crosby was published. It wasn't the content of the book that excited me, but the title. Up to this moment, the industrial world looked at the high cost of improving quality. If you wanted to improve the quality of your products, we thought you needed greater investment and more inspections. Crosby was telling us the reverse. In his book's title was revealed the secret of the Japanese success story – the greater the quality, the lower the cost to produce your products and services, and you now have happier and more loyal customers.

In 1979, he founded Philip Crosby Associates, Inc., with headquarters in Winter Park, Florida. Over the next ten years it grew into a publicly traded corporation with 300 employees around the world and $80 million dollars in revenue. Phil eventually sold his company, rumored for around $60,000,000 to Proudfoot Management Consulting, and ironically bought it back in 1997 rumored to be for around $2,000,000 – not a bad deal.

My goal during the 1980's was to meet and learn from every productivity and quality Guru in the world. I invited these great people to come and speak at my 'Productivity the American Way' conferences that we ran every six months. At one of first of these conferences in Washington, DC[199], I invited Philip Crosby to be one of the keynote speakers. At each conference we had 40 to 50 speakers: industry leaders, consultants, and authors. Miraculously, I only had to pay a speaking fee to the politicians. The legal limit at the time was $2,000 to get a leading political person to speak.[200] Except Phillip Crosby's VP insisted on $7,000. I didn't want to do it – it was against my religion, but I felt that Crosby's name would attract many attendees, so I relented. Ironically, when I met Philip a few years ago in Portland, Oregon, before he died and I told him this story. He said, "Norman, you didn't try hard enough. I would have spoken for free."

Crosby was also noted for saying, "Doing things right the first time adds nothing to the cost of a product or service." His Four Absolutes of Quality Management:

1. Quality is defined as conformance to requirements, not as 'goodness' or 'elegance'.

2. The system for causing quality is prevention, not appraisal.

---

[199] I invited president Ronald Reagan to speak at this conference and received a tentative approval, except at the last moment he attended a famous conference in Japan to re-evaluate the dollar to the yen – the dollar dropped down drastically – he should have stayed in Washington DC.

[200] Over the years we had five US Senators, three congressmen, 50 CEO's of Major Corporations, including Andy Grove of Intel, Herb Kelleher of South West Airlines, Robert Crandall of American Airlines and many more great people keynote our conferences. It was magic!

3. The performance standard must be Zero Defects, not "that's close enough."

4. The measurement of quality is the Price of Nonconformance, not indices.

Crosby's 14 steps to quality improvement:

1. Management commitment
2. Quality improvement team
3. Quality measurement
4. Cost of quality evaluation
5. Quality awareness
6. Corrective action
7. Establish an ad hoc committee for the Zero Defects Program
8. Supervisor training
9. Zero Defects Day
10. Goal setting
11. Error cause removal (ECR)
12. Recognition
13. Quality councils
14. Do it over again

His management style checklist:

- Listening
- Implementing
- Cooperating
- Learning
- Helping
- Leading
- Transmitting
- Following
- Creating
- Pretending

Dr. Noriaki Kano

I met Dr. Noriaki Kano in 1982 when he spoke to our study mission group. I was very impressed with his presentation as we heard about 'Attractive Quality Creation;' the key to success was to not just listen to what customers were saying but to develop a deep understanding of the customers' world and then to address these latent needs. At the time the travelers came from corporate environments that did their best to produce products that they thought the customer would buy as opposed to discovering the needs, aspirations and even those desires not as yet known to the customer. The example given by Dr. Kano is the Konica camera company solving problems of blurry images, under and over exposures, and blank rolls by creating new cameras with auto focus, built-in-flash, and automatic film winding.

Dr. Kano spoke about fulfilling customer requirements. There was considerable risk associated with it if the product/service provider was not aware that there are different types of customer requirements. Without this understanding and measurement, providers risk:

- Providing superfluous quality
- Wowing the customer in one area, and driving them to competitors in another
- Focusing only on what customers say, and not what they think

He suggested that we measure the degree to which the customers' requirements are fulfilled. The dimensions range, naturally, from completely unfulfilled to completely fulfilled.

Also mentioned was the customers' subjective response from being 'irate' to being 'delighted.' This model of customer satisfaction predicts that the degree of customer satisfaction is dependent upon the degree of fulfillment, but is different for different types of customer expectations.

Dr. Kano built a now famous model of customer satisfaction. The model described the complexities of customer needs and their relationship to customer satisfaction in an easy to understand visual format. It provides insight into product and service attributes that are perceived as important to customers and is an important tool for helping teams focus on differentiating features, those that will set them apart from their competitors.

Once again I made a mistake. I told Dr. Kano that I wanted to publish his books in English, but he said, "I haven't written any books." For some years I lost touch with him. Later, he did write some very good books but sadly someone else published them.

I do periodically meet with him. Last time we had dinner in Tokyo he told me that he had fulfilled a wish of his to drive in each of the 50 states.

Kaoru Ishikawa

Dr Ishikawa was the true father of the quality improvement movement in Japan after World War II. He was the principal force and creator of Quality Control Circles and the leader of the Total Quality Control (TQC – later changed to Total Quality Management TQM) efforts that spearheaded Japanese companies to lead the world in quality products. According to Ishikawa, quality improvement is a continuous process, and it can always be taken one step further.

J. M. Juran

Mr. Juran was recognized as the person who added the human dimension to quality—broadening it from its statistical origins. Noted by every quality practitioner for his Quality Control Handbook first published in 1951.

W. Edwards Deming

He was a great teacher, a Professor of Statistics at the Graduate School of Business Administration of New York University and most noted for being the catalyst inspiring the Japanese towards their great quality success. The Deming prize in Japan sparked Japanese companies in their quality improvement efforts. His Plan – Do – Check – Act wheel broke the stereotype that Quality had fixed parameters – it could always be improved.

Yasuhiro Monden

Professor Monden wrote many books on The Toyota Production system and also on Japanese management accounting. He is a professor at the Institute of Policy and Planning Sciences, University of Tsukuba and is also on the Certified Public Accountant's board of examiners. In 1980, he gave what was probably the first lecture on the Toyota Production System in America. Some of his notable books:

Toyota Production System, Industrial Engineering and Management Press (Institute of Industrial Engineers), 1983.

Innovations In Management: The Japanese Corporation, Industrial Engineering and Management Press, (co-ed. with Shibakawa, R., Takayanagi, S. and Nagao, T.), 1985.

Applying Just In Time: The American/Japanese Experience, Industrial Engineering and Management Press, 1986.

Japanese Management Accounting, Productivity Press (co-ed. with Sakurai, M.), 1989.

Shigehiro Nakamura

Mr. Nakamura has taught over 30 different management manufacturing courses at the Japan Management Association in Tokyo. Each course is part of the total process of continuous improvement. He shows clearly how each function in the organization: sales, accounting, logistics, manufacturing, etc. plays an integral part in improving quality, performance and driving down costs.

The New Standardization: Keystone of Continuous Improvement in Manufacturing

Go-Go Tools: Five Essential Activities for Leading Small Groups

Total Productivity Management

Hiroyuki Hirano

There is great power in simplicity and directing your attention to teaching the total elimination of the manufacturing wastes. I liked very much Mr. Hirano's books for they were easy to read and easy to follow. I visited Mr. Hirano in his office in Tokyo and was very impressed with his library of manufacturing books. I remember while he was out of the room I would busily write down every title seen for I was looking for other Japanese books to publish in English.

We took an enormous gamble in publishing his JIT Implementation Manual and first selling it for $3,500 per two-volume set. Amazingly when something is good, it sold and sold very well. The power was in the forms that Mr. Hirano would use on the factory floor.

I don't know about you but when I go into a book store I am always very reluctant to buy a book over $40.00, but when I sit at my desk in the office I have a totally different perspective and will spend hundreds on books, software and training material.

His books:

- ***JIT Implementation Manual: The Complete Guide to Just-In-Time Manufacturing***
- *5S for Operators: 5 Pillars of the Visual Workplace*
- *Putting 5S to Work*
- *JIT Factory Revolution: A pictorial Guide to Factory Design of the Future*
- *5 Pillars of the Visual Workplace: The Sourcebook for 5S Implementation*

Shigeru Mizuno

The book *Management for Quality Improvement: The Seven New QC Tools* edited by Shigeru Mizuno was advanced management techniques to improve quality. I liked these tools but actually never saw them applied. I knew that Florida Power and Light gave copies of the book to 7000 employees to help them win the Deming Prize. With Yoji Akao he developed QFD a method that would design customer satisfaction into a product *before* it was manufactured and co-authored with Akao QFD: the Customer-driven Approach to Quality Planning & Deployment.

Ryuji Fukuda

Dr. Fukuda was a vice president at Sumitomo Electric in charge of their production facilities. He also was a professor of Reliability Engineering at Kobe University and he was most famous for his development of the CEDAC technique. He is the brilliant author of *Managerial Engineering* (my first published book), *CEDAC A Tool for Continuous Systematic Improvement,* and *Building Organizational Fitness.* He was awarded the Deming Literature Award and Sony's highest award for quality.

Dr. Fukuda developed a very simple but very powerful technique fully described in *Building Organizational Fitness* based on the X-Type Matrix. X-Type Matrix is one sheet of paper top where management describes their three to five main objectives for the year such as a 10% reduction in costs, 30% improvement in quality, 50% introduction of new products, etc. Then the division or departmental managers decide what areas they will work on to deliver the objectives. On this one form the managers then can see where they overlap and how they should work together to deliver the targets. CEDAC (an advanced form of the Cause and Effect Diagram) keeps track of the problems, targets and interaction between the groups. Finally the specific measures are shown so that periodic checks can be made to determine if the objectives will be met.

In Stuttgart, Germany I visited one of Dr. Fukuda's clients a Sony TV plant. At first when Dr. Fukuda came to teach the X-Type Matrix to them they tolerated him for he came from Sony headquarters in Japan, but they pretty much ignored him feeling that 'We Germans are much better and don't really need help.' But, a year later when Dr. Fukuda came back they realized the simplicity and also the incredible power rendered to them in this one sheet of paper and they then managed their plant successfully from it.

Since communication with vendors is often a problem, in the material receiving section of the Sony plant was a CEDAC chart listing all of the problems with incoming parts. At their sister plant in England where the TV tubes were made was also a copy of this CEDAC chart up on the wall. The two plants would fax each other daily keeping the chart up to date: problems found, possible causes, intended resolutions, progress being made, etc.

James B. Swartz

It was in 1996 when I received a telephone call from the president of Spraying Systems in Wheaton, Illinois wanting to reach Jim Swartz. I called Jim and said you are wanted; let's go to Chicago to visit them.

In the office of the president, with the corporate controller, VP of Engineering, and VP of Manufacturing, I watched with amazement as Jim communicated with these senior officers. The president had heard Jim speak earlier and was so impressed that he invited him this day. However, instead of, like many others, jumping in with a sales presentation, Jim slowly asked, "What are your most important strategic issues. Tell us about your position in the marketplace. What are your greatest opportunities? What changes would you have to make to seize those opportunities?

And then Jim listened carefully. We were told that Spraying Systems was the world's leading producer of nozzles for every commercial application: for farmers spraying crops, washing cows, drying milk, coffee, detergents, flavorings, air atomizing nozzles producing an extremely fine spray — under 15 microns in some cases — by mixing compressed air with liquid, spray coating, moisturizing, humidification, gas conditioning and dust control, spray guns, painting automobiles and if you wanted to clean a tank, tote, vat, vessel, drum, tanker truck or any other container. But, even though at this time they were the world's leader, to stay the leader they had to speed up their delivery and lower their costs.

Jim thought carefully and finally told them that he could definitely help, but to be fair he wasn't sure that he could free up enough time to be available at this time. Then we walked through the factory and Jim was inspired with the technology seen and also knew that he could help them seize the opportunities they had found. Jim took the assignment and now, eight years later, Jim is still spending significant time with the company. If you visit the factory you would see perhaps one of the finest manufacturing facilities in North America.

From a beginning as a physicist in the late 50's, Jim worked at Delco Electronics in various engineering assignments, including project manager for the development of Fuel Injection Electronics. His career in lean manufacturing began in the late 1970's when he was named manager of an electronic plant. Seeing that high cost operations were being moved to Singapore, Jim mobilized the plant workforce to reduce costs by 23% in one year using lean principles he learned from visits to Toyota. This began a crusade to improve American manufacturing.

Jim is the author of *The Hunters and the Hunted*, similar to *The Goal*; it is a very fine non-fiction novel about manufacturing. His new book, *Seeing David in the Stone*, due out later this year, is another masterpiece. In this book, Jim, helps you understand what the great masters in the past, Galileo, Michelangelo, Fred Smith (Fed EX), Marie Curie, Albert Einstein, Bill Gates (Microsoft), Sam Walton (Wal-Mart), Leonardo da Vinci and others did to find and seize the great opportunities of their time.

Jim works with companies to find and seize the greatest opportunities in their market. He helps them implement a high leverage version of Kaikaku using 12 actions.

Find High Leverage Lean Opportunities:
- Learn lean and agile technology
- Analyze the business situation
- Envision lean opportunities
- Select only high-leverage lean opportunities

Multiply the Power of Lean through Others:
- Find the stakeholders highest meanings
- Co-create opportunity with eager stakeholders
- Sell opportunity to cautious stakeholders
- Find common ground with opposers

Seize Lean Opportunities and Deliver Rewards:
- Design a superior future manufacturing/business system
- Place resources at high-leverage points
- Act rapidly/flexibly in an organized, timely campaign
- Lead stakeholders to seize the rewards

James Bramsen, President, Spraying Systems says:

"Jim is an absolute master of the tightly focused question series to help people understand the situation and also to understand the answer. He makes sure people working with him inculcate the answer and it is their answer, which is the first step in getting something solved. He has an excellent ability to deflect any credit taking on his part. He does not take credit. He makes sure that the credit goes to the people implementing it. This is the way he has worked because he is so good at this; this is why I want him to continue to work in our organization. Jim found very big payoffs and we were happy to make the changes."

There are three keys to opening people's creativity:

1. Respect their acquired expertise. Let them tell you what they know about their work. There is a lot to respect them for.

2. Respect their power over their work and let them know that you need their help. Be humble and be aware of their power to change or to resist change. I need your help!

3. Respect their point of view.

If you want their help to change, you must:

1. Co-create with a small group of eager investors (workers) to get them to lead the opportunity search.

2. Find the higher meanings that will sell the large group of cautious stakeholders (those affected by the change,) because they don't easily change.

3. Find common ground with the small group of opposers, then negotiate with them.

I am happy to include Jim in my Gallery of Great Geniuses.

Bunji Tozawa

Bunji is the president of the HR Association in Tokyo, and has for the past 15 years taught Quick and Easy Kaizen workshops throughout Japan and the Far East. He teaches around 110 workshops a year, every year. He was in Bangkok a year ago and 500 people showed up for his workshop. He has been the inspiration and the catalyst to thousands of companies to implement this simple but powerful process to open every worker to their creative potential.

Quick and Easy Kaizen empowers every worker to recognize problems or potential problems and to come up with solutions and implement those solutions themselves or with their work team. The secret behind this process is for the worker to focus on things around them that they can implement instead of coming up with improvement ideas and expecting someone else to do it for them..

Bunji has also written more then 20 books on Kaizen.

34

Professor Louis E. Davis, Socio-Technical Systems and the Quality of Work Life

"The gem cannot be polished without friction,
nor man perfected without trials."
Chinese Proverb

Through our research we were most fortunate to find Dr. Louis Davis, professor and head of the Center for Quality of Working Life at UCLA. Lou, with an industrial engineering background, was concerned both with the creation of highly effective organizations and with the human impacts of automation. How do you get high productivity? "Flatter, be more responsive and economically viable organization, based on intensive worker participation and balance between the requirements of people and technology"[201]

Dr. Davis had worked very closely with Eric Triste and Albert Cherns from the Tavistock Institute in Scotland, to introduce the concepts of Socio-Technical Systems.

---

[201] University of California In Memoriam of Lou Davis

Socio – Technical Systems blend the best of social systems with the best of technology. That means plants are designed to be highly productive, but also to create an environment that respects the human being fully. Lou detested the assembly line where people would only perform simple repetitive tasks over and over again.

The work of Dr. Davis, Triste, and Cherns, gave birth to the development of self-directed work teams.[202]

It was during World War II that Eric Trist discovered, studying work crews in coalmines in England, that the most productive mine had no supervision at all. The workers had delegated the authority between them, maintained a high spirit as they were serving the war effort through their work and began what we call today 'self-directed work teams.'

In studying Dr. Davis's work I began to realize that we had here in America a methodology equal or superior to the Japanese model but for some strange reason it was not spreading. Even better I thought if we could put socio-tech on top of JIT then we would definitely have the best of all worlds.

---

[202] Self-directed work teams " involve employees in the daily management of their business through work teams. These teams are empowered to take corrective actions to resolve day-to-day problems. They also have direct access to information that allows them to plan, control and improve their operations. In short, employees that comprise work teams manage themselves. Self-directed work teams represent an approach to organizational design that goes beyond quality circles or ad hoc problem-solving teams. These teams are natural work groups that work together to perform a function or produce a product or service. They not only do the work but also take on the management of that work -- functions formerly performed by supervisors and managers. This allows managers to teach, coach, develop and facilitate rather than simply direct and control."
– Ron Williams Quality Digest, November 1995

There was a Skippy Peanut Butter plant in Arkansas that was the most productive plant in the corporation with very little supervision, without a separate quality manager or quality inspectors, where the plant manager's assistant was also the factory nurse. In this plant, workers were assigned to work teams and had full responsibility to manage their work areas. The work team interviewed and hired new employees to join their team, and each new member knew that within six years they would be able to do everything within their area of responsibility, from ordering parts to quality inspection, to machine repair, etc.

There was an Alcoa plant in the state of Washington with a similar story. There was a Procter & Gamble (P & G) plant also noted for its high productivity. These plants were so good that most of the companies using Socio-Tech kept it as a secret. They felt that it gave them a vast competitive advantage. The problem was that they were able to use this system only in new plants and were unable to spread it to the older ones. Most of the plant managers I called would not (or were not allowed to) talk to me, for fear that their competitors would learn too much about them.

I invited Dr. Davis often to speak at our conferences, and convinced Continental Can to set up a new plant under his guidance. Lou also invited me to attend his annual conference held right next to Laguna Beach in California. It was exciting for me to learn that there was a group of people in America vitally interested in finding better ways to manufacture products, and also create a living environment that would enrich people's lives.

"Would you want your children to work in your factory?" This was a question I asked once again at one of my public presentations. Only one person in the room raised a hand and that person owned the company. How many of you would be proud to invite a friend into your house? Why wouldn't you want your

children to work in your plant?   Interesting questions for you to address!

In the first years of World War II, Lou was working at AT&T's Bell Labs in lower Manhattan, where they had just received one of the first radar devices, secretly transported from Britain by submarine. The need to get this radar into large-scale production was urgent. Lou was part of a team responsible for establishing the Bell Labs' assembly line for manufacturing these devices. To do this Lou set up an assembly line, simplifying tasks to get the radar devices quickly produced.   Lou said he also felt ashamed to have been the designer of the repetitive, tedious jobs these women were forced to perform. He made up for this in helping to redesign hundreds of manufacturing sites throughout the world.

According to Jim Taylor, "Lou's view of his profession changed forever at that time. In a way, his subsequent efforts to improve job design became his atonement. He succeeded magnificently, but his many achievements in supporting and creating systems for improving the quality of working life took him, and us, far beyond the mere design of jobs."

> *In December 2002, United Airlines was attempting to avoid going into bankruptcy and appealed to their unions for 'givebacks.' The pilots, flight attendants, and other unions agreed to the cutbacks, but the mechanic's union wouldn't agree.   Why?   They felt that United was not fair with changes in vacation policy and that they wanted improvements in the Quality of Work Life for their members.*[203]

---

[203] A good gauge to see how successful your company is in creating a Quality of Work Life is to ask your workers, which is the best day of the week for them. When the answer is any other day than Friday or Saturday you know you are going in the right direction, or when people stop looking forward to their retirement, you know you are getting close.

> *I am sure that United's management wanted to offer the best quality of work life for their mechanics, but didn't know clearly what that meant or how to deliver it. Quality of work life is probably only attained when workers are empowered to bring change. Socio-Technical systems is one marvelous way to get there, another is Quick and Easy Kaizen.*

The issue of the Quality of Work Life is far from being resolved but Lou Davis had made a major step in the right direction.

35

Failure to change is a vice.

"I want everyone at Toyota to change or at least do not be an obstacle for someone else wanting to change. I also want everyone to write down their change plans for the year."
Hiroshi Okuda, CEO and chairman, Toyota Motors

Toyota does not let 'grass grow under their feet.' Just imagine the most successful company in the world challenging all of their workers to change. The questions to ask are what does Mr. Okuda want in changes from his workers, how can Toyota go about getting those changes, how can they manage rapid change, and what does this mean to other auto manufacturers in the world? It is something to study right now before the differential becomes too great.

In a sense everyone resists change sort of like the yin - yang[204] principle. The individual is afraid to make mistakes. At

---

[204] This Symbol (Yin-Yang) represents the ancient Chinese understanding of how things work. The outer circle represents "everything", while the black and white shapes within the circle represent the interaction of two energies, called

school our grades were less if we made mistakes, a foolish system, for in truth we only learn from our mistakes. In industry we repeat this and discourage people from making mistakes and learning from them. Surely we don't want to make defects and we want to prevent costly mistakes from happening but we also don't want to thwart the creative process.

Then how do you bring change to your organization?

In Japan all school children know that the individual does not cross against the red but a crowd can.

Recognize that the individual resists change and it is the leader's job to inspire people to work in teams, and to challenge them to break 'new ground.'

"...basically the philosophy of corporate management is to endeavor to be a company that maintains strength beyond passage of time. A manager has to endure and strengthen their corporate organization by maintaining a strong and unwavering corporate philosophy. To protect a company from all the drifts, he should never be satisfied by the status quo; should not fear failure; and should introduce a culture of challenge." Hiroshi Okuda, CEO and chairman, Toyota Motors.

In December 2003 Toyota announced a series of drastic changes to the pay structure for all employees. For over 50 years at Toyota and in Japan people were initially hired at a base minimum wage and then each year received automatic pay increases. The increases did not at all correlate to job performance.

"yin" (black) and "yang" (white), which cause everything to happen. They are not completely black or white, just as things in life are not completely black or white, and they cannot exist without each other. They maintain a balance in the universe.

Now the drastic change was that all employees at Toyota would be evaluated yearly for pay increases and that pay increases would be based on merit not on age or length of employment.

When Japanese retire they normally receive a lump sum, maybe $200,000 to $400,000. Now under this new method at Toyota whereby employees will be evaluated yearly on their performance on retirement there could be a difference of 10,000,000 yen, roughly $92,592 at today's exchange rate.

Hiroshi Okuda, CEO and chairman of Toyota Motors is living under his word, "Failure to change is a vice." He is fostering drastic change at Toyota.

36
Summary

"If you knew how much work went into it, you wouldn't call it genius."
Michelangelo

I hope as your read the book that you found things to strengthen and deepen your understanding of Lean. I also hope you will accept the challenge of our age and find ways to enrich the quality of work life for all of the people that work with you and for you.

Lean is an unending journey to be the most innovative, most effective and efficient organization. The Power and Magic of Lean is to continually discover the hidden opportunities existing all around you. There will always be wastes to be eliminated. It seems to grow just like dust on your furniture. And always remember that people have unlimited creative ability but they must be challenged, encouraged, respected and expected to change. Continuous improvement must become your way of life.

Rudi once told me to ask for only one thing in life and that is to grow – to grow to my highest capability. All that really stands in the way is my resistance to change.

I wish you great success in your unending journey.   I welcome feedback on the book.   Did you see the stereogram?   Email me at <u>bodek@pcspress.com</u>.   - Norman Bodek

37

Gary Convis – President of Toyota Motor Manufacturing Kentucky

"Even if you're on the right track, you'll get run over if you just sit there." – **Will Rogers**

Gary Convis was named the first American president of Toyota Motor Manufacturing, Kentucky (TMMK) on April 1, 2001. In April, Convis was one of two Americans named by Toyota Motor Corporation as a Managing Officer.

Before coming to TMMK, Convis spent 16 years at the New United Motor Manufacturing, Inc. (NUMMI) plant in California. He was promoted to the position of Executive Vice President and to their Board of Directors. Prior to joining NUMMI, Convis worked with both General Motors and the Ford Motor Company.

Bodek: *I have enjoyed watching your career progress these past years and was "pleased as punch" when you were selected as president of Toyota, USA. I was most fortunate to have met and worked with Mr. Taiichi Ohno, former VP manufacturing of Toyota, and Dr. Shigeo Shingo, and to be the first to publish their works on the Toyota Production System in English. I have learned greatly from them. This new knowledge developed by these geniuses has and continues to revolutionize manufacturing processes* *around the world. We used to see mountains of inventory and all kinds of non-value adding wastes throughout a manufacturing plant, but wonderful changes have come. The Toyota Production System has focused on improving manufacturing processes, techniques, new tools, new methods, new systems, and words like Kaizen, Jidoka, Muda, SMED, TPM, Lean, standard work, takt time, and others are becoming common words in our manufacturing literature. But, very little has been written about the human side, how people do fit into this lean system, and how the Toyota system has begun to change the very nature of work. I would like to talk to you today about these changes and what they have meant and will continue to mean to the quality of work life.*

Convis: Within North America and globally, if you look at what Toyota is doing they are expanding without acquisitions. They are growing their culture country-by-country, operation-by-operation, which is really a phenomenal situation. The Ford's and GM's of the world are buying Volvo or Saab or different entities. Each of these new acquisitions developed over the years brings their own culture. Toyota is very much different from that, still headquartered in Japan, but gradually, due to their success, are expanding globally has a centralized homocentric culture. I think your point about the human side of lean is very understated and probably underestimated. You have a very good topic.

I would doubt that anybody outside of Toyota could perceive how much time and effort and discussion and sensitivity we have over the human side of our business.

In recent years we have developed what others might call the Toyota DNA. The Toyota DNA is the combination of bringing together two important aspects of Toyota; one is (T.P.S.) Toyota Production System and the other is managing the Toyota Way. In just the last few years Mr. Cho, Toyota's current president in Japan, has put the Toyota Way into a written format, coming from a process of almost ten years from many internal discussions. The Toyota Way, through our global management system, is to realize the human effort so critical to our success. If we look back at our history, the people who created Toyota (mainly our initial leaders Sakichi Toyoda, the founder of the automatic loom in Japan, the forerunner of Toyota, and his son Kiichiro) had certain philosophies and beliefs that were practiced from the very beginning. They didn't really talk much about them. It was more of how they did business. I think people like myself, who have been given added responsibility because we have demonstrated the traits and the knowledge that our senior officers have become comfortable with (to be able to manage the way they really strongly believe people), need to be managed.

Bodek: *Every successful company has certain guiding principles and values that are clearly demonstrated that pulls them foreword. Please tell us what keys have been the bedrock of Toyota's success.*

Convis: There are two pillars; one is continuous improvement, you might not call this a human issue exactly, but Toyota's success rests on the need for all employees, all management, to be looking for and striving for continuous improvement and never being satisfied. I remember back in 1986 at NUUMI when we won a silver JD Power award. We were pretty pleased about it, but GM said, "You did a good job, but look at all of the defects." We were proud to win but we had a lot of room for improvement. Yes, we did really well, but we saw where we could go and it was that challenging environment to never be satisfied. That is one of pillars of the Toyota Way. As human beings we need challenges. Actually, a basketball game would be rather dull if you didn't have a target to shoot at and with somebody keeping score.

To be challenged is a human trait that we all need. Of course, we rationalize on certain days over certain issues. But to be part of winning team drives us and provides us with human satisfaction.

To feel connected to something that is maybe difficult, that in it-self is life in the Toyota Way. We all need to continuously improve in every aspect of what we do. Like Tiger Woods, who uses Butch Harmon to help recreate his golf strokes, we need to continuously challenge and recreate our-selves. You want to continuously challenge to improve yourself, to improve your operations, to benchmark yourself, to be open to say maybe I am OK, but look that is right behind me coming up with a new something.

We believe very strongly in what the Japanese call 'genchi genbutsu,' the foundation of Toyota's engineering strategy, which means go, see, confirm, and be aware with your own eyes. That is why Kiichiro Toyoda actually went to Europe, spending many months over in England, looking at and assessing how they built their automatic loom. He probably knew more about making automatic looms then anyone else in the world, but he spent many months under very rigorous conditions to study what others were doing. It is part of our culture to go and see, and not just to be cheerleaders. We want to recognize what others are doing and also give them recognition for what they are doing. Understand it deeply and also be close by so you can help them, if they need help, offer an idea, and open a door that they don't perceive is available to them.

Bodek: *I strongly agree. I have been to Japan 57 times visiting over 250 plants, leading many study missions. It was for most of us our most important learning experience. Seeing world class companies with your own eyes and asking key questions, often gives you the power to bring change back to your own company.*

Continuous improvement is Toyota's first pillar for success; now please tell us about the other one?

Convis: The other pillar of the Toyota Way is respect for people, and honestly, I think that this is the heart of what your book is going to be. Respect for people! Honestly, if you don't have respect for the people that work for the company, you are in the wrong business. I think that individuals can tell from your body language, from your voice, whether you respect them for what they bring to the party. Just for the fact that they get up every day at 5:00am, and get dressed, and make the effort to come to work, and do a good job, you must respect them for that. What they do and how they do it! Being a responsible manager in the Toyota entity means you have a great responsibility to take care of the people who are donating their lives to the company.

Bodek: *So often I hear others use the 'respect' word, then I go out into the factory and see people acting only as extensions of machines, and given very little opportunity to change and improve their working conditions. Tell us about some of the things that Toyota has done to demonstrate how this pillar of respect works for you and them?*

Convis: I think the real key is having open two-way communications, where the employee feels free and empowered to talk to the boss. We have many ways we do that. We have a hot line call system, where anyone can pick up the phone, the call is registered, and the person does not have to give his or her name. But we have an obligation to respond to that complaint or to that call. We don't shirk any of them.

This afternoon we are having a president's roundtable. We do this once a month and select at random a group of 30 to 40 people to have a no holds barred meeting. We encourage them to ask people on their team or in their group for topics that they would like to bring up and talk about. We encourage people to be very open. We share reality, all of the facts, and our knowledge on an issue that they bring up. We find that they are very intelligent and very concerned about the company and the business. We tell them where we are heading, and what we are doing, and so on.

Another example, last year we invested almost $200,000 to upgrade our communication hardware and software to improve internal communications. We also reorganized some administrative resources and expanded our communications group. We run a small city here with almost 8000 people, and having the ability to communicate with them is very critical. We spend a lot of time and effort and resources to enable us to do that, and to do it well.

Bodek: *Is this new equipment also used to help people grow on the job through your training courses?*

Convis: Yes, we've upgraded the ability for us to do videos very quickly, without a lot of technical difficulty. We are heading to a real-time, on-demand video network system throughout the company. We probably have a library of over 200 videos, and if there is a particular topic that team members want to know more about, the group leader can pull up the video on their computer screen in their office. They can get the story right from the 'horses mouth,' whether it is a policy issue, a procedural issue, or speech I made in the past, or some technical issue that might need further investigation.

Bodek: *What percentage of a person's time will be spent on training?*

Convis: The average is between 40 to 60 hours a year.

Bodek: *What are some of the topics that you've developed videos on, and that workers might be looking into with you?*

Convis: Topics change from time to time. Four years ago we focused on values, sexual harassment issues, and diversity. It still goes on and will always go on. The last few years we have been creating more videos on the Toyota Production System, on standardized work, and on how to perform those kinds of activities. One current issue for us is giving team members more opportunities and more responsibility, called 'personal process operator.' The idea behind this is to make an operator a key individual that would have some key responsibility of taking care of some unique aspect of the process. This can range from a safety issue on the process to certain quality issues on the process. We are trying to have a methodical way of dividing the important aspects of the work, and giving more control to key individuals. Of course, it is all governed by a set of standards. It is not just a bunch of loose opinions going on. The standards are based on Toyota Production System standards we have developed. If there is a difference of opinion, we actually have ways of measuring it and coming back to fundamental basic ways of thinking. Is this the right way or should we go this way?

Bodek: *Wow, isn't that wonderful and powerful, giving individual workers on the floor more and more responsibility over the work processes. That is real respect for the worker and surely adds to the quality of their work life!*

Do you think that the pace of the work in Kentucky is equal to the pace of the Toyota worker in Japan?

Convis: No real differences today. The Japanese workers may be better in certain areas for they have been at it longer. And since their country size is smaller, they enjoy leveraging that with their suppliers. The suppliers in Japan do more work for the plants (due to their nearness to them) and there might be overall a little more added value. I think our team members work really consistently and very dedicatedly and are quickly catching up.

Bodek: *This also is great. From my past experiences visiting GM, Ford, and Toyota, the differences are like night and day between them.*

Convis: We are very up front with our team members that our customers won't pay more for our products just because we would like to have a raise next year. What we try to do is to teach them how to look at a process, and anything that we do needs to be adding value.

Bodek: *So nicely and simply stated, but very rarely taught to workers. Even though many companies today teach Lean manufacturing, very few of their employees, I believe, can make the distinction between adding value and non-value adding.   It is only when you really respect and trust your employees will they then begin to more carefully look at what they do to see if it is something that the customer wants to pay for.*

Convis: It is kind of like being out in your garage. If you are going to do a project, you first are going to get all of your tools together to have them handy. You don't want (in the middle of the job) to have to run down to the hardware store because you forgot something. This same thing is true in our work environment. We want everything to be organized to locate parts and have tooling in the right spot. We want the heavier parts waist high. There are many things we teach. We call it process diagnostics. We teach team members so that they can continuously improve their process and reduce the non-value added work. We feel that is our only way to insure our long-term survival.

Bodek: *Do you have and practice Jidoka the same way here as they do in Japan?*

Convis: Absolutely!

Bodek: *When a worker detects a problem, can they stop everyone around them from working until the problem is solved?*

Convis: They do it every day.

Bodek: *That in it-self gives such power to the worker. To think that 'I can stop everyone else from working when I have a problem or need help.' This gives incredible respect to the individual.*

Convis: In our culture it obviously takes time for everybody to buy into it. It takes fortitude. There are smart people here who know that the line has to run for us to make money, but we have to build quality into our products. We have the knowledge of how the car goes together. We have the right tools. We have the right parts. We have to build the quality in were it belongs. Step by step, overall, we are more efficient for we are not repairing and taking things apart that we have already put together. We are not creating new problems. We live very strongly to that program every day.

Bodek: *Can people rotate their jobs?*

Convis: Yes, we do rotate; typically we rotate four jobs per day. It keeps both the mind and the body pretty sharp. It is a talent you have to cultivate to be astute. You have to be concentrating from one job to another. You have to know how to read the manifest. You have to know where those parts were. You have to know how to do it in our environment. We don't match-build here. We build a different kind of car; practically every other car is different. As compared to say, Honda, where they match-build, it is more challenging for our team members.

Bodek: *One other question. My wife (who is Japanese) was listening to your chairman Hiroshi Okuda on TV who said, "Failure to change is a vice. I want everyone at Toyota to change or at least do not be an obstacle to change." How does that apply to you and the other Toyota members in Kentucky?*

Convis: Mr. Okuda is one of the brightest guys on the planet and in a world environment that doesn't embrace change, he is a very unique individual. As an example, he has recently restructured the traditional Toyota board alignment. They realize that in being global they have to make decisions quicker. They needed to more strategically driven by a smaller but highly developed group of people, so they narrowed the board down to senior managing directors and above, and created a new body called managing officers. I am one of the first three non-Japanese to be given that responsibility, which speaks for the change in it-self. The three individuals have the Toyota DNA; my wife says I am ¾ Japanese.

Bodek: *When I discovered the Toyota Production System in the early 1980's, I was just overwhelmed and spent the next twenty years devoting my life to finding out all about it, and getting as much material as possible translated into English. Mr. Ohno told me that for many years he would not let anyone write down anything about the Toyota Production System. He said that was because it was always changing. But, I felt deeply that he didn't want anyone outside of Toyota to discover what you were doing, for the tremendous economic advantage it gave Toyota over your competitors. He would allow nothing to be written down until he and Mr. Shingo wrote their books explaining it. I was most fortunate to become their American publisher. That was over twenty years ago. What is happening now?*

Convis: As we speak, Toyota is making a great investment in a global production center housed at the Motomachi Plant in Japan. It will pretty much centralize the teaching and the methodology of how we build things, how we manage the process, and how we manage major model changeovers. It is based once again on best practices that have been derived around Toyota, and from benchmarking others. We are going to now grow into this global production center as being how we do business, how we do things.

This is a big change for us from our past mother plant concept.

Bodek: *Please give us an example of what this means?*

Convis: We have a power train group here in TMMK, building L 4 engines and L 6 engines, and we also have an axle operation in power train. Each of the entities has a mother plant in Japan, and what we find is that the mother plant has its own language, its own way of doing things, it own little quirks on how they write standard work, the format they use or the little ways they do things inside power train. When I got here there was not a common language, a common format, and so on, and so forth. Right inside our own four walls we were not standardized. This was created because of mother plant differentiation. Toyota, as they become more global finds it harder to manage and leverage the best practices they find, and to spread them. So they realize that to become a global company, they have to become more capable in teaching our concepts. The global production center will be beyond just teaching. It is also applying it. There will be a very large mock up of an assembly area, a welding area, and logistics handling kanban. It will be the kind of center to develop best practices, and where they can demonstrate them.

Bodek: *Gary, I do thank you deeply for your time and look forward to meeting you soon in Kentucky.*

> *Lean thinking is best defined as creating organizational wealth. Lean thinking:*
>
> - *Adds value by focusing on customers*
> - *Creates flow by focusing on people and processes -- and by developing engaged employees who collaborate to engage customers by understanding and anticipating their needs*
> - *Achieves mastery by focusing on personal and group learning. This is the final element of lean thinking. It encompasses one of the most basic*

human needs: the drive for meaning, growth, and progress.[205]

The interview with Gary Convis was also published in the November 2003 issue of Quality Digest magazine – reprinted with permission.

---

[205] Mike Morrison, Dean of Toyota University – Gallup Management Journal, August 14, 2003, When leaders effectively manage the human difference, they build employee engagement, and align associates' performance to work that drives customer value. This requires managers who can match talent to task, build shared values among team members, and develop all employees to their full potential.

38

Gary Smuda – Technicolor Corporation

It is True! People are Your Most Important Asset.

*"Opportunity is missed by most people because
it is dressed in overalls and looks like work."*
Thomas Edison

Last July, I had the privilege of running a creativity workshop in Detroit, Michigan for a group of managers from Technicolor Thomson Group and others. While I was speaking, I was confronted by Gary Smuda, Director of Duplication Services in Livonia, Michigan for Technicolor, who said:

"Norman, I have been listening for the past two hours and I have not heard anything new!"

At first, I was shocked but somehow held my composure and replied,

"Gary, you are absolutely correct. There is nothing new here but you are not doing it. You are not empowering your employees to be part of the creative process."

Well, as you will see from the following interview, Gary Smuda took up the challenge and has implemented one of the most successful Creative Idea programs in America – he calls this improvement process Quick and Easy TIP's.

Bodek: *Gary first please tell us a little bit about your background in industry.*

Smuda: I have been with Technicolor for twenty years. I actually started in the video business with CBS Fox Video in 1983 and came along with the furniture when Technicolor acquired the Livonia Plant in 1987. I have worked as tape loading supervisor, duplication supervisor, and production scheduler and eventually became the production manager at the Livonia plant. In 1993, I was sent to our plant in the Netherlands in charge of duplication, packaging and distribution as part of a transition team. After returning to the states I was promoted to director of duplication services in 1996. Prior to Technicolor I worked for Ford Motor Company, TOYS R US Inc., and served in the U.S. Army as a combat engineer.

Bodek: *What does your group do in Livonia, Michigan?*

Smuda: We duplicate videocassettes for three of the largest motion picture studios among several video clients and have, since 1987, produced over 1 billion 750 million videocassettes here in the Livonia plant.

Bodek: You are the leaders in the video production industry. Please explain the importance of your Quick and Easy Kaizen TIPS process and what is has done for your employees, for Technicolor and for you personally?

Smuda: As you said in the introduction the first time we met I was very skeptical of all of this. In fact, I asked you during the initial workshop, "What's new here?" At the time when you visited us we were in to the third year of our Lean journey emulating the Toyota Production System. **One of the major parts of the Toyota Production System is their connection with their employees through their suggestion program.** Around six months before your visit we did implement the Technicolor Improvement Program (TIP) and we were soliciting suggestions from our employees. We were not very successful with our program and I was frustrated with it. But, before the end of that first day with you, a light flickered on and two strong messages came through from the Quick and Easy Kaizen training: **one was to go to the operator and ask them what they can do at their workstation to make their job easier and two was to do everything you can to make the suggester the implementer.** And if it was beyond their scope then make them part of the implementation team.

Basically Quick and Easy Kaizen kind of supercharged our implementation program to help us attain our goal of two written suggestions from each of our employees each month.

Since the first of this year I have become the Michigan "Cost Killer" responsible for my site in Livonia and the other two sites in Michigan to come up with cost killing ideas to reduce our indirect labor cost and non-production purchases. Through the TIP program we get many suggestions to reduce costs in those areas. In fact, today Norman I have gone through 237 TIP's. I spent my whole day going through these TIP's and 65% of them have already been implemented, and another 18% of them are in the process of being implemented. The rest either have to be bumped up to a higher level or they weren't really legitimate suggestions.

We do try to attach cost savings to some of the suggestions we have received. For example, today I looked at one about recycling office supplies and file folders. We have a form we use, a TIP form, and someone suggested that we just take used paper flip it over and copy the TIP forms on the back. Some of the TIP's I am looking at right now are on the back of recycled paper. A simple idea but it enlists our employees to pitch in and help save us money. We have had cost savings from $50 to $200 all the way up to $10,000 to $15,000. And they all add up. TIP has been an enormous help in reducing our costs with very little investment on our part. This system encourages people to participate in improvement activities, to be involved, and also allows management to be better connected with their employees.

Supervisors, managers including myself are now walking around the factory with these TIP forms in our back pocket and through our conversations with people we are writing down ideas and making sure that they get credit for them. One of our more clever supervisors trying to figure out how to recycle more things held up a packet of things at his last meeting and said, "How can we recycle this and remember every idea you give me is a TIP?" He got 30 ideas in that meeting. Some supervisors have gone up to their employees and said, "OK, guys and gals you can't go home until you give us a TIP – a joke really, we are not locking doors but he actually got 15 TIPS that day.

Bodek: *That is wonderful. What does it do for your personally in your job?*

Smuda: When we had our first meeting I was really skeptical about it. I was skeptical about getting any ideas. Then I was also very concerned with what are we going to do when we got them. So initially, to be truthful, I was both skeptical and nervous but then those two lights went on in my head. And getting the suggester involved in the implementation has exposed me to more of my employees. I have been trying to make a point to talk to everyone that does put in a TIP and say thank you. I also try to go out and see some of them being implemented. It has opened up another line of communication between myself and the folks that might have been somewhat nervous about approaching management. Although we do have a pretty much open environment here there are some people who just always blend in the background. One of the neat things about the Quick and Easy Kaizen program is that if a group of people put in a suggestion and work on it as a team they all get credit for it. You do have some people that are very quiet and now they get credit for an idea that they would not normally get credit for. This gives me a chance to also talk to them. It brings them out into the forefront. It also is one of the things that allow me to know more about what the workforce is thinking about. Some of the TIP's you get in the program are not necessary a legitimate TIP. Some of them are gripes or concerns and although they are not a suggestion that will make you a lot of money it is an area of concern that needs to be addressed. You get your eyes open to that and you can then deal with it.

Bodek: *Maybe you can tell me a little bit how it works?*

Smuda: Typically we will get a written suggestion, which is first given to the employee's supervisor. The supervisor then looks at it and between the two of them or between the supervisor and his work group they are empowered to immediately implement it. That happens between 50-60% of the time. If it requires the aide or the buy in outside of the group then the supervisor solicits that help. The more help they need the higher up the ladder the suggestion will go to get it implemented. But I would say at least 50% of them are implemented within 48 hours of the suggestion being handed in to the supervisor by the employee.

Bodek: Do the ideas not immediately implemented create any kind of burden on you or your managers?

Smuda: We do have meetings to go over the ideas that are out of the reach of the work groups. There is some management time involved but it is not a burden and I don't see this as a burden for the work group. It is looked at as one of the easier things to manage. We do get some weird suggestions and some things that are not really suggestions and we do have to go back to that person and tell them in a diplomatic way that it is not a legitimate idea but we want to do it in a way that doesn't insult them. It is an additional thing we have to manage but we are getting a lot of good out of it. We don't look at it as a burden.

Bodek: *Who participates?*

Smuda: Everybody, including my boss Mike Karol and his direct reports have the goal to submit a minimum of two improvement ideas per month. We track it and we post it. Our goal is on the average of two suggestions a month per employee. I give my suggestions to Mike and normally they are implemented before he receives them and it works that way all the way from the bottom all the way to the top.

Bodek: Change is difficult at every level. Why all managers in other companies are not jumping on the Quick and Easy Kaizen amazes me? What advice would you have for other managers to discover the power of this marvelous system you are using in Detroit?

Smuda: A lot of managers are probably skeptical about an employee suggestion program. At the last AME conference in Chicago I spoke with a number of senior managers that did not think that it was productive to go through this kind of exercise. I told them of my initial skepticism and how we were not doing very well when we first got started on this process. Fortunately we got in touch with you and went through your seminar. I think the most important thing we got out of that seminar **was asking the employees what could you do in your workspace to make your job**

easier? I believe it was that one thing that gave us a way to connect with the employees. Telling the employees that this process was going to make their job easier allowed us to make quick progress. When they do come up with a suggestion you must act fast to get it implemented. That is the key that proves that you are listening to them. Once management starts reacting to their suggestions and they actually see movement their suggestions become even more thoughtful. You make them part of the implementation process.

What might concern other managers is the thought, "what do we do when we get 2,000 suggestions per month? I can't implement them." And when you have a lot of people reporting to you I am sure you start to feel really nervous about this idea. But when you empower people to implement the improvement ideas the burden is off you. Like I said earlier 65% of the TIPS I looked at today were implemented already and it makes you feel pretty good. One of the major parts of Lean management often neglected by many companies is empowering people to be problem solvers. Most of us come from past cultures where we are the fireman all of the time. **Well now I have 450 firemen out there putting out fires and they are not coming to my door saying we have a problem. They are knocking on my door and saying well we had a problem and this is how we fixed it - that is really cool.**

I think the two biggest things are, to ask people the question what can make your job easier and then get them involved in the process to implement as quickly as you can. And if they need help then make sure they get the help that they need. And down the road there are ways to make it fun. I have some really creative people working with me. We looked at wasted pieces of cardboard and said, "We want to recycle this rather than throw it away – tell us how to do it?"

We received some discs from another Technicolor site where they package DVD's. They were blank DVDs, clear discs of polycarbonate with a hole in the center that are put at the end of a spindle so that the stack of DVDs doesn't get damaged. We were throwing those clear discs away. The replication facility didn't want them back. We held them up in meetings and asked our people do you have any ideas how we can use these things? We were throwing them away. We were paying money to have them taken to a landfill. We asked for ideas and received 12 TIP's on how to use them. We made it kind of a game.

January was safety month in our plant. We asked for and received quite a few safety TIP's during the month. Between November 2001, and January 2003, we worked over one million hours without a loss time accident in Livonia. A huge part of this accomplishment was because of the safety suggestions; many of them were a direct result of this program.

Bodek: *Are there any rewards given to the people?*

Smuda: We do have what we call a Bravo award system where we nominate special suggestions for a special gift. Where suggestions have helped give us exceptional cost savings there is also special monetary bonuses. Also we have Technicolor bucks where the supervisor and on up can give them out to people as a thank you note for a special idea, and all these things are used.

Bodek: *What are some of the effects on quality?*

Smuda: Many suggestions have been related to process and that affects the quality of our products. They have improved our process, which has improved our quality. We have come up with so many slick ideas on how to move product around without damaging it. We now respond quicker to problems. Many ideas reduced movement, eliminated steps where a product could be damaged. We improved the conveyors. We basically redid much of our material handling operation. A new cart was designed for the movement of bulk videotape because of a TIP. It improved the material handling. One big issue for us on quality is to eliminate damage to the videotape before it gets to the equipment that actually winds it into the cassettes. We have virtually eliminated the problem of the videotape pancakes falling on the floor from carts by using a new cart that came from a TIP. Without a doubt it has helped us to improve our quality.

Bodek: *You have been super. I thank you very much.*

The interview with Gary Smuda was published in the June 2003 issue of Quality Digest magazine – reprinted with permission.

39

Professor Doc – Robert Hall

"The greatest risk is not taking one." - Anon

Robert W. Hall is Professor Emeritus of Operations Management, Kelley School of Business, Indiana University. He is a founding member of the Association for Manufacturing Excellence (AME), and is now editor-in-chief of the association's publication, Target.

Dr. Hall was one of the first examiners for the Malcolm Baldrige National Quality Award. Currently, he is a judge for the Pace Award (for innovation among auto industry suppliers), and reviews applications for the Industry Week America's 10 Best Plants competition.

Dr. Hall is the author or co-author of six books:

- Zero Inventories, McGraw-Hill/Irwin, 1983
- Attaining Manufacturing Excellence, McGraw-Hill/Irwin, 1987
- Measuring Up, (with T. Johnson and P. Turney), McGraw-Hill/Irwin, 1990

- Flexibility: Manufacturing Battlefield of the 90s, (with J. Nakane), AME, 1990
- The Soul of the Enterprise, Harper/Collins, 1993
- Kaizen Blitz, (with A. Laraia and P. Moody), John Wiley & Sons, 1999.

Bodek: *Let us please talk about the human side of Lean manufacturing. Toyota has made enormous strides, and many Western companies are attempting to implement Lean but I feel that the West does not fully appreciate the power of involving all of their employees in improvement activities. Could you start off by talking about Jidoka * (automation with human intelligence), which is giving power to the machine and to the individual worker to stop the machine, to actually stop all of the surrounding workers whenever an error or a potential error is detected, which might affect quality or costs. Do any American companies do this?*

Hall: There are many definitions, various kinds of Jidoka. It means literally to "stop to think," most commonly where the worker pulls a chain or hits an Andon signal to stop the machine and then you attempt to figure out what is going wrong. The concept is pretty widespread.

Bodek: *The whole plant stops. Is this true in America?*

Hall: It isn't even true for Toyota anymore. In the new Kyushu plant they divided the plant into five sections and only one-section stops. There is now a buffer of one or two vehicles between the line segments because they didn't think that people were stopping the line enough. The employees did not want to shut the whole plant down so they would scramble and do a lot of things before they pulled the chain. They decided to make it a little more conducive to pull the chain when there was a problem. People were very reluctant to stop an auto line that might have been a mile or a half a mile long.

Bodek: *So, Toyota by dividing the plant into segments was encouraging the workers to more often stop their machine to detect problems or potential problems?*

Hall: At the Toyota Georgetown plant and in most Toyota plants they expect a certain amount of Jidoka time each day. At Georgetown it means two to four percent of the total time. Some of the downtime is not just an obvious problem that was detected, but it might just be an opportunity to study too. Also time is spent at the beginning of a shift or the end of a shift to have stand up meetings, that is think time, think before you work. People are getting clued in as a team if there is a little stand up meeting. It may not last more than a minute or two unless there is something really to talk about. It may be an opportunity for every body to get together! In the ones I've seen, a few of the side meetings are as important as the main meeting because everyone will be there and you can talk to whoever you want right at that time. We call it communicating, think before you work, and we are all clued into what we are going to do, like the football huddle. It is more extensive going all the way back to Ohno's stand in a circle thing; take time to observe what is going on around you in the process, don't just work away but take some time to think about what you are doing and why and so on and so forth.

Bodek: *Since there is an opportunity with Lean to re-look at the very fabric of what work is all about, I am hoping in this book to help people rethink what makes a factory or an office an exciting, humanistic place that people will actually look forward to coming to work.*

Hall: I feel that it all begins with the hiring processes. A lot of the problems I see in companies wanting to go Lean is that they didn't hire people with Lean in mind. It is challenging when you are attempting to be Lean with half the workforce unable to communicate with each other. In the past you might have hired people solely for their hands and what they could do physically without really doing a lot of checking. But can they really work as a team? Are they capable enough? They may not be highly educated but are they willing to think on the job? Are they just inclined to do their job and daydream, or will they really think about the job? Toyota or any company that hires people has to take a lot more time examining their new people. It is beginning. In some of the plants the teams do the final okay before a person is hired. Will this person fit onto this team? They are looking at different things not just dexterity.   There are a lot people in the world that can't do this or don't want to; maybe they could, but their concept of work doesn't fit into a Lean environment.

Bodek: *Bob, that needs a little bit more explanation. In America, unlike Japan, we are a very ethnically culturally diverse nation and that diversity does give us great strength.*

Hall: But, you know Norman, many people have been conditioned at work to think that this is sort of like a part time job. I do my thing at work, and then it is Miller time. I go home and I watch sports.   They have not been conditioned to think that they are really part of a company or a team that is going to do something that is important. It is just that with my little part of the job, if I do it fairly well then I am okay.

Bodek: *But that has so much to do with the climate of the company. The worker often just follows the tune set by management.*

Hall: People can get into it. At least a lot of them will. But you always have a problem both with the managers' expectations and also sometimes with the worker's expectations.

Bodek: *What are the expectations of people doing Lean?*

Hall: If you don't expect more then you certainly will not get more, as a manager or as a leader and people also have to expect it of them selves. The leadership can certainly encourage it and part of the trick is to get people to want to do it. Sometimes bonuses are given to inspire workers, sometimes given very reluctantly, but you sometimes have to do that to get the job done. If workers are reluctant and really want to harass management without violating any of the union contracts they just work the rule; this extra stuff is not in my job description so the hell with you.

Bodek: *What do you feel is missing with Toyota or at American companies to really engage people?*

Hall: The core of creating the right attitude is proper leadership. You can have problems because the workforce has not been well selected for Lean. But, you can do a lot to correct this. **The best leaders are the ones that realize that what you are doing is cultivating the people.** The techniques are all designed to develop people. If the leadership doesn't sort of see that, then Lean will just stagnate. **The whole idea from 5S and on is to reveal problems with the expectations that people are going to see the problems and they will want to do something about them.** They do have the capability of contributing something towards the solution of the problems. With the proper development of people they may at times do a whole lot more than what is normally expected from them. I am constantly amazed at the talents that people have and this is not just in manufacturing plants. I am on the board of a credit union, a fairly sizable one with around 250 employees. Last year at their annual all-employee meeting they put on a whole series of skits. Ten of the employees did a lot of work away from their job to practice acting and dancing to perform the skits. They were really good; to me they looked like professional dancers. If you hadn't told me that they were credit union employees I would have thought that they were paid for the thing. You get those kinds of things **and the various talents that people have should never be underestimated**. Being able to dance might not be able to help you when you are working on production line, but the talents that people have just aren't shown because nobody ever thought anything about it.

Bodek: *What would you recommend should be done for American companies to focus on the human side of Lean?*

Hall: I have a friend Tom Lane, formerly with Cummins Engine, and now a behavioral consultant. He has a unique way to explain it. To develop managers you have to help them suppress a little bit of their masculinity and expose a little bit more of their feminine side, because the masculine instinct is not to develop people but to control them. The feminine side is much more subtle. You can control people in various ways. You don't have to be bombastic about it and be a Donald Rumsfeld type. You can be much more subtle with budgets and standard work. A rigorous work procedure is not the same thing as having a boss thinking they have personalized control. It is awfully hard for managers, at least a lot of them, to make that distinction because there is an archaic tradition, not just here in the US, but in much of the rest of the world including a lot of Japan. Managers feel that this is their company and they manage it to represent and benefit the owners, and therefore I control you.

I tried experiments in a class on teamwork. With a few case examples spread a month apart, I gave a situation where you form teams and those on the team take the role of the employee. The whole class liked the idea. A month later again with the same people we form teams with a different case example but now you are the management. How to you like that? They are now not so sure. They are in a different role. When you probe a little deeper they are not too sure that they can trust the worker. I am okay, but you can't tell about that other SOB. It is very deep and very instinctive. The key part of it is for management to learn to build the trust of the workers and have some confidence in them and trust in them.

Bodek: *Making mistakes it essential to learning but there is always a lot of fears in letting people learn from their mistakes?*

Hall: Yes, of course, turn them lose and let them make some mistakes and still have some confidence in them. If they really make a big blunder or just don't take responsibility that is another thing. Sometimes those things happen but most of the time people really want to do a good job, but they are never really released to do it. They don't feel free to do it. There is a curious paradox here. They must work in an environment that is not chaotic. It has to be structured. You have to know something about what standardization of work means and if you are going to improve you re-standardize or you just get chaos. If you have that discipline going for you that paradox gives people a good deal of freedom to figure out what to do.

Bodek: *Tell us about your last trip to Toyota plants?*

Hall: I went with my Japanese buddy around a year ago to three Toyota plants, three suppliers in the US. We concluded that there were severe problems that Toyota had with the system in the US. **There was the instinct of the staff and the management to control. They thought they were doing employee participation but actually what they were doing was leading them too much and controlling too much.** They would make a suggestion on what needs to have Kaizen attention. They would do the deciding. To them consensus meant that management okayed the project first. If it is then okay with the workers, we have consensus. It is not the same thing as workers actually doing this more spontaneously.

They see that this is an improvement so it is okay. That is a real tough step to take and few Americans in the managerial role can make it. I am not sure that I could. I grew up in an era when manufacturing certainly wasn't that way. **Really turning the workforce loose takes a long apprentice period of learning. How to get comfortable building trust?** Another aspect of this is the turnover issue of managers and sometimes the workers. If you really have high turnover you can't develop the workforce properly. You always have to contend with the new people that are really green. That may not be so bad if you had a simple process and jobs are easy to learn but the more complicated it gets the worse it gets.

And then the other one is the turnover of leadership. At General Electric (GE) it is one of their major problems. I have seen several GE plants and for as long as I can remember they change plant managers about once every two years on average. Then they may change two or three other people at the top of that plant at the same time. You have nomadic plant managers going from place to place trying to gel as a team. Then are they going to influence the culture, sure they are. Several of my wife's relatives work at a GE plant and they all know that whenever this new group starts to change things just wait it out. A few years later they will be gone and we will still be here. Smaller companies may have different versions of that, but GE sort of typifies it. The objective is to move people around and give managers a variety of experience, which has its merits, but there is insufficient attention given to the development of the workforce. They are really developing a culture of improvement or what ever you want to call it. That they delegate to someone, like a director of organizational change or whatever. But as long as the top leadership changes and they are different signals about what they want it is not going to be effective.

Bodek: *Do the Japanese managers have a more consistency of style?*

Hall: Well I think there is more consistency in Japanese management but all Japanese are not agreed on Lean manufacturing. Some of them are as opposed to it as any American manager. If you go to Toyota and other organizations of the same ilk, they do move their managers. They don't move all of them at the same time. A hidden part of the system to me is that they give a lot of attention to building a fairly common culture among the managers. If I am coming from Japan to be an adviser to the American plant manager in Georgetown, I probably won't make a whole lot of waves at first.   I will just see what is going on.   Since I know the system, I see that the person before me was not really bad.   I don't have to do something just to make me look good, unlike GE where getting ahead means I have to be a hero.   So at Toyota the new manager coming in is expected to contribute more to the development of the people and to just continue a process of improvement that existed before they got there and that will be in place when they leave. During their watch if they add their influence to make some significant advances in developing people have done their job.   They don't need to tear everything up, institute a new program or cancel an old program or do something just to pad a resume.

Bodek: *But GE has been the great American model these past years, everyone is emulating Six Sigma.*

Hall: One of the big problems I see with GE's six sigma and to some extent with Motorola is that it gets converted to a managerial status system instead of being part of developing people. At GE if you are not a black belt you probably are not going to be considered these days for higher-level management. What does that do? Well, you got to have some projects that have some wham to them. I have to go through the plant and get some six sigma projects that are going to show well. So when I move to the next place I can be a star. It doesn't develop people. It doesn't have to be totally contradictory to developing people.   You could do it, but since you don't normally have enough tenure, people are stuck trying to rummage up to programs or projects that make them look good and that is what they do.

Bodek: AT GE don't they eliminate the lower 10% each year, which puts all kinds of pressure on people?

Hall: There is always a lower 10%.

Bodek: *But at GE those lower 10% are gone!*

Hall: Yeah, and how do you define the lower 10%?   That gets you into a whole lot of other issues. The assumption is that you are improving yourself. I personally find that doubtful. There are always a few people including at Toyota that just cannot keep up for all kinds of reasons. They degenerate. They can't do the job. People that get into alcoholism or something else. Gives you an HR problem that has to be dealt with. It happens everywhere including Toyota. Just having this arbitrary rule letting go the lower 10% at the end of every year doesn't really accomplish that much. It does stir up a lot of fear and a lot of managers working under fear just reinforces it. I seek to make myself look good instead of developing the people. **At a Toyota system company the manager's performances are measured a little bit on outcome on how the numbers look but a whole lot is based on how well people develop between when you came and when you left. So a manager in that sense is much more of a teacher.** They don't call the Kaizen leader sensei for nothing. They are teachers, very tough teachers. Norman, you have been around some of them. They can be pretty tough at times but they are still teachers. We call them coaches; coaches don't play the game; coaches can't make themselves look good by personally playing the game. They probably aren't going to look good by directly intervening in anything. They look good by whatever style they use trying to get the most out of the people, to let them do it. Some of them might have a pretty good style of it and some of them might be a little bit rough at times.

Bodek: *On my last visit to Japan I heard the chairman of Toyota, Mr. Okuda say,* "Failure to change is a vice. I want everyone at Toyota to change or at least do not be an obstacle for someone else who wants to change!" *What does that mean to you?*

Hall: Toyota is sort of moving on. It is hard to say what he meant exactly by that but from my reading of people around Toyota I get the feeling that they must get a little bit beyond some of the rigidly of Lean. They have to be a little more innovative. It is not that they are bad at innovation **but you don't use the Toyota system as sort of a bible that isn't bendable**. There is no technique in it. There is no recipe and if I just follow it I will be okay. The real test of the workforce is the ability to take a process that is new and different or a product that is new and different and reduce that to something that gets you to **standardize work** in record time. It is not that we have done kaizen for so long that all can get is our one tenth of one percent improvement for this year out of it, that doesn't get it.

I heard a German explain it very well. There is a huge difference in people when they say they have 30 years of experience. One person has the same experience each year for thirty years while the other one had thirty different years of different experiences.

The last time I visited Toyota I knew they were moving towards higher states of change. At the Tahara plant where they will try out a new vehicle, the workforce should be capable of not only doing a pretty good job with production but also at taking a process that has new wrinkles to it, maybe a highbred car that has something different about this, and working through that and getting it down so that, if they had to transfer that production to Thailand, it would go in pretty good shape and the Thais could carry on from there. They want to get away from rigidity with the use of Information Technology (IT). You can use the information system to manage the waste instead of getting rid of it. **You want to dispel the fear of doing something that is different.**

American managers that have done the worst are technique-ish. **The ones that have done the best didn't have an in-depth understanding of all of the techniques but they were really good with the people.** You can always take a people person and coach them on a few things that they didn't know about the technique, but when you take someone who is a smart ass on all of the techniques and doesn't pay attention to the people, didn't get on the floor, didn't socialize with them, didn't make themselves accessible, and didn't try to make sure that they were coming along; they were likely to fail.

40

Don Dewar

*Don Dewar is awarded the Ishikawa Medal (2003)
from the American Society of Quality (ASQ). The
Ishikawa Medal is awarded to an individual or a
team whose work has had a major positive impact
on the human aspects of quality.*

Don Dewar is the President, QCI International. QCI International publishes: *Quality Digest,* a monthly magazine, *Timely Tips for Teams,* a monthly newsletter, *Inside Quality,* a Web site for quality professionals, *Quality Insider,* a weekly newsletter, *Quality Digest E-Update, Inside Six Sigma,* a monthly newsletter, *InsideStandard,* a monthly newsletter, and *InsideMetrology,* a monthly newsletter.

In 1973, he pioneered the introduction of quality circles in the United States. Don has spoken to thousands of people in hundreds of sessions in 25 nations worldwide, and he has authored or collaborated on nearly 300 articles and papers, 46 books and produced 97 training videos. Three of his books have sold over one million copies each.

In 1977, Don co-founded the Association for Quality and Participation (AQP) (formerly the International Association of Quality Circles), and served as its president for three terms. AQP grew to over 10,000 members.

Bodek: *I credit you and Wayne Ricker as the two key people that had the foresight to discover, develop and bring team activities to America.   You broke the mold! We have given these team activities many different names quality control circles, self-directed work teams, quality teams, small group activities, six sigma; they are very similar. They all brought people together in small work groups to improve quality. Now the issue some twenty odd years later is how will these teams function under a lean environment? And can we advance the team concept to help change the human condition at work?*

Dewar: Employee involvement teams – they thought I was nuts to try and teach this, the brave people willing to pick up the gauntlet and go with it – similar to Quick and Easy Kaizen, people with experience come up with ideas. Today, if you don't have teams something is wrong with you. A lot of company's still call it quality circles but the majority don't, they call it employment involvement teams, or safety teams, or productivity groups, six sigma teams, self-directed work teams and so on. The thing I found different with Quick and Easy Kaizen is people involvement. With a quality circle, the leader says you have to pick something to work on, so lets have a brainstorming session. They come up with a list of things that they can work on. They might come up with 20 or 30 or a 150 items, often a huge list of things they could work on. They then go through the exercise to narrow it down to the number one thing to work on. What happens for the next four to six month they are working on that one problem?   All of the other ideas maybe a hundred of them were out there on the charts, hanging on a wall, which would eventually end up in the shredder or carrying dust. Nothing happened with the other ideas. The teams would always get good results and make presentations to management, and I insisted on measurements. But there were still a lot of people that never saw their idea come to fruition. When I first visited Pioneer Electric in Japan they told me about their Quick and Easy Kaizen system. I got so excited about it; anything that could come out of quality circles is dwarfed by what could come out of Quick and Easy Kaizen. You are very conservative when you talk about the savings to cost ratio of four to one. I have a feeling that is probably a lot closer to 10 to 1. In QCC days properly run quality circles it was 6 to 1. I really think Quick and Easy Kaizen has greater possibilities then quality circles.

(Don likes to tell the story how he visited Pioneer Electric on a study mission and was told proudly about their getting one idea per month per employee and then when he came back years later and asked if they were still getting the one per month the manager said no then smiled and said that they were now up to two per month).

At Lockheed a VP did not want me to measure, he was afraid the payoff would be so slow and un-dramatic that senior management would kill the QCC effort. We couldn't even put one word in the company newspaper. Then one day he was having breakfast with the company president and the president was shocked to hear that there was a Japanese consultant over there in the missile division. "No, there is no consultant over there." He just heard about the quality circles. "You mean hourly employees are sitting around and meeting together. What's the payoff? What is our payback?" The VP couldn't give any dollar figures. He left the breakfast meeting very agitated and spoke to me. "I just come back from a 'hella' meeting with the company president. He knows about the circles. He is a little bit disappointed in me. I wish now that I would have let you conduct measurements like you asked to do." I thought for a second. "I got good news for you I have been getting the measurements and we got initially a six to one ratio in cost savings and now in our third year it is now eleven to one." "Oh thank God you didn't listen to me, he said. "Bring whatever you got and I am going to meet the president for breakfast again to talk about what you did."

Lean is an all out war against waste and all out war against non-value added activities. In the quality arena we have to reduce inspection, rework, and get our people involved.

41

Richard Schonberger

'Two caterpillars are conversing and a beautiful butterfly floats by. One caterpillar turns and says to the other, "You'll never get me up on one of those butterfly things."
Scott J. Simmerman

Richard J. Schonberger was one of the first outside of Japan to recognize the power of the Toyota Production System. In 1982 he authored *Japanese Manufacturing Techniques: Nine Hidden Lessons in Simplicity*, New York: Free Press.

Dr. Schonberger is the author or co-author of eight books:

- *Japanese Manufacturing Techniques: Nine Hidden Lessons in Simplicity*, New York: Free Press. 1982.
- *World Class Manufacturing: The Lessons of Simplicity Applied*, New York: Free Press, 1986.
- *World Class Manufacturing Casebook: Implementing JIT and TQC*, New York: Free Press, 1987.
- *Building a Chain of Customers: Linking Business Functions to Create the World Class Company*, New York: Free Press, 1990.

- *Operations Management: Meeting Customers' Demands* (with Edward Knod), Boston: McGraw-Hill Irwin, 7th ed., 2001.
- *SynchroService! The Innovative Way to Build a Dynasty of Customers* (with Edward Knod), Burr Ridge, Ill.: Irwin Professional Publications, 1994.
- *World Class Manufacturing—The Next Decade: Building Power, Strength, and Value,* New York: Free Press, 1996
- *Let's Fix It! Overcoming the Crisis in Manufacturing: How the World's Leading Manufacturers Were Seduced by Prosperity and Lost Their Way,* New York: Free Press, 2001.

Bodek: *It was over 20 years ago when we first met and you were kind enough to keynote a conference of mine in San Francisco. I remember reading your manuscript for Japanese Manufacturing Techniques: Nine Hidden Lessons in Simplicity and I knew that it would become a great best seller.*

I want to add to my book some comments on the people side of lean, improving the quality of work life and I am asking you to help rethink the very nature of work.

Schonberger: Right. : You keep shifting with the times.

Bodek: *In December 2002 the mechanics union at United would not agree on a new contract citing management's inability to provide a quality of work life for their union members. We both know that in the last hundred years, people have been slotted into manufacturing and told, "Don't bring your brains to work, just bring your body and do what you're told."*

And now with Japanese management and an opportunity to re-look at the working environment, what do you think is happening in relationship to the human side of Lean?

Schonberger: Well, I think it's a yes and no issue. Yes, Lean, as the human side is being defined today, involves a lot of Kaizen events that get people working on projects. Front-line people, along with experts, and that's good, but on the other hand, I think that things have been lost.

Employee empowerment isn't quite there as much as it was, maybe ten or fifteen years ago or at least professed to be at that time. And I do find when I go to the Far East, not Japan, but Singapore and Malaysia and so forth still a very strong quality control circle culture that's built in. And this is more continuous employee involvement rather than projects. I'm concerned that there's too much emphasis on projects, and not enough on continuous improvement.

I think that's the Lean community isn't even aware of it.

Bodek: *That's our job. That's why I'm doing this. We have to be more aware of this, and hopefully as I write something, you'll be writing more on this area. I also was very impressed with the work of Dr. Lou Davis and Socio-Technical Systems.*

Schonberger: A lot of academics were similarly impressed.

Bodek: A few consultants were able to do some really great things, but it never moved.

Schonberger: Yeah.

Bodek: *And so, I think there's an opportunity now though with Lean.*

Schonberger: I think there is too.

Bodek: *There are very key things we see from Toyota, like Ji-doka, which really empowers people.*

Schonberger: Well, when improvement is my project.   When improvement is my project instead of continuous, I'm afraid that the staff experts will dominate.   And that's another thing – in addition to the discontinuity of projects.   There's a tendency for the experts to kind of take over like the Japanese experts roving throughout America.

Bodek: *I brought them to America.*

Schonberger: Yeah, and I see what you're doing and I mean with your new approach.   Quick and Easy…

Bodek: *Quick and Easy Kaizen, but I'll tell you, you know it is so hard for me to make any breakthroughs in this society.*

Schonberger: Sure.   Well, it's hard for anybody; there are just too many books and experts and so forth out there.

Bodek: *But this Quick and Easy Kaizen works.   Last year at Technicolor got 13 ideas in March out of 1,500 people and now we are up to over 1,000 a month.   And there are great ideas coming from the workers.*

Schonberger: Yes, but how to get it into the heads of the front-line workforce is a big problem.   I think part of that problem is the performance management system.   I've written lots about this.   We measure people on the shop floor for the wrong things.   We measure things that they have either no interest in or can't relate to easily.

Take productivity of labor.   Most of the cause of productivity, good or bad, is not in the hands of the workforce and yet that's the dominant measure of people on the shop floor. So I think there needs to be a revolution in the kinds of measures that are up on the walls in most companies.

Bodek: *Give me some examples of what you'd like to see.*

Schonberger: Well, I'd like to see the employees own the performance management system. I would like to see them in charge of goal setting. Management should not set the goals. And the things that are displayed on the shop floor, graphs and so on, they have to be within the zone of influence, I guess that's the word I've used in my own writings. They have to be within the zone of influence of the front-line individual and team. If they're outside that, you almost have to bribe the workforce in order for them to relate to it.

Things like yield, and on time, and productivity, and utilization, and all that sort of thing, those are all important, but management thinks that they can post graphs of that stuff up by the workforce and they'll be interested in it. And they really aren't, it's not the kind of thing that they're going to go home and say "Wow honey, we improved the yield today."

Bodek: *Please give me some of the things that they would relate to.*

Schonberger: Well, they can relate to aggravations of the job. The aggravations of the job are what people come home and bitch about to their spouse and their families. And mostly those are things that have to do with reasons why they can't deliver quality, reasons why they can't be on time, reasons why they're standing around waiting when they should be busy and they feel uncomfortable standing around waiting because the boss isn't there or the blue prints are wrong or whatever.

So anyway, instead of really goals and measurement against goals, it should be more tracking, tracking, tracking, and tracking. They should be tracking everything that possibly could go wrong: all the mishaps, all the glitches and hiccups and aggravations of the job. And then that becomes grist for the continuous improvement teams. They go to work, and everybody is a data collector, collecting data all the time.

You know, the companies that do get large numbers of suggestions, and there are some really good ones in the U.S. too, Milliken and Wainright Industries. They're getting over sixty per employee, per year. Better than Toyota, I think. They've both won Baldrige Prizes.

Bodek: *But let's talk more about the tracking. I like very much the Seven Basic tools idea. That focuses, primarily, on quality.*

Schonberger: I think it focuses on everything. It's very important to management and it also is important to the people who do the work. Every operator of a machine, as part of the job is improving the changeover time on the machine. That's their job; it's not the engineer's job. That's a little bit bigger realm of thought for the operator, than just the aggravations of the job. When you are a machine operator and this machine costs $180,000 and every time you set it up and it takes 20 minutes, you reflect on an $180,000 machine that's not working for 20 minutes. So, here's why your job is, for your entire work-life here, to continually think about ways to set it up faster.

Bodek: At Citizen watch I've seen those pictures on the wall showing where they went from 30 to 20 seconds on set-up. Go ahead.

Schonberger: I was just going to ask you, what are some of your ideas?

Bodek: *Well, the idea that I'm really trying to say is, if my children go to work, what kind of a life of work would I want for them? It's surely not what I see at work today.   To me personally it doesn't matter what I do.   I mean, pardon my expression, "I'll shovel shit as long as I have an opportunity to improve what I'm doing."*

It doesn't matter.   If the job stinks, I can rise above it if I have an opportunity to grow and change what I do.   As long as I have an opportunity to be creative at work.   It's what I love about this Quick and Easy Kaizen.   It's Maslow's concept that once you go through the basics, self-actualization will continue to motivate people.   And I call self-actualization the creative part of the individual and we don't feed this in our society at all.   We rarely recognize the need in people to change and grow.

There is a minister in our area Mary Manin Morrisey who said in a speech that a study of 50,000 people showed that only two percent of people in the age groups from 25 to 45 could be considered as highly creative.   While at age seven only 10 percent are highly creative but at age five it is 90 percent.   What happens to us from kindergarten to second grade and then onto adulthood that kills our creative spirit?

As I teach Quick and Easy Kaizen, I can see that everybody has creative potential if they're asked, encouraged to express themselves and given the opportunity to solve problems and implement their own ideas.

I feel the same way as you do that management cannot change the environment.   Management can develop people and challenge them to change the environment, which is the real bottom-up idea.

Schonberger: You know, there's one thing that management is doing right, but they're not building on it and that is creating work cells.

A work cell is a natural home for ideas. I mean, since the hand-offs reveal problems right away. People are so close together and they're cross-trained, they're changing jobs, they get broader perspective. That kind of situation is almost the heart and soul of Lean, all of that creates the perfect opportunity for people to contribute and then companies fail to follow-through and get the job done.

Bodek: *I was talking to Jeffery Liker about standard work and the feeling from Jeffery was that standard work is so rigid. You reach a place in the Toyota system where you have your takt-time and you are so rigid at work that it doesn't allow for the creative flexibility. Where do the Toyota people find time to come up with ideas and implement them?*

Schonberger: Yep. Another way of looking at standards, are engineering standards that are developed through design for manufacture and assembly, you standardize the parts so you don't have a thousand varieties. You allow the engineers to select only certain screws; they can't have fifty different kinds of screws in the machine. Standards of any kind, including standard work, free people from the unimportant so they can concentrate on the important. That's the good thing about standards, but still, I think Jeffery Liker has a point. It can very easily, and probably does, get in the way of freedom, freedom to think and do much.

And that might not be because of standard work, it might be because of the failure like you say, what gives people enjoyment on the job. The management hasn't created an environment where they can take standard work and build upon it. They aren't free to build up on it that easily.

Bodek: *You know we're dealing with a traditional hierarchy where you have a manager. The manager then maybe has seven* *people that report to them. And they might have another fifteen or twenty people under them and then they have five hundred people down below. And the manager directs downward what he wants, the people in the middle try to deliver what the manager wants, and they don't recognize the power of giving people the opportunity to learn and grow.*

Okuda, chairman of Toyota said something recently, which was intriguing, "Failure to change is a vice." He told about a group of mavericks, misfits that were turned loose a Toyota and came up with a fascinating car called something like the 'Wilvi.' They tried to appeal to the age 25 to 35 market in Japan, that is the market that Nissan has done so well with. And this group of misfits given the freedom to be independent thinkers came up with this new car – it looked like an accordion. Okuda said that the Wilvi was not that successful, but it challenged the other five hundred traditional designers to be more creative. And that's what he liked very much.

I'm hoping that we can look more at the nature of work and how should it change? How should it change? What can be done to bring back high skill? You know, that existed earlier?

You are one of the real key people. You were number one in America to bring this Lean effort. Because you were able to communicate it in a way that other people could understand. I brought over a lot of literature, and it was great, and it gave a lot of the specific techniques but it wasn't articulated the same way, as you were able to do.

Don't ever think of retiring.

Schonberger: I wouldn't. (Laughing)

42

Vision Statements

"A leader's role is to raise people's aspirations for what they can become and to release their energies so they will try to get there."
David Gergen

In difficult times, especially during war, leaders can inspire people to unselfishly volunteer themselves to serve a higher purpose even to the extent of putting their lives in danger. Yes, there is inside all of us an untapped 'hero' waiting to rise to the challenge to serve the benefit of humanity. Put us on a team and we will competitively do our best to be an important part of winning the event. Ask us to help neighbors in distress and we will bring forth new energy to help. There is in all of us a much higher place that will respond when called upon.

It is the job of a leader to know how to bring this higher sense of service out of people that work with us. The leader starts by formulating a vision, pointing to the future, stating the values and the fundamental reason the organization exists – to make money for the owner. To give people a place to earn a living is important, but is not enough to inspire people to perform at their highest capability.

The US Declaration of Independence, the US Constitution, and the Bill of Rights have been the guiding light, the force behind the success of our country for over 225 years. Many global companies recognize this same need to establish fundamental principles that will keep employees focused on continually reaching forward and growing for their own personal benefit, but also for the benefit of the customer, the user of their service or product and also for the entire benefit of the world. The following are just a few of the powerful vision statements found in Japan in America.

Kyocera, one of the world's leaders in ceramics, dedicates its corporate resources to three key areas: Information and Communications, Environmental Preservation and Quality of Life. As we grow steadily in each area, creating value through diversification, we hope to contribute to the advancement of society and humankind.

Information and Communications is an expansion beyond their original purpose of making ceramic products. Now they envision using their past experience and talents to produce products and services in a much more expansive arena.

There is the old story that the problem with the railroads were that they limited their vision to railroads, which were once the most powerful and richest companies in America. Now they are struggling to survive with their old equipment. Instead, they should have envisioned themselves as being in the transportation business, expanding and growing through automobiles, airplanes, etc.

Environmental Preservation looks at how Kyocera can succeed financially and also be part of saving the future of this globe we all live on.

Quality of Life helps them look at their corporate purpose to enhance meaning, joy, and well-being to their customers. It also identifies their purpose to improve the quality of work life for their employees while they produce products that improve the quality of life for their customers.

Sony is known for creating products that enrich people's lives. Through Sony Corporation of America and its three operating companies - Sony Electronics Inc., Sony Music Entertainment Inc. and Sony Pictures Entertainment - we are also dedicated to improving people's lives. Our commitment extends to helping local communities, fostering better educational systems, funding research to cure devastating diseases, supporting the arts and culture, helping disadvantaged youth and actively encouraging employee volunteerism. - SONY IN AMERICA: Working Together to Make a Difference

Matsushita Electric Industrial Co., Ltd. (Panasonic and National) is committed to consistently delivering products and services that enhance the quality of life. - In line with this slogan, we aim to achieve the top position in global markets by working to establish businesses that will be pillars for future growth.

Mitsubishi Group of Companies strives to provide a common set of management guidelines:

"Shoki Hoko" - Strive to enrich society, both materially and spiritually, while contributing towards the preservation of the global environment.

"Shoji Komei" - Maintain principles of transparency and openness, conducting business with integrity and fairness.

"Ritsugyo Boeki" - Expand business, based on an all-encompassing global perspective.

Toshiba

We are working vigorously to hand over the irreplaceable global environment to succeeding generations

We always start from the "Voice of Customer" to ensure customer satisfaction.

Sanyo Group's corporate philosophy is the guiding principle in accomplishing the key management policy of ensuring products and services that are indispensable in creating harmony between people and the environment.   Sanyo's priorities are: Customer Satisfaction and Harmonizing with the Environment.

Nikon Corporation - **"Vision Nikon 21" we have reviewed "Nikon's identity" and understood on what ground we stand as a business group.**

- **Nikon is a manufacturer backed by excellent technologies**
  Manufacturers build the foundations for a prosperous society by offering top-quality merchandise.

- **Nikon   exists   thanks   to   consumers**
  If a consumer feels that Nikon products have enriched their life, then we've achieved our mission.

- **Nikon   Exists   due   to   its   uniqueness**
  Nikon's reputation is based on its opto-electronics and precision technologies and

. its ongoing innovations in these areas.

Taking a major change of Nikon's economic and business environment into consideration, we reviewed our previous "philosophy" and have defined Nikon's new "philosophy" as follows:

It is crucial that we be trusted and loved by people worldwide. Nikon exists and prospers in harmony on all levels throughout the world. We maintain pride, faith in our business and encourage an entrepreneurial sprit. One of our goals is to appeal to people all over the world and satisfy them with efficient and useful products and services.

Nikon has set the following "corporate objectives" in order to realize the principles of our "corporate philosophy":
With superb technology as our backbone, we must offer the best quality products and services worldwide.
By restructuring our business and focusing our management resources on growing areas where we can make the most of our strengths, we aim to be the best in each business field.
Accomplish a solid management structure wherein each group company strives to grow, evolve and flourish.
Build agile management that allows us to adapt swiftly to the ever-changing business environment.

Bring further transparency to management.

General Electric - *I never perfected an invention that I did not think about in terms of the service it might give others"* *-Thomas Alva Edison, GE Founder*

IBM - The truest test of any institution's vision, strategy and values is how it does two things: responds to change, or inspires it. Important change. Not just in global markets, but in global politics. Not just in technologies, but in cultures and societies. Not only among employees or clients, but also among their children. In schools, in our air and water. In the ways the technologies contribute to making the world safer, more secure and more prosperous.   As this report has documented, we don't think our role in these social, human, legacy issues is all that different from our role in technical fields or in financial markets.   Frankly, we believe a company with IBM's wherewithal is expected to handle these changes, by investing in their solution, and by applying its resources, expertise and the discipline of its management systems to step up to the tough issues and the coming generation of unknowns.   We believe that a leader leads—guided by principles that endure, and a willingness to change everything else.

"Vision is the art of seeing the invisible."
- Jonathan Swift

Lean Terms

Andon - – signboard, a lighting and audio-visual system that alerts workers where in the factory potential or actual problems are happening and indicates production status in one or more work centers; the number of lights and their possible colors can vary, even by work center within a plant; however, the traditional colors and their meanings are:

> green - no problems
> yellow - situation requires attention
> red - production stopped; attention urgently needed

Andon Board - A visual control device in a production area, typically a lighted overhead display, giving the current status of the production system and alerting team members to emerging problems.

Autonomation – **see Jidoka Autonomation:** Automation with a human touch. Refers to semi-automatic processes where the operator and machine work together. Autonomation allows man-machine separation. Also referred to Jidoka.

Blitz, Kaizen - A blitz is a fast and focused process for improving some component of business a product line, a machine, or a process. It utilizes a cross-functional team of employees for a quick problem-solving exercise, where they focus on designing solutions to meet some well-defined goals.

Cellular Manufacturing - Equipment and workstations are arranged to facilitate small-lot, continuous-flow production. Workers in a manufacturing cell are typically cross-trained and, hence, able to perform multiple tasks as needed.

Cause and Effect Diagram - A problem-solving tool used to identify relationships between effects and multiple causes (also Fishbone Diagram, Ishikawa Diagram).

CEDAC - Cause and Effect Diagram with the Addition of Cards.

Cycle Time - The time required to complete one cycle of an operation. The normal time to complete an operation on a product.

5 S - refers to the five words **seiri, seiton, seison, seiketsu, and shitsuke**. These words are shorthand expressions for principles of maintaining an effective, efficient workplace

- **seiri** – (sorting) eliminating everything not required for the work being performed
- **seiton** – (set in order) efficient placement and arrange ment of equipment and material
- **seison** – (shine) tidiness and cleanliness
- **seiketsu** – (standardize) ongoing, standardized, con tinually improving *seiri, seiton, seison*
- **shitsuke** – (sustain) discipline with leadership

Five "whys - a simple way to arrive at root causes to problems; keep asking "why."

5W1H – Things that need to be specified in any plan of action - who, what, where, when, why and how

Flexible manufacturing system - an integrated manufacturing capability to produce small numbers of a great variety of items at low unit cost; an FMS is also characterized by low changeover time and rapid response time.

Gemba - shop floor, on the line, on site

Heijunka – production smoothing, leveled production

Hosin Planning (Hoshin Kanri) - Also known as Management by Policy or Strategy Deployment. A means by which goals are established and measures are created and cascaded down the organization to ensure progress toward those goals.

Just-In-Time – JIT is a management philosophy that strives to eliminate sources of manufacturing waste by producing the right part in the right place at the right time.

Jidoka - Autonomation - is the concept of adding an element of human judgment to automated equipment. In doing this, the equipment becomes capable of discriminating against unacceptable quality, and the automated process becomes more reliable.

Kaikaku - A rapid and radical change process, sometimes used as a precursor to **kaizen** activities.

Kaizen - Continuous, incremental improvement. Kaizen is changing the method, small changes and changes within constraints.

Kanban – Signboard or signal. Normally the kanban is card placed on carts or boxes to pull production through the factory or between factories. It signals a cycle of replenishment for production and materials, maintaining an orderly and efficient flow of materials throughout the entire manufacturing process. The card normally contains the part name, description, quantity, who produces the part and where and when the part will be delivered.

Lean manufacturing or **lean production** is simply an American term that replaced The Toyota Production System, or Just-In-Time (JIT). Lean manufacturing means that you operate your facilities with the least amount of **waste**, that you are operating at the highest state of efficiency, with the least amount of investment, the lowest number of employees, the highest state of quality, the shortest time line from order to delivery of the finished products, that you neither over nor under produce, and that you deliver the products to your customer neither early nor late – just exactly on time.

Muda - any activity that consumes resources but creates no value; waste, non-value-adding.

Mura - Variations and variability in work method or the output of a process.

Muri - unreasonable / impossible / overdoing – Avoidable strain or irrational use of resources for carrying out work.

Non-Value-Added - Activities which do not add value to the product. Manufacturing is converting raw materials to finished goods: milling, bending, converting, adhering, painting, grinding, designing, drilling, etc. All of the other activities such as transportation, inspection, moving, might be necessary at the moment but do not add value to the finished product. The desire is to either minimize these activities or introduce process improvements that would eliminate them entirely.

One-piece flow - refers to a process in which products proceed, one item at a time, through the various production operations without interruptions or waiting time.

Pareto Chart - A vertical bar chart, which graphically helps to separate effects or causes into the vital few and the trivial many.

Poka - yoke - 'mistake-proofing', a means of providing a visual or other signal to indicate a characteristic state. Often referred to as 'error-proofing', poke-yoke is actually the first step in truly error-proofing a system. Error-proofing is a manufacturing technique of preventing errors by designing the manufacturing process, equipment, and tools so that an operation literally cannot be performed incorrectly.

QFD (Quality Function Deployment) - A customer-focused approach to quality improvement in which customer needs (desired product or service characteristics) are analyzed at the design stage and translated into specific product-and process-design requirements for the supplier organization.

Sensei - instructor, usually refers to an external consultant

Six Sigma - A methodology and set of tools used to improve quality to 3.4 or less defects per million or better. Six Sigma started at Motorola by taking the best tools and techniques from Total Quality Management and adding very cleverly the concept of 'black belts' used in the martial arts to inspire people towards improving quality. It really took off when Jack Welsh, CEO of General Electric, promoted the method in his company.

SMED – abbreviation for Single Minute Exchange of Die; literally, changing a die on a forming or stamping machine in a minute or less; broadly, the ability to perform any setup activity in a minute or less of machine or process downtime; the key to doing this is frequently the capability to convert internal setup time to external setup time.

Standardized work is a precise description of each work activity specifying cycle time, takt time, the work sequence of specific tasks, and the minimum inventory of parts on hand needed to conduct the activity.

Target Costing: Before a company launches a product (or family of products), senior managers determine its ideal selling price, establish the feasibility of meeting that price, and then control costs to ensure that the price is met. The same logic as quality must be designed into products before they are manufactured. Target costing follows the formula: Sales price - Target Profit = Target Cost

Takt time - "Takt" is the German word for the baton that an orchestra conductor uses to regulate the speed, beat or timing at which musicians play. So Takt Time is "Beat Time"? "Rate Time" or "Heart Beat." Lean Production uses Takt Time as the rate or time that a finished product is required by the customer. If you have a Takt Time of two minutes that means every two minutes a complete product, assembly or machine is required to be produced off the line to meet customer demand.

Total Productive Maintenance (TPM) - aims at maximizing equipment effectiveness and uptime throughout the entire life of the equipment.

Value Stream Mapping - Creating a visual picture of the 'Current State' or how material and information flows from suppliers through manufacturing and to the customer. Total lead-time, process cycle times and value-added times are shown. Highlights the sources of waste and helps to eliminate them by implementing a future state value stream that can become reality within a short time.

Visual Control - The placement in plain view of all tools, parts, production activities, and indicators of production system performance so everyone involved can understand the status of the system at a glance.

I want thank NW Lean and Gemba Research for their help on the above terms.

Norman Bodek - Biography

Education: Yonkers, New York Public School system, University of Wisconsin, New York University (BA), and 42 additional credits at New York University Graduate School of Business, and New York University College of Education

Military service: Two years active duty with the U. S. Army Audit Agency and four years in reserve.

Instructor: American Management Associations, Control Data Institute, President Regan's Productivity Conference – Washington, DC, PPORF Conference - Japan, Total Productive Maintenance Conference – Tokyo, Institute of Industrial Engineers, American Society for Quality, APICS, Productivity, Inc. Conferences and Seminars, Dresser Mfg., Union Carbide, AVCO Corporation, Larsen & Turbo - India, Productivity - Madras (Chennai), India, London - England, Jutland - Denmark

Recipient of The Shingo Prize[*] for Manufacturing Excellence and also created the Shingo Prize with Dr. Vern Buehler sponsored by Utah State University

Professional Career: Public Accountant and Insurance Broker, Vice President Data Utilities, New York City, and Barbados, West Indies, President Key Universal Ltd. with offices in Greenwich, Connecticut and Grenada, West Indies

1979-1999 Started Productivity Inc. & Productivity Press with offices in Norwalk, Connecticut, and Portland, Oregon.

Newsletters: PRODUCTIVITY, Total Employee Involvement (TEI), The Service Insider, Quick Change Over (QCO), and Total Productive Maintenance (TPM)

Study missions to Japan, led around 35 missions visiting 250 manufacturing plants

Conferences: Over 100 conferences on productivity and quality improvement including Productivity The American Way, Best of America, Quality, Quality Service, TPM, and TEI

Seminars: Hundreds of seminars on TPM, TQM, TEI, QCO, Visual Management, 5S, JIT and others.

---

[*]For information on the prize: http://www.shingoprize.org/shingo/index.html

In plant training events: Brought over Ohno's assistants from Japan (Iwata and Nakao) and ran Five Days and One Night (now called Kaizen Blitz), Maintenance Miracle, Quick Changeovers, Visual Factory, and benchmark plant visits and seminars with American Manufacturing companies.

Books Published: Dr. Shigeo Shingo's - Toyota Production System, SMED, Poka-Yoke, Non-Stock Production, etc., Taiichi Ohno - Toyota Production System (JIT), Henry Ford – Today and Tomorrow, A New American TQM, Yoji Akao – Quality Function Deployment (QFD) and Hoshin Kanri, Dr. Ryuji Fukuda – Managerial Engineering, CEDAC and Building Organizational Fitness, Shigeichi Moriguchi – Software Excellence, Shigeru Mizuno - Management for Quality Improvement (The 7 New QC Tools), Seiichi Nakajima – Total Productivity Maintenance (TPM), Michel Greif – The Visual Factory, Ken'ichi Sekine – One Piece Flow, Shigehiro Nakamura – The New Standardization, and many other books on world class manufacturing and total quality management.

1990 - Industry Week called him "Mr. Productivity."

2001 – Called "Mr. Lean" in Quality Progress Magazine

1999 - Started PCS Press with a monthly newsletter, consulting, and workshops on Quick and Easy Kaizen and Improving Customer Service.

2004 – Started Kaikaku Press Inc.

Books:

The Idea Generator – Quick and Easy Kaizen,
PCS Press 2001

The Idea Generator – Workbook,
PCS Press 2002

Kaikaku: The Power and Magic of Lean
PCS Press 2004

Articles published in:

Quality Digest Magazine
Solutions – IIE Magazine
Target – Association for Manufacturing Excellence (AME)
Quality World
The Journal for Quality and Participation
T + D Magazine - ASTD
Manufacturing Engineering – SME's magazine
Timely Tips for Teams – monthly
NWLean
HR.COM
And others, over 40 articles published in the last two years.

Radio – ran an interview program in New England.

E-learning – course developed with Society of Manfacturing Engineers to teach Quick and Easy Kaizen.

Bibliography

Akao, Yoji (ed). - *Quality Function Deployment: Integrating Customer Requirements into Product Design* – Productivity Press, 1990
————. *Hoshin Kanri: Policy Deployment for Successful TPM* – Productivity Press, 1991
Akiyama, Kaneo. - *Function Analysis: Systematic Improvement of Quality and Performance* – Productivity Press, 1991
Asaka, Tetsuichi and Kazuo Ozeki (eds.) - *Handbook of Quality Tools: The Japanese Approach* - Productivity Press, 1990
Ballis, John – *Managing Flow: Achieving Lean in the New Millennium to Win the Gold* – Brown Books, 2001
Barrett, Derm – *Fast Focus on TQM: A Concise Guide to Companywide Learning* - Productivity Press, 1994
Basadur, Min - *Simplex a Flight to Creativity* – Paperback Creative Education Foundation, 1995
Belohlav, James A. - *Championship Management: An Action Model for High Performance* - Productivity Press, 1990
Bodek, Norman – *The Idea Generator: Quick and Easy Kaizen* – *PCS Press, 2002*
Boyle, Daniel C. – Secrets of a Successful Employee Recognition System - Productivity Press, 1995
Camp, Robert C. - *Benchmarking: The Search for Industry Best Practices that Lead to Superior Performance* - Productivity Press, 1989
Campbell, John Dixon – *Uptime: Strategies for Excellence in Maintenance Management* - Productivity Press, 1995
Chowdhury, Subir - *Management 21C* - Pearson Professional Education, 2002
Christopher, William F. and Carl G. Thor - *Total Employee*

Involvement – *Handbook for Productivity Measurement and Improvement* - Productivity Press, 1993

Cooper, Robin and Regine Stagmulder – *Target Costing and Value Engineering* – Productivity Press co-published with The Institute of Management Accountant, 1997

Covey, Stephen R. Covey – *The 7 Habits of Highly Effective People* – A Fireside Book, Simon & Schuster, 1989

De Bono, Edward - *Lateral Thinking: Creativity Step-By-Step* – HarperCollins, 1990

————. *Six Thinking Hats* - Little Brown & Co, 1999 paperback

D'Egidio, Franco. - *The Service Era: Leadership in a Global Environment* - Productivity Press, 1990

Deming, W. Edward - *Out of the Crisis* - MIT Press, 1986

————. *Elementary Principles of Statistical Control of Quality* - Nippon Kagaku Gijutsu Remmei, Tokyo, Japan, 1950

————.and Mary Walton - *The Deming Management Methods* – Perigee, 1988

Fisher, Kimbell - *Leading Self-Directed Work Teams: A Guide to Developing New Team Leadership Skills* - McGraw-Hill Professional Publishing, 1999

Fitz-Enz, Jac - *The 8 Practices of Exceptional Companies: How Great Organizations Make the Most of Their Human Assets* – AMACOM, 1997

————.*The Roi of Human Capital: Measuring the Economic Value of Employee Performance* – AMACOM, 2000

————.and Jack J. Phillips - *A New Vision for Human Resources: Defining the Human Resources Function by Its Results* – Crisp Management Library, 1999

Ford, Henry. - *Today and Tomorrow* – Productivity Press, 1988 (Double Day 1926)

Fukuda, Ryuji – *Building Organizational Fitness: Management Methodology for Transformation and Strategic Advantage* – Productivity Press, 1994

————. *Managerial Engineering: Techniques for Improving*

Quality and Productivity in the Workplace – Productivity Press, 1983

————. *CEDAC: A Tool for Continuous Systematic Improvement* – Productivity Press, 1990

Galsworth, Gwendolyn D. - *Visual Systems: Harnessing the Power of a Visual Workplace* - American Management Association, 1997

Grief, Michelle. - *The Visual Factory: Building Participation through Shared Information* - Productivity Press, 1991

Gotoh, Fumio. - *Equipment Planning for TPM: Maintenance Prevention Design* – Productivity Press, 1991

Gross, Clifford M. – *The Right Fit: The Power of Ergonomics as a Competitive Strategy* - Productivity Press, 1991

Hall, Robert W. – *Attain Manufacturing Excellence* – McGraw-Hill Professional Publishing, 1988

Hartley, John R. – *Concurrent Engineering: Shortening Lead Times, Raising Quality, and Lowering Costs* - Productivity Press, 1992

Harrington H., James and Daryl Conner, Nicholas L. Horney – *Project Change Management : Applying Change Management to Improvement Projects* – McGraw-Hill Professional, 1999

————.and Erik K. C. Esseling (Contributor), Harm Van Nimwegen - *Business Process Improvement Workbook: Documentation, Analysis, Design, and Management of Business Process Improvement* - McGraw-Hill Professional, 1997

————.and Glen D. Hoffherr, Robert P. Reid - *The Creativity Toolkit: Provoking Creativity in Individuals and Organizations* – McGraw-Hill Professional,1998

Hatakeyama, Yoshio. - *Manager Revolution! A Guide to Survival in Today's Changing Workplace* - Productivity Press, 1986

Head, Christopher W. – *Beyond Corporate Transformation: A Whole System Approach to Creating and Sustaining High Performance* - Productivity Press, 1997

Hirano, Hiroyuki. - 5 *Pillars of the Visual Workplace: The*

Sourcebook for 5S *Implementation* - Productivity Press, 1995
————. *JIT Factory Revolution: A Pictorial Guide to Factory Design of the Future* – Productivity Press. 1989
————*JIT Implementation Manual: The Complete Guide to Just-In-Time Manufacturing* - Productivity Press, 1990
————. *5S for Operators: 5 Pillars of the Visual Workplace* Productivity Press, 1996

Hobbs, Dennis P. - *Lean Manufacturing Implementation: A Complete Execution Manual for Any Size Manufacturer* - J. Ross Publishing, 2003

Horovitz, Jacques. - *Winning Ways: Achieving Zero-Defect Service* – Productivity Press, 1990

Hutchins, Greg - *ISO 9000: A Comprehensive Guide to Registration, Audit Guidelines, and Successful Certification* - John Wiley & Sons, 1997

Ichida, Takashi (Compiler) – *Product Design Review: A Method for error-free Product Development* - Productivity Press,1996

Ishiwata, Junichi. - *IE for the Shop Floor 1: Productivity Through Process Analysis* - Productivity Press, 1991

Ishikawa, Kaoru - *How to Operate QC Circle Activities*, JUSE, 1985
————. *QC Circle Koryo: General Principles of the QC Circle* – JUSE, 1980
————. *Quality Control Circles at Work: Cases from Japan's Manufacturing and Service Sectors* – Asian Productivity Organization, 1984

Imai, Masaaki - *Kaizen: The Key to Japan's Competitive Success* – McGraw Hill, 1986

Jackson, Thomas L. and Constance E. Dyer – *Corporate Diagnosis: Setting the Global Standard for Excellence* (Based on the work of Shigehiro Nakamura and Dr. Ryuji Fukuda) - Productivity Press, 1996
————. And Karen R. Jones – *Implementing a Lean Management System* - Productivity Press, 1996

Japan Institute of Plant Maintenance, eds.- *Autonomous Maintenance for Operators* - Productivity Press, 1997

————.TPM *Encyclopedia.* Atlanta: Japan Institute of Plant Maintenance – Productivity Press, 1996.

————. *Focused Equipment Improvement for TPM Teams* - Productivity Press, 1997

————.TPM *for Every Operator* - Productivity Press, 1996

————.TPM for Survivors - Productivity Press 1996

Japan Management Association - *Kanban and Just-In-Time at Toyota: Management Begins at the Workplace.* - Productivity Press, 1986

————. *Total Productivity: The New Science of TP Management* (Based on the work of Shigehiro Nakamura) – Productivity Europe, 1996

————. The *Canon Production System: Creative Involvement of the Total Workforce* – Productivity Press, *1987*

Japan Union of Scientist and Engineers (JUSE). - *TQC Solutions: The 14-Step Process* – Productivity Press, 1991

Jones, Morgan D. - *The Thinker's Toolkit : Fourteen Powerful Techniques for Problem Solving* - Times Books, 1998

Juran, J. M, ed. - A *History of Managing for Quality: The Evolution, Trends, and Future Directions of Managing for Quality* - ASQC Quality Press, 1995

Kanatsu, Takashi. - *TQC for Accounting: A New Role in Companywide Improvement* – Productivity Press, 1991

Kaner, Sam and Lenny Lind, Catherine Toldi, Sarah Fisk, Duane Berger –*Facilitator's Guide to Participatory Decision-Making* - New Society Pub, 1996

Karatsu, Hajime. - *Tough Words For American Industry* - Productivity Press, 1988

————. *TQC Wisdom of Japan: Managing for Total Quality Control* - Productivity Press, 1988

Kato, Kenichiro. - *I.E. for the Shop Floor 2: Productivity Through Motion Study* - Productivity Press, 1991

Kaydos, Will. - *Measuring, Managing, and Maximizing Performance* - Productivity Press, 1991

Kirby, J. Philip and David Hughes – *Thoughtware: Change the Thinking and the Organization Will Change Itself* – Productivity Press, 1991

Kobayashi, Iwao - *20 Keys to Workplace Improvement*- Productivity Press, 1990

Liebling, Henry E. – *Handbook for Personal Productivity* - Productivity Press, 1989

Lewis, C. Patrick – *Building a Shared Vision: A Leader's Guide to Aligning the Organization* - Productivity Press, 1996

Lu, David J. - *Inside Corporate Japan: The Art of Fumble-Free Management* - Productivity Press, 1987

Mauer, Rick – *Feedback Toolkit: 16 Tools for Better Communications in the Workplace* - Productivity Press, 1994

————. *Caught in the Middle: A Leadership Guide for Partnership in the Workplace* - Productivity Press, 1994

Maskell, Brian H. - *Performance Measurement for World Class Manufacturing: A Model for American Companies* - Productivity Press, 1991

————. *Software and the Agile Manufacturer: Computer Systems and the World Class Manufacturing* - Productivity Press, 1994

Merli, Giorgio - *Total Manufacturing Management: Production Organization for the 1990s* – Productivity Press, 1990

————. *Co-Makership: The New Strategy for Manufacturers* – Productivity Press, 1991

Miltenburg, John – *Manufacturing Strategy: How to Formulate and Implement a Winning Team* - Productivity Press, 1995

Mizuno, Shigeru (ed.). - *Management for Quality Improvement: The 7 New QC Tools* – Productivity Press, 1988

Ishiwata, Junichi – *IE for the Shopfloor 1: Productivity Through Process Analysis* - Productivity Press, 1991

Kaydos, Will – *Measuring, Managing, and Maximizing Performance* - Productivity Press, 1991

Kelley, Tom with Jonathan Littman – *The Art of Innovation* – A

Currency Book, Doubleday, 2001

King, Bob - *The Idea Edge: Transforming Creative Thought into Organizational Excellence* - Goal/QPC, 1998

Laraia, Anthony C. and Patricia E. Moody, Robert W. Hall - *The Kaizen Blitz: Accelerating Breakthroughs in Productivity and Performance* – John Wiley & Sons, 1999

Latzko, William J. and David M. Saunders – *Four Days with Dr. Deming: A strategy for Modern Methods of Management* – Addison-Wesley Publishing Company, 1995

Liker, Jeffrey, ed. - *Becoming Lean: Inside Stories of U.S. Manufacturers* - Productivity Press, 1997

Louis, Raymond J. - *Integrating Kanban with* MRPII: *Automating a Pull System for Enhanced JIT Inventory Management* – Productivity Press, 1997

Maskel, Brian H. - *Performance Measurement for World Class Manufacturing: A Model for American Companies* – Productivity Press, 1991

————. *Making the Numbers Count: The Management Accountant as Change Agent on the World Class Team* - Productivity Press, 1996

————. With LearnerFirst - *Putting Performance Measurement to Work: Building Focus and Sustaining Improvement* - Productivity Press, 1997

Maslow, Abraham, and Deborah C. Stephens, Gary Heil - *Maslow on Management* – John Wiley & Sons, 1998

Maurer, Rick. - *Feedback Toolkit: 16 Tools for Better Communication in the Workplace* - Productivity Press, 1994

McGregor, Douglas, and Warren G. Bennis – *Human Side of Enterprise: 25th Anniversary Printing* - McGraw-Hill Higher Education, 1985

Merrill, Peter – *Do It Right the Second Time: Benchmarking Best Practices in the Quality Change Process* – Productivity Press, 1997

Michalski, Walter J. - 40 *Tools for Cross-Functional Teams: Building Synergy for Breakthrough Creativity* - Productivity Press, 1998

————. *Tool Navigator: The Master Guide for Teams* – Productivity Press, 1997

————. *40 Top Tools for Manufacturers: A Guide for Implementing Powerful Improvement Activities* – Productivity Press, 1998

Mizuno, Shgeru (ed.) – *Management for Quality Improvement: The 7 New QC Tools* - Productivity Press, 1988

Monden, Yasuhiro. - *Toyota Production System: An Integrated Approach to Just-In-Time* - Norcross, GA: Engineering and Management Press, 1998

————. and Michiharu Sakurai (eds.). *Japanese Management Accounting: A World Class Approach to Profit Management* - Productivity Press, 1990

————. *The Toyota Management System: Linking the Seven Key Functional Areas* – Productivity Press, 1999

————. *Cost Reduction Systems: Target Costing and Kaizen Costing* - Productivity Press, 1995

————. *Japanese Cost Management* - World Scientific Pub Co;, 2000

————. *Cost Management in the New Manufacturing Age: Innovations in the Japanese Automobile Industry* – Productivity Press, 1992

Moriguti, Shigeiti (ed.) – *Software Excellence: A Total quality Management Guide* - Productivity Press, 1997

Nachi-Fujikoshi (ed.). - *Training for TPM: A Manufacturing Success Story* - Productivity Press, 1990

Nakajima, Seiichi. - *Introduction to TPM: Total Productive Maintenance* - Productivity Press, 1988

————.*TPM Development Program: Implementing Total Productive Maintenance* - Productivity Press, 1989

Moser-Wellman, Annette - *The Five Faces of Genius* – Viking Press 2001

Musashi, Miyamoto - *A Book of Five Rings* – (1584-1598) – The Classic Guide to Strategy – The Overlook Press, 1974

Nachi Fujikoshi Corporation. - *Training for TPM: a Manufacturing*

Success Story - Productivity Press, 1990

Nagashima, Soichiro – *100 Management Charts* – Asian Productivity Organization, 1990

Nakamura, Shigehiro – *The New Standardization: Keystone of Continuous Improvement in Manufacturing* – Productivity Press, 1993

————. and Hideyuki Takahasi – *Go-Go Tools: Five Essential Activities for Leading Small Groups- Productivity Europe*

Nikkan Kogyo Shimbun, (eds.) - *Poka-Yoke: Improving Product Quality by Preventing Defects* - Productivity Press, 1989

————. *Factory Management Notebook Series: Mixed Model Production* - Productivity Press, 1991

————. *Factory Management Notebook Series: Visual Control Systems: Visual Control Systems* - Productivity Press, 1991

————. *Factory Management Notebook Series: Mixed Model Production* - Productivity Press, 1991

————. *Visual Control Systems - Factory Management Notebook Series:* Productivity Press, 1995

————. *TPM Case Studies* - Productivity Press, 1995

Northey, Patrick and Nigel Southway – *Cycle Time Management: The Fast Track to Time-Based Productivity Improvement* – Productivity Press, 1993

Ohno, Taiichi. - T*oyota Production System: Beyond Large-Scale Production* - Productivity Press, 1988

————.*Workplace Management* - Productivity Press, 1988

————. and Setsuo Mito - *Just-In-Time for Today and Tomorrow* – Productivity Press, 1988

Ono, Ken'ichi – *Visual Feedback: Making Your5S Implementation Click* - Productivity Press, 1996

Osada, Takashi – *The 5S's: Five Keys to a Total Quality Environment* – Asian Productivity Organization, 1991

Perigord, Michel. - *Achieving Total Quality Management: A Program for Action* – Productivity Press, 1991

Psarouthakis, John. - *Better Makes Us Best* - Productivity Press, 1989

Puri, Subhash C. – *Stepping up to ISO 14000: Integrating*

Environmental Quality with ISO 9000 and TQM –
Productivity Press, 1996
————. *ISO 9000 Certification: Total Quality Management* –
Productivity Press, 1995
Productivity Press Development Team – *Just-In-Time for Operators
Learning Package-* Productivity Press,1998
Regan, Michael D. - *The Kaizen Revolution* - Holden Press, 2000
Robinson, Alan. - *Continuous Improvement in Operations: A
Systematic Approach to Waste Reduction* - Productivity Press,
1991
————. And Same Stern - Corporate Creativity: How Innovation and
Improvement Actually Happen - Berrett-Koehler, 1997
————.and Dean M. Schroeder - *Ideas are Free: How the Idea
Revolution is Liberating People and Transforming
Organizations* - Berrett-Koehler, 2004
Robinson, Charles J. and Andrew P. Cinder. - *Introduction to
Implementing TPM: The North American Experience* -
Productivity Press, 1995.
Robson, Ross E. - The Quality And Productivity Equation:
American Corporate Strategies For The 1990s –
Productivity Press, 1990
Sakurai, Michiharu – *Integrated Cost Management: A
Companywide Prescription for Higher Profits and Lower
Costs* - Productivity Press, 1995
Sarita Chawla and John Renesch – *Learning Organizations* -
Productivity Press, 1995
Scanlan, Phillip M. – *The Dolphins Are Back: A Successful Quality
Model for Healing the Environment* - Productivity Press,
1995
Scholtes, Peter R., Brian L. Joiner, and Barbara J. Streibel - *The
Team Handbook, Second Edition* - Joiner, 1996
Schonberger, Richard J. – *Japanese Manufacturing Techniques:
Nine Hidden Lessons in Simplicity* – Free Press, 1982
————.*The World Class Manufacturing: The Lessons of*

Simplicity Applied – Free Press - 1986

————.Schonberger, Richard J. – *World Class Manufacturing: The Next Decade* – Free Press, 1996

Sekine, Keniche, Keisuke Arai, and Bruce Talbot. - *Kaizen for Quick Changeover: Going Beyond SMED* - Productivity Press, 1992

————.*One-Piece Flow: Cell Design for Transforming the Production Process* - Productivity Press, 1992

————.and Keisuke Arai.- TPM *for the Lean Factory: Innovative Methods and Worksheets for Equipment Management* – Productivity Press, 1998

Shetty, Y.K and Vernon M. Buehler (eds.). - *Competing Through Productivity and Quality* – Productivity Press, 1989

Shiba, Shoji, Alan Graham and David Walden – *A New American TQM: Four Practical Revolutions in Management* - Productivity Press, 1993

Shingo, Shigeo - *A Revolution in Manufacturing: The SMED System* – Productivity Press, 1983

————. *Zero Quality Control: Source Inspection and the Poka-yoke System* – Productivity Press, 1986

————. *. The Sayings of Shigeo Shingo: Key Strategies for Plant Improvement,* - Productivity Press, 1987

————. *Zero Quality Control: Source Inspection and the Poka-Yoke System* - Productivity Press, 1986

————.A *Study of the Toyota Production System from an Industrial Engineering* Viewpoint - Productivity Press, 1989

————. *Quick Changeover for Operators* – Created by Productivity Press from Shingo's SMED System, 1996

————. *Mistake-Proofing for Operators: The ZQC System* - Created by Productivity Press from Shingo's SMED System, 1996

Shinohara, Isao (ed.) - *New Production System: JIT Crossing Industry Boundaries* – Productivity Press, 1988

Shirose, Kunio. - *TPM: New Implementation Program in Fabrication and Assembly Industries* - Japan Institute of Plant Maintenance

————.*TPM for Workshop Leaders* - Productivity Press, 1992

————.TPM *Team Guide* - Productivity Press, 1996

————. And Yoshifumi Kimura and Mitsugu Kaneda – *P-M Analysis: An Advanced Step in TPM Implementation* - Productivity Press, 1995

————. and Keisuke Arai *Design Team Revolution: How to Cut Lead Times in Half and Double Your Productivity* - Productivity Press, 1999

Steinbacher, Herbert R. and Norman L. Steinbacher – *TPM for America: What it is and Why You Need It* - Productivity Press, 1993

Suehiro, Kikuo – *Eliminating Minor Stoppages on Automated Lines* – Productivity Press, 1992

Sugiura, Tadashi and Yoshiaki Yamada – *The QC Storyline: A Guide to Solving Problems and Communicating the Results* – Asian Productivity Organization, 1995

Sugiyama, Tomo. - *The Improvement Book: Creating the Problem-Free Workplace* – Productivity Press, 1989

Suri, Rajan – *Quick Response Manufacturing: A Companywide Approach to Reducing Lean Times* - Productivity Press, 1998

Suzaki, Kiyoshi - *The New Manufacturing Challenge: Techniques for Continuous Improvement* - Free Press, 1987

————.*The New Shop Floor Management* - The Free Press, 1993.

Suzue, Toshio and Akira Kohdate. - *Variety Reduction Program (VRP): A Production Strategy for Product Diversification* – Productivity Press, 1990

Suzuki, Tokutaro (ed.) – *TPM in Process Industries* - Productivity Press, 1994

Swartz, James B. – *The Hunters and the Hunted: A Non-Linear Solution for Reengineering the Workplace* - Productivity Press, 1994

Taguchi, Genichi, Subir Chowdbury and Shin Taguchi - *Robust Engineering: Learn How to Boost Quality While Reducing Costs & Time to Market* – McGraw - Hill Professional, 1999

Tajiri, Masaji and Fumioh Gotoh - Autonomous Maintenance in

Seven Steps: Implementing TPM on the Shop Floor -
Productivity Press, 1997

Takahasi, Yoshikazu andTakashi Osada – *TPM: Total Productive Maintenance* – Asian Productivity Organization, 1990

Tateisi, Kazuma. - *The Eternal Venture Spirit: An Executive's Practical Philosophy* – Productivity Press, 1989

Tel-A-Train and the Productivity Press Development Team – *The 5S System: Workplace Organization and Standardization* – 1998

Todorov, Branimir – ISO 9000 Required: Your Worldwide Passport to Customer Confidence - Productivity Press, 1996

Tozawa, Bunji – *Kaizen Teian 1: Developing Systems for Continuous Improvement Through Employee Suggestions* – Productivity Press, 1992

————. *Kaizen Teian 2: Developing Systems for Continuous Improvement Through Employee Suggestions* – Productivity Press, 1992

————.*The Idea Book: Improvement through TEI (Total Employee Involvement)* – Productivity Press, 1988

————. *The Improvement Engine: Creativity & Innovation Through Employee Involvement* - Productivity Press – 1995

————. *The Service Industry Idea Book: Employee Involvement in Retail and Office Improvement* – Productivity Press, 1990

Tsuchiya, Seiji – *Quality Maintenance: Zero Defects Through Equipment Management* - Productivity Press,

Uchimaru, Kiyoshi, Susumu Okamoto and Bunteru Kurahara – *TQP for Technical Groups: Total Quality Principles for Product Development* - Productivity Press, 1993

Watson, Gregory H. - *Benchmarking Workbook: Adopting the Best Practices for Performance Improvement* - Productivity Press, 1992

Wellington, Patricia - *Kaizen Strategies for Customer Care: How to Create a Powerful Customer-Care Program—And Make It Work* –Financial Times Prentice Hall Publishing, 1996

Womack, James P. and Daniel T. Jones – *Lean Thinking, Banish Waste and Create Wealth in your Corporation* – Simon &

Schuster, 1996

————. and Daniel T. Jones, and Daniel Roos. - *The Machine that Changed the World: Based on the Massachusetts Institute of Technology S-million dollar 5-year Study on the Future of the Automobile* - Rawson Associates, 1990

Yasuda, Yuzo. - *40 Years, 20 Million Ideas: The Toyota Suggestion System* - Productivity Press, 1991

* The above list includes all of the books I published at Productivity Press, most have my introduction. In addition we published 60 books in our Management Master Series each around 60 to 75 pages.

"Only by much searching and mining are gold and diamonds obtained, and man can find every truth connected with his being if he will dig deep into the mine of his soul." - **James Allen**

Index

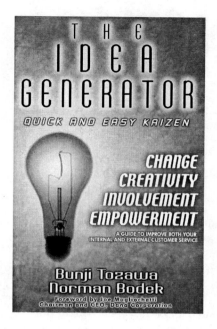

"*The Idea Generator* brings continuous improvement down to Earth--and raises up to the heavens the importance of everybody documenting every implemented idea, however small. It's a message too few understand." - **Richard J. Schonberger, Author or World Class Manufacturing: The Next Decade**

"Lean systems will degrade without ongoing improvement from every employee through a myriad of simple, quick changes. What brings lean structures to life is people—people engaged in continuous improvement. Tozawa and Bodek provide deep insights into this fundamental ingredient of high performance companies." - **Prof. Jeffrey K. Liker, University of Michigan and author of The Toyota Way**

In down times, having an idea program will make the difference. It creates a competitive advantage. **- Gary Corrigan, VP Corporate Communications, Dana Corporation**

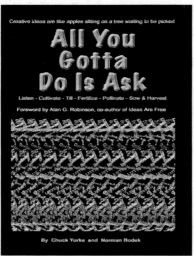

Yes, All You Gotta Do Is Ask Your Employees to make their work easier, more interesting and to build their skills. The result is happier people, reduced costs, improved quality, improved safety, better customer service and faster throughput. Subaru in 2003 received 108.1 ideas per employee and saved $5,246 per employee.

"A simple approach and a very powerful message centering on the brain-power each employee can bring to work and how leaders can tap into it." – **David Veech, Manager Lean Certification Programs, University of Kentucky**

"From the Suggestion Box to the Toyota Production System--All You Gotta Do Is Ask has a lot of good ideas to save an organization time, effort, and money. It is well worth reading!" - **William C. Byham, Ph.D. , Chairman, DDI and author of Zapp!: The Lightning of Empowerment : How to Improve Productivity, Quality, and Employee Satisfaction**